The Silent Man

The Silent Man

Alex Berenson

W F HOWES LTD

This large print edition published in 2009 by
W F Howes Ltd
Unit 4, Rearsby Business Park, Gaddesby Lane,
Rearsby, Leicester LE7 4YH

1 3 5 7 9 10 8 6 4 2

First published in the United Kingdom in 2009
by Hutchinson

A CIP catalogue record for this book is available
from the British Library

ISBN 978 1 40743 738 5

Typeset by Palimpsest Book Production Limited,
Grangemouth, Stirlingshire
Printed and bound in Great Britain
by MPG Books Ltd, Bodmin, Cornwall

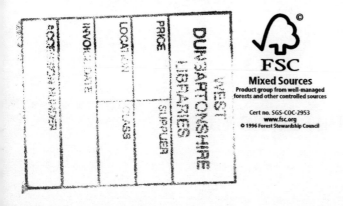

For Jackie

There rose from the bowels of the earth a light not of this world, the light of many suns in one.

—*The New York Times*, September 26, 1945, describing the first nuclear test

A small group of people, none of whom have ever had access to the classified literature, could possibly design and build a crude nuclear explosive device. They would not necessarily require a great deal of technological equipment or have to undertake any experiments. Only modest machine-shop facilities that could be contracted for without arousing suspicion would be required . . . The group would have to include, at a minimum, a person capable of searching and understanding the technical literature in several fields, and a jack-of-all-trades technician. Again, it is assumed that sufficient quantities of fissile material have been provided.

—United States Congress, Office of Technology Assessment, 1977

PART I

CHAPTER 1

CHELYABINSK PROVINCE, RUSSIA

A weaker man would have found Shamir Taghi's pain unbearable. The average American, used to popping Tylenol and Advil for every ache, would have found Shamir Taghi's pain unbearable.

But Shamir wasn't American. He was a Kazakh who lived in Russia, and he was fifty-eight years old, and he was dying of cancer. Lung cancer that had reached his bones. He felt as though he were being cut open from the inside out, tiny claws tearing apart his ribs.

Yet every day Shamir faced his pain. No morphine or hydrocodone for him. Those were expensive drugs, and he was a poor man. Instead he gobbled down aspirin, brought by his son Rafik from the pharmacy in Makushino in big white bottles with peeling labels. For all the good the pills did him, they might as well have been filled with sugar.

Before the cancer came, Shamir had been a strong man, 200 pounds, his muscles swollen by a lifetime of work. Now he weighed 140 pounds. He couldn't eat, couldn't bear to swallow. He couldn't even smoke anymore, his only sin.

The pain. There were no words for it.

But it would be ending soon.

A week before, his son had brought a man to see him. A light-skinned Arab who came recommended by the imam of the local mosque. A quiet man, well schooled in the Book, which meant more and more to Shamir as his death approached. The man knelt on the concrete floor of Shamir's apartment and took his hand.

'Father,' he'd said, and Shamir had looked at Rafik before realizing his mistake. 'Father, do you want the Prophet to smile on you at your death?'

Shamir nodded.

'Then will you do something for me? For all Muslims?'

The Kamaz Tanker truck roared down the two-lane road at sixty-five miles an hour, its driver's-side wheels exactly on the centerline. A quarter-mile ahead, an oncoming Lada pulled to the side, giving the tanker plenty of room to pass. High in the cab of the Kamaz, Nikolai Nepetrov smiled as the Lada moved over. Nepetrov was used to playing highway chicken, and winning. What driver would take on a tanker loaded with eight thousand gallons of gasoline?

For five years, Nepetrov had run gas from the massive Sibneft refinery at Omsk to stations in Chelyabinsk, five hundred miles west. He was thoroughly sick of the trip. On maps, the Omsk-Chelyabinsk road looked like a four-lane highway. In reality the road was two lanes most of the way, clogged by army convoys that rattled along at thirty miles an hour. In fact, Nepetrov had been stuck behind a convoy this morning. He'd finally passed it a few miles back, on a short stretch where the highway really was four lanes.

The Lada disappeared behind him, leaving empty pavement ahead, two lanes with thick firs on both sides. Nepetrov popped in the clutch, downshifted, stomped on the gas. The hardy hum of the engine rumbled through the cab. He put his hands high on the truck's oversized wheel and began to sing, loudly and well: *Po ulitse mostovoi, shla dyevitsa za vodoi . . .*

'*Along the paved road, there went a girl to fetch water, there went a girl to fetch water, to fetch the cold spring water.*' A Russian folk tune, one of his favorites. His voice echoed through the cab. '*Behind her a young lad is shouting:* "Lass, stand still! Lass, stand still! Let's have a little talk!"'

Nepetrov felt a pleasant itch in his crotch as he imagined the young woman, wearing woolen tights against the cold. She held a wooden bucket as she bent over the well, her legs slightly apart . . . Perhaps when he dropped off this fuel he would reach into his pocket for a few hundred rubles, find a woman for his amusement. Though his lass would be wearing too much makeup and stink of all the other men she'd had that day.

Outside, thick gray clouds blocked the sun. The temperature had fallen since morning, the first real cold snap of the long Siberian winter. Nepetrov wore a hat and leather driving gloves. He preferred not to use his heater. The cold kept him awake. He put aside the lass with the bucket and slipped into a new song.

'*Down the Volga, Mother Volga, over the wide sheet of water, there rises a thunderstorm, a huge thunderstorm . . .*'

The road was still clear, aside from a big tractor dragging a load of bricks toward him. Nepetrov upshifted and feathered the gas pedal, watching with satisfaction as the speedometer rose to 120 kilometers – 75 miles – an hour.

'*Nothing is to be seen on the waves, there is only a small black ship.*'

Shamir gripped the wheel of the tractor, watching the big tanker truck rumble at him. Even the wind couldn't soothe his burning bones. With every rut in the road, the claws inside him dug deeper.

Whatever came next, he'd be leaving this pain behind.

Five . . . The big truck was about three hundred meters away and steaming along. Shamir edged the tractor toward the center of the road, real estate that the truck had already claimed. 'Now's the time, father,' the Arab had told him a few minutes before, after getting a call on his mobile phone. 'We'll be with you. We'll all be watching you.'

Four . . . The truck could have moved back into its lane to give Shamir room. Instead it veered toward Shamir, bearing down on him, trying to force him to the edge of the road. Its air horn fired a long blast in warning.

Three . . . Shamir pulled the tractor slightly to the right as if he were getting out of the truck's way. The air horn blasted again.

Two . . . '*Allahu akbar.*' God is great. The words emerged in a whisper from Shamir's ruined throat.

One . . . He twisted the wheel hard left.

'There is only a small black ship – NO!'

Suddenly the tractor blocked the road ahead. Nepetrov had only bad choices. Jerk the wheel hard left and skid into the trees. Stamp his brakes and jackknife the tanker behind him. He chose to do nothing at all, hoping that he might somehow smash the tractor into pieces and survive. Perhaps he would have, if not for the bricks the tractor was hauling.

The crash killed Shamir instantly. Nepetrov wasn't so lucky. The force of the collision split the cab from the tanker. The cab rolled forward, and for a wild moment Nepetrov saw the pavement coming up at him through the windshield. Then the cab flipped onto its side, bouncing down the road, breaking apart. It trailed metal and glass and coolant for seventy-five feet before finally it stopped.

Behind the cab, the tanker slid forward, its undercarriage grinding against the road, kicking up a sea of sparks. It smashed into the back of the cab and stopped. For a moment the two pieces of the truck rested beside each other, a parody of the vehicle they had once been.

Inside the cab Nepetrov tried to get his bearings. Still alive, though he couldn't understand how. His seat belt had saved him. That crazy farmer on his tractor. Why hadn't he moved? No matter. Now . . . he needed to get out. He reached for the belt. But his arms weren't working. In fact, as he looked at his right wrist he saw a bone poking through his skin. Though it didn't hurt, didn't bother him at all. What about his legs? He tried to wriggle in his seat, but he couldn't move. Caged like a chicken. A chicken on the way to the slaughterhouse.

Bang! The cab jolted forward as the tanker hit it. 'No,' Nepetrov whispered.

The tanker didn't have an automatic fire protection system or the other safety equipment standard on its cousins in Western Europe and the United States. It was a Molotov cocktail on sixteen wheels. Now it was lit.

Hanging from the seat, coughing blood, awaiting the inevitable, Nepetrov began to sing. '*There is only a small black ship with glistening white sails—*'

Behind him, the tanker blew up, over sixty thousand pounds of gasoline. The blast wave swallowed Nepetrov and his next verse forever, tearing him apart instantly, or as close to instantly as possible, a death merciless and merciful at once. He never knew he'd been part of anything but a freak accident.

A tiger, a Russian Humvee painted camouflage green, led the convoy. Two uniformed men sat in front, faces tense, breath visible in the cold. A BTR-80, an armored personnel carrier, followed the Tiger. The BTR was wide and tall, with eight oversized wheels and an angled front deck to deflect rocket-propelled grenades.

Then a truck, a Ural 4320 with a special cargo compartment, its walls made of inch-thick steel. Two men shivered inside the unheated cargo hold, their AK-47s held loosely at their sides. Beside the men, two big steel boxes lay on either side of the hold, twenty-four feet long, four feet high and nearly as wide. Chains connected the boxes to the floor of the truck. Each box held a short-range SS-26 missile, called the Iskander by the Russian army, a nuclear-tipped weapon with a range of about three hundred miles.

During transport, the Iskander's nuclear bomb was removed and boxed separately, in a steel case about the size of a small trunk. The cases were carried alongside the missiles in the cargo hold. The warheads they held were the most precious and destructive treasure ever created, weighing just three hundred pounds but with the power to tear the heart out of a city.

The men in the back of the Ural knew that the warheads were engineered to be impervious to fires, earthquakes, meteorites, and everything else the universe might throw at them. If terrorists put a bomb under the road and blew a hole in the Ural's cargo compartment, the explosion might kill the soldiers. But the warheads would not go off, not without first being armed – a procedure that required codes that no one on this convoy had. The safeguards were as close to perfect as human beings could devise. In the two generations since the United States detonated the first nuclear weapon, nations around the world had conducted hundreds of nuclear tests. But no bomb had ever exploded by accident.

And still, as they sat shivering under the fluorescent lights of the hold, the men wondered: How would it feel? If a dozen somethings went wrong, and the trillion-to-one odds came to pass? If one of the warheads blew, exploding with the power of 200 kilotons of explosive? Two hundred kilotons . . . 200,000 tons . . . 440,000,000 pounds. Exploding not ten feet from where they sat. How would it feel? *What would they feel?* The answer, they knew, was that they would most likely feel nothing at all.

But somehow that fact provided little comfort.

Behind the Ural, the convoy continued.

Another Ural. Another Tiger. Two more Urals. Finally a second BTR and two final Tigers. Ten vehicles in all, carrying forty men and eight missiles. They rolled slowly, a concession to the weak winter light and the lousy road. The convoy's commander, Major Yuri Akilev of the 12th GUMO, the military unit responsible for the security of Russia's nuclear weapons, knew this route well. He had budgeted eight hours to cover the three hundred miles from Ishim to the Mayak nuclear plant, their destination. They'd made fine time until early afternoon, when the road ahead had filled with traffic. After a few minutes of waiting, Akilev sent up a sergeant to find out what had happened. The man reported that there'd been an accident ahead. A tanker truck was burning and blocking the road.

Akilev wasn't surprised. Like many Russians, he saw life as a series of meaningless accidents laughed at, if not actually encouraged, by an angry God. But he wished the crash hadn't happened on this stretch of highway, too narrow for him to turn his vehicles around.

For hours, he and his men waited, passing the time by cursing the drunkenness of Russian drivers, the foolishness of Russian engineers, and the ugliness of the local women. Akilev warned his men to remain alert, on the tiny chance that the accident was somehow a setup to block the road so terrorists could attack his convoy. But he wasn't overly worried. His men were well-trained, and his BTRs were equipped with 14.5-millimeter machine guns that could stop anything short of a tank. If he truly needed help, he could get reinforcements by helicopter in two hours at most. He could defend himself for two hours.

Anyway, where would terrorists go even if they did manage to steal a bomb? The whole of the Russian army would be chasing them. In the last year, Akilev had led convoys down this road a dozen times, so often that his cargo almost seemed routine. Russia moved its nuclear weapons far more frequently than the United States did. The Russians had no choice. The chemical propellant that fueled their missiles was toxic, prone to corroding warhead shells. So Russia constantly needed to refurbish its arsenal, moving weapons from bases to the giant plant at Mayak, the heart of the Russian nuclear complex.

Yes, the trip almost seemed routine. But not quite. Akilev was always happy when he reached Mayak and his cargo became someone else's problem.

Finally the tanker fire burned out and the local road crews roused themselves to clear the highway and free his trucks. The sun was already down by the time the convoy began moving again. Akilev had hoped to reach the Mayak plant by sunset. Instead, he and his men would ride well into the night. They had to move slowly after dark. The highway was unlit and they couldn't chance an accident.

Akilev would rather have stopped for the night, but he had no choice. There were no bases between here and Mayak. Anyway, the convoy was due by midnight. Never mind that the plant would effectively be closed by then. The convoy was due, and as long as it arrived by 11:59 p.m., Akilev would get credit for a job well done. If he crossed the gate at Mayak at 12:01 a.m., on the other hand . . . Akilev shook his head. No one had ever accused the Russian army of having sensible rules.

Grigory Farzadov sat in his decrepit kitchen, sipping peach brandy from a chipped glass, watching the LCD timer on his microwave count down toward zero. He wore no pants or shirt, only gray underwear that billowed around his giant haunches. The temperature outside had fallen close to zero, but a film of sweat covered his belly and legs.

Grigory was a hulking shambles of a man, a cross between Frankenstein and Mr Potato Head, with big soft hands and pitted skin. He'd never been married or had a girlfriend. He'd never even had sex without having to pay for it. He had been cursed with a fine mind and a fiercely ugly body. He wished every day for the reverse, but the choice wasn't his to make. Fate made fools of men. He'd been born alone, and he'd surely die alone.

Beep. Beep.

Dinner was ready. Grigory lumbered up and extracted a pepperoni pizza from the microwave. He cut the slices into small bites, savoring each forkful. His movements were oddly dainty, in sharp contrast to his size – and his surroundings. Leaky pipes had discolored the kitchen's walls and loosened the plaster from the ceiling. The rest of the apartment wasn't much better. The electricity cut out sporadically, always when Grigory had just settled in to watch television. At least the heat worked, but too well. From November through April, he kept the windows open, and still he sweated.

Worst of all was his next-door neighbor Mikhail, a worthless drunk who divided his time between watching pornography and battering his wife. One particularly ugly night a year earlier, Grigory had knocked on Mikhail's door and threatened to call the police. A half-hour later, he heard Mikhail outside his door, shouting, 'Out, you fat coward!' The ranting continued until Grigory made the mistake of opening up. When he did, Mikhail pulled him into the hallway and jammed a pistol under his chin.

'If you ever interfere with me again, you elephant—' Mikhail shoved Grigory down and launched a glob of spit at his face. As Grigory curled on the concrete floor, Mikhail kicked him, his steel-tipped boots leaving bruises that didn't fade for weeks.

But Mikhail wasn't a problem anymore, Grigory thought. No. His new friends had taken care of Mikhail. Grigory shivered, suddenly cold despite the overheated apartment, and poured himself another glass of peach brandy. Very soon he would need to make his decision. Though it was really no decision at all. He tossed the brandy down the sink. He would need to be sober tonight.

★　　★　　★

For this life Grigory had trained in operations research for six years at Ural State University in Ekaterinburg. He hadn't been at the top of his class. Those men went to energy companies like Gazprom. The middling students, like Grigory, weren't so lucky. They became engineers for Rosatom, the ministry that controlled Russia's nuclear weapons plants and storage depots. Grigory worked at the weapons depot at Mayak as a manager in the PC&A unit, responsible for the protection, control, and accounting of nuclear material. He lived in Ozersk, the 'closed city' – protected by checkpoints and a barbed-wire fence – that surrounded Mayak.

Grigory didn't have many friends. But for most of his life he'd been close to his cousin Tajid. Like Grigory, Tajid lived in Ozersk and worked at Mayak, as a security guard. On the long cold nights when the very walls of his apartment mocked his loneliness, Grigory often found his way to Tajid's. He always took a bottle of Stolichnaya and a fresh orange for Tajid's wife by way of apology for the intrusion. He and Tajid sat in Tajid's kitchen and drank until Grigory staggered home.

But over the last three years, Grigory had become less welcome at his cousin's apartment. Tajid had fallen in with a bunch of Kazakhs. They claimed to be taxi drivers, but they hardly worked, from what Grigory could see. They spent their time drinking coffee and reading the Quran.

Tajid and Grigory had both been born Muslim, but they'd never practiced the religion growing up. In their youth, the Communists had frowned on organized religion. Today, the Russian government still discouraged Islam, though it wasn't illegal. Employees at Mayak were warned against becoming overly involved with 'foreign religious groups,' which everyone knew was code for Islamic fundamentalists.

'What do you want with those peasants?' Grigory asked his cousin one winter night. 'They aren't even Russian.'

'They follow the true path, cousin. Come, see for yourself.'

'Look at me. You think I have any reason to believe in God?' Grigory laughed. 'A drink, cousin?'

'I told you I don't drink anymore.'

'Suit yourself.' Grigory threw back a shot of vodka.

The next time Grigory showed up at Tajid's apartment, Tajid wasn't alone. One of the Muslims was there, too. Tajid looked at the bottle of vodka Grigory held. 'Give me that,' he said, his voice low and angry.

Grigory handed the bottle over and watched in horror as Tajid tossed it out his window.

'Never bring alcohol to my home again.'

'Cousin—'

'Go. Now. You bring me disrepute.'

Grigory hadn't known what to say. Tajid was his oldest friend. His only friend, really, aside from

16

the old men at the city chess club, who were as lonely as he.

He'd left Tajid alone for a few months. Then, finally, he'd worked up the courage to return to his cousin's apartment – this time carrying no vodka, only a bag of dates. When he knocked on the door Tajid hugged him, surprising him.

'I was just thinking of you, cousin.'

Over a cup of strong sweet coffee, he'd told Grigory why.

At first, Grigory had believed, wanted to believe, that Tajid was joking. But after Tajid insisted he was serious a second time, and a third, Grigory had stopped arguing.

'It's impossible,' he'd said to deflect his nervousness. 'Can't be done.'

'Of course it can,' Tajid said. 'You've said so yourself many times.'

Indeed, Grigory and his cousin had often talked about the problems at Mayak. Rosatom had dramatically improved the defenses of its nuclear plants since the 1990s, when guards didn't show up and warheads were stored in warehouses protected only by cheap padlocks. But weaknesses remained, especially in the hours after new warheads arrived. Having finished the dangerous work of moving warheads, convoy commanders were eager to sign over their shipments and leave. Sometimes too eager.

'I don't want to be involved in this.'

'But my friends already know about you. Your job at the plant.'

17

'Tajid.' Grigory felt a sinking sensation in his belly, a hopeless feeling that would become uncomfortably familiar. 'What do they know?'

'Only your name and your job.'

'My name?'

'My cousin, you can do this.'

'Even if I could find a way—' Grigory broke off, hardly able to believe he was even pretending to consider the suggestion. 'How do you know the men proposing this aren't agents of the FSB' – the Russian Federal Security Service, the successor to the KGB – 'or the GUMO?'

'My sheikh vouches for them.'

'That might be enough for you, Tajid, but I need more.'

'Your neighbor Mikhail, does he still bother you?'

'Today and every day. Worthless scum. Why do you ask?'

'We'll talk soon, cousin.'

A week later, Grigory came home to find his apartment unusually quiet. He soon realized why. No porn actresses were screeching in fake pleasure next door.

Mikhail's body was found the next day, dumped on a back road outside Chelyabinsk. He'd been shot between the eyes. Worse, he'd been stabbed over and over, his ears and tongue cut off, or so the rumors went. Grigory heard the news and poured himself a glass of vodka, waiting for the phone to ring. He didn't have to wait long.

18

'You heard what happened to your neighbor?'

Grigory was silent.

'When can we meet?' Tajid said.

'Whenever you like.'

'An hour, then. At the Moscow' – a rundown café on the edge of Ozersk.

Tajid hung up and Grigory threw back his vodka. The drink warmed his belly but his mind was still cold. Tajid's men had proved in the most emphatic way possible that they weren't police agents. They'd also sent Grigory a lesson in what might happen to him if he didn't cooperate. Two doves with one arrow.

Tajid sat in a corner of the Moscow with another man, a light-skinned Arab, small, clean-shaven, and neatly dressed, his only distinctive feature his almond-shaped brown eyes. He wore a black leather jacket and a thin gold bracelet. In all, he looked more like a junior member of the *mafiya* than the jihadi Grigory had expected. But then this man would want to blend in, Grigory thought.

'Your cousin speaks highly of you,' the Arab said in Russian, extending his hand. 'I am Yusuf.'

Grigory couldn't pretend he was a brave man. Nonetheless he screwed up his courage. 'Yusuf. This thing you propose to take . . . what will you do with it?' Even now, Grigory could not make himself say *bomb*.

Tajid frowned. 'Cousin, you've only just arrived and already—'

'Let him ask,' Yusuf said. He looked at Grigory. 'Truly I don't know. But I promise you this. We won't use them inside Russia. Part of my job is to get them out.'

'Them?'

'We need two.'

'Madness.'

'Madness or no, we need two.'

'Let me ask you something else, then.' Grigory spoke with bravado he did not feel. 'Since we are friends now, speaking frankly as friends do.'

'Go on.'

'You understand these devices have locks? What the Americans call permissive action links? They cannot be used without the proper codes, and the codes cannot be broken. Not even by the most skilled cryptographer. So you must know that whether you steal one of these, or two, or a hundred, they're useless to you. Unless you have some way of breaking into the Kremlin for the codes.'

'Grigory, you're very smart. I'm merely a technician. I have a shopping list. And I would like your help in filling it.'

'I don't think it's possible, Yusuf. I would tell you, I swear.'

Yusuf patted Grigory's shoulders. Despite himself, Grigory flinched. 'Consider all the alternatives. There's always a way. Meanwhile—'

Yusuf reached into his jacket and slid a thick white envelope across the table. Grigory peered inside. A wad of green hundred-dollar bills, the new kind, counterfeit-proof, secured with a red rubber band. Grigory tried to hand the envelope back to Yusuf but the little Arab raised a hand.

'Yours,' he said. 'Whatever you decide. If you help us I promise ten times more.'

'Very generous of you,' Grigory said. 'Now I can buy all the vodka I like.' His tone was ironic, but Yusuf didn't seem to notice.

Yusuf stood, touched Grigory's arm. His fingers were as weightless as the devil's. 'We'll meet again soon. I hope you can work with us.'

Sure enough, a week later, Grigory heard the knocking on his door, a light rapping, so soft that at first he hoped he was dreaming. But the knocking continued, and Grigory opened the door, knowing what he'd see.

'Cousin,' Tajid said. Yusuf stood beside him, holding a leather satchel.

They came in and sat around the plastic table in the kitchen. 'Would you like coffee?' Grigory said. He poured himself a glass of vodka. Let them watch him drink.

'Your cousin says you're an excellent chess player,' Yusuf said.

'Mediocre at best.'

'I'm sure you're lying. We must play.'

'Whenever you like.'

'So have you given any thought to my proposal?' Yusuf opened his satchel and extracted two oranges and a long curved knife with an ebony handle in a leather sheath. He slid the sheath off, revealing the sharpest blade Grigory had ever seen. Under the fluorescent kitchen lights the blade gleamed silver.

The devil, Grigory thought. Truly, he's the devil.

'Tajid tells me you like oranges,' Yusuf said.

'Doesn't everyone?'

'Not me,' Yusuf said. 'They're too fleshy. Something almost human about them.' He worked the blade through the first orange, slicing it in half, then quarters, his movements fine and careful.

Then a frenzy seemed to come over him and he cut faster and faster, turning the fruit into a pulpy mess, not recognizable as an orange at all, its juice dribbling off the table onto the crackled linoleum floor. 'I get excited,' he said. 'It was the same with your neighbor.' He stood and moved behind Grigory, the knife poised in his hand.

'Please,' Grigory said.

'May I use your sink?'

'I'll help. I promise.'

'I can do it myself.' Yusuf washed the blade gently, humming to himself.

'I mean with your project. I'll help.'

Yusuf dried the knife, sheathed it. 'This is wonderful news.'

'You don't have to pay me.'

'Of course we'll pay, Grigory,' Yusuf said. 'We keep our word.'

22

'But—' Grigory hesitated. 'Shall we talk about this now?'

'Why not?'

'So. I don't want to disappoint you' – Grigory looked at the knife – 'but this isn't as simple as you imagine. We've tightened security, switched to the American system. No one enters the warehouses alone. Ever. Always two men, with a third watching on a camera. And you need a reason to enter.'

Yusuf swept up the mess of the orange, threw it in the sink, and sat down beside Grigory. 'Even you? Your cousin says you're very senior.'

'Not so senior. Why do you think I live here? Anyway, the president himself must have a partner when he visits the depot.'

'Depot.'

'What we call the warehouses where we keep the weapons.'

'Do you always have the same person with you? Someone for me to talk with?'

'To improve security, the pairings are random. Also—' Again Grigory hesitated. He didn't think he'd ever feared anyone as much as this man.

'Yes,' Yusuf said.

'I work nights now. Along with Tajid. I audit the work we've done the previous day. It's paperwork. The plant is basically closed. There's no reason for anyone to be inside the depots. The guards check them at the beginning and end of each shift. Otherwise they're not touched. We figure the less they're entered, the better.'

'But you could go inside. If you had a reason.'

'Perhaps. But I'd be watched.'

Yusuf idly peeled the second orange. 'Surely there's another way.'

Tajid coughed. 'What about when the convoys come, cousin? Didn't you say—'

'I know what I've said. But the convoys never arrive at night.'

'But if they did?' Yusuf popped an orange slice in his mouth.

'I thought you said you didn't like oranges.'

'Who doesn't like oranges? Especially in this miserable cold.'

Now the devil can laugh about his joke, now that he's won, Grigory thought. Aloud he said, 'The same rules are supposed to apply when a convoy arrives and we move warheads in or out of the depots. Always two men. But sometimes we get sloppy. The pairings aren't always random. The convoy commanders want to hand over the material and be gone.'

'So if a convoy came late, you would receive it?'

'It's not my job. But the man who would, he's a drunk. He sleeps all night.'

'So you could receive it. And you could pick your partner.'

Grigory drank down his vodka and poured himself another glass. 'But none of this matters, you see. The convoys arrive during the day. Always.'

'The convoys, do they always take the same route?'

'In theory, no, for security reasons. But effectively, yes. In winter there's really only one road they can use.'

'And you know when they're due to arrive?'

'For production purposes, we must. You aren't thinking of attacking a convoy, are you? It's impossible. You'd need hundreds of men.'

'No. Delaying it.'

'But how?'

'Leave that to me.'

'In that case. If you could. It's possible—' Grigory turned over the scene in his mind. 'Not guaranteed. I would need some luck. But it's possible.'

'Can you find the dates of the next convoys and show me their route by tomorrow?'

'Yes.'

'Until tomorrow, then.' Yusuf flipped his satchel over his shoulder and stood. Tajid followed. When they'd left, Grigory sat at his kitchen table. The devil had left a stink of oranges and Grigory knew that for the rest of his life, which he feared wouldn't be long, the fruit would never again cross his lips.

Grigory grabbed a rag from under the sink, wiped furiously across the kitchen table, hoping to rid the kitchen of the sweet orange smell. What was he doing? How could he consider helping these men steal a special weapon? No, no euphemisms now, no pretty names. It wasn't a special weapon. It was a nuclear bomb.

But then, what choice did he have? He would be signing his own death warrant if he told the police what Yusuf planned. Even if the police believed him and arrested his cousin and Yusuf, Yusuf's friends would find him afterward. They would gut him front to back and toss his innards in the trash.

Anyway, what he'd told Yusuf was true. Without the codes, the weapons were useless. And Yusuf couldn't possibly get the codes. Could he? No. Impossible. The codes were more heavily guarded than even the weapons themselves.

Grigory finished mopping and tossed aside the rag. He wouldn't say anything to the police, not yet. Perhaps later, when he had more evidence . . . but he knew he was lying to himself. This was the moment to go to the police, not later. The further this went, the harder it would be for him to get himself out.

Fine. He would help. He would hope that Yusuf stuck to whatever bargain they made and didn't kill him as soon as Grigory handed over the warheads. In the worst of all cases, if he learned that Yusuf had somehow gotten the codes, he would tell the police everything he knew.

'Only a fool trusts the devil,' Grigory said to the empty kitchen. He took another slug of vodka, but this time the drink was bitter in his throat.

The days had gone quickly after that meeting, too quickly for Grigory. He gave Yusuf the dates when the next five convoys were scheduled to arrive.

The little Arab disappeared for a few days and Grigory hoped he might be gone for good. And one night he looked at the envelope filled with hundred-dollar bills. He put on his best black shirt and covered himself in cologne, a new bottle he'd bought a day before. Hugo Boss, it was called. Grigory didn't know it, but it sounded fancy. Then he extracted twenty of the bills and made his way to the Paddy O'Shea, a knockoff Irish bar that had somehow become the fanciest nightspot in Ozersk. The Russians felt a kinship with the Irish, their cousins in heavy drinking, gloomy novels, and depressive behavior. The Paddy played true to every Irish stereotype imaginable, throwing in a few Scottish stereotypes for good measure, like the set of fake bagpipes hanging from the ceiling of the bar. Grigory ordered shots of Jameson at 100 rubles – about $5 – each for everyone at the bar. He pulled the wad of hundreds from his pocket, making sure the women in the place saw it. They did, and they forgot his pocked skin. For one night, he felt beautiful.

When he woke the next morning, the two hookers he'd brought home were gone. So was the envelope with the rest of his money. He'd hidden it, but not well enough. When he staggered into the bathroom to vomit, he discovered that they'd even taken his bottle of cologne. He knelt over his toilet, throwing up whiskey and Guinness, a thick brown ink that rolled down his chin and stuck to the sides of the toilet. He knew he should be ashamed, but he wasn't, not a bit.

In the next month, convoys came and went. Grigory allowed himself to exhale. Maybe Yusuf had seen the difficulties he faced.

The knock came on a quiet afternoon. Outside, the sun had set. On the concrete plaza of the apartment complex, kids were playing in the dark. Grigory expected to see his cousin, but when he opened the door, Yusuf was alone.

'Is there still a convoy this Thursday?'

'I'll double-check tonight, but yes. But the convoy is due in the afternoon.'

'*Inshallah*' – God willing – 'it will be late.'

'The later the better.'

'I understand. Now explain again how you will do this.'

Grigory did. Even as he said the words, he wondered if he'd have the courage to go ahead. Yusuf must have sensed his uncertainty, for when Grigory finished he was silent. Finally he sat next to Grigory on the lumpy couch. He was much smaller than Grigory. And yet he radiated a strength that Grigory couldn't hope to match.

'After you're finished, I'll meet you here. We'll go on from there.'

'At best you'll have only a few days. After Tajid and I don't show up at work, they'll open the boxes as a matter of course. Certainly, by the middle of next week they'll sound the alarm. We'll be the most wanted men in Russia.'

28

'That will be plenty of time. *Inshallah*.' Yusuf stood. 'You aren't a believer, Grigory. I hope one day you will be. In the meantime, this will prove our sincerity.' He reached into his pocket for an envelope like the other one he'd given Grigory. He tossed it beside the chess set where Grigory traced out positions from his books. 'Go with God,' he said.

In return, Grigory said . . . nothing. This man takes my tongue along with everything else, he thought. Without a word he reached out for the envelope.

Now Thursday had come, far too quickly. Maybe he'd be lucky. Maybe the convoy would already have arrived, and the steel boxes would be locked in the depot where he couldn't get to them.

Yet somehow Grigory knew he wouldn't escape so easily. He wasn't a superstitious man, and he certainly wasn't religious. He was a scientist. But the devil had tapped his shoulder and asked him for a game of chess, and he had no choice but to play. He had to see this through.

He finished his microwaved pizza and cleaned his plate. He pulled on his pants and found a clean blue shirt in his closet. He turned on the taps to wash his face and found the usual trickle of lukewarm brown water. He clipped on his badge, grabbed his thick winter coat, laced up his boots. And as he walked out the door, he felt almost relieved. What would be would be.

CHAPTER 2

SILVER SPRING, MARYLAND

They sat in a circle in the basement room, crutches and prostheses laid by their chairs. The night outside was cold and clear, but the narrow baseboard heaters, and the body heat of a dozen men, kept the room uncomfortably warm. A refrigerator stocked with soda sat in one corner, and the men held Cokes and coffee cups.

They'd been silent for almost a minute when a young man in a gray T-shirt whispered a single word: 'Overpasses.'

Grunts of recognition from the rest of the circle. The man looked around uncertainly, as if he'd surprised himself by speaking at all. His name was Paul Redburn, but he'd introduced himself as Stitch, tribute to the seventy stitches sewn into his stomach. And so Stitch he was.

'Tell us, Stitch.' This from the group's informal leader, Kyle Stewart, a marine sergeant who'd come home two years before – against his wishes – after taking a sniper's bullet in the neck in Ramadi.

'How you were talking about stuff that makes you crazy,' said Redburn. 'All out of relation to what it should. Like when somebody from high school says how they almost signed up and then they got some lame bullshit why they didn't.'

'I want to wreck them,' Stewart said. 'Not afraid to say it.'

'For me it's overpasses. Every half-mile on 202, there's an overpass. And every time I drive under one . . . every time . . . I wonder if some haji's watching, gonna grab his phone, call his buddies so they know I'm coming.'

'Or just toss a grenade down on the roof,' said the man to Redburn's right. Freddie Sanchez, an army private who had lost his right leg when a bomb blew out his Humvee in Baghdad.

'That is so,' Redburn said. 'And you know, some days are easier, some days I can just about do it. Then some days I have to pull off, find another way to get where I'm going.' He fingered the small silver cross that hung from his neck. 'Just like everything else.'

'I almost wrecked a few months ago,' Sanchez said. 'On the Beltway. First time on a highway since I got back. I was in the slow lane, taking it easy. It was fine for a while and then I spotted this bag of trash on the side. And I thought . . . I didn't think at all. Just went left. Put some space between me and that IED.' Sanchez ducked his head, looked at the space where his leg should have been. 'I'm saying I was back there. Not like

31

I was imagining it. I was *there*. I almost took out this Toyota, chick driving, two kids in the back.'

'You didn't, though,' Stewart said.

'No. I didn't. But the worst part was, when I saw what I done, I was so damn mad at that chick in the Toyota. My heart was taking off in my chest. My head, I wanted to—' Sanchez broke off. Sweat glowed on his forehead under the fluorescent lights. The room was silent again as the group waited for him to say what he had to say. These men were used to waiting.

'I'm just glad my gun's locked up in my closet,' Sanchez said finally. 'If I had that thing on my hip, everybody on the road would be in a lot of trouble.'

Every week, they met in a church in downtown Silver Spring. The Central Maryland Iraq and Afghanistan Veterans Group, a big name for a simple organization. Between twelve and twenty guys showed up, usually. A half-dozen regulars. The rest floated in and out. They came here to talk about the things they didn't want to say to their wives or girlfriends, the things that only other soldiers could understand. They had plenty to say, John Wells thought.

Most soldiers came back from Iraq and Afghanistan basically intact. But ten thousand men and women had been hurt badly enough to require serious surgery. Others had memories they couldn't shake, of buddies blown apart, civilians killed in raids gone wrong. The wounds in their minds didn't necessarily match the injuries the world could see.

The amputees sometimes joked that life was easier for them. No one ever doubted their sacrifice. They never had to apologize for having bad days.

'Thanks, Freddie,' Stewart said. 'Hour's almost up, got to give back the room. But before we do—'

He turned to Wells. 'Jim, you been here a bunch of times, but you don't say much. Anything you'd like to get off your chest?'

Wells shook his head. 'I guess not,' he said. To avoid distracting the other men, Wells used a fake name at these sessions. Everyone in America had learned his name two years before, when he stopped a terrorist attack on New York, but his face was still a mystery to most people. The CIA had managed to keep pictures of him out of general circulation, though a few old ones were floating around the Web.

Stewart leaned forward, offering Wells a deceptively soft smile. 'Mind if I ask, Jim, where'd you serve? Reserves? Guard? You're a little gray for active duty.'

'If it's all the same, I'd rather not say.'

Stewart slid his chair a half-foot closer to Wells. A couple of the other regulars leaned in, too. They'd planned this, Wells thought.

'Can't let you off that easy, Jim. Can't have men who aren't vets in here.' Stewart wasn't smiling anymore. 'Can't have accountants sneaking in, listening so they got something to say on singles night at the Marriott. Man might get hurt that way.'

'No one ever accused me of being an accountant

before,' Wells said. He searched for a way to be honest without saying too much. 'I was a Ranger back in the nineties and that's the truth,' he said.

'No war then.'

'I've seen war.'

'You ever been to Iraq?'

'Afghanistan,' Wells said. He didn't add that he'd fought for both the Taliban and the United States. 'Listen, Sergeant, it does me good being here. But I understand. You don't trust me, I won't come back.'

'Just tell us something,' Stewart said. 'So we know.'

All right, Wells thought. You want me to talk—

'I'll tell you about a dream I have,' he said. 'I'm in an apartment. Over there. Windows taped over. And I'm supposed to be a hostage. Wearing an orange jumpsuit. And my throat's getting slit when the clock hits midnight. *I know this*. I know what's meant to happen.'

Now Wells was the one sweating. He wiped a hand across his forehead.

'Only I'm not the hostage,' he said. 'I've got the knife. And these guys, these four guys, they're the ones tied up. They're begging me. And I hear Johnny Cash singing. "*I hear the train a-comin', it's rollin' round the bend.*" "Folsom Prison Blues." And then the clock hits midnight and I start cutting.'

Wells took a breath. 'I'm cutting, and it's slow going. You ever put a knife in someone? And I'm trying to make myself stop, but I can't. And then I look at the guy I'm cutting. And—'

Wells broke off. A few seconds later, Stewart spoke, very quietly. 'You?'

'Yeah. Me. But that's not the worst of it. The worst of it is that when I wake up, I look over at my fiancée and I—'

Again Wells found himself unable to speak.

'You want to hurt her?' Stewart said.

The men in the circle looked at him steadily. Wells knew they would wait as long as he wanted. He felt their patience under him, holding him, and then he could speak.

'I would never . . . It's not even a thought. It's more like a word. *Knife. Cut.*'

'Does it keep you up?' Stewart said.

'It's not like I have it all the time.'

'You ever said anything about it to her?'

Wells shook his head.

'You think she knows?'

The question surprised Wells, but he knew the answer. 'She knows. Maybe not exactly, but she knows.'

The florists were closed, but on his way home Wells found a dozen roses at Whole Foods. When he opened the front door, he heard Exley singing to herself in the kitchen. He padded in, hiding the bouquet behind his back, and found her at the table, surrounded by travel guides for South America. She was wearing a red sweater that matched the roses.

He tipped back her head, kissed her, handed over the bouquet as smoothly as he could. She put a hand to his face, ran it down his neck. He felt his pulse against her fingertips.

'When did you turn into such a romantic?' she said.

'About halfway home.' He still couldn't get used to the idea that they lived in a house, their house, one they owned together, with an eat-in kitchen and rooms for her kids when they visited. An upstairs and downstairs. A garden.

This was the first house, the first piece of real estate, he'd ever owned. Exley had pushed for it. So had the agency, which said they needed a detached house, someplace a security detail could watch them full-time without bothering the neighbors too much. Wells hadn't argued, and now they owned a house and were planning romantic getaways to South America. Yuppies. And still Wells's restlessness – and his dreams – showed no signs of fading.

Wells was beginning to think they never would. He'd spent the better part of a decade working undercover to infiltrate al-Qaeda for the CIA. He'd come back to the United States to stop a massive al-Qaeda attack with Exley's help. More recently he and Exley had helped avert war between the United States and China. The missions had saved untold lives.

But Wells didn't know the men he'd saved, only the ones he'd killed. Some had been villains by

36

anyone's definition, terrorists targeting civilians. But others had merely been doing their jobs, protecting themselves, following orders they didn't necessarily agree with or even understand. Chinese policemen. Afghan guerrillas. He couldn't pretend they were his enemies. He'd killed them all because he'd had no choice. He'd killed them—

'For the greater good,' he said aloud.

'What greater good?' Exley said.

'I was hoping you could tell me.'

Now he was trying to put his head back on, gather his strength. Because he knew. The world wouldn't stay quiet very long.

Exley stood, busied herself cutting rose stems, putting the flowers in a cut-glass vase. 'How were the guys?' she said.

'I finally talked a little,' Wells said.

'Anything you want to tell me?'

As an answer, he stood, wrapped an arm around her and another under her legs and picked her up. Wells was six-two and muscular, twice Exley's size, and he lifted her easily. She cupped his face in her hands, locked her blue eyes on him.

'Got the trip all planned yet?'

'Close,' she said. 'You sure you don't want to help?'

'I'm not making decisions these days,' he said. 'I'm in a decision-free mode.'

'No decisions at all? So I can do what I like with you.'

'Absolutely.'

'Then why don't you take me upstairs?'

'Yes, ma'am.'

He'd just put her down on the bed when the doorbell rang.

'Ignore it,' she said. She pulled her sweater off. Underneath she was wearing only a thin white T-shirt that clung to her nipples. She tugged him down. He'd begun to slip off her T-shirt when the bell rang again.

Downstairs he flipped on the porch lights and peered through the front door's bulletproof glass. A tall black man in a long blue overcoat stood on the porch. Adam Michaels, the head of the CIA security detail that watched the house.

Wells didn't particularly like the idea of being guarded this way, but he understood the need, especially when Exley's kids visited. Anyway, Michaels and his guys were discreet.

'Sorry to bother you, John,' Michaels said.

'No bother.'

'Can I ask you and Ms Exley to come outside, take a look at somebody?'

The man stood under a streetlight. He was white, wearing jeans, a Yankees cap, black gloves, and a thin leather jacket that didn't look like much good against the cold. Two of Michaels's men watched him, their hands close to the pistols on their hips.

Wells looked him over, carefully. 'Never seen him before.'

'Me, neither,' Exley said.

'Who is he?' Wells said.

'Nobody, probably,' Michaels said. 'But we've seen him five, six times the last couple days. Walking by the house, front and back. Slow and careful. Like he's casing it. This time we stopped him, asked him what he was doing.'

'It's a free country,' Wells said.

'That's what he said,' Michaels said.

'What's his name?'

'Says it's Victor, but he's got no ID. From his accent, he's probably Russian.'

Wells walked over to the man, examined him closely. Nope. Definitely a stranger. Wells stuck out his hand. The man hesitated, then shook it.

'Victor,' Wells said. 'I'm John Wells.'

'Nice to meet you.' The Russian accent was unmistakable.

'You looking for me? Because I'm right here.'

'Why would I be looking for you? I don't know you. Just walking when these men grab me. Make me stand here and it's cold.'

'You know a Spetsnaz named Sergei Tupenov?'

'Never heard of him.'

'Me, neither,' Wells said. 'Victor. You like the Yankees?'

'Sure.'

'Big fan?'

'Sure.'

'Who's their shortstop?'

Victor frowned. 'Shortstop? What kind of question is this?'

'Fair enough,' Wells said. 'You have a nice night. See you around.'

He walked back to Michaels. 'Anything?'

'Nope,' Wells said.

'Any good threats come your way the last few weeks?' Exley said.

'On you two?' Michaels said. 'Course not. Don't you know everybody loves you?' Michaels paused. 'Seriously, the usual nonsense. I'm more worried about the ones we don't get.'

'True enough,' Exley said.

'So if you don't recognize him, guess we have to cut him loose.' Michaels turned to Victor. 'Get out of here,' he said. 'And do me a favor. Don't come back. Find another block to walk.' The Russian glared at them, then walked off, slowly.

And as Wells watched Victor go, he heard Johnny Cash, singing in the night. *I hear the train a-comin', it's rollin' round the bend . . .*

CHAPTER 3

The Mayak complex stretched across hundreds of acres, encompassed dozens of buildings, and was protected by three separate layers of security. Foreigners, and most Russians, were barred not only from Mayak, but from Ozersk, the city that surrounded the plant. During the Soviet era, Ozersk hadn't appeared on maps, or even had a name. It had been called Chelyabinsk-65, for its location, sixty-five kilometers from Chelyabinsk, the province's capital. After the USSR collapsed, the Russian government had acknowledged Ozersk's existence and allowed foreigners into the city. But now a new cold war – or at least a cold peace – was dawning. The Kremlin had again closed the gates to Ozersk and its other nuclear cities.

Of course, plenty of outsiders, like Yusuf, evaded the outer city checkpoints with fake identification and found their way into Ozersk. But a second level of security protected Mayak. The plant had its own guard force, an electrical fence, and closed-circuit cameras at every entrance. To further improve security, only managers like Grigory were

41

allowed to bring their cars into the plant. Ordinary employees were required to park outside the perimeter and ride buses around the complex.

Finally, a third layer of fencing, guards, and high-intensity lights surrounded the 'special area,' the depots where warheads were stored. Only employees with at least five years' experience were allowed in the special area. And except for convoy trucks, all vehicles were barred from the area. The plant's managers worked just outside the special area, in a hulking three-story concrete building whose narrow deep-set windows gave it the look of a maximum security prison.

Grigory Farzadov turned his Volga sedan off the four-lane avenue that connected the front gates of the complex with the special area, and rolled into the headquarters parking lot. Unlike senior managers, he didn't have a designated spot, but working at night meant he could always park near the front doors. A good thing, too, since the parking lot was covered with an inch of black ice, a combination of water, dirt, sand, and grease that froze in November and didn't melt until April. Every year Grigory took at least one nasty fall, found himself on the ground with his knee or his wrist aching, just short of broken. This cursed place, where even walking was a chore. If he succeeded tonight, he would take Yusuf's money and go somewhere warm, someplace where he wouldn't have to wear mittens six months a year.

If he succeeded tonight. And Yusuf didn't kill him afterward.

Inside the front doors, a bored guard glanced at Grigory's badge and waved him in. The guard's name was Dmitri. He and Grigory had been hired around the same time, fifteen years before. As much as the cameras and fences, the long tenures of men like Grigory and Dmitri guaranteed Mayak's security. No one new was allowed anywhere near the depots. But that familiarity had a downside. The insiders couldn't really imagine one another capable of theft or sabotage. Tonight Grigory would take advantage of that blindness.

'Evening,' said Grigory. 'How are you?'

'As usual, thanks. Yourself?'

'This beastly cold. Looking forward to spring.'

'Already?'

'Today and every day,' Grigory said. He remembered Mikhail and stifled a shiver. He'd condemned his neighbor to a frightful death with the same four words.

Grigory had arrived for his shift early, as always. He busied himself with paperwork for a few minutes before walking down the hall to the office of Garry Pliakov, the deputy manager of operations. Pliakov oversaw the handling of all special nuclear material – the phrase that both Russians and Americans used for plutonium-239 and uranium-235, the two atoms that formed the core of nuclear weapons.

The Russian nuclear bureaucracy still hadn't

gone completely digital; Pliakov's office was thick with personnel reports, orders from Rosatom's headquarters, details of convoys arriving and departing, the papers neatly organized in folders on the shelves around his desk.

'Wasn't a convoy due today? I don't see the paperwork,' Grigory said.

'Those bastards are late.'

Yusuf had kept his promise. Grigory wasn't surprised. 'What, they stopped for a drink?'

'They say an accident blocked the highway. They're hoping to arrive by ten o'clock. You know what that means. A cold night for you, unless Oleg' – the night manager at the plant – 'decides to stay sober.'

Pliakov smiled. He was a decent man who invited Grigory to his apartment for a drink once a year or so. For a moment, Grigory's resolve wavered. Could he really betray all these men he'd worked with for years? Then he remembered the way that Yusuf had torn apart the orange.

'No need for Oleg,' Grigory said. 'I'll do it.'

'Of course. Check the cucumber crates and then into the north warehouse.'

The special area had two storage depots. The north one was a low concrete building that held a couple hundred warheads that were still in active service but had been brought to Mayak for repair. The south warehouse was larger and dug deep belowground. It provided permanent storage for decommissioned and obsolete warheads. Though if the new cold war really got hot, they could always be put back into service.

'I know the procedure. I signed one in a couple of years ago.'

'Good. I'll send over the codes in a few minutes, before I go.' In yet another security precaution, the codes to open the cucumber crates – Russian jargon for the boxes that held the warheads – were not carried on the weapons convoys. Instead, they were sent to Mayak over the secure private network that linked Russia's nuclear facilities. Even if terrorists attacked the convoy and stole the boxes, they wouldn't be able to unlock them and would have to cut them open to get to the warheads inside.

'All right. See you tomorrow, Garry.'

'Tomorrow.'

No night had ever passed so slowly. Over and over, Grigory's eyes migrated upward, to the clock over his desk. Each time they did, he was shocked at how slowly its hands had moved. Five minutes. Ten minutes. Two minutes. Through his narrow window, he saw that snow had begun to fall.

At nine o'clock he wandered down the hall to check on Oleg. The night manager lay on the couch in his office, a bottle of vodka half hidden under a cushion, his shirt untucked and pants unbuttoned, his potbelly rising and falling with each breath. When Grigory walked in, his eyes fluttered open and he treated Grigory to the patronizing smile he'd given Grigory a thousand times before. The smile that said, maybe vodka has turned my liver to rot, but I've got a wife and family waiting for me and you go home every morning to nothing but your own empty hand. Or maybe Grigory was projecting. Maybe Oleg was just thinking of his next drink. Even so, Grigory wouldn't miss that smile.

Oleg mumbled something.

'Yes?'

'The lights,' Oleg said. 'Make yourself useful for a change. Turn them off. And close the door. I don't want you looking at me. What if you get hungry?'

'Of course, boss.'

Grigory turned off the lights and went back to his office. When he checked again a few minutes later, he heard Oleg's heavy snores. No, Oleg wouldn't be a problem.

Ten o'clock. Weren't they supposed to arrive by now? Where were they? He walked over to the security center, a windowless room where guards monitored the plant's alarms and cameras.

Tajid nodded as Grigory walked in. He was fiddling with a screen that had gone dark. Monitors broke all the time, but the failure of this particular screen was no accident. It was one of three that watched the north weapons depot. Without it, the men in here would be partly blinded to what was happening in the warehouse.

'Hello, cousin,' Tajid said. He looked perfectly

normal. The room looked perfectly normal. Another endless night at Mayak. Grigory still couldn't quite believe what he was about to do. He pointed to the darkened monitor.

'You broke it watching pornos?'

'We don't need pornos,' said Arkady Merin, the senior night security officer. 'We use our imagination. And sometimes Tatu.'

Against all regulations, a fat black tabby lurked in the security office. Two winters before, a guard had found the cat in the special area during a blizzard. In her search for shelter, she'd somehow gotten through the electrified fences. She wasn't wearing a tag, and she ought to have been put down. But Arkady had taken a shine to her and made her the mascot for the guards. He named her Tatu, after a pair of Russian lesbian singers popular a few years back.

'Anything happening?'

'Quiet as a virgin in a whorehouse,' Arkady said. The perimeter and inner gates were staffed around the clock, but the operations center emptied out at night. This evening, only three men were on duty – Arkady, Tajid, and Marat, a fifty-something guard with a gritty, phlegmy smoker's cough that for the last few weeks had gotten worse.

'When's that dammed convoy due?'

'Eleven, they're saying.'

'Another delay?'

'One of the BTRs had engine trouble.'

'They're cursed. And such a night for it.'

'Could be worse. Could be February.' Arkady turned back to his monitors.

'Call me when they arrive,' Grigory said. 'Our esteemed boss is dreaming up new and better ways to manage and doesn't want to be disturbed.'

'Dreaming up? Such wit, Grigory,' Arkady smiled.

Grigory left. Hanging around wouldn't look natural. He needed to look natural. But back in his office, he couldn't work. He gave up trying and sat at his desk, watching the second hand tick. He knew what he was about to do was wrong, beyond wrong, and yet he couldn't stop himself. He never would have guessed he could break the rules so easily. Perhaps every man carried a beast inside him.

A few years back, a serial killer had worked his way through Chelyabinsk, killing dozens of prostitutes before one escaped from his truck and called the police. The killer – Grigory couldn't recall his name, but he was an electrician, he'd strangled his victims with thick black cords – grinned his way through his trial, and when the judge asked him if he had anything to say, any apologies to offer, he shook his head. 'You're lucky you caught me, for I would have gone on forever,' he said. 'You can't imagine how it feels.'

At this moment, Grigory thought he could.

The phone rang. 'They're here. At the main gate.'

'Thanks, Arkady.'

48

Grigory grabbed his coat and the paperwork he would need, including the single sheet of paper that held the codes to unlock the warhead boxes. Easy, he told himself. No rush. The delivery was a minor break from routine, nothing more. He walked slowly to the security office. 'Come on, Tajid. Enough pornos tonight. Let's greet our visitors.'

The first test. If Arkady raised a stink about the fact that Grigory had asked his cousin to be his partner on the delivery, they'd fail right away. But Grigory didn't expect Arkady to object. He wouldn't want to go himself, and sending old Marat into the cold would be callous. Sure enough, Arkady was feeding Tatu and hardly looked up.

'Have fun, Tajid,' he said.

'A real humanitarian, you are.' Tajid grabbed his coat and gloves and followed his cousin out.

First test passed.

Outside, the freezing wind hit Grigory full in the face. The snow was still falling, lightly now, covering the ground with a thin white rime.

Grigory was wearing a heavy down jacket and a sweater and woolen gloves, but he hadn't bothered with proper boots or a hat tonight, and the wind found his feet and face and attacked them. Human beings weren't meant to live this way. Maybe for a year or two, but not decade after decade. Not their whole lives.

Fortunately, the Volga started easily. Grigory had replaced the battery a few weeks before. Tajid and Grigory sat in silence for a moment, blowing on their hands, their breath filling the car. 'No second thoughts, cousin?' Grigory said.

'None. You?'

'I'm not thinking at all.'

'Probably that's best.'

Grigory put the Volga into gear and drove down the deserted avenue to the main gate. The convoy sat in a parking lot just inside the guard posts, the Ural trucks glowing under neon arc lights. The Volga looked like a toy beside the BTRs and Urals. Grigory parked beside the convoy and stepped out. A trim man wearing the single silver star of a major greeted him. Despite the cold, he wore only a thin wool coat and a hat with fur earflaps. He extended a hand.

'Major Yuri Akilev.'

'Grigory Farzadov. You've had a long trip.' Grigory's heart was pounding, but his voice sounded normal.

'The cards turn ugly and the bottles go dry,' Akilev said. 'No reason to expect anything else.'

'A man after my own heart,' Grigory said. 'That's it. A thousand years of history right there.'

'Even so, I'd like to get my men inside.'

Grigory pointed down the security fence at a squat two-story concrete building a few hundred yards away. 'Our overflow barracks. You can send the BTRs and Tigers there while we unload.'

'Is there food?'

This major was a good commander, concerned about the welfare of his men, Grigory thought. 'Not at this hour, but they'll have hot showers and warm beds.'

'That'll do.'

'But make sure you bring a couple of extra men with you to unload the crates.'

Akilev passed along the order to his sergeant. A moment later, the armored personnel carriers and three of the Tigers rumbled off, leaving just Grigory's Volga, the commander's Tiger, and the four Urals that held the bombs.

'Follow me.'

Grigory stopped the Volga at the guard post that protected the entrance to the special area. The post hut was made of thick concrete blocks, hardly bigger than a tollbooth, and had entrances on both sides of the restricted zone. The guards inside the hut theoretically would be the last line of defense in case of an all-out assault on the plant. In reality, the hut was the most boring place to work at Mayak, especially at night, when the special area was locked down and empty. Between 8 p.m. and 6 a.m., the post was staffed by a single guard, who slept most of the shift.

Through the thick window of the guardhouse, Grigory saw cheap black boots resting on a desk.

'Who's on duty tonight?' he said to Tajid.

'Roster said Boris Hiterov.'

'With the hair.'

'Yes.'

Boris Hiterov. A lifer. No better or worse than the average guard. With any luck, he'd have taken a couple of shots of vodka to help him sleep. Grigory cranked down his window. The second test was about to begin.

BEEP! Grigory leaned on the Volga's horn. Inside the hut, the boots kicked up with almost comic speed. Hiterov opened the window, just a crack. He was a big man, though not as big as Grigory, with dark brown hair that he wore up in a sort of pompadour. He was very proud of his hair.

'Boris!' Grigory yelled. 'We're here.'

A puzzled look settled on Hiterov's face. 'Who's that?'

'The convoy! Let us in, you damned fool!' The insults were key here. Grigory wanted to remind Hiterov of his place in the plant's hierarchy.

'Yes. But Grigory, you know the rule.'

Indeed Grigory did. Even if he hadn't, the black-lettered sign in front of him was clear. *No private automobiles. Official vehicles only.*

'If you think I'm leaving this car and walking, you've drunk away the last of your brains.' The north warehouse was about three hundred yards away, not really a long walk, but the cold night was working to Grigory's advantage.

'Why don't you ride with the convoy?'

'The commander's Tiger is full. Maybe you'd like me to sit on his lap.'

'But if anyone finds out—'

'No one will. Open the gate and go back to sleep, you wretch.'

Hiterov slammed the window shut. The electrified gate slowly rolled back, its wheels screeching in the cold.

Second test passed.

To keep American spy satellites from seeing their exact locations, both the north and south warehouses had been concealed under metal sheds as big as airplane hangars. Grigory drove into the north shed now, followed by Akilev's convoy. Inside, the shed was bright as a sunny afternoon, thanks to arc lights mounted high on its girders.

The weapons depot, a windowless concrete building one hundred feet long and sixty feet wide, sat in the northeast corner of the shed. The entrance to the depot was a wide steel door with no visible locks or opening mechanism. Four surveillance cameras focused on it. A half-dozen others watched the rest of the shed. But the cameras couldn't see everything, Grigory knew. He parked near the door to the shed, got out of his Volga, and turned to Akilev.

'Have your trucks park here and unload the cucumber crates. I'm going to get you out of here as quickly as I can.' Grigory spoke firmly, as if he were the major's superior officer. He had to be in control, give Akilev no room for questions. He felt sharp and strong, as if he'd burned through the first rapid-fire moves of a chess match and settled into the midgame. He'd arranged the board as he liked. Now he needed to press forward.

'As you say.' Eager to get some sleep, Akilev's men quickly unloaded the warhead crates. Meanwhile Grigory called to headquarters to tell Arkady that he and Tajid would be entering the warehouse. The steel door to the depot was three feet thick and could be unlocked only from head-quarters – another security measure.

Arkady picked up after five rings. 'Sleeping, Arkady?'

'Of course not. Everything on schedule?'

'Cold as your wife's tits. Otherwise fine.'

'My wife has no tits,' Arkady said. 'Let me know when you've checked the crates.'

Grigory hung up and turned to Akilev. 'Ready to be done with this?'

'More than you know.'

From his pocket Grigory unfolded the sheet that held the codes to unlock the warhead crates. He punched a twenty-two-digit code into the numeric keypad attached to the lid of the crate nearest him. The magnetic lock popped open and Grigory opened the crate. The warhead sat naked and sterile, a cylinder about two feet long and eighteen inches in diameter, held firm by the rubberized interior of the cucumber crate. A string of numbers and Cyrillic letters, painted in red, gave the warhead's serial number and its specifications. Halfway up the cylinder, a control panel stuck out, a simple metal plate with three switches side by side: Armed/Not Armed; Full Yield/Half Yield/Low Yield; Airburst/Groundburst. Beside the plate, the warhead's locking mechanism, two eight-digit combination locks and a circular keyhole. Everything about the bomb was simple and low-tech, designed for reliability and ease of use by frontline soldiers who were likely to be under attack as they readied the warhead for launch.

'Hardly looks like it's worth the trouble,' Grigory said to Akilev.

'Harmless as a Gypsy curse.'

Grigory closed the crate, which locked automatically. They moved on to the second crate, the third, and on down to the eighth. All the boxes were full.

'Well done, Major.'

'You thought I'd lost one?'

Grigory grabbed the file that held his inventory receipts from the Volga. He dated and signed the papers and handed them to Akilev. 'Sign here,' he said.

'But aren't we supposed to wait until the boxes are inside the warehouse?'

Third test. 'If you like,' Grigory said. 'But me and Tajid will need at least two hours to put the crates in their proper places. I thought you and your men might want some rest. Your choice.'

'Can we help you move the crates inside the depot?'

'I'm afraid not. Not that I don't trust you—'

Yes, Grigory thought. Turn back the question of trust on him.

'I understand. And you don't mind if we leave. You're certain.'

'Not a bit.'

'All right.' Akilev signed the papers and handed them back to Grigory. 'Thanks for this. It's been a very long day.' He whistled sharply to his men. They jumped into the Urals, which started with a heavy diesel thump. A minute later, the Tiger and the trucks had disappeared from the shed, leaving Grigory and his cousin alone.

Third test passed.

To his surprise, Grigory felt no excitement. He was relaxed, yet hyperaware of his surroundings. The grain of the pavement beneath his feet, the cold air against his face, the hum of the arc lights above his head – he saw and heard everything at once. This must be how God feels, he thought.

He called Arkady. 'The crates checked out.'

'Has the convoy gone? On the monitors—'

'I told them they could. No need to make them wait for us.'

'But how will you—'

'We drove in.'

'Grigory, you know that's not allowed—'

'So write me up. But meanwhile open the damn door, so we can put them away and be done.'

Arkady hung up. A few seconds later, the big

56

steel door creaked open. Grigory and Tajid hefted two crates onto a forklift beside the door. Grigory drove into the cool depths of the warehouse, Tajid walking slowly behind him. Dropping the crates off took twenty minutes. When they were done, they loaded two more crates and repeated the procedure.

Fourth test. The third set of crates had come from the truck that had been nearest the Volga. Grigory waited until the cameras mounted on the rafters of the shed were facing away from him. The cameras made long, slow loops around the warehouse. For Grigory, who knew the pattern, they were easy to avoid.

Quickly, Grigory popped the trunk of the Volga and pulled out a pair of steel toolboxes, two feet by two feet by three feet, each half-filled with hard rubber balls the size of large marbles.

Toolboxes in hand, Grigory strode over to the crates and again keyed in the codes to unlock them. He reached into the first crate and grabbed for the cylinder. He had never actually touched a warhead before. To save weight and space, the damn thing didn't have handles, and Grigory wasn't sure how to lift it. He wedged his fingers underneath and began to pull. The warhead slipped back, nearly breaking his hands, and he fired curses at his cousin.

'Come on, you oaf. Help.'

On the second try they lifted the cylinder and transferred it into the toolbox, arranging the rubber balls so that it wouldn't roll around. Quickly, they repeated the operation with the second crate.

Grigory snuck a look at the cameras on the ceiling. Still safe. He and Tajid slipped the toolboxes into the trunk, one over each wheel well. The lightbulb inside the trunk was dead, and the trunk was dirty with old newspapers and bottles of antifreeze and a spare tire and wrenches and a jack. Grigory covered the toolboxes with blankets and slammed down the lid. A thorough search would spot the boxes, but a flashlight quickly shined over the trunk wouldn't. So he hoped. He closed the Volga lid and looked around. The cameras were still pointing away.

Fourth test passed.

With the warheads in his trunk, Grigory's self-confidence began to flag. Until now he'd been playing a game, outsmarting Arkady and Boris Hiterov and Major Akilev, which wasn't hard, since none of them knew they were playing at all. Bringing the Volga in was a technical infraction, nothing more.

Now, though, he'd crossed the border into something else. What if he'd been caught in some elaborate setup? What if the FSB had recruited Tajid to betray him? What if a force of agents waited outside the fence at this moment—

'Cousin,' Tajid said sharply, knocking Grigory from his reverie. 'Let's be done.'

So they went back into the warehouse, first with the two empty crates and then the final two. Grigory heart pounded in his chest. He was grateful for the cold air.

Then they were done. Grigory called Arkady, who answered on the second ring. This time he'd been awake, awaiting the call, Grigory figured. A bad sign.

'We're done. Thank God. I think my balls have frozen.'

'Fine, then.' Arkady sounded annoyed. Grigory hung up and stepped away as the steel door slid closed. The shed was empty, the forklift beside the door. The place looked exactly as they had found it.

Grigory and Tajid slid into the Volga. Grigory hoped no one would notice that the car was sitting lower now. 'Do you really believe we'll get out of here, cousin?'

'*Inshallah*. It's God's will.'

'If you say so.' Grigory turned the key and the Volga started immediately.

But when they arrived at the guard hut, the fence was still closed.

'Damn Boris.' Grigory honked. The rear door of the hut opened and Hiterov stepped out, holding a flashlight. Its beam caught Grigory in the eyes. Grigory felt his bowels tighten.

Grigory rolled down his window. 'What's this, Boris?'

'I have to check the car. Arkady's orders.'

Fifth test. This one unexpected. Grigory felt as he did playing chess when an opponent found a weakness and counterattacked, leaving him naked. Grigory opened the door, stepped out of the car. 'Come on, Tajid. Into the cold while he finds the bombs we've stolen.' He hoped he had the right tone of sarcasm in his voice.

'You think I want to be out here?' Hiterov whined. Nonetheless he leaned into the car, shined the flashlight over the front seats, then into the back. 'Now the trunk.'

Grigory unlocked the trunk. Hiterov poked the beam of his light inside.

'What a mess. Don't you ever clean this thing?'

'Only on nights I'm screwing your wife in the backseat.'

With his free hand, Hiterov poked ineffectually at the papers and antifreeze bottles. Grigory imagined how he would explain the war-heads to the police and the FSB. An experiment, a test of the plant's security. Maybe he'd tell the truth, try to trade his life for Yusuf's, though he'd still wind up in a Siberian jail until he died.

Finally, Hiterov stood up. He hadn't found them. He hadn't noticed the toolboxes, hadn't even moved the blankets.

'Inspection over. Tell Arkady I did as he asked.'

'Tell him yourself.' Grigory and Tajid slipped back into the Volga as Hiterov disappeared into the hut. The gate opened and Grigory put the Volga into gear and rolled out.

60

Fifth test passed. Game over. Checkmate.

The rest was simple. They checked in at headquarters and handed over the paperwork. Arkady complained about the way Grigory had broken the rules, and Grigory apologized dutifully. Four a.m. came, the end of Grigory's shift. 'See you, Tajid,' he said to his cousin, whose shift didn't end for another hour. 'Have a good weekend, Arkady.'

'You and your mother, too.'

Grigory walked out of headquarters and into the frigid night. The lights of the buildings around him glowed brightly, but nothing moved. In the distance, somewhere outside the gates of the plant, a truck rumbled. He walked toward the Volga. It wasn't too late. He could still turn around, confess to Arkady, explain the theft as a crazy practical joke . . .

Too late, not too late, too late . . . Forget it. He'd won. Now he wanted his reward, whatever it was. He settled himself inside the Volga, slipped key into ignition.

'*Inshallah*,' he said. The foolishness that contented his cousin. God willing. What a strange thing to say. As if God had anything to do with this game they were playing. He pursed his lips, said it again. '*Inshallah*.' He drove off, toward the plant's main gate, two stolen nuclear warheads in his trunk.

CHAPTER 4

ZURICH

Cottage cheese.

Cottage cheese and melon. Cottage cheese and low-fat granola. Cottage cheese and an egg-white omelette . . . In the last three months, Pierre Kowalski had eaten cottage cheese all the ways it could be eaten. Now he was eating it again, spooning the rubbery white junk into his mouth. He choked it down with a glass of Evian, trying to pretend it had any taste at all.

'This is no way to live,' he grumbled in French across the table at Nadia Zorinova, his girlfriend, a twenty-two-year-old whose pert nose and ice-blue eyes were currently gracing the cover of Spanish *Vogue*.

'Now you know how we models feel.' Nadia smirked at him with her million-dollar lips. 'Soon you'll be ready to walk the runway.'

Nadia. This mansion on Lake Zurich, another in Monte Carlo. A yacht complete with its own helicopter pad. A billion dollars spread in banks around the world. The ear of defense ministers and presidents from Buenos Aires to Bangkok. Kowalski had everything he wanted. Everything but this . . . cottage cheese.

Kowalski never wanted to see cottage cheese again, not unless it was sitting next to a steak. A thick filet mignon, medium rare, in a pepper-corn sauce, accompanied by a bottle of burgundy. He picked up his plate, Wedgwood bone china, and spun it across the room like a $600 Frisbee. It crashed into the fireplace and exploded in a thousand shards, scattering cottage cheese and grapes across the floor.

Nadia's smirk widened. 'Pierre, you mustn't keep destroying the china.'

'It's replaceable.' Like you, Kowalski mentally added. Though Nadia had her charms. A few weeks earlier, she'd just missed being cast as an underwear model for Calvin Klein.

'Would you like something else?'

'Do you plan to cook it for me?'

Three months before, Kowalski had brought his personal physician, Dr Émile Breton, to his mansion for a physical. The appointment was not entirely routine. For weeks, he'd found himself unable to . . . perform, despite Nadia's most tender ministrations. He'd never suffered that problem before. Quite the opposite, in fact. Years before, his endowment had earned him the nickname 'Cinquante,' French for 'fifty,' a reference not to the American rapper but to the .50-caliber sniper rifle, among the most powerful firearms ever made.

So Kowalski's troubles left him puzzled. Perhaps his advancing age? Whatever the problem, he expected that Breton would take care of it with a prescription for Viagra or some similar elixir. The doctor had other ideas. He weighed Kowalski, drew blood, insisted that Kowalski come to his office for a treadmill stress test. And then he returned to Kowalski's mansion to deliver the bad news in person.

'Pierre. You must change your diet, begin to exercise. You've gained ten kilos' – twenty-two pounds – 'in two years.'

'You've been saying the same thing for as long as I've known you.' Kowalski smirked. 'Would you like lunch, Doctor? It's quail today, in a sauce of figs.'

'This isn't a joke. Your cholesterol, your weight, your glucose. Disastrous, all of it.'

'Aren't there those balloons?'

'Angioplasty. Yes, you may need that as well. But unless you take your diet more seriously, it's only postponing the inevitable. Your arteries are nearly blocked. Why do you think you're having such trouble with that delightful girl out there?'

Kowalski's smile faded. 'Now I see I have your attention,' the doctor said.

'What about the pills?'

'If you don't lose at least twenty-five kilos' – almost sixty pounds – 'Viagra will be useless.'

'You're beginning to depress me.'

'Forty kilos would be even better. Tell your chef to throw away the quail, cook some vegetables.'

'Forty kilos? That's nearly one-third of my weight.' Kowalski weighed 130 kilos – almost 290 pounds.

'I know.' He handed Kowalski a card: H. W. Rossi, *spécialiste de diète*. 'If you're serious about remaining alive, call him. I've seen him work miracles with men like you.'

Indeed, under the watchful eyes of Rossi, who seemed to survive solely on vegetables and an occasional piece of broiled trout, Kowalski had lost thirteen kilos in three months. Over the last few weeks, his libido had even started to return. Even so, the diet wore on him. Kowalski had always been a master at presenting a smooth face to the world. Now, though, he found himself irritable, prone to silly tricks like flinging plates across the room.

Yes, the diet was bothering him. The diet. And the knowledge that John Wells was still alive.

Kowalski was the world's largest private arms dealer, a conduit for weapons from Russia, France, and the United States to armies all over the developing world. His father, Frederick, had gotten into the business in the late 1950s, recognizing that the newly liberated nations of Africa would need weapons and that Europe had millions of guns left over from World War II, moldering in warehouses.

The business took off in 1975, when Frederick brokered a deal between France and a young Iraqi dictator named Saddam Hussein. By then, Kowalski was at Oxford, studying political science. A few months before Kowalski graduated, Frederick asked when he would join the firm.

'Never,' Kowalski said.

Frederick looked at his son with the cool dark eyes that were a family trait.

Kowalski felt the need to explain, though he didn't want to offend his father by questioning the morality of the business. 'I want to make my own success.'

Frederick raised his hand. 'Pierre. *C'est bon.* When you change your mind, you'll find an open door.'

It will never happen, Kowalski thought. 'Thank you, Papa,' he said aloud.

But his father was right. After five years of working in Paris for Lazard Frères, the investment bank, Kowalski had grown supremely bored. These pompous executives in their hand-tailored suits thought they ruled the world. But the men who really ruled, the generals who held whole nations in their grip, didn't pay lawyers to squabble at each other. When they saw something they wanted, they took it. If they made a mistake, they didn't get a fat severance package and a new job a few months later. They paid with their lives.

And those men – they came to his father for help. All over Africa, Latin America, the Middle East,

Frederick Kowalski was treated like royalty. Pierre was disgusted, too, with the hypocrisy he saw every day in business. These companies, with their trade associations and their codes of ethics, as if they cared about anything but their profits. At least the Africans didn't hide their greed. On his fifth anniversary, just as his boss at Lazard told him he was on track to become a partner, Pierre handed in his resignation.

Two days later, he was back in Zurich. When he appeared at his father's office on Bahnhofstrasse, Frederick smiled.

'Come to join me?'

Pierre nodded, feeling slightly abashed. Until now he hadn't considered the possibility that he might have waited too long, that his father might be angry at him, might even reject him.

'What took so long?' Frederick said.

The business became Kowalski *père et fils* a few years later, and Kowalski took over when Frederick suffered a stroke in 1999. Besides his daughter, Anna, a regular in the pages of the fashion magazines, Kowalski *fils* had two sons from his first and only marriage. So far, neither had shown interest in becoming part of the trade. But Kowalski expected they'd change their minds soon enough.

Like his father, he ran the business on a few simple principles. He never promised customers weapons he couldn't deliver. He never stored his merchandise on Swiss soil. He always made sure he was paid up front. He never worked twice with anyone who tried to burn him.

And he never made threats he didn't intend to keep.

Several months before, John Wells had attacked Kowalski at a rented mansion in East Hampton, New York. Wells had . . . Kowalski didn't even like to remember what Wells had done. Handcuffed him, shocked him with a stun gun, covered his head with duct tape. He was lucky he hadn't suffocated. Wells had worn a mask, but Kowalski had learned his identity a few weeks later. Now he wanted revenge, the revenge that he had promised the masked man in his bedroom that night. On Wells, and Exley, too, who'd helped Wells.

'*You must know you're making a terrible mistake*,' Kowalski had said at the time. '*Whoever you are . . . Even if you think you're safe. I'll break the rules for you.*' Now Kowalski meant to keep his promise. Wells would pay for what he'd done.

A hand touched his shoulder, snapping him out of that summer night. Nadia stood beside him. 'Pierre, are you all right? Your face was so . . . black.'

He kissed her cheek. 'Too much cottage cheese.'

A light knock on the door. Anatoly Tarasov, Kowalski's head of security, a former Russian Spetsnaz officer, entered. A walking tornado, capable of extraordinary violence.

'Have you finished?' Kowalski said to Nadia.

'Yes.' Her lunch had consisted of two pieces of melon and a boiled egg, and yet she seemed satisfied. He couldn't imagine how.

'Then wait for me in the drawing room. Today we'll go for a shop.'

She kissed him and glided out. Tarasov waited until she was gone, then closed the door and sat beside him. 'You like her.'

'She's sweet,' Kowalski said. 'Sweeter than most of them.'

'Or a better actress.'

'Perhaps. Have you news on our friend?'

'You won't wish to hear it. The CIA has two teams, two men each, watching the house where he and the woman live.'

'Around the clock?'

'Around the clock. One team in front, one in back. There's a third in plainclothes that comes and goes.'

'What about their vehicles?' Putting a bomb underneath a car was the easiest way to assassinate someone.

'Garaged. They travel to work in separate cars most days. The woman drives a Dodge minivan, and Wells a Subaru. Sometimes he rides a motorcycle, but not in the winter. Two of the guards follow in a chase car.'

'Are their cars armored?'

'It doesn't seem so. At Langley, they're untouchable, naturally. They also have a private office in a place called Tyson's Corner. But they spend most of their time at the agency now. And the private building has its own security. One of the CIA guards has a post outside the door and the other watches the cars. There's a third guard in their office.'

'Could we reach them there?'

'They never open the door when there's anyone else on the floor, and there are cameras on the corridor.'

'How about the elevator?'

'Such a confined space isn't ideal. If Wells gets a hand up—'

'I understand.' They would have only one chance at Wells and Exley. Kowalski didn't want to waste it.

'Also, the guards at the house have noticed our scout.'

Kowalski's stomach began to ache. 'They've blown it already? Markov said these were his best men.'

Ivan Markov was recently retired from the FSB. Kowalski had given Markov $2 million up front to kill Wells and Exley, with the promise of another $3 million for a successful job.

'Nothing's blown, Pierre. Our man was asked an idle question by the agents outside the house. He gave an idle answer. Nothing more. We shouldn't underestimate the CIA. Perhaps they cannot catch bin Laden, but they are perfectly capable of watching a house in Washington.'

For a moment Kowalski wondered whether he

ought to call off this assassination. He had known all along that Wells and Exley were not ideal targets. They were high-profile, and Wells was more than capable of defending himself. Still, Kowalski had figured that Markov's men would finish the task quickly.

A few days of watching, then a few pounds of explosive attached to the undercarriage of Wells's car. A three-man team. No elaborate surveillance required. And when he'd given Markov Wells's name, the general had actually smiled. The Russians didn't like Americans much these days, Kowalski thought.

But now . . . this job was turning messy.

'What do you think?' he asked Tarasov.

'I think that once you begin a mission like this . . .' Tarasov trailed off. But Kowalski understood. The Russians respected strength. Bombings, poisonings, assassinations, Siberan prison camps – Russian leaders used every weapon at their disposal to remain in power, without apology. If Kowalski backed off, Markov would not be impressed. He would pass the word to his old bosses in the Kremlin: Pierre Kowalski has gone soft. The Russians were Kowalski's most important business partner. He couldn't afford to look weak to them.

And yet . . . he had built this mansion, built his empire, by thinking clearly, never letting emotion cloud his business dealings. Only women had the luxury of setting reason aside in their decisions.

He didn't need to kill John Wells. Why take this risk?

'Thank you, Anatoly.' Kowalski nodded to the door. 'Come back in a quarter-hour.' He needed a few minutes alone. A few minutes to think.

Tarasov reappeared fifteen minutes later.

'So the home is impossible,' Kowalski said. 'And also the office.'

'Not impossible, but—'

'Then we will hit them in between, I think.'

'I thought you might say that.'

'Will Markov want more men?'

'He believes in three-man teams.'

'And these men?'

'The best, Pierre. I know them myself.'

'Good,' Kowalski said. 'Now let me find that girl before she gets herself into trouble.' He pushed himself from the table and padded toward Nadia. In the desperate weeks to come, he would ask himself more than once whether he would have made a different decision if he hadn't been so damned hungry.

CHAPTER 5

Wells awoke to Exley's hands on his back, sliding across the base of his spine, over his hips, up to the thick muscles in his shoulders. Outside their bedroom the sky was dark, no sign of dawn in the winter night.

'Time is it?'

'Five-thirty.'

'Have you been awake long?'

'Hush, John.'

He tried to turn on his side, but she pressed him down.

'I'm treating you. Close your eyes.'

Wells closed his eyes and tried to float, though weightlessness had never come easy to him. Except on his motorcycle on a good clean road. And hiking through the Bitterroots growing up, leaves crunching under his feet, the comforting weight of a rifle on his shoulder, the sky blue and wide and cloudless, the tips of the mountains painted with snow that never melted. Above him eagles and falcons circling, spreading their wings to catch thermals. Exley's hands pulled him up and Wells left his gun behind and rose to meet the raptors.

He made great mile-wide loops, peering at the mountains below until the sky turned black. He wondered what had happened to Exley. But no matter where he turned, she was gone.

He woke again to the blare of the radio by their bed: 6:45. The sky outside had turned gray and the WTOP announcer was promising a blustery cold day. Exley was gone, and the shower was running. He wandered into the bathroom.

'Come in here. I'll wash you.'

Exley liked to mother him sometimes, pretend he couldn't take care of himself. Wells wondered sometimes whether all women had this instinct. Maybe she did it to cut him down, make him more manageable. Or maybe she just liked him clean. Living in Afghanistan, he'd gone weeks, even months, without washing himself properly. Old habits died hard.

'I can handle it.'

'Get in here.'

'Why is it I think you're looking for more than a shower this morning?'

At that, a hand reached out from the curtain and tugged him in.

Afterward, she sat beside him on the edge of the bed. She was flushed and pink, her mouth open, her lips swollen. Wells was breathing hard, too.

'So good today,' she said.

'You always say that.'

'No, it's true. I'm just glad we have our own house now. So I can make all the noise I want.' She kissed his cheek.

'Let's get dressed. Or we'll never get out of here.'

'Then let's not. Let's stay in here forever. Make a little world, just us.' She wrapped her arms around him. Her blue eyes shone and he knew she was serious. Like him, she'd devoted her life to the agency, given up everything – her first husband, her kids, her friends.

But since Wells had come back from China, she'd begun to pull away from the CIA. She was more engaged in planning their vacation than with anything happening at Langley. She kept extending the trip, too. First they were going to South America for two weeks. Then a month. Now she was talking about visiting Africa, too, six weeks in all. He'd joked that she should look into Antarctica.

Wells couldn't blame her, not after everything that had happened over the last two years. But quit? Retire? He couldn't imagine it. The job was all he knew how to do.

The job was all he was. He disentangled himself from her.

'Tomorrow,' he said. 'Tomorrow we'll stay in here forever.'

'You promise, John.'

'I promise.'

Exley headed back into the bathroom to put her face on. But do you love me, John? Do you *really*?

Do you even know what the word means? Loving Wells was like throwing quarters down a mineshaft. She could hear the faint echo when the coins hit bottom, but she had to listen hard.

Not that she could complain. She'd made this choice, or more correctly the choice had made her. She couldn't imagine ever being with anyone else. She would take as much of him as he could give. And maybe, one day, she'd find the key and he'd be hers for good.

Not likely.

Back in the bedroom, Wells was doing push-ups, the scar on his back twitching with each rep. He was nearly forty, and he'd taken a lot of abuse the last two years, but physical therapy and constant exercise and his natural strength had saved him. He still looked like the football player he'd once been, his muscles laced atop one another like illustrations in an anatomy textbook.

'Come on, sit on my back,' he said.

'What are you, fourteen? You just showered. Now you're going to be sweaty again.' Nonetheless she kneeled atop him while he finished another twenty reps. Wells was showing off, she knew, but she couldn't help herself. He was never more endearing than when he was acting like a big kid. And she found touching him this way nearly irresistible. He finished and she stayed on him, not wanting to move.

'Up,' he said. 'You're going to break me.'

'You asked for it.' She ran a finger across the sweat on his back. 'Come on. Let's get dressed, go to work. Such as it is.'

Exley's Dodge Caravan was six years old and had a deep dent in its back fender from a tailgating cabbie. Inside, the carpets were grimy and cluttered with broken pens, coins, half-filled bottles of diet soda. Its heaters poured out an indefinable but vaguely unpleasant odor.

'You ever going to get something nicer?' Wells said. 'A seventy-two Pinto, maybe.'

'Didn't you used to say that Western materialism disgusts you?'

'Western materialism? Western? Have you checked out the Indians and the Chinese lately? I give up.'

'Really?'

'No, but I make an exception for cars. So sue me.' In fact, Wells had just bought a Subaru Impreza WRX, a turbocharged rice rocket that didn't look special but could go from zero to sixty in just over four seconds. 'Seriously, you've got to do something about this thing. It belongs on *Pimp My Ride*. Maybe I'll send them a video.'

'How do you know about *Pimp My Ride*?'

'I'm hip.'

At that, Exley laughed. 'You are many things, John, but hip isn't one of them.'

★　　★　　★

Washington was notorious for its traffic, but even by those standards the city was having a miserable morning. Constitution Avenue went bumper to bumper at 18th Street, a full five blocks from the ramp to the Roosevelt Memorial Bridge, one of the main routes connecting D.C. and Arlington.

Wells flicked on the radio only to hear that someone had ditched a car at the end of the bridge, by the exit ramp to the George Washington Parkway. The 14th Street Bridge was messed up, too, thanks to a car fire that had started around 6 a.m. The fire had quickly been put out, but the incident was still being investigated. Wells turned off the radio. 'We should have stayed in bed.'

'Told you so.'

A Ducati zipped by on the left, a beautiful bike, low and red, sailing through the narrow aisle of asphalt created by the stopped cars in each lane. The driver and passenger were bundled against the cold, wearing thick gloves and black helmets with mirrored face-masks. They peered at the minivan as they rolled by.

'I believe they're laughing at us,' Wells said. 'That bike is probably worth ten times as much as this thing.'

'Let them laugh. It's freezing out there.'

'If we'd taken my bike we'd be there already.' Harley and Honda sold the romance of the open road in their ads, but cutting through traffic jams was one of the underappreciated pleasures of riding.

'Who rides a motorcycle when it's thirty degrees?'

'You've got me to block the wind.'

'Nothing blocks the wind in weather like this.'

Wells's cell phone rang – Steve Feder, who ran their security detail during the day. Feder was riding shotgun in their chase car, a black Chevy Suburban directly behind them. 'Should I turn on my flashers, get us out of here?'

'Not unless there's something you think we need to be concerned about,' Wells said. He looked back and Feder gave him a little wave, Queen-of-England style.

'Nothing specific.'

'Then it's all right. We can wait like everybody else.'

'Fair enough.' *Click.*

Twenty minutes later, they'd gotten only to the block between 20th and 21st Streets, the Federal Reserve building filling the block to their right, protected by big concrete stanchions. Wells didn't pretend to understand what went on in there. The light ahead turned green and they shuffled forward a few car lengths.

'Maybe they finally got it out of the way.'

'Maybe,' Exley said. 'What're you thinking?'

Wells nodded at the Fed. 'Looks solid, doesn't it? All these big, gray buildings.'

'It's held up awhile.'

'Maybe we've just been lucky.'

'It's a solid ship. And there's a lot of us running around looking for leaks.'

'Is that what we are? Sounds glamorous.'

In the distance behind them, Wells heard a motorcycle engine. Then another.

And suddenly he knew.

Who rides a motorcycle when it's thirty degrees?

Accidents on two bridges.

Too many coincidences this morning.

If he was wrong . . . no harm no foul. He'd call it paranoia and have something to talk about at the support group this week. But he knew.

He looked back, but his view was blocked by the bulk of the Suburban. He leaned forward and examined the passenger-side mirror. There. A red sportbike on his side, cutting between the traffic and the curb. Maybe ten cars back, three hundred feet in all, including the gaps between vehicles. Closing, slowly and steadily.

'Jenny. Check your mirror. Do you see a motorcycle?'

Exley leaned forward, peeked at her mirror. 'Sure. A black bike. Back a ways.'

The red bike was 150 feet away, five car lengths. With his left hand, he unbuckled his seat belt. Then Exley's. With his right, he reached under his jacket. He carried his Glock in an armpit holster under his left shoulder.

The traffic inched forward. On his side, the red bike was now only about three car lengths behind. Wells pulled the Glock, the big pistol solid in his hand. Time seemed to slow, a good sign. His reflexes were accelerating. Because he was right-handed, he'd have to get out of the van, expose himself, if he wanted a clean shot. Not what he wanted. But he had no choice.

'Open your door, Jenny. NOW.'

Wells couldn't take the time to look at her, but he heard her door open. He reached across his body and opened his own door with his left hand, blocking the path of the bike.

In one smooth motion, he swung himself out of the minivan, left leg over right, and dropped to his knees, the gun in his right hand. He knew he had almost no time to decide. If he was wrong, he was about to kill a couple guys who were trying to beat traffic.

The bike was a red Ducati carrying two men. Just like the one that had passed them before. It was maybe fifty feet away, rolling slowly beside the Suburban chase car, nearly stopped, and then—

Then the passenger on the bike reached down and flicked something under the body of the big SUV.

'Grenade!' Wells yelled.

The Ducati revved toward him. He fired. The bike came fast, but the bullet was faster. The shot caught the rider in his right shoulder and the bike twisted right but stayed up, its front wheel barely ten feet from Wells. Wells shifted his aim and fired again. The mirrored faceplate of the helmet shattered.

The rider's head jerked back and his body slumped in death and his hands came off the bars. The bike started to go down—

And there were two explosions under the Suburban in quick succession—

Boom! Boom!

The Suburban lifted off the ground—

BOOM!

A larger explosion followed as the SUV's gas tank blew—

Thick black smoke filled the air—

Wells kept shooting, aiming now at the second man on the Ducati, who was reaching under his jacket. But the bike was skidding down, giving Wells a clean look. Wells took his time and caught the guy with a shot to the side of the head. His helmet twitched. He fell off the back of the bike and hit the asphalt with a heavy dead thump.

Wells was already shifting his focus. Two grenades. Two motorcycles. He braced himself against the side of the minivan and spun. On the far side of the Caravan, by its left rear wheel, another rider stood, his bike between his legs, a pistol in his gloves right hand.

The pistol jerked twice in succession, *crack-crack—*

'John!' Exley screamed, a high hopeless sound—

Wells fired through the minivan, his only choice, knowing that if he missed, he risked killing an innocent driver in the cars behind the shooter—

And missed.

The rider turned toward Wells and fired. The round smashed through the van's window—

And missed.

Wells sprang left, looking for a cleaner shot, a shot that wouldn't be blocked by the van's second row of seats. The rider reached under his jacket with his left hand. Wells fired, separated from the guy only by the width of the van—

The 9-millimeter slug from Wells's Glock caught the guy full in the chest, tore open his leather jacket. Its force jerked him back, standing him upright. But he didn't go down. *Bulletproof vest*, Wells thought. He ducked as the guy lifted his pistol and fired two shots, wild and high, then threw down the pistol and again reached into his jacket.

Wells slowed himself. Last chance. If he missed this time, the guy would toss a grenade under the van and cook Exley.

He aimed carefully through the van and squeezed the trigger.

Crack. Through the van, Wells saw the rider's face-plate shatter. The guy fell backward, his helmet cracking against the roof of the BMW behind him, dead already.

Wells ran around the van to the driver's side. Exley lay in the front seat, moaning, slumped forward.

'John.'

'Just stay still.'

Already he could hear sirens. Behind them, the

Suburban crackled and burned, throwing off gobs of smoke that stank of gasoline and charred flesh. The agents inside were surely dead. Five dead here this morning. As long as it wasn't six.

He didn't see the wound. He pulled up her sweater. There it was, blooming red on her white shirt, the right side, just above the waist. Maybe the liver, Wells thought. If it was the liver, they'd better get her to a hospital quick before she bled out. He pressed down on it and she moaned again. Her warm blood seeped between his fingers. A bad one.

He put his hand to her cheek and listened to the sirens draw close. And he wondered who'd done this to them. He wondered who would pay.

CHAPTER 6

BLACK SEA

In the dark, Grigory Farzadov couldn't see the waves. But he could hear them, banging against the hull like living beasts. Thump. Thump. Thump-*thoomp*. In the last hour, their intensity had steadily increased. And yet Grigory didn't mind. He'd grown up thousands of kilometers from the ocean. He'd never seen the Pacific or the Atlantic. He didn't even know how to swim. But all his life he'd envied those lucky souls who lived on the water. Now he was one of them. Sort of.

His cousin wasn't so sanguine. As the *Tambulz Dream* – the little fishing trawler that had been their home for a day – rocked sideways, Tajid laid a hand on his stomach and gripped the dirty steel rail that ran around the cabin. He'd already vomited once. Meanwhile Yusuf sat in a corner, cursing under his breath, his eyes dead and flat as ever. Grigory was sure that if he looked hard enough he would see smoke coming off Yusuf's head, and smell the faint stink of sulfur.

Though maybe the smell was just the Black Sea, a famously dank waterway. The sea lay between six countries – Russia, Georgia, Turkey, Romania, Bulgaria, and Ukraine – and had possessed a bad reputation for at least three thousand years. Technically, the Black Sea and the Mediterranean formed a single body of water, linked through the Bosphorus, the narrow strait that divided Istanbul. But the sparkling waters of the Mediterranean had little in common with the Black Sea. The complex currents that connected the two left the Black Sea's depths a toxic stew, thick with salt and hydrogen sulfide, poisonous to fish.

The sea's surface was hardly more pleasant, regularly racked by storms powerful enough to split oil tankers in half. Even so, anchovy and sturgeon lived in the sea's upper layer, and fishing trawlers set out each day to catch what they could. This ship was one of them, a simple vessel, about a hundred feet long, its hull a faded blue, its one-story cabin white. Grigory knew nothing about boats, but even he could see that this one had seen better days. One of its cabin windows was missing, replaced with wooden planks. The engines growled madly when the captain pushed the throttle forward. Besides Grigory, Yusuf, and Tajid, the trawler carried a crew of three, the captain and two younger men who seemed to be his sons.

More than that, Grigory didn't know. He wasn't even sure where they were headed, though he assumed somewhere on the Turkish coast.

Yusuf wasn't saying, and Grigory had learned the hard way not to ask.

Still, their escape had gone smoothly so far, Grigory had to admit. When he arrived at his apartment building at 5 a.m. on the night of the theft, the sun still hours from rising, there was Yusuf, sitting in an old Nissan sedan. As soon as Grigory parked, Yusuf was at his window.

'You have them.'

'A pleasure to see you, too.'

'You have them.'

'It was more trouble than I expected.' Grigory was enjoying himself now.

'If you don't have them, you'd better tell me now.'

'Of course.'

'Of course, you have them? Or of course you don't? Grigory, I swear—'

'They're in the trunk.'

To Grigory's surprise, Yusuf clapped his hands. 'Congratulations, Grigory.' Yusuf pulled the Volga's door open and tugged Grigory out. Grigory wondered whether the little Arab planned to cut his throat. Instead, Yusuf hugged him, wrapping his arms around Grigory's bulk like a circus clown trying to saddle an elephant.

'Ready to go?'

'My bag is upstairs.'

'Then get it.'

Grigory hadn't found much in his apartment

worth taking. In a cheap nylon bag, he'd packed a half-dozen books, two pornographic DVDs starring the American Jenna Jamison, a few shirts and sweaters and long underwear, and both of his chess sets, his good wooden one and a little magnetic travel set. He'd taken his passport, though he couldn't see what use it would be. Soon enough he'd have a new name and nationality. Or be dead.

Grigory rode the creaking elevator downstairs for the final time and tossed the bag into the backseat of the Volga. Yusuf grabbed his arm. 'Show me, Grigory.'

Grigory popped the trunk of the Volga and moved aside the junk to reveal the toolboxes. Yusuf flipped open the boxes and stood in silence over the trunk. 'They don't look like much,' he said at last.

'What did you expect? A ticking clock? Something glowing?'

'They're real?'

Grigory laughed, a crazy giggle that set his flabby stomach bouncing. All he'd gone through, and now this.

'They don't impress you, Yusuf? They're real. More real than anything else in this stupid world, I'd say.'

'All right.' Yusuf snapped the boxes closed. 'We'll put them in my car, leave this heap.'

'Whatever you like.'

They shifted the bombs to the Nissan, and Grigory

threw his bag in as well. 'Shall I drive?' Grigory said. 'Since we're partners now?'

'You'll drive if I'm dead. Maybe not even then.'

'I was joking, Yusuf. You've heard of jokes?'

'Quiet.'

Grigory slid into the Nissan, which stank of cheap air freshener. They drove to Tajid's apartment and waited for him to arrive. Then the three of them drove out of Ozersk. Grigory craned his neck left and right as they left the city, feeling like a kid taking his first big trip. He didn't expect to be back.

Just outside Samara, southwest of Chelyabinsk, they were filling up at a dingy petrol station when a Toyota sedan stopped in front of them. Yusuf trotted to it and slipped into the passenger seat. Grigory had always known that Yusuf couldn't be acting alone, but this was the first proof he'd seen. He poked at his cousin, who was dozing in the backseat.

'Tajid, who's that?' Grigory pointed to the Toyota. 'Have you seen Yusuf with anyone before?'

'No questions, cousin. Don't you understand that by now?'

When Yusuf returned, Grigory couldn't help himself. 'A new friend, Yusuf?'

Yusuf said nothing.

'Who was that, anyway?'

Yusuf backhanded Grigory across the face, hard, then tugged his ear until he thought it might tear off.

'Come on, Yusuf,' he said. 'Please. *Please.*'

Yusuf looked back at Tajid. 'Control this overripe turd,' he said. 'Or I will.' He put the car in gear as Grigory sniffed at his armpits. He didn't smell great, it was true. Too bad the whores had taken his cologne.

West of Samara they turned south and followed the Volga River. Near Saratov, with the sun already down again, Yusuf's cell phone rang. He listened for a moment. '*Nam,*' he said, Arabic for 'yes.' '*Nam.*' Without another word, he hung up. They drove into Saratov – a million-person city on the Volga – and Yusuf threaded his way through the streets unerringly, despite the dim streetlights and honking traffic. Suddenly, Grigory understood that Yusuf had taken this trip before.

These men, whoever they are, they've practiced, he thought. This theft had been planned for months. Maybe years. Such preparation seemed beyond Yusuf. He was dangerous, but no great thinker. For the hundredth time, Grigory wondered who was running this operation, and what the ultimate plans were. Blackmail? Or did they intend to use the bombs?

Yusuf turned left onto a narrow street fronted by an eight-story apartment building as ugly as Grigory's own. He drove past it and parked in the courtyard of a two-story brick building covered in peeling yellow paint. 'Come.' Yusuf stepped out of the car and opened the door of the apartment nearest the Nissan. He popped the Nissan's trunk, and he and Grigory grabbed the toolboxes and hefted them into the apartment.

Inside, the apartment was filled with lime-green furniture. The television, a boxy wooden monstrosity, played silently, a game show, the Russian version of *Deal or No Deal*. The place was tidy but not really clean. The floral-patterned wallpaper peeled at the corners. A cheap chandelier hung crookedly from the ceiling, half its bulbs burned out. Grigory sensed that an old man lived here, hanging on but too tired or weak to clean the place. There were no pictures, no books or newspapers, no hints of the owner's personality at all, aside from a prayer rug in the corner.

No one was home, but the owner, whoever he was, had left them supper, mounds of black bread, and jam and butter, and slices of grayish boiled beef. Aside from the bread and jam, it wasn't much of a meal. Grigory didn't care. He was famished. He hadn't eaten since the night before. He couldn't remember going so long without a meal. Fortunately, there was plenty of bread, and Grigory slapped jam on it until he was full, ignoring Yusuf's dark looks. In this, at least, he would indulge himself.

After dinner, Yusuf pulled a digital video camera and tripod from his bag. He set them up in the living room, facing the chair in the corner. Grigory's anxiety rose. He didn't know what this nonsense was about, but it couldn't be good.

When he was done, Yusuf tapped the chair. 'Grigory,' he said. 'Sit. We're making a film.'

Grigory's mind turned to the death videos he'd seen from Russian soldiers in Chechnya, where the hapless victims gave their names and ranks before being gutted. Yusuf clapped his hands peremptorily. 'Come on. I promise it's nothing.'

So Grigory arranged his bulk in the chair and looked at the unblinking camera eye. Yusuf handed Grigory a sheet of paper. 'Memorize this and say it. And make sure your ID from the plant is visible so everyone will know it's you.'

Grigory read the sheet. 'But this isn't true. And they'll know it. They know they didn't give me the codes. Why do you want me to say it if it isn't true? I'll be a fool.'

'When we make our demands, we're going to include this. To increase the pressure.'

'Demands?'

'Of course we wouldn't use the bombs. We're selling them back. One billion euros each, two billion for both' – more than three billion dollars.

'You're not going to blow them up?'

'How could we? We don't have the codes. But this way they'll be under extra pressure to make a deal.' Yusuf laid a hand on Grigory's shoulder, and despite himself Grigory flinched. 'Come on, Grigory. Don't make me frighten you. Don't think too much about it. Just say what's on the sheet.'

'If you say so.' Grigory tried to ignore the tightness in his belly that told him he was a greater fool than ever. He memorized the words and spoke to the camera. He needed a few takes, but finally Yusuf pronounced himself satisfied.

'We'll make a star of you yet, Grigory.'

Before bed, Yusuf and Tajid prayed. They hadn't kept to the usual schedule, five times daily. Grigory supposed they were allowed to break the rules on this mission so as not to attract attention. Grigory kneeled with them, listening to the words but not reciting them.

Then they sacked out on the floor of the living room. Grigory didn't think he would sleep, but he did. He dreamed he was swimming in a pool filled with cologne and slept straight through until 5 a.m., when Yusuf kicked him awake. 'Let's go.'

'Can't we hang around, watch TV?'

Yusuf squeezed his hands together. 'A joke, right?'

'Very good.' Grigory knew he was making a mistake inciting the devil this way, but he didn't much care. Yusuf would kill him or not, and a joke or two wouldn't much matter either way.

'You're lucky for my orders,' Yusuf said.

They headed south toward Volgograd, the former Stalingrad, site of some of the fiercest fighting in all of World War II. The Nazis and Soviets had battled for eleven long months for the city that bore Stalin's name, both sides ordered never to surrender. By the time the fighting was done, almost a million men on each side were dead and the city was ash. And yet the cargo in their trunk could do just as much damage as all those men, Grigory thought. Secret armies, these bombs were.

By late afternoon the land turned hilly, and to the southeast Grigory could see the mountains of the Caucasus, big gray slabs of rock that disappeared in the haze. It was night when they reached Novorossiysk, on the coast. A day and a half had passed since Grigory drove out of Mayak with the bombs in his trunk. Grigory hoped they would leave Russia tonight. They didn't have much time left. In another day or two, someone would be assigned to make sure that the weapons were present. Of course no one would think that a bomb was really missing, but with him and Tajid gone, they'd check anyway, just to be sure. And what a surprise they'd have.

Novorossiysk was a gray industrial city, the biggest Russian port on the Black Sea. Apartment buildings crawled up the hills that rose from the coast. The air stank of oil from the storage tanks on the harbor, round white behemoths a hundred feet high. They passed along its edge and turned southeast along the narrow coast road. The hills jutted up to their east and the sea lay to their west. The road was dark and slick and Yusuf drove carefully, both hands on the wheel.

'You know, even if we get in an accident, they won't go off,' Grigory said.

'Are you ever quiet? You're worse than a woman.'

Half an hour later, outside Gelendzhik, Yusuf pulled onto the grounds of a deserted hotel closed for the winter. A rutted road rose up a hill toward the hotel, a concrete building with a few ugly frills. Behind the hotel, a dozen cottages sat among leafless trees. Beside the cottage farthest from the hotel, Yusuf cut the engine and they sat in the dark. The rain had stopped, but the air was cold and damp. They waited in silence, listening to the cars on the coast road, and to their breathing.

They passed an hour that way. The car grew cold, but Yusuf didn't seem to mind. He closed his eyes and dozed lightly. Grigory tried to do the same, but he couldn't. Each time he closed his eyes, he saw everything that had happened since Friday, the convoy arriving, the masterful way he'd played Major Akilev, the way Boris had checked the trunk . . . It was as if he'd been born two days ago, and everything before that hardly existed.

'Tajid,' he said. 'When Boris checked the car, were you nervous? Was your heart pounding?'

'I suppose.'

'That's all you can say? You suppose. These bombs in our trunk, our lives facing us, and what did you think? Wasn't your heart pounding?'

'You know what,' Yusuf said abruptly. 'I never knew before. But two days with you have shown me. There're only two kinds of people in the world.'

Grigory waited for Yusuf to explain, but he said nothing. 'Shall I guess? The fat and the thin?' Silence. 'Men and women?' Silence. 'The strong and the weak?' Silence. 'The tall and the short.' Silence. 'Come, Yusuf, give us your wisdom.'

'Those who can keep their thoughts to themselves,' Yusuf said. 'And those who can't. Sometimes I could cut your throat for a few minutes of peace.'

'Only sometimes?'

Grigory never got to hear Yusuf's reply, because at that moment a car scraped up the hotel driveway. It was the same Toyota that had stopped beside them at the petrol station the day before. The Toyota parked next to them and a man stepped out, an Arab by the look of him, darker than Yusuf. He wore a cap and a heavy jacket. The man was in charge, Grigory saw immediately. Yusuf treated him with a deference he wouldn't have given Grigory even if Grigory had put a gun to his head.

Yusuf and the man walked behind the Nissan, and Yusuf flipped up the trunk lid. A minute or so later, the trunk lid was lowered. The man sat in back beside Tajid and pulled off his cap, revealing a nearly bald head – unusual for an Arab. He was in his thirties, medium height, with a neatly trimmed goatee, wide dark eyes, a handsome round face. He looked gentle, though Grigory was certain he wasn't.

They drove down the hill, leaving the Toyota behind. At the coast road, Yusuf swung left, to the southeast. 'I won't ask you how you did it, but it's a great accomplishment,' the bald man said.

'At last,' Grigory said. 'Someone understands.'

They made good time for a while, but then the road became a true coastal serpentine, rising and falling along the swooping contours of the hills. Yusuf drove slowly, and after two hours they'd traveled barely seventy kilometers – forty miles. But neither Yusuf nor the man in the back showed any impatience. Grigory figured they must have driven the route before and knew how long it would take.

Russians called this strip of the coast their Riviera, and during the summer, this road was jammed with vacationers. Now the houses and hotels scattered through the hills were mostly dark, closed for the winter.

Just past midnight, Yusuf swung off the road, to the right, down a narrow track that hugged a steep cliff down to the sea. When they reached the base of the cliff, they were in a campsite beside a narrow, heavily forested cove. The main road stretched high above them on a concrete bridge supported by a dozen pillars. With trees all around them and thick gray clouds blocking the moon, they were invisible from the road.

'I hope you've arranged a boat,' Grigory said. 'Otherwise it's a long way to swim.'

No one bothered to answer.

'Hard to believe the Olympics will be in Sochi

in 2014, isn't it? Though I don't suppose any of us will be there.' Silence. Grigory sighed. 'All right, then. Tell me this, Yusuf, since you're such a philosopher, dividing the world into categories. What's the harm in a bit of chatter?'

'Nothing.'

'At least he speaks! Go on, then.'

'As long as you've got something to say. Which you don't.'

'And who made you emperor?'

'My knife.'

'Yes, because you have a weapon, you can do as you please, insult me or anyone you like. Some world this is.'

'Shh,' the bald man in the back said. 'Listen.'

In the silence, Grigory heard the distant rumble of a boat engine.

The man in the back swung open his door and the others followed. Yusuf popped the trunk and they pulled up the toolboxes and their bags. By the time they were done, the boat had arrived, a black motorboat with an open deck. Grigory couldn't imagine it would get them across the Black Sea. Nonetheless they transferred everything to the boat, and then Yusuf and the bald man hugged briefly and whispered in Arabic.

The motorboat's captain clapped his hands together, obviously anxious to be gone. Yusuf and Grigory and Tajid stepped into the boat. '*Allah yisallimak,*' the bald man said to them all.

God keep you safe. He waved at them as the boat turned and headed for the open sea. And then he disappeared.

They lost sight of the coast within an hour, and Grigory began to get nervous. But the captain steered confidently, occasionally checking the GPS tacked to the dash of the boat.

The fishing trawler was running without lights and Grigory didn't see it until they were almost on top of it. They drew up alongside and someone inside threw down a rope. The motorboat's captain tied the two boats together. The men in the trawler hauled up the toolboxes in a reinforced net and then sent down a rope ladder. Grigory wasn't sure he would make it up, but somehow he did, the ladder creaking under his bulk. Tajid and Yusuf followed. The motorboat turned back toward the coast and the trawler rumbled into the sea.

The sun rose and set again and all the while they headed west. Grigory passed the time by amusing himself with his magnetized chessboard, even playing a couple of games with the ship's captain. At midday the seas picked up, and by nightfall the waves batted the boat like a cat playing with a mouse. About then, Tajid threw up.

But Grigory, to his surprise, felt fine. Another unexpected talent. First he'd stolen the bombs. Now this. A new day for Grigory. He closed his eyes and imagined his future. He'd take the money they gave him, go on a diet, and—

He startled as someone tapped his shoulder. Yusuf. He was smiling, a thin smile that pulled at the corners of his mouth and frightened Grigory.

'Let's play chess,' Yusuf said.

So Grigory set up the board and they played, twice. Yusuf played well, but Grigory beat him both times. Yusuf's smile never faded.

'Let's go,' Yusuf said when they were done, nodding at the door that led to the storage room behind the main cabin.

'What?'

'It's time, Grigory.'

Grigory didn't have to ask what he meant. 'Please, Yusuf,' he whispered. His bowels came loose and he thought for a moment he would soil himself.

'Don't beg,' Yusuf said. 'I'm giving you the chance to do this properly, with dignity.'

'But you promised, and I've done everything you asked.' *It's the* chess, Grigory thought madly. *He's angry about the chess. If I hadn't beaten him—*

'You knew how this would end, Grigory. It's the same for all of us.'

Yes, of course, all of us, but why now for me? *Whynowwhynowwhynow* . . . the words clung together in Grigory's mind, all question and no answer.

'I should have turned you in.' So many chances, so many wrong choices.

'Come on.'

Yusuf carried a pistol to go with his knife. Grigory knew he couldn't escape. The sea surrounded them. And he couldn't swim. So he pushed himself up and took the two steps to the storage room. Yusuf closed the door behind them. A single bulb lit the space, which was empty aside from a rusty anchor and a few nets balled up in the corner, stinking faintly of the sea's sulfurous brine. A fitting place to die.

'Lie down,' Yusuf said.

'Is this about the chess?' Grigory couldn't stop himself. 'We can play again. As much as you like. You'll win, I promise.'

'Lie down. On your stomach with your hands above your head.'

'I will. But tell me. Was what you said about blackmail true, or do you plan to use them?'

'You think we've gone to this much trouble to give them back?'

'Then what about the video? Why did you make me do that?'

'Down, Grigory.' Yusuf's voice was at once soothing and commanding, as if Grigory were an unruly dog who needed a firm master.

'But you don't have the codes.'

'Lie down.'

And Grigory did. A plastic tarp covered the floor. For him. His coffin.

'Do you want to pray, Grigory? It's never too late. Allah is always listening.'

'Fuck you and your crazy Allah.'

'I want to read you something. A poem that was written for Sheikh bin Laden.'

Grigory heard Yusuf unfold a piece of paper. Then:

How special they are who sold their souls to God,
Who smiled at Death when his sword gazed
  ominously at them,
Who willingly bared their chests as shields.

Grigory's heart pounded wildly. He was dying for *this*? For a moment, he wanted to stand and fight. But he knew he wouldn't even reach his knees before Yusuf finished him.

'Are you ready to bare your chest?'

Grigory turned his head and spat on the tarp. Not much of a protest and half the saliva rolled down his cheek, but at least he would die a man, not a beggar. 'Fuck you, I said.'

'Your choice. Close your eyes.'

At the base of his skull, where his hair touched his neck, Grigory felt the tip of the pistol graze his skin. It pulled back, then touched him again, higher this time. Yusuf must have done this before; he was placing the pistol so Grigory's skull wouldn't deflect the bullet. To his surprise, the pistol was warm, not cold, and then Grigory remembered it had been lying in Yusuf's armpit. Such a strange last thought—

★   ★   ★

The pistol barked, and Grigory Farzadov was dead. Tajid followed. To Yusuf's annoyance, where Grigory had accepted his fate with a certain poise, Tajid blubbered like a child. He moaned about his family and promised that if Yusuf just let him be, he would never ever say anything to anyone. It was all the same, though, all the same in the end, because Yusuf had the gun.

When he was done, Yusuf and the fishermen wound up the two bodies in the tarp and wrapped thick steel chains around them and threw the whole package into an old anchovy net. They put the luggage that Grigory and Tajid had brought with them into another net and weighted that one down as well. Then they dumped both nets overboard. Yusuf could have prayed for the cousins, but he didn't. Grigory didn't deserve Allah's blessing and Tajid's whining had irritated him. The nets sank into the water and the waves kept coming, as if Grigory and Tajid had never existed at all. And the boat and its cargo turned south and made for the Turkish coast.

CHAPTER 7

Wells stalked the first-floor corridors of George Washington Hospital, long strides cutting through the clean white halls. He reached the double doors that marked the entrance to surgery, turned, paced back to the entrance.

The hospital was on 23rd and I, seven blocks from the shooting. The first ambulance had come in five minutes, the first cops two minutes later. Wells flashed his identification at them, shook off their questions, told them they could find him at GW if they needed him. Then he sprinted up 21st, wishing all the while that the hospital was farther away so he could keep running.

He'd made enemies of some of the most dangerous men in the world. Then he'd refused to take the most elementary precautions. He and Exley drove unarmored cars, took the same route to work most days. If he'd been on his own, his happy-fool act wouldn't have mattered . . . but he wasn't.

When he reached the hospital, Exley was already in surgery. No one would be able to tell him anything for at least an hour, the nurses said. So Wells walked the halls, expecting someone would tell him to stop moving, sit down. But the orderlies looked at his agency identification and the blood on his hands and his empty shoulder holster and didn't say a word.

A hand touched his shoulder. He turned to see Ellis Shafer, his boss.

'John.' Shafer gave Wells an awkward half-hug and led him to a door marked by a brass sign that said 'Family Room B.' Inside, they sat on uncomfortable plastic chairs around a battered wooden table. Wells wondered at the conversations that had taken place in here, well-meaning doctors and their hard truths. *I'm sorry, but we've tried everything . . .*

'What happened, John?'

Wells told him.

'Was the Russian there today?' Wells had told Shafer about the strange incident with the Russian outside their house.

'They were wearing helmets.'

'You didn't check? Afterward?'

'I had to keep pressure on her so she didn't bleed out.'

A light knock. The door opened – Michaels, the head of Wells's security detail. He squeezed Wells's arm, set a laptop on the table.

'I'm sorry, John. We should have done a better job. My guys—'

'Your guys never had a chance.'

Michaels grimaced. Wells balled up his hands, dug his fingernails into his palms. 'Didn't mean that how it sounded. Just that it all went down so quick. They were pros, whoever they were.'

Michaels pulled up a photograph on the laptop. A fleshy face, black eyes shiny and dead, hair still tousled from the helmet he'd been wearing. The collar of his leather jacket was just visible at the bottom of the screen. Then a second photo, a full-body shot, the corpse curled against the curb where Wells had shot him two hours before. Blood trickled from a corner of his mouth. Wells knew him immediately. The Russian who'd come to the house the week before.

'He was on the red bike,' Michaels said. 'The passenger.'

'We have a name?'

'Not yet. We're running their prints against immigration.' Michaels pulled up more images, the other two men that Wells had shot. 'You know them?'

Wells shook his head.

'You sure?'

'I'm sure.'

'Because maybe you want to settle this yourself, but I've got a stake. Two of my guys. Even if they never had a chance.'

Wells said nothing. At this point, he didn't plan to tell Michaels that though he didn't know his assassins, he had a pretty good idea who'd sent them.

'Any of them carrying ID?' Shafer said.

'No. But the bikes had temporary Georgia tags. And one of the guys had a Marriott keycard in his pocket. We're checking every hotel within a hundred miles and we'll go from there. The first guy was carrying a key to a Pathfinder. We haven't found it yet.' Michaels drummed his big fingers on the table. 'We don't have to do it now but we're going to need an official statement, John. For us, the D.C. police, the FBI.'

'Sure.'

'Shouldn't take long. With all the weapons we found on them—'

'I told you it's no problem.'

'I'll let you know when I hear more. I'm sorry, John. I mean it. We owed you better.' Michaels disappeared into the hall.

Shafer waited until the door was closed.

'You think you know who did this, don't you?'

Wells said nothing.

'Don't play with me, John. I've known her longer than you have.'

'Yes, I think I know.'

'So tell me.' Shafer waited. 'Of course. I get it. Your fault and you're the only one who can fix it. The man of steel. Don't you see this is how you got into this mess?'

'You just love being the smartest guy in the room, don't you, Ellis.'

'Let me help you.'

Wells shook his head. The silence stretched on

as an ugly fifties-style clock above the table clicked away the seconds. Finally, Shafer stood, reached for the door.

'All right. Play it your way.'

'Pierre Kowalski. I think.'

Shafer sat. 'Why? He's lucky we didn't bust him for helping the Chinese.'

'I never told you what I did when I broke into his house.' Wells explained how he'd tied Kowalski up, humiliated him.

'You wrapped his head in duct tape,' Shafer said when Wells was done.

'I made sure he could breathe.'

'That was thoughtful.'

'So you see.'

'Yeah, I see why he might be pissed.' Wells saw the unasked question on Shafer's face: *Why? What were you thinking?* Even now Wells couldn't fully unlock his motivations. He knew only that he hated Kowalski. To sell weapons, to profit from death, couldn't be denied or explained away.

'Even so, maybe it wasn't him,' Shafer said. 'Maybe it was al-Qaeda.'

'Qaeda would have put a truck bomb in front of the house. Kowalski was furious that night I taped him up. Told me he'd get me no matter what. And we know he's got contacts in Russia. These guys this morning, they were pros. You get it now, Ellis? You see why I think I may have to do this myself?'

'I get it.'

Neither of them needed to say the obvious: These days, Russia was going out of its way to prove that it didn't need the West. In 2006, when a former KGB operative was poisoned at a London restaurant, the Kremlin had basically refused to help Scotland Yard investigate. If the connection between Kowalski and today's assassination ran through Moscow, the CIA would have a tough job convincing the Russians to cooperate.

'It's not so bad, John,' Shafer said. 'Two of our own died today. Practically in front of the White House. We can't ignore that kind of provocation. If we can lock it down, find the link, the big man will put a lot of pressure on the Kremlin.'

'If we can lock it down.'

'Promise me one thing. Whatever you do, tell me. Ahead of time. At least give me a chance to give you some advice. Since I am the smartest guy in the room.'

'All right.'

'Now let's find out how your girl's doing.'

'Our girl,' Wells said.

'Our girl.'

But the nurses had no news. Exley was still in surgery.

'What does that mean?' Shafer said.

'It means she's still in surgery. Are you a relative, sir?'

Wells leaned into the nurse. 'Ms Exley is my fiancée. So, please, if you have any information—'

'I don't. You probably won't hear much for a while more.'

'Thank you.'

'Fiancée?' Shafer whispered as the nurse walked away. 'Was it a special invisible ring? Because I didn't see it.'

'She didn't care about the ring.'

'You really don't understand women at all.'

And you don't understand Exley, Wells didn't say. She would have been happy with a Cracker Jack ring. Though maybe Shafer was right. He'd managed to stay married for thirty years; Wells had barely lasted two.

'Were you going to make it official?' Shafer said. 'Or did she not care about that part either?'

'New Year's, we were saying. Something simple, our way. Just before the South America trip. The trip was the honeymoon.'

'You didn't tell me.'

'We didn't tell anyone. Just her kids. Not even our exes yet.' Wells turned away from Shafer, leaned his head against a wall, closed his eyes. The white plaster was cool and reassuring.

'Ellis, what am I gonna say to her kids?'

'That you love her. And that she's going to be fine.'

When Wells opened his eyes, Vinny Duto, the CIA director, was beside him. Around Duto stood five sides of beef, the director's security detail.

Duto extended a hand, and Wells saw no alternative but to take it. Since the Times Square mission, when Duto had questioned Wells's loyalty, Wells could barely stand being in the same room as the man. The feeling was mutual, he supposed. Duto viewed him as arrogant, untouchable, a loose cannon. Maybe Duto was right.

'I'm sorry, John. Truly. How is she?'

'Still in surgery.'

Duto gently rested a hand on Wells's shoulder. 'Mind coming out to the car so we can talk in private?'

The car was a heavily armored Suburban with run-flat tires, a specially raised undercarriage, and inch-thick glass that could stop an automatic rifle round. Wells followed Duto into the backseats.

'John,' Duto said. 'I want you to know that we will do everything we can here. Everything possible to catch whoever did this.'

Wells stared out the Suburban's smoked windows, watching as a heavyset woman picked her way down the sidewalk toward the hospital. A thin cold rain was falling, and the media hordes had already arrived, the camera trucks and long-lens photographers. The D.C. police had set up a block-long perimeter around the hospital to hold them at bay. Good. Wells had no appetite for their nonsense.

'You have a pretty nice ride here, Vinny. I was just telling Jennifer this morning we needed to trade up.'

Again Duto put a hand on Wells's shoulder. This time Wells shook him off. 'Whatever it takes, we'll get these guys.'

'Or have a good excuse if you don't.'

Duto's mask slipped for a moment and Wells saw the anger underneath it, the tightness around his eyes and the angry curl of his mouth. The agency's job was to predict chaos, and prevent it wherever possible. The lawyers, the top-secret classifications, the chains of command, all of them were efforts to bring order to a world that insisted on anarchy. More than anything, Duto hated to be surprised, hated unexpected questions from his bosses. This morning, he'd gotten lots of those, Wells was sure.

'What I'm saying is, if the Russians are involved we've got to play this carefully. But it will be our highest priority.'

'I get that part,' Wells said. He bit his lip to stifle his next sentence: And when Medvedev tells you to stuff it, that he'll never let an American investigative team on Russian soil, what will you do then? Threaten to nuke Moscow if he doesn't change his mind?

'Any ideas who did this?' Duto said.

'There're a lot of people who don't like me.'

'So let us investigate, get the evidence.'

The evidence is dead, Wells didn't say. It's lying on Constitution Avenue. I killed them a little too good. Should have let one live so we could talk to him.

Wells looked out at the camera trucks. 'The media's gonna go crazy on this. You going to tell them that this was aimed at Jennifer and me?'

'No,' Duto said. 'And we're going to ask anyone who figures it out to keep you out of it. Your name will just add to the fire here.'

'You want to tamp it down as quick as possible so you can investigate better,' Wells said.

'This isn't just from me. The president told me directly, fifteen minutes ago, that he values our relationship with Russia. And that he wants us to be on firm footing, whatever we do. Assuming you're correct about the nationality of the men.'

'So what do you want me to do?'

'Let us figure out who was paying these guys,' Duto said. 'Build a case. Do it the right way. And then we'll nail whoever did this.'

'I hear you,' Wells said. 'On one condition.'

'What's that?'

'You'll share everything you get with me.'

'Of course, John.' Duto extended his hand and they shook. Wells wondered if Duto knew that Wells had no intention of sitting back and letting the agency and FBI screw this up. Probably. He might not even care. He'd sent the message, officially. The Suburban was probably bugged. Just in case anyone ever wanted proof of this conversation. Now Duto was safe, whatever Wells did.

Back inside the hospital the hours passed miserably. David and Jessica, Exley's kids, showed up, along with Randy, Exley's ex-husband, had brought them. The kids hugged Wells, but Randy didn't even shake his hand. He was everything

113

Wells wasn't. Wearing business casual, a little paunchy, with close-cropped hair and a black laptop bag. He'd loved Exley, Wells knew. Maybe he still did. He stared across the waiting room at Wells, his eyes shouting an accusation: *You did this. Your fault.*

Finally, around 2 p.m., a man in clean blue scrubs emerged from the double doors that marked the entrance to the emergency rooms. His surgical mask dangled from his neck and his eyes were tired, but he moved confidently.

He looked around the waiting area and signaled to Wells. Randy also rose and the three of them stood in an unfriendly huddle.

'I'm Dr Patel. Are you both relatives?'

'I'm John Wells. Her fiancé.'

'When did that happen?' Randy said.

'We were planning to tell you.'

'And you are?' Patel said to Randy.

'Her ex-husband.' He pointed to David and Jessica. 'Those are our kids.'

'In that case, Ms Exley's injuries were quite severe. She's fortunate she arrived at the hospital so quickly. The bullets were fired from behind, at an angle. They entered through her back.' Patel touched his back to indicate where the wounds had been. 'One damaged her lower spine, the L-two and L-three vertebrae. The other pierced her liver. That was our immediate focus, since liver injuries bleed heavily. Indeed, Ms Exley lost several pints of blood, but we've now stanched the bleeding and

I believe she's out of immediate danger. We've left the damaged vertebrae alone. She'll need a second operation to repair her spine tomorrow. But I would say her long-term prognosis is favorable. As you may know, the liver is adept at renewing itself.'

'Thank you,' Wells said.

'Thank God,' Randy said.

Patel raised his hand. 'Understand. Even if the second operation goes smoothly, she has rehabilitation ahead to regain full use of her legs.'

'She's paralyzed,' Randy said.

'We believe it's temporary. There's severe inflammation around the spinal cord, but the nerve bundles appear intact. The swelling ought to fade over time and she'll regain motor control. But there are no guarantees with this type of injury.'

'Can we see her?'

'For a minute.' Patel nodded at Exley's kids. 'I wouldn't recommend letting them see her yet. She's quite tired.'

'Quite,' Randy said. He turned to Wells. 'Happy, John? Get everything you came for?' His breath was middle-manager minty and he had a forced grin on his face, the smile of a vampire about to plunge his teeth into a victim's neck. Wells took a half-step back, wondering whether Randy would really be foolish enough to swing at him in here.

'Gentlemen,' Patel said. 'Are you all right?'

'Fine and dandy,' Randy said.

'All right. Mr Wells, please come with me.' To Randy: 'You can wait here, sir, with your children.'

Wells followed Patel down a wide corridor and into a room marked 'ER Recovery 1.' As soon as he stepped in, Wells understood why the doctor hadn't wanted David and Jessica to see Exley. Her eyes were closed and sunken, her face drawn, exhausted, nearly white under the room's harsh lights. Monitors beeped around her, measuring her pulse, respiration, and other vitals. Bags of solution fed a tube into her arm. Two more tubes, one slowly pulsing with clear liquid, the other bright red with blood, poked from the gauze that covered her stomach. His dear girl. And this was his fault, his and his alone.

Wells wrapped her hand in his. Her pulse fluttered fast and weak in his palm. Her eyes opened, slid shut, opened again and found him.

'John.' Her voice was dull and dry.

'Jenny.'

'Where?'

'You know if I'm here, it can't be heaven.' Her eyes flickered and he saw that she hadn't gotten the joke. 'It's GW Hospital.'

'The motorcycles.'

He squeezed her hand.

'Yes. I'll tell you later. The whole story. Are you okay? In pain?'

She grunted, a soft sigh that seemed to indicate that her consciousness had been dulled beyond quotidian concerns like pain.

'You'll be fine,' Wells said. 'Better than new. I promise.'

She closed her eyes. Patel touched his arm. 'She needs to rest.'

'Jenny. David and Jessica are outside.' He kissed her cheek. 'We'll all be waiting. I love you.' She didn't answer.

She started to bleed again an hour later. The nurses called Wells over and whispered the bad news. She was back in surgery. He endured another two hours of miserable waiting before Patel emerged again, not as dapper or as confident this time. His shoulders slumped, and he spoke so quietly that Wells had to lean in to hear him.

'It's not surprising, given the severity of the initial injury. We have it controlled now, but we had to give her more blood.'

'Can I see her?' Wells was alone now. The nurses had moved Randy, David, and Jessica to a separate waiting area.

'Certainly not tonight. Tonight she rests. Possibly tomorrow.'

Wells left a few minutes later, sitting in the back of an ambulance, the only sure way to get through the media cordon. He emerged at his house to find three Suburbans parked in front. Two men sat inside each of the SUVs, peering out. Two more men were on the porch, all wearing Kevlar flak jackets. Agency guards. Michaels had told Wells to expect them. Wells supposed he understood the logic. But he hated the idea of having the house he shared with Exley turned into a fortified garrison.

The guard nearest the front door raised a hand as Wells inserted his key into the lock. 'Mr Wells. Leon Allam,' he said. He raised his identification.

'Good to meet you,' Wells said.

'Mind if we come in with you? Just to be sure everything's cool.' Allam had a soldier's tight haircut, and his Kevlar looked ridiculous over his suit and tie. Wells tried not to dislike the guy. He was just doing his job.

'I'm sure it's fine.' Wells turned the key in the lock. 'I'll holler if I need you.'

'Yes, sir. But I'd be a lot more comfortable if I could come in.'

Wells felt his temper rise. 'You asking or ordering?'

'I'm asking.'

'In that case, you can come in. As long as you and your men agree to trade in those flak jackets for bulletproof vests that'll fit under your suits. No need to scare the neighbors.'

Allam paused. 'All right, sir. If Mr Michaels agrees.'

'And stop saying "sir." I can't stand it. I'm John.'

Wells turned the lock in the door and Allam grabbed his arm.

'I'd like to go in first, secure the entry.'

'Secure the entry. By all means.' Wells restrained himself from pointing out that anyone inside the house would be well aware by now that they were coming in. He stepped out of the way and Allam pushed open the door and jumped inside.

'Secure!' he yelled a few seconds later.

'Where do they get you guys?' Wells murmured to himself.

A few minutes later, with Allam downstairs, Wells stepped into the shower and hit himself with a blast of frigid water. He wanted to hurt himself, run in the dark until his knees burned and his feet blistered, but the shower would have to do for now. He needed to catch up on the investigation. He dressed, packed a kit bag. He would sleep at Langley until Exley came home. He couldn't bear to spend his nights in this empty house, with her gone and the guards outside.

He refused Allam's offer of a ride in an armored Suburban and instead took his little Impreza out from the garage. But Allam insisted that the Suburbans ride shotgun front and back, their emergency lights flashing as the convoy rolled out.

And as they flew toward Langley with the Suburbans running their sirens at eighty miles an hour, Wells realized that even if Exley recovered completely, and for the sake of his sanity he had to believe she would, their lives wouldn't be normal for a very long time. This attack had destroyed whatever privacy they had left. They'd live in a bubble for the foreseeable future.

Another reason to make Kowalski pay.

★ ★ ★

119

At Langley, Shafer briefed Wells that the CIA and FBI had set up a joint task force, eighty agents, with the promise of more to come if they were needed. Following the card key, the investigators had tracked the Russians to the Key Bridge Marriott in Arlington. The Marriott staff reported that the men had checked in six days before, to rooms 402, 403, and 404. They'd used a single credit card, a MasterCard from Bank Zachodni in Warsaw. They'd kept to themselves, saying they were visiting Washington on business and expected to stay about a week, possibly longer. They'd parked only the Pathfinder, not the motorcycles, which they'd apparently stashed elsewhere. They'd asked for quiet rooms. When they'd checked in, the clerk had gotten a plate number for the Pathfinder from them, which caused a brief whirr of excitement at the agency, but when the agency ran the number, it was fake. In all, no one at the Marriott found anything odd about them. They weren't American, but so what? People from every nation in the world had business in Washington.

While the hotel staff was questioned, rooms 402, 403, and 404 were searched to their foundations, every piece of furniture removed and disassembled. So far, the investigators hadn't found much. In 402, a Russian copy of *The Da Vinci Code*, lightly read. In 403, a pack of Marlboro Reds, crumpled and empty, and an empty pack of matches from Reverse, a Moscow nightclub. The agency's Russia desk, which was assisting the investigation, reported that Reverse was known to be popular with Russian intelligence officers. In 404, a bottle of vodka, half-empty, and three clean glasses.

But no passports, real or fake. No cash. No computers. No cell phones. No Pathfinder in the Marriott's parking lot. The assassins had apparently planned to ditch their motorcycles, pull off their masks, take a cab or the Metro to the Pathfinder, and disappear. With their faces hidden and the motorcycles bought under fake names, their tracks would be lost.

Wells had rendered that plan inoperative. The task force now had faces and fingerprints from the corpses. Investigators were checking the prints against the FBI national criminal database, as well as the prints that foreign visitors to the United States were required to provide when they entered the country. The criminal database hadn't matched any hits. The immigration records had, for two of the men. They'd entered the United States three weeks earlier, on a nonstop Delta flight from Warsaw to Atlanta. They had valid Polish passports with valid U.S. tourist visas, issued a few weeks before in Warsaw. They were brothers, and their names were Jerzy and Jozef Godinski, according to the record.

Already, Langley had asked the Polish government, which unlike the Kremlin was a good friend of the United States, to help it track down the men – if they existed at all. Everyone at Langley figured that both the names and the passports would be fake. As for the third man, the passenger on the Ducati, his fingerprints didn't match any on file. Which meant he'd come in on a foreign diplomatic passport. Or illegally over the Mexican border. Or by car from Canada, where fingerprint checks were not yet routine. Put another way, the investigators had no idea how he'd gotten in. Not yet, anyway.

'So that's what we know,' Shafer said when he was done.

'Have we called the Russians yet?'

'No proof they were Russian yet. The credit card's the best lead so far. Until we find the Pathfinder.'

'You think they stowed everything in it?'

'They had to keep their passports and cells somewhere. Unless they had a safe house. And if they had a safe house, why stay at a hotel?'

The maintenance staff found a cot and brought it to Wells's office on the sixth floor of the Old Headquarters Building. But when Wells closed his eyes, he couldn't sleep. He swore he could smell her, her lemony perfume. Near midnight, Shafer walked in. 'Come on. Get dressed.'

'Did they find something?'

'I'm taking you home. To Casa Shafer. We'll have a beer, watch TV, pretend today never happened.'

'I'm fine.'

'No, you're not. Get dressed. I promise, you'll

have lots of time for whatever bloody revenge fantasy you're cooking up.'

'You promise?'

'I promise.'

CHAPTER 8

Finding the Pathfinder didn't take long. Fifteen hours after the attack, just about the time that Wells and Shafer got home, a D.C. cop spotted the Pathfinder parked in Northeast, two blocks from the Rhode Island Avenue Red Line metro stop.

Inside the Pathfinder's glove box were two Polish passports, $12,000 in cash, and a disposable cell phone. The passports had been issued two months before. They were the same ones the would-be assassins had used to enter the United States through Atlanta. A few hours later, four thousand miles away, the famously bad-tempered agents of the WSI, the Polish military intelligence service, arrested the clerk who'd issued the passports. He confessed immediately – a wise choice – but insisted he'd had no idea what the men who'd bought the passports had planned to do with them. They were Russian, he said, and paid cash.

Meanwhile, the phone was handed over to the wizards at the National Security Agency. The phone shouldn't have yielded any information. It was a disposable. Its call registers had been deleted. And it hadn't even been used to place any calls. But through some magic Wells didn't claim to understand, the NSA's engineers found records for two incoming calls in the phone's memory. Both had been received the night before the assassination attempt. They were sixteen-digit numbers, international, country code 7, city code 495. Moscow, Russia. When the agency first tried to trace them, neither existed. Like the northern Virginia extensions that led to CIA headquarters, they couldn't be found in conventional telco databases.

The next day, Walt Purdy, the American ambassador to Russia, asked for a meeting with the Russian interior minister, Aleksandr Milov. Without mentioning the cell phones, Purdy said that evidence connected Russia with the terrorist attack in Washington.

What evidence? Milov asked. Had the assassins been definitely identified? Not yet, Purdy conceded. But the assassins were traveling on false Polish passports, and the passport clerk who issued them said the men were Russian. Would Russia allow the United States to send its own agents to Moscow to investigate further leads?

First, Milov said, allow him to express the Kremlin's outrage at the attack. In broad daylight. And so close to the White House. Terrible. Of course the Russian government would offer whatever help it could, Milov said. Of course, of course, of course.

But . . . unfortunately . . . the Kremlin could not allow American investigators on Russian soil. To do so would violate Russian sovereignty and be an affront to the FSB, which was certainly as skilled as the FBI. *At least* as skilled. In any event, Milov was certain that no Russians would ever commit an attack. The Poles were notorious liars and probably trying to deflect attention from their own guilt.

Nonetheless, the FSB wanted to prove its goodwill. If the United States would share the evidence it had gathered so far, the FSB would gladly send its own agents to Washington to aid the investigation. They could be on their way on the next Aeroflot flight. A joint Russian-American effort to combat terrorism. No? Well, then, the Kremlin would wait for instructions from the United States . . .

'And yadda yadda yadda,' Shafer said, when he'd finished telling Wells what had happened. They were in a conference room at GW Hospital. Exley had just undergone surgery to clean up her spine. The early report from the doctors was positive. The center of her spinal cord was undamaged. Her rehab would be difficult but she should be able to walk again.

'They gave us nothing?'

'Pretty much. But I do have some good news from Fort Meade—' the NSA. 'They think they can trace the Moscow end of the call to a specific address.'

'Even though the numbers don't exist?'

'Correct. And even if they're never used again. Don't ask me how.'

'I wasn't planning to.'

'But there's a catch. Even if they can track it, they say we can't ever disclose what they've found, either publicly or privately, to the Russians. NSA doesn't want the Kremlin to know how far we can get inside their phone networks.'

'And how far is that?'

'All the way, give or take.'

'But even if we can't go public with it, we'll know.'

'Apparently. Though if the numbers track to some ninety-year-old *babushka*, we may have to reconsider.'

'We'll have a name.'

'Maybe a company, maybe a person. What then? Planning a trip to Moscow?'

'I haven't decided.'

'You have. It's obvious. How about a better idea? Help her get better and let everyone else work this for a while.'

'Ellis Shafer, giving the team-player speech. Did Duto put a chip in your brain?'

'Don't be stupid. The whole agency wants what you want.'

'And what's that?'

Shafer paused.

'I was going to say justice. But you don't want justice. You want a scalp.'

Wells didn't disagree.

'You always told me violence was a last resort for you. That you'd never killed unless you had no choice.'

Wells closed his eyes and looked at the faces of the men he'd killed. In Afghanistan, in Atlanta, in New York, in China. 'It's been a last resort an awful lot,' he said. 'Rarely as deserved as this.'

'Prosecutors have a name for this, what you're planning: "with malice aforethought." Premeditated murder. First degree. Exley told me you were thinking about quitting after what happened in China. Maybe you should have.'

Wells said nothing.

'What? You think she shouldn't have said? She has to pretend you're a robot, too?'

'I'm fine, Ellis.'

'She had to tell someone.'

'And who did you have to tell?' Wells hated being talked about this way.

'No one. It ends with me. But ask yourself this: Will going to Moscow put the dreams away, give you an honest night's sleep? Let the rest of us handle it.'

'Wise advice from the desk jockey of all desk jockeys. You know better than anyone that if I don't push, it won't happen.'

'We lost two of our own. You're wrong.'

'We won't piss off the Kremlin.'

'Give it some time. Us. Me.'

Now Wells stood, pushed past Shafer, moving

128

the smaller man out of his way with an easy hand on Shafer's shoulder. He opened the door.

'Let me know when we get that name, Ellis.'

A day later the NSA reported that both numbers led to the same six-story office building in central Moscow. The building had four tenants, all connected to the Russian military, the FSB, or both. One was a security company that provided protection for American multinationals doing business in Moscow. Another seemed to be a front company for the Russian army, like the ones the Defense Department used to hire software programmers who didn't want to work full-time for the government. The third was little more than a shell corporation, probably used to move money out of Russia. None of them were likely to have been involved in the attack.

But the fourth caught Wells's attention. Helosrus Ltd. The agency's file on Helosrus was slim but damning.

'Helosrus is owned by Ivan Markov, former assistant chief of operations for the FSB, Markov maintains a close relationship with current FSB officers, some of whom are said to be silent partners in Helosrus. The company's legitimate business consists of providing guards for executives at companies with close ties to the Russian government, such as the natural gas monopoly Gazprom. Its agents have a reputation for being aggressive and eager to use force.

'Helosrus is willing to accept jobs that other security companies will not, including extra-legal operations. A confidential source within the Russian government reports that the FSB has used Helosrus operatives to harass Russian opposition parties. The extent of this harassment is unknown.

'Helosrus also conducts operations outside of Russia. The nature of these operations is unknown. In July, a confidential source for another foreign intelligence service reported that Helosrus operatives were responsible for the plane crash that killed Sasha Kordevsky.' Kordevsky had made, or stolen, billions of dollars in the Russian oil business before losing the Kremlin's favor and being forced into exile in London. His Gulfstream had crashed into a mountain following the World Economic Forum, the annual meeting of business, financial, and political leaders in Davos, Switzerland. 'The source offered no evidence to back his claim. Of note, Swiss aviation authorities ruled the crash an accident after a thorough investigation.'

The pieces fit, Wells thought. Kowalski got his weapons from Russia. Of course he would know Markov. They'd probably done business together. And Wells knew firsthand from his previous run-in with Kowalski that Kowalski looked to Moscow when he needed help on dangerous jobs.

But this time Kowalski had overreached – and left fingerprints. As he read over the Helosrus file,

Wells wondered why Kowalski had made such a foolish mistake. Presumably, he'd figured that his hired assassins would escape cleanly and that the CIA and everyone else would assume that Muslim terrorists were behind the attack, given Wells's history with al-Qaeda.

For the next ten days, Wells readied himself for Moscow. As a rule, he hated trying to disguise his identity, but this time he had no choice. He couldn't exactly show up at the Helosrus offices and ask to see Markov.

So he dyed his hair black and didn't shave. He bought an unlimited pass to Solar Planet in Washington, and every day he stood inside a tanning booth for three ten-minute sessions. Wells was a quarter-Lebanese by birth, and two weeks under the UV rays turned his skin nearly as dark as it had been during his years in Afghanistan and Pakistan. With his dark hair, scruffy beard, and olive skin, he suddenly looked more Arab than American.

Along with the tanning, Wells started eating as he never had before, junk and more junk – French fries, chocolate bars, double cheese-burgers, doughnuts, ice cream, milkshakes. The first couple of days were fun, and then his body rebelled and he had to force the food down his throat. After one particularly greasy piece of fried chicken he found himself doubled over a toilet.

But he gained more than a pound a day, sixteen pounds total, and wound up with the beginnings of a double chin and a spare tire. Between his new face and the flab on his chin and his gut, he became a new person. Of course, Exley and Shafer and anyone who really knew him wouldn't be deceived. But Ivan Markov had never seen him, except in photographs. And he didn't have to fool Markov or his men for long. Just long enough to get a meeting with them, somewhere nice and private.

On his ninth day of eating and tanning, Wells stopped by the basement offices of the agency's Directorate of Science and Technology. He left with several unusual pieces of gear – not available in stores, as the engineers liked to joke – as well as five new passports in five different names. Two were American, one French, one Lebanese, and one Syrian.

He drove into D.C. and gave one of the American passports to a courier service that charged him $400 and promised a Russian tourist visa in two days or less. His new Lebanese passport came with a fake Russian visa and entry documents of its own. Those couldn't get him through Russian immigration, but for what Wells was planning they would be handy anyway.

After three days at George Washington, Exley was moved to the Walter Reed Army Medical Center, where she could be more easily guarded. Her back and her left leg hurt terribly from the damage to the nerves in her spine, and she could stay on her feet for only a few minutes at a time. Wells visited her every day, spending hours with her in the afternoons, after her rehab sessions, which she refused to let him watch. He turned her on her side and rubbed her back for as long as she would let him.

Despite her pain, she quickly weaned herself from the morphine drip and Vicodin that the doctors offered her. She didn't need to tell Wells why. Her father had been an alcoholic, and she feared becoming addicted to anything. But she couldn't conceal the price she paid for refusing the medicine. Her eyes were wet with tears when she came back from rehab sessions.

As her second week in the hospital began, he brought in *Bonfire of the Vanities*, one of her favorite books, and read aloud for her.

'As if reading his mind, Maria said, "You're behind the times, Sherman. Real estate brokers are very chic now."'

Exley smiled wanly. 'Maria's supposed to sound southern, John. Not retarded.'

'I was going for southern.'

'I hope your Arabic's more convincing.'

'So do I.'

She raised a hand to his face and ran it over his scruffy beard. 'You've been going native for a week now and I've been pretending not to notice. Want to tell me?'

133

Wells put the book aside and looked into her tired eyes. 'Want to know?'

'I want you to shave off that beard and stay here and work on your southern accent.'

Wells didn't say anything.

'You think you're doing this for me, but you're not. You're like an addict. It tears you up, but you can't stop.' She looked at him, and he found he couldn't meet her eyes. 'Argue, John. Yell. I don't care. Just let me know somebody's in there listening.'

She was right and she wasn't. Wells had never felt quite this way before. Even if he was wrong, and he probably was wrong, he couldn't stop himself. He wanted these men to pay for what they'd done to Exley. Even if she didn't. And he'd told Shafer the truth. These men deserved to die more than most of the men he'd killed. They'd set out to murder him, and they'd failed. When he came for them, they would know exactly why he'd targeted them. And that would be a great relief.

'I can't let this pass, Jenny. I know I should, but I can't.' Wells reached for the book. 'Come on, let's read some more.'

'All right, John. We won't talk about it anymore.' Exley closed her eyes. 'But promise me. You won't tell me when you're leaving. No heads-up.'

He squeezed her hand.

'No heads-up,' she said. 'I mean it.'

★   ★   ★

The visa came through the next morning, and he booked himself a first-class ticket on that afternoon's Aeroflot flight 318, Dulles to Moscow nonstop. It was round-trip, with the return two weeks away, though Wells hoped he wouldn't need that long. He drove home, packed, made his way to Langley to see Shafer. He'd talked with Shafer only in passing in the days since their argument, mainly so Shafer could update him on the progress of the official investigation into the attacks. The FBI was working to trace the path the assassins had taken between Atlanta and Washington and determine whether they'd had support from conspirators inside the United States. Meanwhile, the WSI and the agency were trying to find out how the assassins had entered Poland and where they had lived in Warsaw while they waited for their fake Polish passports. The task force was aiming to find conclusive evidence that the assassins were Russians, so that the White House could demand the Kremlin's cooperation without having to reveal how the NSA had unearthed the Helosrus phone numbers. Unfortunately, progress had been slow so far. The FBI hadn't found any evidence of conspirators in the United States, and the Poles hadn't been able to track the men's movements in Warsaw. Going directly to the Russian government with the information from the cell phone would have been far simpler. But Russia could make life difficult for the United

States in innumerable ways, from covertly supporting Iran's nuclear program to reducing its oil output and driving crude prices even higher. And so the White House had let Duto know that it wasn't anxious to confront the Kremlin unless the FBI and CIA came up with hard proof of Russian involvement in the attack. Wells felt a familiar bureaucratic stasis settling in. In situations as complex as this one, any action carried risks. Doing nothing was the safest course.

'I'm on my way to Dulles,' Wells said to Shafer.

'You're losing her, John,' Shafer said. 'She's disappearing before your eyes.'

'Can we not talk about that?'

'Then why are you here?'

'I may need your help in Moscow.'

'Why would I help you when I don't want you to go at all?'

'Because you'd rather I don't get killed.'

'Maybe. So sit for a minute, tell me what you're planning.'

Wells explained. When he was done, Shafer shook his head vigorously, sending a small cloud of dandruff flying. 'You've got no shot,' Shafer said.

'You must know someone. You always do.'

'I'll think about it,' Shafer said.

'Tell her I'm gone,' Wells said. 'She asked me not to tell her.'

'John—'
Wells walked out.

There was no traffic on the way to Dulles. And the flight to Moscow left exactly on time.

PART II

CHAPTER 9

ZURICH

The sapphire nestled in the V of Nadia's black silk dress, glowing as blue as her eyes.

'Pierre,' she said. 'It's perfect.'

'Perfect,' the Tiffany's saleswoman purred.

'Perfect.' What else could Kowalski say? *Perfect* was the perfect word to describe the necklace, the stone perfectly settled between Nadia's perfect breasts. He could survey the bankers strolling down Bahnhofstrasse to their 100-franc lunches. Nine out of ten would agree that Nadia and her sapphire were perfect. The tenth would be blind.

Kowalski steered the saleswoman – Frederica, middle-aged and trim, her brown hair neatly bobbed, a more suitable match for him than Nadia would ever be – to the counter in the back room, where Nadia couldn't see them. Unlike lesser items, the necklace had no price tag.

'*Six cent mille,*' she said, knowing the question. Six hundred thousand francs translated into about

141

$570,000. Absurd, even by the standards of the $5,000 handbags and $10,000 dresses he regularly bought Nadia.

'But the stone is flawless,' she said. 'It will never lose its value.' Frederica cocked her head and peeked into the front room. 'And look at her.'

Kowalski followed Frederica's gaze. Nadia caught him looking and smiled and folded her white swan arms across her stomach, lifting her breasts slightly so that the sapphire settled between them like a new-born about to suckle. She was jaw-dropping, breathtaking, all of her. The irony, of course, was that she would have looked just as good in a potato sack. The jewelry and the couture dresses helped less beautiful women, but they were wasted on her.

This thought had occurred to Kowalski before. Normally it pleased him enormously. But not today. Nothing was pleasing him today. For weeks, nothing had pleased him. Not since—

Frederica laid a hand on Kowalski's arm. 'What do you think, monsieur?'

'It is beautiful,' Kowalski admitted. He handed Frederica his black Amex card, idly wondering how much she would make on the sale. 'Run it through, madame,' Kowalski said. 'But quickly.'

Kowalski didn't like being in public anymore. Not even in the heart of Zurich, one of the safest cities in the world. Not even with the door to Tiffany's locked and his bodyguards outside. After all, John Wells had gotten to him in the Hamptons when he'd had five guards protecting him. And that was *before* Wells had a real reason to hate him.

Frederica disappeared into the back. The Tiffany's on Bahnhofstrasse didn't do anything as déclassé as conducting business where customers might see it. Kowalski walked back to Nadia, who wrinkled her nose at him as if she didn't know what he'd decided.

'Pierre? Did you decide?'

'Kitten. Even I have limits. But I spoke to Frederica and we're getting you a very nice charm bracelet. You know, the silver.'

Nadia's hands fluttered up to her neck.

'But it's so pretty, Pierre. And you said—' She broke off. She looked like a puppy whose favorite toy had suddenly gone missing. Kowalski reached for her and squeezed her against him.

'Of course it's yours. You know I don't deny you.'

'Pierre.' She wrapped her arms around him and kissed him. They stood that way, a parody of a diamond ad, the fat middle-aged man clinging to the young sylph, until Frederica came back with the receipt.

Kowalski was in his office that afternoon when Tarasov, his head of security, appeared. 'May I?'

'Come.'

Tarasov walked in, followed by a tall, thin man in a red and blue tracksuit. The man was one of the ugliest creatures Kowalski had ever seen, with patchy blond hair and tiny deep-set eyes. 'This is Dragon, the man I mentioned. Dragon, meet Monsieur Kowalski.'

'Pleased to meet you,' Dragon mumbled in sixth-grade French.

'You prefer I call you Dragon, or Monsieur Dragon?' Kowalski knew he shouldn't mock this man, his newest employee, but he couldn't help himself. *Dragon.* Had anyone ever looked less like a dragon?

Dragon tucked his hands under his arms. 'Dragon is fine,' he said. 'There's no need for formality.'

'Dragon it is,' Kowalski said.

'I've explained the terms to Dragon and he's agreeable,' Tarasov said.

'It will be an honor,' Dragon said.

'*Bon,*' Kowalski said. 'Please wait outside, Dragon. And close the door.'

Dragon left, and Kowalski turned to Tarasov.

'That's him? Your famous shooter? He doesn't look like much.' Kowalski had told Tarasov to beef up security, and not with the musclebound cretins who had been so useless in the Hamptons. Tarasov had come back with Dragon, supposedly the deadliest shooter anywhere between Zagreb and Athens. Not just one of the deadliest, *the* deadliest. Kowalski wondered how he'd gotten the title. It wasn't as if the Serbian paramilitaries could have held a competition. Or maybe they had, back in the 1990s, during the nasty little wars that had torn up the Balkans.

'He's the best,' Tarasov said.

'Didn't you say that about Markov's men? Let's hope he's more successful with Wells than they were, if it comes to that.'

'I'll take responsibility.'

'Anatoly. You take responsibility for nothing but spending your salary. If I want empty words, I'll turn on the television. Just get that Dragon some suits. I don't want him running around like a Serb gangster. Even if that's what he is.'

Tarasov left, and Kowalski was alone. He stared at the Zürichsee – Lake Zurich – and the mountains that rose gently behind the lake to the south. The sun had already disappeared to the west, behind the city. Across the lake, factories and homes glowed placidly in December twilight. But the view didn't soothe Kowalski.

In 1980, not long after he joined his father in the firm, Kowalski had struggled to close his first major deal, with a cocky general from Suriname who'd brought his mistress along with him for the trip. The general didn't want to negotiate, he told his father.

'I've put together a package that suits his needs, but he insists it's too expensive.'

'Yes?'

'The list is thirty-two million, but I've told him we're flexible. We could go as low as twenty-seven and still make a profit. I don't see why he won't negotiate. Too busy with his mistress.'

'Pierre, I could have handled this myself. You know why I let you?'

'No, Father.' Kowalski had wondered himself.

'What's our most powerful weapon?'

The question puzzled Kowalski. 'I suppose the APCs with the mounted cannons—'

'Pierre. I see they taught you nothing at Lazard. Our most powerful weapon is information. How big is General Pauline's budget?'

'The dossier said twenty-one million.'

'Correct. And our source told us that was a strict limit. So why are you offering a package for thirty-two million?'

'The Sikorskys I recommended suit his needs better than—'

'He can't afford them. And when you press him, you make him feel poor. Now call him, before he leaves Zurich. Get him what he needs at twenty-one million.'

'But the Sikorskys—'

'Don't pretend you can tell the difference between a Sikorsky and a mosquito. You may know all the specs, but you're not a soldier. Always remember that.'

Until the end of his life, Kowalski's father could make him feel like a misbehaving child.

'And even if you could tell the difference, do you think General Pauline could? He's not fighting the American marines. He's chasing rebels around the jungle until both sides are too bored to keep fighting. Most of what we sell sits in hangars until it's rusted out. It's there to make the generals and the defense ministers and presidents feel better about themselves, to puff up their chests. This man has come all the way to Zurich to make a deal. Not to be embarrassed in front of his woman. Let's use the knowledge we have to accommodate him.'

'Yes, Father.'

Kowalski had never forgotten that lesson. He spent millions of francs a year to cultivate informers in armies and intelligence services all over the world. But at this most crucial moment, his sources in the United States had proven useless. The Americans had kept any information about their investigation into the attack from leaking, not just to the press but to the ex-CIA agents and retired army officers who were Kowalski's sources in Washington. Had the agency learned of Markov's involvement? Publicly, the men had been identified only as 'foreign nationals,' not Russians. They had been traced to the hotel where they'd been staying, but no further. But was the United States actually further along? And what about Wells? Had he guessed Kowalski's role in the attack? Too many questions without answers. Damn Markov and his men for their bungling. For his part, Markov had told Kowalski that he wasn't worried. Easy for him to say. He was holed up in Moscow, untouchable as long as the Kremlin didn't turn on him.

Markov had the Kremlin. Kowalski had the

Dragon, another overpaid Eastern European eating his food and taking up space under his roof. His own fault. He'd made this mess.

His landline trilled. Thérèse, his secretary.

'Monsieur,' Thérèse said. 'A call from Andrei Pavlov. Shall I take a message?'

Pavlov was a deputy director at Rosatom, the Russian nuclear agency. Two years before, he and Kowalski had sold the Iranian government centrifuges to enrich uranium, a highly profitable deal.

'Put him through.'

The line fell silent. Then: 'Pierre, my old comrade.'

'Andrei.'

For fifteen minutes Pavlov blathered about a new Rosatom power plant and the money he'd made trading oil futures. 'Of course it would be nothing to you, Pierre, or to the Abramoviches of the world, but for a man like me it's a real fortune.' Finally, just as Kowalski was about to lose all patience, Pavlov said casually, 'So. I don't suppose you heard about our missing material?'

Missing material? Rosatom would only worry about one kind of missing material. And the fact that Pavlov had waited so long to mention it, and then mentioned it so casually, signaled that Rosatom must be very worried indeed.

'Just the rumors,' Kowalski said.

'A minor matter. A kilo or two of low-grade stuff. Maybe three.'

'Yes, of course.' Kowalski stretched his bluff. 'But I heard it was HEU.' Highly enriched uranium, suitable for a nuclear weapon, not the less-enriched kind used to generate electricity in power plants.

'No, not HEU. Somewhere in the middle. But whoever has it may be bragging, saying it's the good stuff, enough for a bomb. And you know, the Americans will make a stink if someone finds it before we do. And sometimes you hear about things.' Pavlov cleared his throat. 'Anyhow, if you hear anything, if you could see your way clear to let us know, we wouldn't forget it.'

Kowalski decided to push for information. 'This stuff, when did it get lost? And where?'

'Last seen in Mayak a couple of weeks back.'

Mayak. The biggest nuclear weapons plant in the world. Another sign this was more serious that Pavlov was letting on. But Kowalski didn't want to ask any more questions. Pavlov had probably said more than he'd meant to already.

'I'll ask some people,' Kowalski said. 'If I hear anything, I'll call you. And promise you'll come to Zurich soon. Nadia and I must take you to dinner. She misses her countrymen.'

'Delightful.' Pavlov hung up and Kowalski considered for a minute, remembering a phone call he'd received a few months before, one of the few offers he'd ever turned down flat. He wondered if he could afford to spare Tarasov with Wells on the loose. On the other hand . . . he had to know if Pavlov's call meant what he suspected.

He called Tarasov. 'Anatoly. Get your passport. You're going to Moscow.'

CHAPTER 10

HAMBURG

On the Reeperbahn, Hamburg's legendary nightlife strip, the hookers were having a slow night. They stood in their usual spot, in front of a small public courtyard between kebob stands and novelty shops specializing in fake pistols and dull knives. They shuffled in their boots, a dozen miserable women, each an even ten feet from the next. Even whores couldn't escape the German passion for order.

Hamburg's true red-light district was a few blocks south, on Herbertstrasse, a single street sixty yards long where the prostitutes sat in shop windows as they did in Amsterdam. Only adult men were allowed on Herbertstrasse, and high wooden fences on both ends kept out women and children. Despite the ugliness of the trade, the street possessed a certain hard glamour. The prostitutes posed on their stools in lace bras and panties, watching men swirl on the pavement beneath them. Police monitored Herbertstrasse, and the prostitutes there registered with the city and were tested regularly for HIV. But the discount hookers on the Reeperbahn had no glamour at all. They wore puffy down jackets and tight jeans, and their faces were young and unformed, yet already worn. They looked like high school juniors who had fallen asleep in their beds and woken up in hell.

A steady stream of tourists and sailors and locals walked by the courtyard. The women gave them all the same treatment, a whispered invitation, half-coo, half-hiss. Any man foolish enough to stop found himself in a whispered tête-à-tête with a hand on his arm. But it was only 10 p.m. and a drizzle dampened the air, and the men were still mostly sober and mostly saying no. So the women smoked and stamped their feet to stay warm and ran their hands through their bleached blond hair and waited for business to improve.

Near the back of the courtyard, Sayyid Nasiji watched the whores' dance. He'd never understood the German attitude toward these women. A police station stood only a couple of blocks away. Why did the German cops tolerate this dismal scene? How had these women fallen so low? Where were their families?

Nasiji didn't delude himself. Muslim nations had prostitutes, too. But at least Muslims were ashamed of the flesh trade and tried to stop it. The Germans seemed almost proud that women were selling themselves in public. They jammed the Reeperbahn. And the crowd wasn't just sailors or ugly old men with no choice. Students and office workers came here to dance at the clubs speckled among the strip parlors.

Yet Nasiji liked Germany. He'd attended college at the Technical University of Munich, five hundred miles south of here. He'd initially planned to specialize in nuclear physics. But he was Iraqi, and his professors warned him that most nuclear power plants probably wouldn't hire him. So he stuck to chemical engineering. Still, he spent most of his free time in the university's nuclear labs.

Nasiji had grown up in Ghazaliya, in western Baghdad. His father, Khalid, was a brigadier general in Saddam's Republican Guard. Khalid had risen far enough in the ranks to build a two-story concrete house and buy a used BMW 735i, his pride. But he had cannily avoided trying to reach the top of the Guard, dodging the bloody purges that swept away his bosses every few years.

Nasiji was the second-oldest of five kids, the favorite of his parents. His intelligence was obvious from his first days in school. After he graduated first in his high school class, Khalid encouraged him to study in Europe, getting him a visa to Germany and permission to leave Iraq.

Nasiji's family was moderately religious, and Nasiji had grown up praying each week at the big Mother of All Battles Mosque in Ghazaliya. In Munich, he kept his faith, praying five times daily, never eating pork or drinking.

But Nasiji was hardly a fanatic. By the spring

of 2001, his last year in Munich, his friends had grown outspoken about their hate for Europe and the United States. A couple even talked about quitting school and joining the jihadis training in Afghanistan. Nasiji wasn't interested. He preferred to spend his time studying. And though he never argued with his friends, he thought that complaining about the West was a waste of breath. He was a visitor to Germany, after all. He would follow its customs and laws, and hope for the same respect from the Germans if they visited Iraq.

After graduation, Nasiji came back to Baghdad. He was home on September 11 when Khalid called with word of the attack. Nasiji and his brothers ran to the television and watched as the Trade Center towers burned. Amir, the oldest and most anti-American of Nasiji's brothers, shouted gleefully when the first skyscraper went down.

'This makes you happy?' Nasiji asked Amir.

'Should I weep? Poor America. Did you forget what they did to us in 1991, Sayyid? All those years in Germany made you soft? They deserve what they get, the Americans. No jobs, empty stores – they're to blame. These stupid sanctions. Beggars on the streets. There were never beggars before.'

Nasiji couldn't disagree. After the Gulf War in 1991, the United States and United Nations had imposed sanctions that had crippled Iraq's economy. Nasiji hadn't found a job since coming home, though the Technical University was among the top schools in Europe. Even so, he knew he couldn't let his brother's words go unchallenged. 'So our economy stinks. Killing those people, ordinary men going to work, what good does that do for anyone?'

'Remember five, six years ago, before you stopped brawling? Back in school, when every afternoon we looked around for Shia to beat? You know what you said to me then?'

'That was a long time ago, Amir.' Nasiji preferred to forget his days as a fighter.

'You loved it. And then one day you just stopped. You never did tell us why.'

'Forget it. What did I say?'

'That sometimes it's necessary to tell the world you exist. And the best way is with a closed fist.'

'I was sixteen, Amir.'

'Even so. When the Americans bombed us ten years ago, they killed plenty of ordinary people. I don't remember seeing them shed any tears. Now they understand how we feel. We've told them we exist.'

'I had American professors in Munich. They were always fair.'

'You're so naive. Look at Egypt. They use Arabs against Arabs. Muslims against Muslims. And the way they help Israel. One Yid is worth a million of us. You watch. They'll find some way to turn this against us. They'll come and steal our oil.'

Amir's words seemed eerily prophetic to Nasiji in the months that followed, as the United States geared up to attack Iraq. The protests, the United Nations votes, nothing made any difference. The American tanks came to Kuwait and then over the border.

For the Nasiji family, the invasion was a disaster. Khalid lost his job as a general when the Americans disbanded the Iraqi army. As a high-ranking Baathist, he was barred from working for the new government. Some of Khalid's fellow Republican Guard officers began organizing resistance to the occupation. Khalid refused. 'Let's see what happens,' he told his family. 'Maybe it's for the best.' Then the violence started. In November 2003, a cousin of Nasiji's was killed at an American checkpoint. Another died in a suicide bombing.

The next month, Amir joined a cell of Sunni insurgents. Sayyid tried to stop him, but Amir insisted. 'They'll kill us all if we let them,' he said. He lasted four months. In April 2004, an American sniper shot him at 3 a.m. as he planted a bomb on the highway that connected Baghdad and Fallujah.

Fouad, the youngest of the brothers, died next. After Amir's death, Fouad joined a local militia to fight the Shia who were taking over Ghazaliya block by block. Three months later, Fouad disappeared. A week later, kids found his body in a soccer field, his fingers hacked off, his face covered with cigarette burns.

In Muslim tradition, the family held Fouad's funeral as quickly as possible, just one day after his body was found, at a mosque in Khudra, a Sunni neighborhood just south of Ghazaliya. Around the coffin, the women of the family screeched and moaned, an unearthly, terrifying lament of loss that seemed to demand a response from the blue sky overhead. Khalid wore his Republican Guard uniform to the funeral, a pointless gesture of defiance against the Shia who had killed his son. Once he had filled out the green uniform proudly. Now it hung loose on his shoulders and one of the sideboards had come askew. He mumbled the same words to all the men who greeted him at the funeral. 'Too soon for this. Too soon.' He had turned old, Nasiji saw.

The ceremony took less than an hour, and afterward the family piled into Khalid's BMW to head back to Ghazaliya. As they were about to leave, Nasiji hopped out, deciding to ride home with his cousin Alaa instead. The choice saved his life.

On an overpass over the main western highway out of Baghdad, two Toyota 4Runners forced Khalid's BMW to a stop. Four men jumped from the Toyotas, AK-47s poised, shooting even before their feet hit the pavement. They blasted out the BMW's windows and kept firing. Thirty seconds later, they were gone.

Nasiji reached the overpass a few minutes later. The BMW's metal skin was pockmarked with too many holes to count. Blood and bone and gristle festooned the interior. The shooters had fired so many rounds at such close range that Khalid's skull was almost gone and the green of his uniform had turned black with blood.

On the sedan's hood the killers had left a mocking present, a wall clock whose background was a picture of Saddam. In the old days, Saddam had presented favored members of the Baathist Party with trinkets like the clock as signs of his affection. A note lay beside the clock, crudely scrawled Arabic: '*All Baathists die! Revenge for the Shia! Iraq for Iraqis, not Saddam's vermin!*'

As his brother Amir had reminded him on September 11, Nasiji knew how to fight. He was only five-nine, but he had a middleweight's build – lean, muscular, and quick. Growing up, he and his brothers had gained a reputation as bullies. They knew that their father could save them from trouble with a word to the local cops.

During brawls, Nasiji used his speed to overcome bigger kids, ducking inside their looping punches and hitting them until they ran or went down. He was the fiercest of his brothers, always ready for a fight. Yet he'd grown almost afraid of the excitement he felt when he knew a brawl was coming, the way his mouth grew dry and his hands seemed to swell.

One afternoon, a Shia teenager from Shula, a slum north of Ghazaliya, bumped into Nasiji's sister in a local market. The contact was accidental, but Nasiji didn't care. As the Shia – Nasiji never did find out his name – walked home,

Nasiji pushed him onto a side street off the main road.

The Shia was skinny, not a fighter. Nasiji looked around to be sure no one was watching, then dragged the kid into a garbage-strewn alley invisible from the road. He punched the Shia in the stomach until the boy doubled over. The kid's shoulders heaved as he gasped for breath.

'You're nothing,' Nasiji said. 'Say it.'

'I'm n-n-nothing.'

The kid looked up. Nasiji caught him across the face with a straight right, snapping back his head. The boy collapsed onto the broken concrete.

'Please,' he said. 'I didn't do nothing.'

'Give me your hand,' Nasiji said. The Shia limply raised his arm. Nasiji grabbed the boy's hand and twisted his pinky sideways until it snapped. The kid pulled back his arm and screamed, a sharp animal cry. Nasiji lined up to kick him. And something more. *Hurt him*. He didn't know where the words came from, but suddenly he had an overwhelming urge to hear the boy scream. Nasiji looked around for a brick, a stone, anything. *Kill him*. The Shia must have seen the madness in Nasiji's eyes, for he scrabbled backward, his legs kicking wildly.

'Allah. Please. I beg you. I'm sorry. Whatever I've done, I'm sorry.'

Nasiji looked away from the boy to find a brick. When he turned back he saw for the first time how pathetic the Shia really was. The kid's T-shirt was dirty and his sneakers didn't match. Tears and snot flowed down his face. Nasiji's rage faded and a heavy shame filled his belly. He stepped back. 'Filthy cur. Go back to Shula and never touch a girl in Ghazaliya again. We don't want your fleas.'

The kid scrambled and ran. Nasiji walked out of the alley, his head pounding, heart beating so quickly that even an hour later it hadn't returned to normal. What if a rock had been handy? What if he hadn't had those few seconds to collect himself?

Nasiji told no one about what had happened that day, what he'd almost done. He stopped fighting and devoted himself to studying. For a decade, he pushed aside his murderous thoughts, locked down the beast inside him.

On the overpass in Ghazaliya, beside the bloodied bodies of his father and mother and sister and brother, he opened the cage.

He joined the Sunni militia battling the Shia for control of Ghazaliya. But he quickly tired of fighting other Iraqis. The Shia weren't to blame for this madness. Everything had been fine until the invasion. The United States had destroyed Iraq. Nasiji saw the truth now.

So Nasiji left Ghazaliya for Tikrit, Saddam's hometown, where former Baathists were organizing the Sunni insurgency. He was easily accepted. Everyone in Tikrit knew what had happened to his father. Nasiji had only one quirk.

He had no interest in operations against the Shia. Only Americans.

He quickly gained a reputation as fearless and vicious. In early 2006 he led an ambush against an American convoy traveling through Mahmoudiyah. His men killed three soldiers and kidnapped two more, hiding them in a farmhouse a few miles south of Fallujah. Nasiji interrogated the men for a few days, but they didn't have much to tell. He told them he'd let them go if they begged for their lives. They knew he was lying, perhaps, but they couldn't help themselves.

He watched their mouths move as they spoke, but he couldn't hear them at all, only the little voice in his head whispering, *Kill them.* When their pleas were done, he blew out their brains and left their bodies in a field for dogs to eat. Then he uploaded the video to a jihadi Web site, to prove to the world that Americans were weak when they didn't have tanks or helicopters to protect them.

After the Mahmoudiyah operation, Nasiji's anger curdled into something calmer and nastier. Over the course of a year, he and his men had killed two dozen soldiers with ambushes and roadside bombs. A good haul. But hardly enough to make a difference in this war. The American bases were impenetrable. He could only pick soldiers off one by one as they traveled in convoys. Eventually he'd be shot in a firefight, or the Americans would learn his name and seek him out. Inevitably they'd get him. Besides, how would killing even a hundred soldiers make a difference? The Americans didn't care how many of their soldiers died here, or how much damage they caused.

'*Ordinary people die all the time here and they don't care*,' his brother Amir had said on September 11. '*Now they understand*.'

But Amir had been wrong. The Americans hadn't understood the message of September 11 at all. To teach them, Nasiji would need to give them a lesson they would never forget. He would need to use the knowledge he'd gained in Munich to turn their cities into lakes of fire.

Nasiji went back to Tikrit with an unusual request. He heard nothing for two weeks, and he wondered if he'd overreached. Then, near mid-night, as he rested in a house in Ghazaliya, his phone trilled. 'Sayyid. It's arranged. For tomorrow.' The voice belonged to a Syrian he knew only as Bas. 'Tell me where you are.'

Nasiji gave his location.

'I'll send a car at six a.m. Whoever you're with, don't tell them. Just go.'

'Of course. Bas?'

'Yes.'

'Thank you.'

That night Nasiji hardly slept. Curled on his metal cot, his AK laid neatly on a sheet on the concrete floor beneath him, he folded his arms behind his head and wondered: Would the sheikh listen to him? He was nothing, a jihadi like a million others. He closed his eyes and saw his father's BMW on the overpass. What he'd first seen that day wasn't the bodies or even the bullet holes, but the puddles of oil and gas leaking from the car. As if he hadn't been willing to look into the BMW itself, as if the fluid took the place of the blood he knew he'd see when he looked up—

And then he had, he had looked up—

No. Enough. Put it aside. 'Not what they've done to you,' he murmured to himself. 'What you'll do to them.' He passed the night half-asleep, his eyes fluttering open every few minutes. He was glad for morning.

Six a.m. came and went, and then seven. Nasiji worried that his driver had been ambushed or arrested. But as he was about to call Bas, a white Toyota Crown with tinted windows pulled up outside the house.

Four hours later, Nasiji found himself in a house south of Ramadi, kissing the hand of a heavy man in a dishdasha, the flowing white robe favored by Saudis.

The man was Sheikh Ahmed Faisal. He and his cousin Abdul were third-tier Saudi princes – and the biggest source of cash for the Iraqi insurgency. The Faisals did in Iraq what Osama bin Laden had once done in Afghanistan, funneling in cash and jihadis to fight the United States. Abdul rarely left Riyadh, but Ahmed came to Iraq every so often to track the progress of the war.

Ahmed raised his hand. 'Please sit,' he said. The Saudi's black beard was neatly trimmed, his robe immaculate, making Nasiji conscious of his own scruffy beard and dirty jeans.

'Thank you, Sheikh,' Nasiji said. 'This visit is an honor. Every day, all of us in Iraq appreciate your great kindnesses.'

'I've seen the video from Mahmoudiyah. If we had more soldiers like you, the Americans might be gone already.' Ahmed spoke a refined classical Arabic that Nasiji had heard only on Al Jazeera. The sheikh tapped the silver case on the table between them. 'Cigarette?'

'No, thank you. I'm sure you have many men more important than me to see, so I won't take much of your time.' Quickly, Nasiji outlined his plan.

When he was done, Ahmed lit a fresh cigarette and took a deep drag. 'Young man,' he said. 'Many others have had this idea. They've all failed.'

'I have certain advantages.'

'Your training. Yes. If not for that, I would not have met you.'

'If I get the material, I won't waste it.'

'But there's something else. You must understand the consequences of this. When the moment comes, you won't have doubts?'

'Has anyone told you what happened to my family?'

The Saudi nodded. For a few seconds the room was so quiet that Nasiji could hear his own breathing. 'These Americans,' Ahmed said finally.

'They need a taste.' Nasiji didn't tell the sheikh that if his plan succeeded it wouldn't destroy just New York or Washington, but all of America. That vision might have been too much even for this man.

Ahmed stubbed out his cigarette. 'Let me ask you, then. What will you need?'

'To start? A Canadian or American passport, a real one. Also one from Europe. Safe houses in Germany and Russia. Men I can trust in both places. And money, lots of it.'

'It's a long list.'

'It'll get longer as we get closer.'

The sheikh nodded.

'Most of all, we need someone in the United States we can absolutely trust, someone with a bit of land. A few acres so we won't be bothered.'

'Inside the United States? Why?'

'We'll need to assemble the bomb there. The material itself isn't very noticeable, but the finished weapon is.'

'Do you really think you can do this?'

'I can't promise success. But it's not impossible. Acquiring the material is the most difficult part. If God wills that . . .'

'*Inshallah*,' the sheikh said. '*Inshallah*.' He clapped his hands together. 'All right. First, let's get you out of Iraq before the Americans find you.

We'll meet in Amman in a week and talk more about your plans. You'll have the chance to revenge your family, I promise you that.'

To his astonishment, Nasiji felt his eyes well with tears. He turned away so the Saudi couldn't see his face.

For the next three years, Ahmed Faisal kept his word to Nasiji. All over the world Faisal and his cousin knew men who wanted to support the jihad. In Montreal, the director of an Algerian community center. In Berlin, the owner of an Afghan restaurant. In Sarajevo, a used-truck dealer. In Chelyabinsk, an imam. All willing to help Nasiji without question. They put him up in their homes, so he didn't leave a paper trail. They passed along cash. A few provided more crucial support. The Canadian passport in Nasiji's pocket identified him as Jad Ghani of Montreal. Nasiji didn't have to worry that an immigration officer would identify the passport as fake – because it wasn't.

Jad Ghani actually existed. He was mildly retarded, lived at home, and had been born in Montreal the same year as Nasiji. Jad's father, a fervent believer, had been more than happy to apply for a passport for his son, using photos of Nasiji. And so Nasiji had a genuine Canadian passport, which would easily get him through border controls anywhere in Europe or the United States.

Nasiji's first big break came when Faisal put him in touch with Yusuf al Haj, who'd served for six years as an engineer in the Syrian army. Yusuf had two great virtues. He spoke excellent Russian. And he was a stone-cold psychopath. The Syrians had discharged him for beating an enlisted man nearly to death when the soldier argued with an order he gave. But Nasiji knew how to deal with madmen. He'd seen Iraqi jihadis as crazy as Yusuf. The key with them was never to show weakness. They were wolves, these men. If they smelled doubt or fear, they would turn instantly.

Slowly, Nasiji put together his network. He arranged a transport system and put together a workshop in the United States. Along the way he discovered certain weaknesses in his plan that he now believed he'd fixed.

But without the material, his plans meant nothing. He'd be practicing dry runs and designing dummy bombs for the rest of his life. Russia was his best bet, he knew. The North Koreans couldn't be trusted, and the Pakistanis were so paranoid about what the Americans would do to them if their bombs went missing that the security of their stock-pile was actually quite good.

So Nasiji and Yusuf traveled across southern Russia, pretending to be traders who wanted to export Russian motorcycles to the Middle East. For months, they got nowhere. They traveled freely into the closed cities, but the bases where the bombs were held were another matter. Then the imam in Chelyabinsk told them of a security worker in Ozersk who might be willing to help.

Nasiji plotted the theft but left Yusuf in charge of handling the Farzadov cousins. If the Russians unearthed the plot, Yusuf was replaceable. Anyway, Yusuf had a talent for this work. He frightened people so much that they would agree to almost anything just to keep him calm.

Nasiji had decided on the Black Sea route because he wasn't sure what the Russians would do once they discovered the theft. They wouldn't want to cause a worldwide panic, so they probably wouldn't make a public announcement. But they might try to close their borders, and the Kazakhs might cooperate with them. Best to get the material into Europe quickly.

Despite everything, Nasiji had scarcely trusted his eyes when he saw the twin bombs in Yusuf's Nissan. He pulled a handheld radiation detector from his pocket to be sure. Yes. The radiation signature was faint but distinct. They were real.

He reached inside the toolboxes and touched the cylinders, one hand on each, the steel cold under his fingers. An electric charge ran through his body, as if he were conducting current from one warhead to the other.

'*Now I am become death, the destroyer of worlds,*' Nasiji said.

'Hmm?'

'It's what the Americans said when they blew up the first bomb.'

'Someone said that?'

'Oppenheimer. A Jew American physicist. It comes from a book of Indian prayers. The fireball went up and Oppenheimer said, "Now I am become death, the destroyer of worlds."'

'That's how I felt, too, when I saw them. Only I wasn't sure how to say it.'

'Do you know what the scientists call them?'

'Bombs?'

'*Gadgets.*' Nasiji said the word in English.

'Gadget?'

'It doesn't translate well into Arabic. It means, a sort of toy. A mechanical device.'

'Why this word?'

'Don't you see? It's a joke. Such a powerful weapon, and they call it a *gadget*. Like it's a mobile phone.'

'*Gidgit.*' Yusuf smiled, trying to play along.

Nasiji closed the trunk. 'You've done well, Yusuf.'

After the trip over the Black Sea, which gave Yusuf the chance to dispose of the Farzadov cousins, the bombs arrived in Turkey. Yusuf watched over them in a rental apartment in an Istanbul suburb for four days, and then the next step was ready.

For a year, Nasiji had been buying toolboxes and cabinets from a factory in central Turkey. He bought them in lots of eight hundred, enough to fill a forty-foot shipping container, and sent them by ship to Trieste, Italy, and then on to Hamburg, where he sold them at cost to German hardware stores.

Nasiji wasn't trying to start a hardware business. He wanted to build a pattern of shipments, a key to avoiding scrutiny by customs agents. Hundreds of thousands of containers came through Trieste each year, far too many for customs authorities to examine. So the agents concentrated their efforts on new shippers, shippers who had a history of evading duties, and shippers from countries that were known to be problematic, like Nigeria. Anyone outside those categories – say, a once-a-month shipper from Istanbul with a clean record – had a better chance of being hit by a meteor than being randomly searched.

The Turkish tool cabinets were delivered to a warehouse in Istanbul's bustling harbor district. There Yusuf added his own packages, stowing them inside crates 301 and 303. The crates were packed in a container that was put aboard the UND *Birlik*, a ship that regularly ran the Istanbul-Trieste route. Five days later, the container was offloaded at Trieste and transferred to a truck for the drive to Hamburg. As Nasiji had expected, no customs agent ever even looked at the container.

Now Nasiji and the container had arrived in Hamburg.

In the courtyard on the Reeperbahn, one of the whores finally found a customer, a young man in a denim jacket. She wrapped her arm in his and they walked toward the little streets where love hotels provided cheap beds by the hour. The man's eyes slid over Nasiji as they walked past, but he didn't break stride. No surprise. Nasiji could hang out in the courtyard all night and no one, not even the whores, would bother him. Strangely enough, despite the noise and constant traffic, he found the Reeperbahn a good place to think.

Nasiji wondered when the Russians would publicly disclose the theft. Ahmed Faisal, who had connections in the Saudi intelligence agency, had told him that the FSB had issued a bulletin asking Interpol and the United States to detain the Farzadov cousins. Still, Nasiji believed he was well ahead of his enemies. Grigory and Tajid were no longer around to spill their secrets. Now only three men knew exactly where the bombs were: Nasiji himself, Yusuf, and the man he was about to meet. And so even the cold Hamburg drizzle couldn't dampen his mood as he waited for his contact, a man who called himself Bernard.

Bernard's real name was Bassim Kygeli. He'd emigrated from Turkey in 1979 and quickly realized that Germans preferred to do business with Bernard, not Bassim. So he was Bernard on his business cards and in his corporate records. Starting with rugs and trinkets, he built a successful import-export business. Over the years, he progressed to furniture and then machine tools. He brought a bride from Istanbul and together they had three children. They lived in a two-story white house in Hamburg's wealthy northern district, halfway between the airport and downtown.

Yet as the years progressed and his wealth grew, Bernard became more angry, not less, at the United States and Germany. The Americans kept Muslims down and then congratulated themselves for their humanity. The Germans had been American lapdogs for so long that they had no opinions of their own anymore.

In the late 1990s, Bernard realized he would be more valuable to the jihadi cause if he kept a low profile. He donated thousands of euros a year to the relief organizations that supported Palestinian refugees. That wasn't illegal and there was no harm in it. But he stayed out of Hamburg's radical mosques, and he never gave money directly to jihadi charities. As a result, his name didn't show up on any terrorist watch lists. The CIA and the FBI; the French DGSE; MI-5 and -6; even the BND, the German intelligence agency – none had ever heard of Bernard Kygeli.

And so Bernard was incredibly valuable to Sayyid Nasiji. Sure, Nasiji sometimes grew frustrated with the man, who had no idea of the risks Nasiji took. Still, he always felt better after a night in the guest room at Bernard's house, drinking sweet tea and eating the delicious dinners that Bernard's wife made, kebobs and hummus and grape leaves stuffed with rice.

The thought of dinner reminded Nasiji that he hadn't eaten all day, and he was more than happy to see Bernard's black Mercedes sedan pull up to the curb in front of the whores, who quickly swarmed the car. Nasiji pushed through them and slipped inside the car, ignoring the whores' backtalk.

Bernard eased the Mercedes away from the curb. 'Tell me again why we must meet on the Reeperbahn, Sayyid?'

'Because our friends at the BND would never expect it.'

'Maybe you just like the girls.'

'Hardly. How are you, my friend?'

'The same. Watching the Kurds make fools of us Turks.'

'While the Americans laugh.'

'Yes. Meanwhile, Helmut' – Bernard's oldest child and only son – 'spends his nights at cafés. Says his screenplay is almost finished.' Helmut had quit the University of Hamburg a year before, supposedly to make movies. Nasiji had met him twice. He was a foppish manchild who stank of sweet cologne.

'You ought to kick him out.'

'I have. Last week. I hope it's not too late. My fault, you know. I never should have named him Helmut. It was the old days. I was trying to pass.'

Nasiji had heard these laments before. 'How are your other two?'

'The girls? Like all women.' Bernard steered the Mercedes into one of the tunnels that cut under the Elbe River. The Elbe had been the source of Hamburg's wealth for centuries, the waterway that linked Germany to the North Sea and the rest of the world. Most of the city lay north of the river, while the giant port complex was located to the south.

'How's Zaineb?' After Helmut, Bernard had gone back to traditional Muslim names for his kids. Zaineb was the older of Bernard's two daughters. Nasiji had only met her once. She was petite, with fine dark hair and a throaty laugh like a bus engine, a laugh that seemed to indicate she found the world impossibly funny. In another life Nasiji would have married her.

'She's fine.'

'Is she around this evening?'

'Visiting a cousin.'

'Away again.' Bernard wanted Zaineb to have nothing to do with him, Nasiji thought. Though he couldn't blame the man. 'Maybe one day I'll get to see her again.'

'Of course.'

'You Turks are such liars.'

'No worse than you Iraqis.'

They emerged from the tunnel on the south side of the river, to the port zone, block-long docks crosscut by canals, as much water as land. On the wharves, shipping containers were stacked in five-high piles. Cranes towered hundreds of feet overhead. Giant container ships, among the largest structures ever built, rested silently in the canals, gleaming under high-intensity spotlights. The biggest ships were a quarter-mile and could carry 200,000 tons of cargo – the equivalent of 100,000 cars.

'It's like a race of giants has taken over,' Nasiji said. 'And then left again.' Indeed, aside from an occasional security guard, the wharves were empty.

'The boats have gotten bigger and bigger,' Bernard said. 'After a while you don't think about it.' They passed over a bridge, to the southern half of the port. Here the canals were narrower, the ships and cranes slightly smaller. Bernard turned right and drove beside a high wall until he reached a guardhouse. The guardhouse's window opened and a fiftyish man with long hair leaned out.

'Yes?' Bernard lowered his window and the guard nodded. 'Oh, hello, Bernard. Good evening.'

'Georg.'

The gate swung open.

'He knows you,' Nasiji said.

'He should. I've owned this warehouse for fifteen years.'

Bernard turned down a dead-end road that led to a locked fence. Behind it was a brick warehouse and a parking lot littered with a half-dozen containers. High on the building, a red-lettered sign proclaimed: 'Tukham GmBH, Bernard Kygeli, Prop.' Bernard unlocked the fence and parked outside the warehouse. He keyed in an alarm code and stepped inside. Nasiji followed.

'No one's watching it?'

'My men would wonder if I asked them to guard a shipment of cabinets, Sayyid. Don't worry. It's fine.' Indeed the long padlock on the end of the container was still locked. Bernard picked up a crowbar and broke it off with a flick of his wrist.

Ten minutes later, they'd dragged out crates 301 and 303. Nasiji popped them open, opened the tool cabinets inside, and . . . there they were.

'May I touch?' Bernard said. He reached down—

'*NO!*' Nasiji screamed.

Bernard jumped back. 'What?' He scuttled backward, away from the warheads, a hand raised protectively.

Nasiji laughed. 'Sorry, Bernard. I couldn't resist. It's perfectly safe. Touch them, kick them, run them over. Doesn't matter. They can't go off.'

Bernard closed his eyes and ran a limp hand over his forehead. 'Damn you, Sayyid. My heart . . . my doctor says—' Bernard leaned against a crate and waited for the spasm to pass. 'So, the ship goes in two days. You're sure you want to do it this way? It seems overly complicated. Why don't you let me send them?'

'I told you, I tried that once myself, a dummy run from Russia, said it was motorcycle parts, and the Americans opened the box.'

'That was Russia. I can send them from Hamburg directly to New York or Baltimore. You see how easy it was from Istanbul.'

'I don't want to take a chance at customs. I want to use your boat. This way, Yusuf and I watch over them directly, then our friends drive them in from Canada.'

'I don't agree, but it's your choice. Now let me show you what I have for you.'

In the back left corner of the warehouse, empty crates and pallets were neatly stacked before a metal cage, its gate protected by a heavy combination lock. Bernard pushed aside the pallets, opened the lock. The men stepped inside the cage, which held two dusty wooden crates, one square, the other long and narrow, both covered with Chinese characters. Bernard grabbed a crowbar and popped the top of the longer crate, revealing two steel tubes packed tightly inside. They were identical, each about six feet long, painted dark green. Their back ends flared out like rocket nozzles, and small sights were attached to their tops, just above their breeches. They were Russian-designed SPG-9 Spear recoilless rifles. Like the AK-47, another brilliant Russian weapon, they were easy to use, built for deserts and jungles, low-tech but effective. The Red Army had first put the SPG-9 in service in 1962, and it had been killing people ever since.

'You leave these here?' Nasiji said. 'In the open?'

Bernard had grown a touch tired of having Nasiji second-guess him. 'You think my men touch that lock if I don't say so, Sayyid? Now lift with me.' They grabbed the barrel and heaved it up.

'Not too bad.'

'No. This is the new SPG, a bit shorter and lighter, about forty kilos' – ninety pounds. 'I suppose I sound like a salesman. But you already have two heavy crates, so I wanted to keep it as light as possible.'

Bernard broke open the second crate, revealing a dozen steel canisters, each painted black, just over two feet long, but narrow, like stretched-out soup cans or oversized bullets. 'The rounds. New design from the Polish, the highest velocity available. Near five hundred meters a second.'

Nasiji picked up a round. The canister was light, no more than six kilograms. He passed it from hand to hand. Standard theory said that the pieces of the uranium pit needed to come together at three hundred meters a second or more to lessen the risk of preimplosion. The problem was that every extra gram of weight that he added to the round would reduce its acceleration and slow its top speed. He'd have to be very careful to keep the pit, and the reflector around it, as light as possible.

'What about the beryllium?' Nasiji said.

Bernard shook his head. 'Much harder than getting these. Almost as hard as getting those nasties out there, believe it or not. Only one reason anyone would want that quantity of beryllium and everyone knows it. There are only two people I trust enough even to mention it to, and they both said no. I can't push. It won't help anyone if my name shows up on a list of people looking to get dual-use material. Anyway, isn't it just insurance?'

'Probably. Until I get inside the bombs and do the math, I won't know for sure.'

'Then I'll keep trying. Meanwhile, let's get back to my house so you can sleep. You'll thank me when you're on the North Atlantic.'

CHAPTER 11

MOSCOW

Wells stood under the glowing ultraviolet rays, trying not to feel silly as the minutes ticked by. Outside, night had fallen and the temperature was just above zero. But inside Ultra Spa, the sun never set.

Wells was the only man in the place and had drawn a suspicious look from the cashier when he arrived. But she took his rubles and led him down a dingy tile hall, past saunas and a tiny lap pool, to a room where a half-dozen stand-up tanning booths crackled with an electrical hum. Wells stripped down to his boxer briefs, earning an appreciative look from the cashier despite the slight gut he'd put on. She put a hand on his arm as she chose a booth and punched in his time, fifteen minutes. She gave him a pair of goggles and in he went.

He wondered if any spy manual anywhere mentioned tanning salons. Doubtful. But he had no choice. He needed to keep his skin as dark as possible, no easy task in Moscow at the end of

December. He intended to approach Markov as Jalal Sawaya, leader of a radical Lebanese Christian independence group, the Flowers of Lebanon. Jalal wanted to hire Markov's men to blow up the head-quarters of the Syrian intelligence service in Damascus, revenge for Syrian-backed car bombings in Beirut. He had 250,000 euros – almost $400,000 – in his suitcase to prove he was serious.

So went Wells's cover story, anyway. In his saner moments, he knew it was thin. Worse than thin. Gaunt. The Flowers of Lebanon did exist, but they hadn't been heard from in years. The Syrians had dismembered them very efficiently. Jalal Sawaya was a figment of Wells's imagination, though the name was common enough in Lebanon. Further, even if Markov did believe that Jalal was real, he would surely wonder why Jalal had approached him and not a terrorist group closer to home.

But Markov didn't have to be planning to accept Jalal's offer, or even to believe the story. As long as Markov agreed to meet with Jalal, even if it was only to steal the money he carried, Wells would have his chance.

Even before he arrived on Russian soil, Wells got a hint that his beard and olive skin wouldn't be an asset in Moscow. Though he was in first class, and booked under the name Glenn Kramon with his new American passport, the Aeroflot attendants were slow to serve him. He'd wondered if he was imagining their attitude, until an attendant called him to the front galley ninety minutes into the flight. 'Mr Kramon, the captain wishes to speak with you.'

The captain was a tall man with close-cut hair and a wide Slavic face. 'You are Mr Kramon?'

'Yes,' Wells said.

'You are Egyptian?'

'American. Want to see my passport?'

'You are Muslim?'

'I'm a Unitarian,' Wells said. For some reason, Unitarian was the first denomination to pop into his head. He hoped the captain wouldn't ask him any doctrinal questions. Did Unitarians believe in faith or works?

'What is Unitarian?'

'Christian. What is this, Twenty Questions? Don't you have a plane to fly?' Wells knew he should keep his mouth shut, but his temper was rising.

'Your passport, please?' Wells handed it over. The captain flipped through the pages and finally nodded. 'Thank you. Please go back to your seat,' he said, as if Wells had demanded to speak to him, not the other way around. For the rest of the flight, the attendants ignored Wells entirely.

At Sheremetyevo-2 immigration, the cool reception continued. 'Passport?' the agent said in English. He was a trim man with hostile brown eyes and a mustache that curled over his upper lip. Wells handed over Kramon's passport and the entry/exit card that all visitors to Russia were required to fill out.

'Visiting Russia for vacation? Now?'

'I got a good fare.'

'What hotel?'

'The Novotel. Found it on Expedia. I can show you the reservation.' Wells began to sort through his computer bag.

'Forget it.' The guard flipped through his passport, scanned his visa, and typed into his terminal. He tore off half of the entry card and handed the other half back to Wells. 'Entry card. Don't lose.'

'Thanks.'

But the guard had already turned his attention to the woman in line behind him.

A half-hour later, Wells checked into the Novotel, lay down on his bed, fell asleep before he could even get his clothes off. He woke drymouthed and tense, certain he'd heard someone scratching at his door. He flipped off the bed, moved noiselessly to the door, pulled it open. The hallway outside was empty. Wells brushed his teeth, undressed, went back to bed, closed his eyes, and resolved to dream of Exley. But if he did he couldn't remember.

The next morning Wells opened his second suitcase, a big, green, hard-sided Samsonite plastic case, the kind that hadn't been in style for at least thirty years and that inevitably banged its owner's shins and left them black and blue. Wells flipped it open, tossed out the clothes and shoes inside. At the base of the case were four almost invisible indentations, the tops of flathead screws that had been machined into place. With his Swiss Army knife, Wells unscrewed them. Underneath was a compartment eight inches long, four inches wide, four inches deep. It held Wells's Lebanese passport and five hundred bills of 500 euros each – 250,000 euros in all, tamped into two packets, each no larger than a narrow paperback book. Wells silently thanked the European Central Bank for deciding to put the 500-euro bill – sometimes called the 'bin Laden,' because it was so rarely seen – into circulation, though he couldn't imagine what the bureaucrats at the bank had been thinking. Who but gamblers, drug smugglers, and spies needed a bill worth almost $1,000?

Besides the money and the passport, the concealed compartment held a few other necessities that Wells had requested from the agency's Division of Science and Technology. Unfortunately, they didn't include a gun, which would have been too dangerous to try to smuggle in without a diplomatic bag. Wells took the Lebanese passport and twenty of the bills – 10,000 euros in all – and tucked them in his pocket. He left everything else, replaced the panel, and repacked the suitcase.

A few minutes later, Samsonite in hand, he headed for the Mendeleevskaya metro station beside the Novotel. The station, like most of those in the Moscow subway, had been designed to double as an airraid shelter. Its platform was several hundred feet underground, reached by an escalator whose base couldn't be seen from its top. Wells found the long ride down oddly calming.

The Freudians and the Buddhists would love these tunnels. One endless line of Muscovites silently descending into the earth, another rising from it, death and resurrection played out endlessly in miniature.

Wells took the gray line to Borovitskaya and switched to the red. At Park Kultury, he moved to the circle line, riding it six stops before crossing the platform and reversing direction. Basic counter-surveillance. The subway cars were Soviet-era, made of blue corrugated steel with big windows, and they emerged from the tunnels with a pressurized whoosh as if they were powered by air and not electricity. They came every two minutes or so, making the switches very easy. After an hour of riding the trains, with four different transfers, Wells was sure that he hadn't been followed. Not that there was any reason for him to expect surveillance. He was on an American passport, after all, and Americans visited Moscow even in December. Finally, he switched to the gray line and rode south another seven stops to Yuzhnaya.

When he emerged from the train, he was far from the glitter of Moscow's city center. Brownish snow covered the streets, and the apartment buildings were mostly cheap concrete left over from the Soviet era. The wind picked up and cut through his jacket and jeans. He looked at the little city map he'd brought and made his way to the Petersburg, a little one-star hotel almost in the shadow of the MKAD, the ring road that surrounded Moscow.

The hotel's lobby was hardly warmer than the street, and the front desk was empty. Wells rang twice on a little bell before a woman in her mid-thirties wandered out. She had dark skin and a mustache and wore a puffy blue jacket against the cold.

'Yes?' she said.

'You have rooms?' Wells said.

'Of course,' she said.

She didn't ask for his passport, but he handed it over anyway. The Lebanese this time. The room was 1,200 rubles a night, about $50, one-eighth the price of the Novotel. For that, Wells got a soft double bed and a plastic shower that ran a trickle of lukewarm water. No keycards here. The door had a big brass lock that an experienced thief, or even a savvy twelve-year-old, could force in seconds.

Wells stowed the suitcase in the tiny closet and headed out. He would sleep at the Novotel, but he wanted to keep his options open. At an outdoor market, he bought a two-pound tub of cheap, oily peanut butter and a loaf of Russian black bread. Then he found Ultra Spa. He intended to stay as fat and dark as possible.

The next morning, Wells made his way to the building that was home to Markov's company. The offices were in the middle of the Arbat district, the center of old Moscow, a half-mile west of the Kremlin, in a refurbished apartment building two blocks down from the Canadian embassy. Two security cameras watched the front entrance. Four more monitored the edges of the building. A big man stood just outside the entrance doors, which were made of heavy dark glass like a cheap ashtray and blocked any view of the lobby. A gate to the south side protected a parking lot that held a half-dozen Mercedes and BMW sedans and a Hummer H1.

Wells didn't break stride. Besides the Aeroflot incident, he'd drawn some tough looks on the subway. Chechen terrorists had repeatedly attacked Moscow since 2000, and Arabs were not loved here, not unless they came from Saudi Arabia and wanted to discuss how to keep the price of oil high.

Wells had arrived in Moscow with only a vague plan to get to Markov. He'd figured on finding the bars and clubs where junior FSB officers hung out, reach out to private security firms whose investigators might know Markov, grease the skids with some of the money in his briefcase. But now that he was here, the odds against that plan seemed impossibly long. As an Arab, even a Christian Arab, he was immediately distrusted. He'd need months to overcome that suspicion. If Shafer couldn't help, Wells would be reduced to trying to break into Markov's house or assassinate him on the street.

He e-mailed Shafer, explaining. A day later, Shafer replied with a name, phone number, and two sentences. *Nicholas Rosette. He has a temper. Don't lie to him and don't piss him off.* Wells and Rosette arranged to meet at a shopping mall in northern Moscow the next afternoon. 'I'll be the Frenchman in the beret,' Rosette e-mailed.

With a day to burn before the meeting, Wells wandered through central Moscow, the boulevards and narrow streets around the Kremlin. The city was loud and busy and shockingly rich. The GUM mall, which stood across Red Square from Lenin's tomb, was filled with Hermès and Dior and Cartier and dozens of other snotty stores. The fact that $4,000 purses were being sold a hundred yards from the mummified founder of Communist Russia struck Wells as deeply ironic. But the Muscovites in the mall didn't seem to care. They wandered happily, shopping bags heavy in their hands. Wells considered buying Exley some official Russian Olympic gear from the 2014 winter games in Sochi – he was supposed to be a tourist, after all – but changed his mind when he saw the price tag on the hat he was fingering: 2,200 rubles, almost $100. For a baseball cap. Wells checked the math three times in his head, figuring he'd made a mistake. Who was buying these trifles? And why? Russia was supposed to be poor, a broken third-world country. Oil had turned its fortunes in a hurry.

The mall that Rosette had chosen for their meet was outside the downtown core, near the end of the green metro line. The place wasn't in the same league as the GUM, but it was still plenty prosperous, with an IMAX movie theater and an array of stores that would have been familiar at any suburban mall in the United States. Though no Star-bucks. For some reason, Moscow didn't have any. Wells was meeting Rosette at the local equivalent, a place called the Coffee Bean. Wells ordered two black coffees, found a seat against a wall where he could watch the door, and waited.

And waited. Rosette showed up forty-five minutes late. Wells didn't recognize him at first. He was in his early sixties, wearing a finely cut blue suit, his hair a distinguished silver. The beret he'd promised poked from his overcoat pocket. Wells wouldn't have guessed he was French, but he didn't look Russian either. German, maybe, or Swedish. Rosette took his time ordering and finally wandered over to Wells's table. Up close, he wasn't so impressive; he had a fleshy face and a drinker's nose, the skin cut with thin red stripes like a contour map.

'Come,' he said to Wells in English.

They walked through the mall, a conspicuous pair. Rosette was nearly as tall as Wells, and better dressed than any other man in the mall. Wealthy Russian women dressed absurdly well – hence the luxury stores at the GUM – but the men tended to favor tracksuits and jeans.

'So why did you bring me up here?'

'I thought you might want to see Moscow,

Mr Wells,' Rosette said. 'Besides, I had shopping to do.' He laughed a little French laugh, *humph-humph*.

So the joke's on me, Wells didn't say. 'Call me John.'

'Fine. Call me Nicholas. St Nicholas.'

'Nicholas, then. Let me ask you. If you didn't know who I was, how long would you need to figure me out?'

'Pretty soon, maybe. The hair, the tan, not bad, and it looks like you gained a few kilos, too, but it only goes so far. What's your comic book?'

'Comic book?'

'What we French call the cover story.'

Wells explained.

'And you want to meet Ivan Markov. You know this isn't a good idea. Did Shafer tell you about me?'

'No.'

'I'm a DGSE man' – Direction Générale de la Sécurité Extérieure, the French intelligence service – 'for a long time. Too long.'

'Here?'

'Here, there, everywhere. Now here again. Long enough to see the Russians go from strong to weak and back to strong. I liked them better when they were weak. All this' – Rosette looked around the mall – 'brings out the worst in them. A suffering Russian is noble. A rich Russian is a pig. A pig with a Rolex who can't even tell time.'

'If you say so.'

'Any other questions?'

'How do you know Ellis? If you care to tell.'

They'd looped around the mall and were back at the Coffee Bean. Rosette led them to a corner and sat.

'Many years ago Ellis did me a favor,' he said, quietly. The tables around them were empty, but even if they'd been full no one but Wells could have heard. 'In the Congo. Though at the time it was called Zaire.'

'Shafer served in Africa?' Wells couldn't picture Shafer anywhere but the Washington suburbs.

'He told me that one day I would repay him. I thought he was wrong. Now you come here, with your beard and your ridiculous cover. A Lebanese freedom fighter. Truly a comic book. And Shafer says it's time for his favor. Why Markov? You think he did this attack on you and your girlfriend?'

'I want to talk to him.'

'Talk? Is that all?'

Wells shrugged.

'You're right. I don't want to know.' Rosette stood. 'I'll set it up. Be sure to get out fast after your talk. These men here, they aren't nice.'

'I'm used to that.'

'Congratulations.'

'You don't like me much, Nicholas.'

'You're complicating my life.'

'Then why help me?'

'Not everyone in Moscow favors Markov. Some people won't mind if your conversation with him gets heated.'

'So you're using me.'

Rosette sat back down and leaned into Wells and pursed his thick lips. Wells immediately regretted his words.

'*I'm* using *you?*' Though Rosette's voice stayed quiet, his fury was unmistakable. '*You* ask for *my* help and I give it to you and then you pretend I've wronged you. Only an American could be so stupid. You're all the same with your false naïveté.'

Rosette exhaled heavily. Wells smelled the alcohol on his breath, heavy red wine under the coffee.

'Markov has enemies, but he has friends, too. Otherwise he wouldn't have lasted. If it comes out that I helped you, when it comes out, I'll be stuck in some foolish Russian squabbles that are best avoided. Not how I meant to end my career.'

'I'm sorry—'

'I haven't finished yet, Mr Wells. John. I'm sure you're very good at what you do. Dressing like an Arab and playing bang-bang. Americans always want to come in with their guns and fix the world and leave. But this game you've stuck yourself in, it's much trickier. It doesn't end when you say. It goes on and on, and when you've forgotten you ever played at all, it comes back to destroy you.'

I've done all right so far, Wells thought. *And so has the United States. And last I checked, France had a second-rate economy and a third-rate army and got attention mainly for the sex lives of its president.* But he kept his mouth shut. He'd said too much already.

Rosette stood for a second time. 'Your boss, Ellis,' he said. 'He saved me from Mobutu. Maybe you've heard of Mobutu? Maybe you skimmed a history book? Maybe you saw a documentary on him on CNN? Between the commercials?'

'You sure can lay it on thick.'

'Mobutu Sese Soko. I made a mistake with a girlfriend of his. He had so many. It was hard to keep track. And even after his men arrested me, I didn't take it seriously. I thought being white would be my protection. But in those days Mobutu thought he was God. Maybe in Zaire he *was* God. You understand? He spoke and the rivers filled with blood. That sounds like God to me. Even being white was no guarantee. But that little Shafer saved me. To this day, I don't know how. And I promised him I would repay him if I could. And now he asks me for this favor for you. And because Markov has enemies as well as friends, it's possible. So I'll vouch for you. But if Markov sees through this comic book of yours and puts a bullet in you, a whole magazine, I won't shed any tears for you. I'll pour a glass of burgundy and tell Shafer we're even. Understand?'

'Clear as crystal,' Wells said.

Despite the lecture, Rosette kept his word. The following morning he e-mailed Wells to meet him at 1:30 p.m. at the ice rink at the Hermitage Gardens on Karetny Ryad Street, a mile north of the Kremlin. Wells gave himself plenty of time for countersurveillance, three subway lines, two cabs, and a long walk. He was certain he hadn't been traced. As certain as he could be, anyway, considering he was in the home city of what was probably the best intelligence service in the world.

The Hermitage Gardens rink was easy enough to find, filled with kids and teenagers who skated endless loops to the cheery lyrics of Rihanna and the Spice Girls. Again, Rosette was a few minutes late. A countersurveillance technique, or just rudeness? Wells wasn't sure.

'We skating?' he said when the Frenchman finally arrived.

'Alas, no.' Today Rosette was dressed down, a heavy wool coat and a thick fur hat. Now he did look Russian, at least to Wells.

They found a cab and rode in the heavy traffic for half an hour before pulling off the third ring road near a huge stadium. They made a left and a right and stopped outside a subway entrance.

They stepped out and Rosette guided Wells toward the entrance to a huge flea market. All around them women carried plastic bags filled with junk. Their faces were heavy, their skin gray under cheap fur hats, their steps exhausted. The booths of the flea market were endless, but the products weren't. Every shopkeeper had the same dull gray pots and pans of paper-thin steel, the same dull sneakers, their color fading even before they took a single step, the same dull jeans, dyed a heavy overripe blue. Lenin's tomb belonged here, not opposite the GUM.

'Don't let the Ritz-Carlton and the GUM and the Bentley dealership across from the Ministry of Defense fool you,' Rosette said. 'This is how most of them live. Especially outside Moscow. A million of them steal all the oil money. A few million more get rich servicing the thieves. Everyone else drinks and waits to die.'

'Sounds like fun,' Wells said.

'Not so different than America.'

'You ever been to America?'

'All right,' Rosette said. 'We'll save that for another time. Tonight you meet Roman Yansky. You know him?'

'The name, sure.' Yansky was Markov's second-in-command, a former commander in the Spetsnaz.

'I called him this morning, gave him the comic book, the whole sad story. I said I knew your family from Beirut and that your father had been a source for me. I said that I'd recommended Helosrus to you. He wasn't very interested until I told him that you were most assuredly stupid enough to have brought the money with you. He says he will meet you tonight at the Ten Places club but you must bring fifty thousand euros. Eleven p.m. To prove your sincerity, he said. I think he kept a straight face when he said it, but since we were on the phone I can't be sure.'

'The Ten Places club?'

'A private place on Tverskoy. Not far from the ice skating rink where we met. Very exclusive.'

'All right.'

'You understand he may just take whatever you bring and shoot you. Or he may take you to your hotel to pick up the rest of the money and then shoot you.'

Or you may have blown my cover, and he'll shoot me whether he gets the money or not, Wells didn't say. Rosette was proving useful, but Wells was beginning to dislike him as much as Vinny Duto.

They walked out of the flea market. Rosette led Wells to his car, an Opel parked near the metro stop. For the next hour Rosette drove around the quiet streets of Khamovniki, the Moscow neighborhood around the flea market, practicing their cover stories: where and when they'd met, how they'd stayed in touch, the payoff that Rosette expected for setting up the meeting.

'Enough,' Rosette finally said, stopping beside a subway station and waving Wells out. 'This foolishness won't take more than a few minutes. He wants your money, nothing else.'

After he was done, Wells headed over to the Petersburg hotel for a nap. He felt refreshed and sharp when he woke. He didn't know why, but he was sure that he would succeed tonight, convince Roman to get him to Markov. And then? Then he would do what came naturally.

But a few minutes later, his certainty faded. He understood he'd been lying to himself, pushing himself forward despite the obvious flaws in his plan. *There's no such thing as a false sense of well-being.* Wells couldn't remember where exactly he'd read those words, but they weren't true. It wasn't too late, he knew. He could still call off the meeting, let Rosette curse him out, fly back to Exley tomorrow.

And leave Markov untouched? Miss this chance? *No.*

Wells opened up the false compartment in his Samsonite and counted out fifty of the 500-euro bills, 25,000 euros in all, and stuffed them in his jacket. Then he taped fifty more bills to the bottom of the night table next to the bed. He left the rest of the bills in the suitcase and sorted through the other equipment he'd brought: three ballpoint pens. One was actually a tiny stun gun, capable of delivering a single massive shock. The other two hid spring-loaded syringes filled with ketamine and liquid Valium, a mix that worked as an exceptionally fast-acting anesthetic.

Wells slipped two of the pens – the stun gun and one of the syringes – into his jacket pocket, then grabbed his suitcase and walked down to the lobby and rang the front bell and shivered in the silent lobby until the mustached woman emerged.

'Can you hold this for me?' Wells lifted the suitcase. 'Just tonight.'

Ten places didn't have a velvet rope or a sign to mark its entrance. Just two massive men standing in front of a gleaming steel door, and a few unlucky

197

would-be clubgoers standing beside them, stamping their feet against the cold. The bouncers frowned when Wells approached, but when Wells gave them Roman's name they opened the door and waved him in. Wells found himself in a steel passageway twenty feet long. At the far end, two large men blocked another metal door. To the right, a bottle blonde sat behind a pane of inch-thick glass in a cashier's office.

'Cover is one hundred euros,' she said.

Wells handed over a 500-euro bill. 'Keep the change,' he said, earning only a small smile. A 400-euro tip didn't go far at this club.

In front of the second door, one of the bouncers patted him down while the other ran a handheld metal detector over him. When they were done, the cashier pressed a red button and the steel door clicked open. The bouncers stood aside to let Wells pass.

Inside, the club was small, but even gaudier than Wells had expected. A half-dozen women in G-strings and pasties shimmied on a platform hoisted over the center of the room. Three more stood behind the bar, serving drinks. The dance floor was in the center of the club, only about twenty feet square, but packed. At 100 euros a head, somebody was getting rich. Rosette sat with Roman, a big man in a black leather jacket, at a table near the back. As Wells approached, Rosette stood and kissed him on both cheeks.

'Jalal,' he said in Arabic. 'So good to see you.'

'Nicholas,' Wells replied in Arabic. 'My old friend.'

'They don't have clubs like this in Beirut.'

'No, they don't. But maybe one day. When the Syrians are gone and peace comes back.'

'We hope.' Rosette nodded to the man in the leather jacket. 'Jalal, this is Roman.'

Wells extended a hand and Roman enveloped it in his own giant paw. The Russian was Wells's height, six-two, and had a boxer's squashed nose and small ugly eyes. They sat and Rosette lined up three shot glasses and filled them from a Stoli bottle in an ice bucket beside the table.

'A toast.' Rosette spoke in Russian. When he was done, Roman laughed and the three men emptied their glasses. Wells hadn't drunk vodka straight since college. The liquid was cold and warm at the same time and left a pleasant burn in his throat.

'What did you say?' Wells said to Rosette.

'Old farmer's toast. I want to buy a house, but I haven't the money. I have the money to buy a goat, but I don't want one. So here's to having wants and needs come together.'

'The wisdom of the Russian serf.'

'Very deep. And now I must go. I hope the marriage is happy, both families approve.'

Rosette disappeared onto the dance floor. Wells sat in silence for a minute, watching the dancers. The worldwide cult of fast money spent stupidly. The worldwide cult of trying too hard.

Moscow, Rio, Los Angeles, Tokyo, New York, London, Shanghai – the story was the same everywhere. The same overloud music, the same overpromoted brand names, the same fake tits, about as erotic as helium balloons. Everywhere an orgy of empty consumption and bad sex. Las Vegas was the cult's world head-quarters, Donald Trump its patron saint. Wells had spent ten years in the barren mountains of Afghanistan and Pakistan. He never wanted to live there again. But if he had to choose between an eternity there or in the supposed luxury of this club, he'd go back without a second thought.

Roman the Russian poured another shot for them.

'Drink,' he said in Arabic, rough but under-standable.

'You know Arabic?'

'I was in Libya three years. A military adviser.' He raised his glass. 'To our friend, the crazy Frenchman.' They drank.

'Do you know why this is called Ten Places? You're supposed to be a billionaire to be in here. Ten places of wealth. A one and nine zeros. Of course, a billionaire in rubles isn't the same as a billionaire in dollars, but even so.'

'I'm afraid I don't qualify.'

'Well, then, let's go.' Roman stood and Wells followed. They walked through the club, the dancers parting for Roman, careful not to touch him. But instead of taking the stairs to the front

200

entrance, Roman led Wells to an exit behind the bar. They walked up a dimly lit staircase to an unmarked door.

'Go on,' Roman said. Wells pushed it open and emerged into an alley by the side of the club. Outside, a black Maybach waited, the oversized Mercedes limousine, with two men in front.

'Put your hands on the trunk and spread your legs,' Roman said. Wells did. Roman frisked him, thoroughly. 'Empty your pockets.'

In his pockets Wells had only his special pens, a cell phone, his Lebanese passport, his packet of euros, and his wallet. All in Jalal's name, of course.

Roman pocketed the phone and the packet of euros, gave back everything else, opened the Maybach's door and steered Wells into the back. The sedan rolled off. Roman unzipped his jacket and slouched in the seat beside Wells. His hand hung loosely over a pistol tucked into a holster on his right hip.

'Jalal, tell me what you want.'

Wells did.

'And Rosette recommended us.'

'He said he'd worked with you.'

Roman frowned. 'I want to believe you, Jalal. And the Frenchman and I have known each other a long time. But this plan of yours. You ask Russians for help against the Syrians, our allies.'

'Who else should I ask? The Americans? The Jews? Since 1975 the Syrians do what they want to us. We bring a million people to protest in

Beirut, one Lebanese in five, it doesn't matter. Have you ever been to Lebanon? Once it was beautiful. I'll go to hell itself and ask the devil if he'll help me.'

Roman pulled a sheet of paper from his jacket and unfolded it. He flicked on the Maybach's backseat light, looked between the paper and Wells as though he were watching a tennis match. Finally he handed the sheet to Wells.

And Wells found he was looking at—

An old picture of himself. A printout of a photograph available on the Internet. His college yearbook headshot from Dartmouth.

Wells allowed a puzzled look to settle on his face. Best to stay relaxed. Even if Roman had already decided to kill him, he wouldn't do so in a moving car. Too risky. 'What is this?'

'You.'

'Not me.'

'No? Your cousin, maybe? Thinner, a little cleaner? You don't see the resemblance?'

'Not really.' Wells handed back the paper. 'Who is it?'

'John Wells. The American spy.'

'I am who I say,' Wells said. 'See.' He reached into his pocket for his Lebanese passport and wallet.

'Don't bother me with that.'

'I don't see what this has to do with me. If you don't want to make a deal, that's fine. I'll find someone else.'

'That's all you have to say?'

'What else can I say? I am who I am. You've talked to Rosette.'

Roman tucked away the photograph, plucked out a cell phone and made a call. He spoke quietly in Russian for a few seconds, listened, spoke again. Wells couldn't understand the words, but he knew now that Ivan Markov was too cautious ever to see him. At best, these men would take his money and put him on an Aeroflot flight to Damascus, let the Syrians have him.

At worst . . . at worst he'd been in tighter spots. Though this was close. Three on one, and the three all had guns. Wells only had the two pens . . . and the final surprise in his wallet. He put his passport away and tucked his wallet loosely against his hip.

Roman hung up, reached into his pocket for the packet of euros he'd taken from Wells. He thumbed through it, shook his head.

'I said fifty thousand. This is twenty-five.'

'I didn't think I should bring it all at once.' A real spy would have handed over all the money at once, kept the transaction smooth. Wells had hoped his amateur act would help convince Roman he was who he claimed to be. But at this point, he doubted anything he did would matter.

'You don't understand your position very well. Where's the rest?'

'My hotel.'

'Where?'

Wells told him. Roman barked an order in Russian and the Maybach swung south.

'This is it?' Roman said when they reached the hotel. 'Not very impressive.'

'I'm saving my money for you.'

'What room? And where's the money?'

Wells told him. Roman said something to the bodyguard in the front seat. He nodded and got out. Wells reached for the door.

Roman clapped a hand on him. 'You and I wait here.'

Wells didn't argue. He had found out what he wanted to know. Roman was big, not fast. The Maybach was an exceptionally wide car and Roman had needed almost a full second to reach across to get him. Plenty of time for Wells. They sat silently in the back of the car until Roman's phone rang for a second time. He had a quick conversation in Russian, hung up, and turned to Wells.

'You seem relaxed, Jalal. Why aren't you nervous?'

'Why would I be nervous?'

'I accuse you of being an American spy. You deny it calmly. I ask you where you've hidden your money. You tell me.'

'It's not mine.'

'Whose then?'

'It belongs to the Flowers.'

'You come to a country, you don't speak the

language, you think you can hire men you've never met for this mission? You're very stupid. Or you have something else in mind. Either way you're too dangerous for me to deal with.'

Wells was silent, weighing his options. If he moved too soon, he'd destroy any chance at Markov. If he waited too long, he'd die. Coming here had been a mistake. He saw now. He'd always trusted his instincts, but this time they'd betrayed him. Or maybe he'd ignored them in his fury. Either way he'd made the most basic mistake. He'd underestimated his enemies, overreached, trapped himself.

He saw only one way out.

Three minutes later, the bodyguard returned, holding the other packet of euros. Roman looked away, up at the guard. As he did, Wells drew a credit card from his wallet with his right hand. With his left hand, he reached for one of his special ballpoint pens, the stun gun.

The bodyguard handed the bills to Roman, who flipped through them.

'This is it?' he said to Wells.

'The other twenty-five thousand, yes.'

'Rosette said you had more. He said you had two hundred fifty thousand.'

'Not in the room.' Wells felt his pulse rise.

'Where, then?'

'You must think I'm a fool.'

'Call it a fee. For wasting our time.'

Wells pretended to consider the offer. 'I'll get it.' Wells reached for the door, and again Roman reached for him.

'You're not—'

But Roman never got to finish his sentence, or say anything else at all.

As he grabbed Wells's right arm, Wells twisted toward him. With his left hand, Wells jabbed the stun gun through Roman's black wool Armani pants and into the meat of his thigh. The electricity flowed and Roman yelped, a clotted grunt of pain, and twisted back and reached down for the stun gun to tear it away from his leg. The simplest of errors. Roman should have gone for his pistol. Instead he'd become fixated on the fire in his leg. He would pay for that mistake with his life. As he reached down, Wells slashed upward with his right hand, the hand that held the card.

Unfortunately for Roman, the card wasn't a typical MasterCard. Its top edge was actually a steel blade sharp enough to cut glass. Wells sliced the blade into Roman's neck, under his chin, through skin and fat and muscle. At the same time, he dropped the stun gun and wrapped his left hand around the back of Roman's neck and jerked Roman's head forward, pulling his neck deeper onto the blade, cutting the carotid in half. Roman screamed, the pure high terror of a desperate animal. His hands flew up as he tried to stanch the blood pouring out of his neck.

But he had no chance. His eyes rolled up as bright red arterial blood pumped out and he began to die a messy death. He slumped forward onto Wells, his body shielding Wells from the bodyguards.

Wells slid his left hand down Roman's back and reached for Roman's pistol. He grabbed it and dropped the safety and aimed across the back of the Maybach and fired three times, the shots echoing in the car. With Roman's body blocking him, Wells couldn't see where he was shooting, but with only six feet between him and the guard, he didn't care. He heard the guard scream and thump against the side of the car. He shifted the pistol toward the driver's seat and pulled the trigger three more times, catching the Maybach's driver as he turned toward Wells. The driver twitched in his seat and groaned and fell silent.

And then Roman's groans were the only sound in the car. He seemed to be trying to speak, but Wells wasn't sure. The guttural sounds he made were the static from a radio at the edge of the dial, half-heard words fading into haze. Was he apologizing, begging for mercy, promising revenge? No matter. He had nothing left to do but die. He would die and Wells would live.

Wells reached into Roman's jacket pocket and grabbed his cell phone and Roman's own cell phone, both slick with blood. Wells pushed Roman onto his back on the floor of the Maybach and stepped out of the car. Lights had flickered on in the apartment buildings beside the hotel, but no one was on the street and there were no sirens yet. Wells tossed his jacket, soaked with blood, into the back beside Roman. Then he dumped the driver's body on the ground. He slipped in behind the wheel and left the driver and the bodyguard behind. He tried not to listen, but he couldn't escape hearing every gurgling breath as Roman wound down to silence.

Fortunately for Wells, the local Moscow police, unlike the FSB, were understaffed and underpaid, slow to respond to crimes outside the golden district around the Kremlin. Wells headed south and east and didn't hear the first distant sirens until he'd been driving for seven minutes, easily enough to get him outside the danger zone. He drove for a few minutes more and then ditched the Maybach in an alley off a narrow street that was just a couple yards from a metro station. The car would be found by morning, but he had no choice.

Wells cut the lights and sat in the silent Maybach. He wanted to explode, to put a fist through the window, but he controlled his anger. He'd played the fool too many times already tonight. He'd blown his chance at Markov and at Kowalski, too. He'd killed three men and missed the real target. He'd made it impossible for the agency ever to investigate the attack on him and Exley. How could they approach the Russians about Markov? At best, both sides would pretend that the twin attacks in

Washington and Moscow had never happened. At worst, depending on how much juice Markov had with the Kremlin, Russia might feel the need to retaliate for what Wells had done, and the FSB and CIA would get drawn into tit-for-tat killings. Not what the world needed.

Well, at least Nicholas Rosette would be able to tell Shafer that he'd repaid his debt for whatever had happened in the Congo all those years before.

Wells washed his hands and face of Roman's blood as best he could with the dregs of a water bottle the Maybach's driver had carried. The driver's overcoat, long blue wool, was on the seat beside him. Wells grabbed it and stepped out and pulled on the coat, hiding his bloody shirt and pants. As long as no one looked too closely, he'd be all right. He walked toward the subway, listening to the distant sirens. He dumped Jalal Sawaya's passport into a sewer grate. Jalal was as dead as Roman and his bodyguards. Wells would book a ticket on Delta in the morning, the first flight out, and depend on an American passport and the name Glenn Kramon to get home.

CHAPTER 12

NORTH ATLANTIC OCEAN

The field was striped orange and black like a cartoon tiger's stripes.

All the players wore army uniforms. The man dribbling the ball was a general. Nasiji could tell from the stars on his shoulders. Defenders came at him, but he flung them aside and no referee seemed to care. The general had no face, but even so Nasiji recognized him. Khalid, his father. Nasiji raised a fist to cheer—

And suddenly the field turned into a wide Baghdad street, rising toward an overpass. Not that way, Nasiji tried to say. Go around. But he couldn't get the words out of his throat and then the road pitched sideways and Nasiji knew what was about to happen and—

A hand squeezed his shoulder. He flung up a fist, nearly striking Yusuf. *Yusuf?* Baghdad disappeared as Nasiji got his bearings. Nothing had changed. He was lying on a narrow bed in a windowless cabin, its walls a drab gray. At his feet, the desk where his books were strapped down so they wouldn't go airborne when the waves got fierce. And in the corner, the crates. Of course the crates. The two big ones that held the bombs, the long narrow one that carried the SPG rifles, and finally the small one that held the rounds.

Nasiji ran a hand over his fevered face. The dream had left him sick. The dream or the waves. He'd rather be anywhere, even fighting the Shia in Ghazaliya, than this ship.

'Sayyid,' Yusuf said.

'I'm fine,' Nasiji said. 'Tired of this useless ocean, is all. Ready to land so we can work.'

Yusuf nodded, though he didn't seem convinced. Nasiji sat up and put a hand against the wall to steady himself. The swells were worse this morning. The worst part was that he could have avoided this misery. Bernard had warned him back in Hamburg, but he hadn't listened. No matter. Soon enough they'd be back on land.

'Do you need the bucket?' Yusuf said.

A soft rap on the cabin's door. Haidar, the little Algerian who brought their meals, stood outside. 'Sirs, the captain asks you to come up at eleven hundred. Would you like breakfast?'

The boat rolled lightly to the left, then harder to the right. Nasiji's guts rose into his throat. He squeezed his eyes shut and groaned.

'Not today, I think,' Yusuf said.

For nine days, the *Juno* had sailed west at a steady sixteen knots across the Atlantic. For most of the trip, the sky had been a leaden gray, bringing squalls of rain, snow, and a harsh icy sleet. Nasiji and Yusuf rarely left their cabin. Haidar brought them meals, thick meat stews and mashed potatoes, strange food that sat in Nasiji's stomach and cramped his bowels.

To pass the time, he studied the physics textbooks he'd brought on board, readying himself for the bomb-making problems he would soon have to solve. When he'd read all he could, he played chess with Yusuf on the little magnetic board that had belonged to Grigory Farzadov until his detour to the bottom of the Black Sea. Nasiji thought of himself as a solid player. But to his irritation, he lost to Yusuf as often as he won. The Syrian knew dozens of openings, and Nasiji always seemed to be playing from behind.

Now, as Haidar closed the door to their cabin, Yusuf picked up the board. 'A game? Or are you too sick?'

'Sure,' Nasiji said.

Yusuf set up the pieces and sat beside Nasiji. 'Promise something, Sayyid.'

'What's that?'

'If I win, you'll tell me how we're going to make them work.' Yusuf nodded at the crates, which were attached to the floor of the cabin with thick steel chains.

'That again.' For days, Yusuf had asked Nasiji to explain the plan. Nasiji had refused, for no particularly good reason. He supposed that part of him enjoyed twitting Yusuf. 'All right. But I play white. And if I win, or even if we draw, you'll stop asking about it until we get to the United States.'

'Fine,' Yusuf said. When the game began, Yusuf pummeled him with an opening Nasiji had never seen before. After only an hour, Nasiji had no choice but to concede. Yusuf put the board away with a satisfied smirk.

'Don't we need to go upstairs, talk to the captain?' In fact it was only 10:15.

'Sayyid, you promised.'

'Where do you want me to start?'

'How do we blow them up, Sayyid? We don't have the codes.'

'Strange,' Nasiji said. 'Everyone's obsessed with the codes. Not just you. The Russians would have told the whole world what we'd done if they thought we had them. Every police, every customs agent, every soldier from Moscow to Washington would be looking for us. Instead they're keeping quiet. It's our biggest advantage.'

'So do we have the codes?'

'We don't have the codes. We have something more important.'

'What could be more important than the codes?'

'*The bombs*. What's the hardest part of building a nuclear weapon, Yusuf?'

Yusuf paused, seeming to wonder if Nasiji was asking a trick question. Finally he said, 'Getting the stuff, the nuclear material.'

'Correct. The design is easy. The uranium is the

hard part. But these bombs have all the uranium we need.'

'So we put our own explosives around the bombs and set them off?'

'Unfortunately, it's not that easy.' Now that Yusuf had made him open up, Nasiji was enjoying the chance to explain what he'd worked out for himself and kept secret for so long. 'You understand the basics of how these bombs work?'

'Not really, no.'

'Inside, they have uranium and plutonium. Those are atoms, heavy ones, and unstable. If they break up, they release little particles called neutrons. Then those neutrons hit other atoms and split them up, too. That releases more neutrons. It's a chain reaction. And all along, the splitting up of the atoms is releasing energy, too. That makes the explosion.'

Yusuf looked at the crates. 'But they don't go off on their own?'

'No. To start the chain reaction, you need to smash the bomb together.'

'Why?'

'It's complicated, but when you push the bomb together you increase the chances that the neutrons will crash into atoms and split them apart. Everything happens very quickly. After just a few cycles of splitting, so many neutrons are loose that the reaction is uncontrollable. It doesn't stop until the power of the explosion tears apart the uranium at the core and the bomb destroys itself.'

'And this takes a few seconds?'

'No, much faster. More quickly than you can imagine, a fraction of a second. But in that time we release tremendous energy and radiation. The equivalent of thousands of tons of explosive, millions of kilograms, much bigger than any conventional bomb.'

'*Millions* of kilograms?'

'Just so. Imagine one truck filled with regular bombs. One of these bombs is like a thousand of those. And that would be a small one.'

Yusuf's head swiveled between Nasiji and the crates in the corner. 'And we have the material. So we can make our own bomb.'

'Correct. There should be more than enough uranium in these two bombs to make one of our own.'

'But I thought you said these are hard to make.'

'Some bombs are easier than others. These bombs, it's complicated and I'll explain more to you when it's time to disassemble them, they actually each have two bombs inside. Conventional explosive, plastic, sets off the first bomb. Then the first bomb sets off the second. It's very elegant, this design, and efficient. All the bombs today use it. But the explosive charges on the first bomb have to be placed perfectly and blown up in precise order. Or else the nuclear explosion won't happen. The bomb will *fizzle*.' Nasiji said the last word in English.

'*Fizzle?*'

'The pieces don't come together quickly enough. And then it splits apart before the chain reaction can really take off. It still blows up, but with much less power. Our bomb will be a different design, what's called a gun type. Instead of a single ball of uranium surrounded by explosives, we split uranium into two pieces—'

'In half?'

'Not exactly. The two sides have different shapes. One is a hollow cylinder, like a piston in a car engine. The other is the right size to fill the cylinder exactly.'

Yusuf smirked. 'Male and female.'

'Sure. We put the two sides about two meters apart. We fire one side at the other with the Spear. They smash together. The chain reaction takes over. And – *boom*.'

'No *fizzle*.'

'No *fizzle*. The one the United States used to blow up Hiroshima, the Little Boy, was this kind. The Americans were so confident in the design, they never tested it. They just dropped it. And it worked.'

Yusuf was silent. He rubbed his fingers on his temples like a student grappling with algebra for the first time. 'Hmm . . .' he finally said. 'So we'll take all the uranium in these two warheads, the four bombs inside, and put it together into one of our own.'

'Yes, my friend. Just so. Our bomb won't be as big as either of these bombs, but it will still be big enough.'

'How big?'

'*Inshallah*, as big as the one in Hiroshima. Fifteen

kilotons or so. That bomb killed one hundred thousand people, vaporized a square kilometer.'

'But . . . I still don't get one part. We're going to take these bombs apart, saw them open, to get to the uranium inside. What if they have, you know, traps?'

'They might. We won't know until we get them open. Nobody's ever done this before. But remember, these bombs have been designed so they don't go off even if they're damaged in a fire or a plane crash. They're very stable. And even if there are traps, I think I have a way to deal with them.'

'What's that?'

'You'll have to win another chess game.'

Yusuf reached for the board, but Nasiji waved him off. 'Not now. Let's get to the wheelhouse.'

Nasiji didn't know much about ships, but even he could see that the *Juno* was a well-run vessel. It was twenty years old, but it looked newer. Its crew washed down its corridors and communal areas every morning. Even so, ever since the coast of Britain had disappeared behind them the previous week, Nasiji hadn't felt comfortable. He could never quite forget the water that surrounded them.

'Can you believe anyone would do this for pleasure?' he said to Yusuf as they climbed the stairs that led to the wheelhouse. 'Sail, I mean?'

'Why not? All those big yachts floating around. Someone must like it.'

'Not me.'

'I figured that out by now.' Nasiji could hear the smirk in Yusuf's voice.

The wheelhouse was empty when they arrived, except for the captain, Haxhi. He was Albanian, and of course Muslim, a squat man with wide legs and a thick chest. A low center of gravity came in handy on these waves, Nasiji thought.

'Gentlemen, how are you? A bit green.'

'Fine.' Nasiji found himself irritated that his seasickness had become a shipwide joke. 'Where is everyone?'

'Sometimes I like to be up here alone.' Haxhi showed them a map of the North Atlantic mounted on the back wall of the wheelhouse. 'I have good news and bad news. First, the good news. We're on schedule for tonight. Our current location—'

Haxhi pointed to a spot east-southeast of Newfoundland, an L-shaped Canadian province that jutted into the Atlantic. They planned to bring the crates ashore in a cove on the southeastern coast of Newfoundland, near Trepassey, a village of nine hundred, really not much more than a few dozen houses clustered against the ocean and the big gray sky.

'We're about four hundred kilometers from the landing point. We should be off the coast in twelve hours. Just before midnight. After that, another ninety minutes.'

Nasiji reached for the satellite phone in his jacket. He didn't like using these. They were easy

218

for the Americans to track. But he'd bought the phone only a few weeks before and only used it twice. And as far as he knew, no one was looking for him. Anyway, this was a call he had to make. He punched in an American number with a 716 area code – upstate New York – and a few seconds later the connection clicked in.

'Hello?'

'Doctor?'

'*Nam.*'

'We'll be in tonight. Around one a.m. You have the location.'

'Of course.'

'Good. We'll see you tonight.'

'*Inshallah.*'

'*Inshallah.*'

Nasiji ended the call and tucked away the phone. 'Thank you, Captain.'

'You forgot the bad news.'

'What could that possibly be?'

Haxhi motioned to the glass windows at the front of the wheel-house. In the distance, heavy clouds, more black than gray, filled the horizon. 'Those.'

Nasiji was miserable for the next few hours. He stayed in the wheel-house for a while with the captain and Yusuf. Finally he staggered back to his cabin, where he filled the bucket beside his bed with vomit – twice. Haidar, the steward, came by with Dramamine, which Nasiji accepted, and Xanax, which he turned down. Better to suffer than to put himself in a haze. But when he closed his eyes and tried to sleep, his dreams were black poems, unfinished stanzas that always ended at the same place, the overpass where his family had died.

Just before nightfall, Yusuf rejoined him in the cabin. The *Juno's* crew was entirely Muslim, and the call to prayer came over the ship's intercom five times daily, as Muslim law required. At sunset, the call for the fifth and final daily prayer – the *mugrib* – came, and Yusuf knelt on the floor of the cabin. Nasiji watched.

'You didn't want to pray?' Yusuf said when he was done.

'I didn't want to throw up.'

'Why do you think Allah's chosen us for this mission, Sayyid?' Yusuf had never raised the question before. It seemed to be as close as he could come to questioning his faith, or the morality of what they were doing, Nasiji thought.

'Because he knew we were strong enough to carry it off.' The easy answer.

'Does he speak to you?'

'Do I look like a prophet, Yusuf?'

'But you're certain.'

'Yes. We're his instrument.' If divine sanction would soothe Yusuf, then Nasiji would give it to him. Let Yusuf think what he wished, as long as his hands stayed steady. Nasiji didn't need God's voice in his ear to know why he'd undertaken this quest.

220

'Do you imagine what it will be like when we set it off?'

'Of course.'

'Does it scare you? Killing all those people.'

'No. Not for this life or the next.' This was true. 'Never forget it was the Americans who set off the first bomb. You know the *Enola Gay*?'

'What is that?'

'The plane the Americans used to drop that first bomb on Hiroshima. The pilot who flew it was called Paul. He lived a long time, until he was more than ninety. One day I saw an interview he gave. They asked him if he felt sad about what he'd done.'

'And was he?'

'Not at all.' Nasiji tried to remember exactly what Paul Tibbets had said. 'He said, "We've never fought a war anywhere in the world where they didn't kill innocent people. That's their tough luck for being there."'

After nightfall the waves lessened and Nasiji slept, waking to a light tapping on their cabin door. 'The captain says it's time,' Haidar said. Nasiji's watch read 23:30.

When they reached the wheelhouse, Nasiji saw that the rain had stopped. But thudding clouds covered the sky and the black waves beneath them were topped with white foam. 'Ready for the little boat?' Haxhi said.

'How long will it take?'

'Ninety minutes, maybe. It's twenty kilometers' – twelve miles.

'We can't get closer?'

'There's not much chance the Canadians will notice us here. Closer in . . .'

'Fine.'

'It won't be the most pleasant hour of your life, but you'll be fine. Believe it or not, this is average weather for the North Atlantic in January.'

'Who's bringing us in?'

'Me and Ebban' – the first mate – 'I told you you'd be safe and you will. At least on the water. Land is another story.'

'That part I'll handle.'

'Let's go, then.'

The lifeboat was lashed with cables to the freighter's port side, a high-sided steel boat, painted black, with a small outboard engine. Haxhi and his men had already pulled off the heavy green plastic tarp that covered it and laid the warhead crates inside. They were wrapped in plastic and strapped to the sides of the boat with thick ropes. As Nasiji watched, they wrapped the long SPG crate in plastic and wedged it snugly under the lifeboat's benches. The fourth and smallest crate, the one that held the rounds, they also wrapped in plastic and tucked under the front bench.

Nasiji stepped forward gingerly toward the lifeboat, eyeing the black waves below. He could hardly believe that this little boat, six meters long, would get them to shore. Haxhi handed him a life jacket, orange and battered. He snapped it over his windbreaker. A blast of harsh Atlantic wind cut through his gloves and sweater and settled mercilessly into his lungs.

'Step back and keep clear,' Haxhi said.

Nasiji stepped back and Haxhi yelled 'Now!' to Ebban, the first mate, another Albanian, who stood beside a spool of cable attached to the side of the *Juno*'s superstructure. Ebban turned the handle on the spool. The cable, which was wound through braces attached to the side of the lifeboat, played out. Inch by inch, the lifeboat slid toward the edge of the *Juno* as Haxhi guided it toward a gap in the steel railing.

Bang! The lifeboat cleared the side of the deck and slipped down, clanging against the side of the *Juno*. Holding the railing with his right hand, Haxhi reached back with his left to Nasiji. 'All right, two big steps and in.'

'Jump?'

'You can't miss.'

Nasiji took Haxhi's hand, stepped through the gap, and fell—

Into the boat. He regained his feet and pulled himself forward to the front bench. Yusuf followed. Then Ebban and finally Haxhi.

'Go,' Haxhi shouted back to Haidar, who had taken over the spool from Ebban. The boat lurched downward, foot by foot, into the water below. It landed with a huge splash and rocked sideways, clanging hard against the *Juno*. Ebban loosened the cables and freed it. In the back, Haxhi started the outboard. The engine grunted twice and then kicked into action. Haxhi pushed the motor down and steered the boat away.

The black outline of the freighter quickly disappeared behind them. The slap of the waves and the hum of the outboard were the only sounds. After about twenty minutes Nasiji saw the first sign of land – a light, faintly visible through the clouds, tracking from right to left before him, disappearing, then returning. On each pass, the light was slightly stronger. A lighthouse. Proof they hadn't left solid ground entirely behind.

Nasiji was feeling almost comfortable. Then the wind picked up and the clouds thickened and the light before them disappeared. The waves rose and slapped against the side of the boat. One broke over and caught Nasiji with a flume of water so cold that for a few seconds he could hardly breathe. Snow began to blow sideways across the boat, leaving them nearly blind. Nasiji huddled low in the center of the boat, one hand on each of the crates.

'Where did this come from?'

'It happens. It'll pass.' But Haxhi's voice had a new tension. Haxhi muttered something to Ebban. The first mate moved to the front of the boat and began to chatter at Haxhi about the direction of the waves and the wind. Haxhi tacked aggressively, running the boat against the side of the waves instead of coming at them directly. With no light, he checked the GPS frequently now.

The wind picked up more, then gusted suddenly—

And a big wave, the biggest Nasiji had seen yet, swept in from the port side—

And the boat rocked hard and Nasiji thought they might capsize—

And the crate beside Nasiji's left foot began to wobble—

And as the boat swung up and bounced down again, somehow the crate came loose from its ropes—

And Nasiji tried to steady it but he couldn't keep hold of it and another wave crashed into the boat and knocked him down and he had to forget the crate and wrap his arms around the cold metal seat as tightly as he could to keep from being thrown out—

And the crate tumbled, loose now, the wood crashing against the boat's steel, and rolled sideways and perched for a fraction of a second on the gunwale of the boat—

And then fell out as another wave knocked into them – and splashed into the water and sank—

'*NO!*' Nasiji yelled—

And as he did, he heard Ebban scream '*Allah!*'—

And twisted his head forward to see Ebban clinging to the front of the boat, losing his grip—

And falling into the water.

★   ★   ★

Just as suddenly as it had hit, the worst of the squall seemed to pass. The boat steadied. The waves grabbed Ebban and pulled him away. He fought, trying desperately to make his way toward them as the waves thrashed him.

'Here!' he screamed to them. '*Here!*'

Haxhi swung the tiller sideways to turn the boat. Nasiji stepped toward the back of the boat and reached for his arm.

'What—'

'We've lost one already. We can't afford it.'

'Help me!' Ebban's voice was high and terrified. 'Please!'

'He's my first mate,' Haxhi said uncertainly. 'I've known him—'

'He'll freeze to death even if we can rescue him,' Nasiji said. Yusuf inched toward Haxhi, one hand on the long curved dagger that had so frightened poor Grigory Farzadov.

Haxhi took one last glimpse at Ebban and turned away. 'God forgive us, then,' Haxhi said. 'All of us.' He turned the lifeboat toward shore and gunned the engine.

An endless minute passed before Ebban's screams faded. In the boat the three men were silent, even when the wind lessened and the snow stopped and the lighthouse spotlight broke through the clouds again.

We're Allah's instrument, Nasiji had told Yusuf this afternoon. But Allah had deserted them this night. Three years of work, the perfect theft, destroyed by a knot tied too loosely and a freak squall that had passed as fast as it came.

They still had one bomb left. How much uranium did it hold? He was hoping for thirty kilograms. But he didn't think he could build a gun-type bomb with thirty kilograms of uranium. *That's why I stole two. I needed two. I had to have two. And I did. But now I don't.* Maybe, with a beryllium reflector . . . but he had no beryllium. Well, tomorrow morning he'd ask Bernard to try again for some. Meanwhile they still had to get this bomb off this boat and over the United States border and then begin the tedious, dangerous work of exposing the core.

For the next half-hour, Nasiji sat at the front of the boat, his head bowed into the wind, as the outlines of the granite headlands of Newfoundland finally emerged through the clouds and Nasiji, like the Vikings and the English and all the explorers before him, caught his first glimpse of a new world. The English had come to conquer North America. They'd succeeded only too well. Now Nasiji was here to give their bastard descendants a lesson in humility.

As they closed on the land, Nasiji glimpsed a few lights from the houses of Trepassey. The village ran along a road carved into the side of the coast, behind and above the outcropping where the light-house stood proudly alone. But they were still at least two kilometers – more than a mile – from the village, and even as Nasiji recognized its shape,

Haxhi slowed the boat's engine and steered them west and out of sight. Slowly, he steered toward a little half-moon cove that was shielded from the eye of the lighthouse by a crumbling cliff. They entered the cove and the waves shrank and the Atlantic sighed and released them at last. Though its waters had extracted more than enough tribute tonight, Nasiji thought.

Haxhi beached the lifeboat and killed the engine. The SUV, a big Ford, sat at the inner edge of the cove. The Ford rolled forward on the big flat stones that formed the beach and stopped beside them. Bashir, a tall man with thick black hair, emerged and walked toward the boat as Yusuf and Nasiji jumped out. 'My brothers,' he said.

CHAPTER 13

ZURICH

The steak filled Kowalski's plate, a cowboy's wet dream, an inch thick and marbled through with rich fat. A slab of grass-fed Kobe beef straight off the Swiss Air nonstop that connected Tokyo and Zurich. Seared in butter on the oversized Viking range in Kowalski's kitchen, delivered directly to the dining room, still cooking in its own juices, sizzling and succulent, medium-rare.

Kowalski had dreamed of this piece of meat ever since that infernal dietician Rossi arrived in his life with his broiled fish and his tofu salads. Today he had decided to defy Rossi and indulge himself. A steak, the best money could buy, and a bottle of burgundy.

So why wasn't he hungry?

Kowalski cut off a tiny corner of the steak and lifted it to his lips. And yet as he looked at his plate, he saw nothing but Roman Yansky's corpse, his neck sawn nearly in half, his body drenched in so much of his own blood that he seemed to have been painted red. Kowalski had asked Markov to e-mail him the photographs that the FSB and the Moscow police had taken of the scene. Now he wished he hadn't. He felt like a condemned prisoner eating his last meal. He choked the steak down with a swig of wine and pushed his plate aside. Maybe he ought to become a vegetarian.

'Pierre,' Nadia said soothingly. 'Are you all right?'

Her fingers fluttered involuntarily to the sapphire necklace he'd bought her from Tiffany's, as if she needed to remind herself why she was here with him.

'It's that fool Rossi,' he said. 'I hear him in my head. Fish, fish, and only fish. Nonsense, I know. But I can't shake it.'

'You've been good,' she said. 'There's no harm in a steak now and then. I've been reading this book called *The Secret*, an American book—'

Kowalski stifled a groan at the thought of Nadia reading.

'Alessandra gave it to me.'

'What is this, Models' Book Club?'

'And it says that the secret to happiness is to wish for what you want, to realize and self-actualize—'

'Please, Nadia. I have enough trouble actualizing anyone else, much less myself.'

'Hush. Yes, realize and self-actualize and your dreams will come true. Like this.' She lifted the necklace, and despite himself Kowalski was stunned by its brilliance. 'I walked by Tiffany's and wished for it a dozen times, and now . . . here it is.'

A dozen wishes and 600,000 francs, Kowalski thought. 'Only a dozen wishes? Imagine what you could have had for a hundred.'

'No, Pierre. This was what I wanted.' She spoke unironically and with absolute certainty. He wasn't sure whether she didn't get the joke or simply refused to engage it. Or maybe she believed every word she was saying. After all, the sheer genetic good luck of having been born beautiful had carried her from a village in eastern Ukraine to this mansion.

She seemed to read his mind. She smiled, a brilliant open smile that had sold lipstick from Sydney to Stockholm. 'Why not wish for a necklace? If I don't get it, I'm no worse off than before.' She reached across the table and pushed his plate toward him. 'Now you've wished for your steak and it's come and you must enjoy it. Before it gets cold.'

It was a philosophy both idiotic and irrefutable. Kowalski couldn't help but eat. As long as he kept his mind off Roman Yansky, the meat actually was quite tasty. He had nearly finished it when his phone trilled. Tarasov.

'Yes, Anatoly?'

'We've just landed.'

'Good.' Tarasov's flight from Moscow had twice been delayed by heavy snow in Zurich. 'Be in my office in an hour.'

★   ★   ★

231

Kowalski and Tarasov stared in silence at the Zürichsee. A thick white blanket of snow covered the ground, hiding the southern shore of the lake and giving the illusion that the water extended to infinity.

Finally, Tarasov cleared his throat.

'Where should I begin?'

'He killed those men as if they were children.' Somehow Kowalski couldn't bring himself to say Wells's name, as if the mere act of speaking it would make Wells appear in this room like a genie.

'Not children, Pierre. I knew Roman fifteen years.'

'Then *how*?'

'He and they are the only ones who know for sure. And they can hardly tell. So it's only guessing now. They were ready for trouble. They weren't sure who he was but they didn't trust his story, even though the Frenchman had vouched for him. He was frisked at the club, the Ten Places, before he met Roman. The doorman is certain he wasn't carrying a knife. Yet somehow he got to Roman, cut him open. Shot the other two with Roman's pistol.'

'He's very quick,' Kowalski said, remembering that night in the Hamptons. 'He sees and decides and moves all at once—'

'Put me in a room with him and we'll see who is quicker,' Tarasov said. But his voice wavered.

'You don't even believe your own words,' Kowalski said.

'He didn't get what he wanted. Markov's still alive.'

'I'm sure that's comforting for Roman and the bodyguards. You encouraged this, Anatoly. Last summer you told me to go after him.'

'And last week you told me that my only responsibility was spending my salary.'

Kowalski's chest clenched. Was this the heart attack Dr Breton had promised him? Finally the pain faded, though he felt flushed and short of breath. Tarasov laid a hand on his arm.

'If I die of a heart attack, do you think our American friend will call us even?'

'Shall I call your doctor?'

Kowalski sat down heavily. 'Forget it. Just tell me what Markov told you.'

'Well, he disappeared quickly,' Tarasov said. 'He was probably on an American passport. The Frenchman who vouched for him left the day after the attacks, on a diplomatic passport. They've both vanished.'

'So what has Markov done? Gone to the FSB?'

'He doesn't feel he can.'

Markov was in a tough spot, Tarasov explained. He couldn't finger Wells for the murders without admitting that he and Kowalski had been behind the attack in Washington. He feared if he confessed that attack, his friends at the FSB would be furious. They'd surely want revenge, but on whom? Wells, for killing Russians in the middle of Moscow? Markov and Kowalski, for the initial attack? All three?

So Markov was keeping his mouth shut. He'd told police investigating the attack that he had no idea who had targeted his men. Everyone knew he had plenty of enemies. As a result, the Moscow police, not the FSB, were leading the investigation, and were naturally focusing inside Russia. Anyway, the FSB had other concerns at the moment, Tarasov said.

'Other concerns?'

'I'll get to those.'

'So Markov's bought some time. For him and us. Does he know how Wells found him?'

Tarasov shook his head. 'He thinks the American investigation must be further along than anyone knows.'

'Does Wells know about me?'

'Markov has no idea. He thinks we should just keep our mouths shut for a while. Let Wells be. He says Wells must know that he can't get to us now,' Tarasov said. 'And if he keeps on, the results will be disastrous for America and Russia both. Markov killed two CIA men in Washington, Wells killed three of Markov's in Moscow, so they're even.'

Kowalski considered. 'Maybe Wells would agree that he's even with *Markov*. But he won't feel that way about me. If he thinks I ordered the attack, he won't stop until I'm gone. In fact—'

Kowalski broke off as Markov's next step became obvious to him. He wondered if it was equally obvious to Markov. Probably. Probably

Markov was trying to find Wells even now. To confess. To apologize. And to give Wells a name. Pierre Kowalski. You remember him, naturally? Yes, he hired me. Perhaps you'd guessed already. But I thought you would want to be certain.

And after that call . . . Wells would have only one target left. He couldn't get to Markov. He'd pushed his luck in Moscow too far already. But Zurich wasn't Moscow, and Kowalski didn't have the Kremlin protecting him. Worst of all, Kowalski didn't have anything to give to convince Wells to quit hunting him. Maybe he ought to try Nadia's suggestion and just wish for Wells to disappear.

Kowalski reached into his desk for a battered pack of Dunhills. He hadn't smoked for years, but tonight seemed like a good time to start again. Maybe he could smoke and eat his way into a heart attack and deny Wells the pleasure of killing him.

'So no one knows where Wells is?'

'Probably Washington. Maybe your friends there can find him?'

The Dunhill was stale, and after a single puff Kowalski tossed it aside. 'Not yet. One thing I'm sure of, now that he's on the scent, he won't let up. We won't have to go after him. He'll come to us.'

'All right,' Tarasov said. 'As for the other thing—'

'What other thing?'

'The uranium.'

'Of course.' Kowalski had been so focused on Wells

that he'd forgotten the reason he'd sent Tarasov to Russia in the first place. 'What about it?'

'No one's talking much. Not even my oldest friends. But I think you were right. They've had a bad loss, more serious than they told you.'

'How bad? A kilo? Two kilos?'

Tarasov rubbed his neck tiredly. 'It seems impossible. But I think they might have lost a bomb. Or at least enough material to make one.'

For the second time in five minutes Kowalski felt as though a big hand had reached through his ribs into his chest and given his heart an unfriendly squeeze. *A nuclear weapon was missing?*

'You said lost. Lost or stolen?'

'Stolen.'

'Are you sure?'

'No one will tell me for sure. But they're going full-blast down around Chelyabinsk. Half the FSB is there. Lots of arrests, lots of Muslims getting knocked around.'

'What else?'

'They've put all their bases on lockdown. And the Mayak plant. They're inventorying all their weapons. This I know for sure. And on the highways into Moscow they've set up rolling roadblocks. Not constant. I don't think they want to frighten people.'

'No one's noticed?'

'You know the media there. If the Kremlin says don't talk about something, they don't.'

'Anything else?'

'They've asked Interpol and even the United States to look for a man named Grigory Farzadov. They're saying he's a smuggler. But he's not a smuggler. He's a manager at the Mayak plant. He and his cousin disappeared several weeks ago and haven't been seen since. The cousin also works at the plant. Or worked.'

'Are they Russian?'

'They must be, to have worked at the plant.'

'Anything else?'

'Not just now.'

'All right. Thank you, Anatoly. Leave me now. I need to think about this.'

At the door, Tarasov turned. 'Do you think it's possible?'

'Don't we both know by now that anything's possible?'

A few minutes later, Nadia peeked in.

'Are you all right, Pierre?'

'Yes, angel. Come in.'

She sat beside him on the couch and ran a hand over his face. She wore yoga pants and a tight black wool sweater. If Kowalski hadn't been so worried about a heart attack, he would have popped open the bottle of Viagra he kept in the desk drawer and taken her right then. Tried to, anyway. 'I know I'm not supposed to ask about business, but is something wrong?'

'I'm dealing with a very unpleasant man,' Kowalski said.

'You've tried to talk with him.'

'It isn't like that.'

'You should try. You're very persuasive, you know.' She kissed his cheek.

'But in business, Nadia, you need leverage. You understand?' Kowalski wasn't sure why he suddenly felt the need to explain himself, but he did.

'Sure. You give him something, he gives you.'

'And I don't have anything to give him.'

But even as he spoke, Kowalski realized he might be wrong. If Tarasov was right, he might have something very valuable indeed for Wells.

CHAPTER 14

Wells wound down the handle of his Honda and poured west on 66 through the Virginia exburbs at eighty miles an hour. Tonight he had become tiresome even to himself. The burned-out cop downing whiskey at an empty bar, moaning that he'd never make detective. The third-rate poet sipping cappuccino in Starbucks, bitching how he'd never get published. And Wells tonight, the world-weary spy sucking down gasoline and ruing his fate. *I saved the world and all I got was this lousy T-shirt.* Usually he heard songs in his head as he rode, but tonight even the asphalt and the wind were too bored with him to talk.

To complete his misery, Wells hadn't dressed properly for the cold. He could barely keep a grip on the handlebars. The scar tissue in his back had turned into a solid block of ice, and his bad left shoulder – worked over by the Chinese a few months before – felt about ready to pop loose. He wasn't a machine. Though he pretended he was. And everyone seemed to believe him.

In the Honda's lone eye Wells saw a sign for an

exit a mile ahead. He closed his eyes and counted ten. Then five more. One . . . two . . . three . . . four . . . five. Before the darkness could take him too far, he looked up. He'd ridden blind almost a half-mile. He laid off the gas, gearing down into fourth. The bike was solid and quick under him. Whatever his sins, he still knew how to ride. At the bottom of the ramp, he swung left under the highway. He'd seen a Denny's sign on the other side of the highway and that sounded about right.

The restaurant was empty, aside from a table of teenagers joking loudly about whatever teenagers joked about these days. The boys had tight haircuts and the girls wore sweatshirts that even Wells could tell weren't fashionable. No doubt they lived farther out on 66, maybe even somewhere on 81. To the south and west of here, Virginia turned country fast.

One of the kids was dipping, spitting into a Coke can under the table. He wore a U.S. Marines T-shirt stretched tight across his chest. Wells wanted to ask the kid if he was really enlisting, and if so why he'd decided to sign up, what he hoped to find. But he kept his mouth shut. The world needed soldiers, and if the kid wanted to become one, Wells could hardly tell him he was making a mistake.

No one in the place noticed Wells, and for that he was happy.

The waitress came over, fifty-five, with a smoker's lined face and brown eyes and heavy shoulders and sensible black shoes. She smiled at him, a big creased smile, as she placed a glass of water on the table. And Wells felt even more of a fool. This woman was probably living in a trailer up in the hills trying to make ends meet, and *she* was taking care of *him*.

She looked at the helmet. 'You all right? Cold night for riding.'

'That it is.'

'Well, you know you can stay in here till you get warm. As long as you like.'

'I look that bad?'

'Tired, is all. What can I get you?'

Wells ordered coffee and scrambled eggs and hash browns. No Grand Slam for him, he didn't eat pork, the last trace of his Muslim identity. Then he indulged himself with a chocolate milk-shake. The food came fast. The ride had left him with an appetite, and he inhaled the shake and ate every scrap of food. The waitress – Diane was her name – kept her word, filling up his coffee cup but otherwise leaving him alone, leaving him to think over the last few days.

Getting out of Russia the morning after the murders had been easy. The agent at Sheremetyevo flipped through his American passport and looked him up and down, taking in his freshly pressed shirt and the TAG Heuer watch he was wearing to complete his cover. Just another American. Without a word, he stamped the passport and Wells was free to go.

241

But his arrival in New York was another story. As soon as the immigration agent at JFK scanned his passport, Wells knew something was wrong. Her smile faded, then returned at higher wattage. To keep him happy until the guards arrived, he assumed. Sure enough, a door at the end of the long hallway opened and three big men in blue uniforms strode his way.

'Can you come with us?' the lead uniform said.

Wells didn't argue. They frisked him, took his shoes, wallet, belt. Then they shunted him to a narrow holding cell, windowless and concrete. A guard checked him every hour, peeking through a steel panel in the door. Wells didn't mind the holdup. He closed his eyes and napped on the narrow steel cot. He found himself in a crumbling mosque, looking through a crack in the ceiling at the blue sky above. He knelt to pray and saw beside him Omar Khadri, the terrorist whom Wells had killed in Times Square. Khadri finished his prayers and turned to Wells. *You've lost your way*, Khadri told him. *You've lost the faith and you'll pay*. Khadri's teeth were fangs and he—

Wells tired of the dream. He knew he was dreaming and decided to wake and did. Instead of sleeping, he examined imperfections in the concrete, looking for patterns in the meaningless whorls.

'Waiting for me to pass a baggie?' Wells said to the guard about six hours on. 'May take a while.'

'Someone'll be here soon enough.' The guard clanked the panel shut.

Two hours more passed before the door finally opened. Wells popped up. Shafer and two guards stood outside. Wells shrank into a corner. '*Noo!*' he yelled. The guards took a half-step back.

'Send me to Guantánamo,' Wells said. 'But don't leave me with him.'

'John, enough,' Shafer said.

'This guy's into crazy stuff. I'm serious. Cattle prods, nipple clamps—'

'If you don't shut up, I'm leaving you here.'

'Fine,' Wells said sulkily.

'This is John Wells,' Shafer said to the guards as Wells slid into his shoes. 'Bet you didn't think he'd be such a jackass.'

Neither of them spoke until they reached the New Jersey Turnpike and Shafer said, 'Duto wanted to teach you a lesson, leave you in the Hotel JFK for a couple of days. I told him it wouldn't be much of a lesson.'

Wells didn't respond. Shafer was right, of course. Shafer knew that ten years in the Northwest Frontier had taught him patience.

'You stepped in it this time, John.'

'Ellis, watch the road.' Shafer was driving a black agency Suburban, and, illegally, flashing the red lights mounted in the grille as he cut through traffic. 'As far as I can see, the agency still owes me a couple of favors.'

'I'm not talking about the agency.'

'Please, no Exley advice, Ellis. Stick to Duto. Does he know where I was?'

'*Of course* he knows.' Shafer sounded irritated at the question. 'And he knows about Markov.'

'What about the Russians? Have they fingered me?'

'Strangely enough, no. At least they haven't said anything to us.'

'Markov's staying quiet.'

An eighteen-wheeler blasted them with its airhorn as Shafer cut in front of it.

'You're the worst driver I've ever seen. And that includes the jihadis.'

Shafer slowed down, turned his head, stared at Wells. 'I hope this little trip of yours was worth it.'

'It wasn't.'

'I know.' Shafer flicked on the radio, WCBS 880, the all-news station in New York, and they listened to the world's hum. Two dead soldiers in Iraq, a big oil find off the coast of Brazil, some starlet arrested again, the Giants getting ready for the NFC finals. Last and least, a triple murder in the South Bronx, drug-related, the police said. No news on Wells's own triple murder in Moscow, but why would there be? Every minute, people everywhere died too soon. Three dead in Moscow, two in Bangkok, four in Johannesburg, one in Newark, an endless tide of mayhem, far too much for a single radio station to track. The police would always be in business.

'Not much happening,' Wells said aloud.

'Maybe there is.'

'How's that?'

'I'll let Duto tell you.'

When they reached the Beltway, Wells thought Shafer would swing east, toward 295, the feeder road that led to central Washington and Exley. Instead he turned west, the highway to Langley. It was near midnight and the road was nearly empty and they made good time. In barely fifteen minutes they'd crossed the long flat bridge that spanned the Potomac and turned onto the Georgetown Pike.

'Now?' Wells said.

'Duto wants to see you.'

'When did he start working so hard? When did you turn into his errand boy?' Wells wanted to see Exley, not Vinny Duto.

'Let's get it over with.'

Just past midnight, they walked into Duto's office, a square room with a heavy wooden desk and views over the Langley campus. The windows were bulletproof glass, tinted, and three layers thick for security. The furniture was generic chief executive, a mahogany desk and heavy brown leather chairs. Wells wondered whether Duto had chosen the decor in a deliberate effort to connect with the agency's WASPy history, the Ivy League mystique that had permeated the place during the 1950s, when half the CIA seemed to have gone to Yale. Duto had actually attended the University of Minnesota, where he'd graduated in three years with a history degree. Oddly enough, Wells was the only Ivy Leaguer in the room. Shafer had gone to MIT.

An oversized wooden bookcase across from Duto's desk was filled with military histories, beginning with Thucydides' *History of the Peloponnesian War* and stretching through the millennia. The titles of the newest books, about the Iraq war, didn't inspire confidence: *Fiasco, Imperial Life in the Emerald City, Generation Kill* . . . The books were slightly out-of-order, as if Duto had actually read them. Wells wondered. He'd never thought of Duto as intellectually curious.

'John.' Duto was reading a black-bordered file and didn't rise from behind his desk, didn't extend a hand.

Wells sat. 'Commandante Duto.' Duto didn't smile. He scribbled a note on a yellow legal pad and flipped the file closed.

'I know what you're thinking,' Duto said. 'You're thinking, you can drag me in here at midnight, yell at me, make me sit through this, but you can't touch me. After what I've done, I'm untouchable. But you're wrong. It'll be ugly as hell, but I can get rid of you.' Duto's tone was steady.

'Vinny—' Shafer said.

'This is between me and him, and if you don't like it, the door's behind you,' Duto said to Shafer, without breaking eye contact with Wells.

'Understand this, John. If what happened in Moscow comes out, you'll have to go. We'll protect you, we'll tell everybody you had PTSD and snapped. Maybe it's even true. We'll make sure you never get charged with anything. And it'll be a real tragedy, losing John Wells, the hero of Times Square. But that'll be that. Can't have a guy who just murdered three Russians on the U.S. government payroll.'

'I guess we're skipping the small talk,' Wells said.

'And if you've thought it through at all, which I'll bet you haven't, since thinking ahead isn't your strong suit, you're probably figuring that worst case, even if we fire you, you'll get by. Because you've always gotten by. But ask yourself, John, if you didn't have this, what would you do? Be a mercenary? Be a stuntman, maybe?'

'Stuntman,' Wells said. The idea was oddly appealing.

'How about a mercenary? You see yourself protecting some billionaire in Mexico City?'

'Maybe I'll move back to Montana and fish.'

'You may think you want to stop, but you're way past that now.'

The intimacy of Duto's tone irritated Wells. 'When did we get to be such good friends, Vinny?'

'Guys like you, there's only one way out. Two ways, but they're the same. You get too old, or you die.'

'Isn't that true for everybody?'

'You don't even see what we do for you. We're

247

the reason you can look in the mirror and say, I did it all for the good guys. Life and liberty and the pursuit of happiness. May not be much, but it's something. Without it, you're just a stone-cold killer.'

'If you're my moral compass, I'm in worse shape than I thought.'

'Then leave right now, go to Moscow or Beijing or wherever. Plenty of people would be glad to hire a man with your talents.' Duto waited. 'No, John? I didn't think so.'

'You made your point,' Shafer said. 'No need to rub his face in it.'

'You think I don't like you, John,' Duto said. 'And I don't. You've been twitchy ever since you came back and you're getting worse. But lemme tell you a secret. I think I'd still rather have you playing for us.'

A vote of confidence. Not exactly what Wells had expected to hear.

'But can I make a request? Next time, at least give us a chance. Make killing three guys the last resort. Not the first.'

'I get it.' Wells hated the idea of apologizing to this man. But what could he do? Duto was right. In third grade, tossing a baseball with his friends in the street in Hamilton, Wells had broken the window of a neighbor's house. He still remembered the glistening sound of the glass shattering, how the pride he'd felt at the unexpected strength of his arm had faded into fear. *I did wrong. It was an accident, but I did wrong and I have to tell.* Tonight he had the same feeling. 'I'm sorry, Vinny,' he said. 'Three guys dead and I didn't even get the one I came for. I apologize. Nothing else to say.'

The apology seemed to surprise Duto as much as Duto's endorsement had surprised Wells. 'It's all right,' Duto said finally. 'You had reason.'

'Nobody's gonna believe this,' Shafer said. 'Lions and lambs together. Though I can't tell who's who.' He stood, stretched his arms out toward Wells and Duto. 'Group hug? Circle of trust?'

'Quiet, Ellis,' Duto said.

Wells wasn't sure what came next. He'd apologized, but his visceral dislike for Duto remained. 'So,' he said. 'Where does that leave us? With the Russians?'

'Smiling and lying,' Duto said. 'Same as ever. So far the FSB hasn't fingered you, at least to us.'

'You think it's possible they don't know?'

'Maybe Markov is keeping his mouth shut because he knows he can't let on it was you without admitting that he's behind the attack here. If you'll leave Markov alone it all might disappear.' Duto leaned forward. 'Can you live with that? If not, we're right back where we started.'

Wells looked away from Duto, scanning the bookcase. He'd blown his chance at Markov forever. The man wouldn't leave Moscow for the next ten years. Anyway, Markov was just a functionary, an order-taker for Kowalski. He'd tried to kill Wells and failed. Now Wells had done the same to him.

'Done.'

'Simple as that,' Duto said.

'Simple as that.'

'What about Pierre Kowalski?'

Wells shouldn't have been surprised, but he was. Of course Duto knew. Shafer must have told him, probably by way of explanation for the reason why Wells had been so sure the killers were Russian.

'What about him?'

'You'll let us take care of him, instead of going at him yourself?'

After the apology he'd just made, Wells didn't see a choice. 'Okay.'

'You sure?' Duto waited.

'I'm sure.'

'Good. Because if you're back on the reservation, I have something for you. What's been keeping me here tonight.'

Duto handed Wells a thin folder, red with a black border. Just six pages inside, but by the time. Wells was done reading, he understood why Duto was still at the office.

Weeks earlier, the Russian Ministry of Defense had warned a NATO liaison officer in Moscow that five hundred grams, just over a pound, of highly enriched uranium had disappeared from the Mayak weapons plant. The smugglers were believed to be Grigory Farzadov and Tajid Farzadov, cousins who lived in Ozersk. Photographs and basic biographical data on the cousins were attached. The Russians did not believe there was an immediate threat and asked NATO not to publicize the theft, but they urged the United States and Europe to increase security at ports and border crossings.

As was standard operating procedure, NATO had passed the report on to the Terrorist Threat Information Center, the joint FBI-CIA working group based at Langley, for evaluation. The center had classified the report as moderate-to-high priority. Russian nuclear material regularly went missing, and five hundred grams was not nearly enough uranium to make a nuclear weapon. Further, unlike plutonium, enriched uranium was not useful for dirty bombs. Nonetheless, the fact that the Russians had reported the disappearance at all was unusual. 'Is there more to this?' one agency analyst had written.

The question had been prescient. Thirty-six hours before, the Russians had given NATO what they called an 'update' on the theft at Chelyabinsk. Suddenly their estimate of the missing material had increased from five hundred grams to five kilograms – eleven pounds.

'This what you were hinting at back in the car?' Wells said to Shafer.

Shafer nodded. 'Heard the basics this morning, but I haven't seen the details.'

Wells handed him the file. 'What happened? Did the Russians miss a zero?'

'We just don't know,' Duto said. 'When you were in Moscow, did you pick up any unusual vibes, anything that might have been related to this?'

'There was a lot of security in central Moscow. I got stopped a bunch. I put it down to my beard and my coloring. But maybe it was this. And one of the guys who stopped me had a radiation detector, one of those clip-on ones that look like a pager.' Wells paused. 'Who else knows?'

'All the European agencies. For two days we and they checked every trace, every wire, every humint' – human intelligence sources, also known as informants – 'every message board, every bank account in our databases. Nobody's found anything. Anywhere. No references to nuclear material, no unusual transactions, no hints that anything's coming.'

'Reminds me of Khadri,' Wells said. 'He kept his mouth shut too.'

Shafer finished reading and handed the file back to Duto. 'That's the whole report? Nothing scrubbed?'

'That's it,' Duto said.

'Then how come there's no figure for the enrichment? Was it eighty percent? Ninety percent? Ninety-five?'

'The Russians haven't told us.'

'Have we asked?' Shafer said.

'Of course. This is all they'll give us. Op sec' – operational security – 'or so they say. They think the Farzadov cousins aren't in Russia anymore, and they're probably right. Once the FSB is on you, there aren't too many places to hide over there.'

'These guys have terrorist ties? Russian mafia?'

'The FSB won't say.'

'Religion?'

'Tajid is a practicing Muslim, but Grigory seems to be secular.' Duto looked at Wells. 'How about you, John? Anything you want to know?'

'Is what's missing enough for a bomb?'

'Not according to Los Alamos,' Duto said. 'They say the minimum amount of HEU necessary to make a bomb is fifteen to twenty kilos. And that's with some very sophisticated tools. Terrorists would need even more.'

'That's slightly reassuring,' Wells said. 'Unless these guys stole fifty kilograms instead of five. Do we think the Kremlin would tell us if the threat was imminent?'

'We hope,' Duto said. He didn't look hopeful.

'So what now?' Wells said. 'For Ellis and me, I mean.'

'I don't have anything specific for you. Stay ready, that's all.'

'We aim to please,' Shafer said.

'John—' Duto stopped. 'I already know the answer to this. But you know these guys as well as anyone. If they got one, would they use it?'

Wells thought back to the hate of the United States he'd seen during his years in the mountains. Hate, fueled by religion, and by the bitter truth that Americans had so much and the people of Afghanistan and Pakistan so little. The anger had only increased since the United States invaded

Iraq. So many jihadis, so eager to die, to strap bombs to their chests and tear themselves to pieces. They killed by the ones and twos, and when they were lucky, by the dozens.

'Suicide's the tough part,' Wells said. 'Once you decide to cross that bridge, why not take as many friends along as you can?' Wells almost laughed but didn't. 'Would they use it? Like you said, you already know the answer.'

So Wells had it backward. The meeting with Duto turned out to be relatively painless. But talking with Exley was impossible. When they left Langley that night, Wells figured Shafer would take him home. Instead, Shafer turned toward his house.

'Appreciate the offer, Ellis, but I'd rather sleep with Jenny.'

'She doesn't want to see you.'

'If you won't take me, I'll get a cab.'

'Give it time, John. She begged you not to go, not to leave her, and you went anyway.' Shafer paused. 'I know what you want to do, run home, tell her you love her, everything's going to be all right. But trust me, whatever you say will seem meaningless to her right now. What she wants is for you to prove that you can listen to her.'

'I do—'

'Then *listen*. She'd rather you stay away.'

'But—' Wells snapped his mouth shut. He couldn't argue with Shafer's logic. 'How long?'

'I think it'll be easier once she's out of rehab,'

Shafer said. 'I'll talk to her in a day or two. Believe me. This is better.'

So Wells slept in Shafer's basement for a night before moving to an anonymous safe house in Vienna, Virginia. Like all safe houses, the place was entirely without personality, white walls and cheap wooden chairs and generic Manet posters in black frames, the real-estate equivalent of purgatory. Shafer asked if he wanted guards, but Wells refused. He'd had enough security for a while, enough guys with guns around.

The house did have two handy pieces of equipment in its basement, a treadmill and a Nautilus machine. Wells worked out for three hours a day, aiming to lose the fifteen pounds he'd put on for the Russia trip, hoping to rid his body of any vestige of that failed mission. Every day for a week, he asked Shafer if Exley was ready to see him. Every day for a week, Shafer said no. Every night, Wells sat by the phone, willing himself not to call her. Four times, he dialed all but the last digit of her cell before hanging up, feeling as lonely and foolish as a lovesick geek aching for the prom queen.

At night, alone in the house, he wondered if Exley would join the rest of the friends and family he'd left behind. Heather, his ex-wife, remarried now. Evan, his son, whom he hadn't seen in more than a decade. He found himself Googling them, hoping to find scraps of their lives on the Internet, wondering if he should go back to Montana, try to see his boy. But he'd tried visiting Heather and Evan once before and the trip had ended badly. For now, anyway, Exley was all he had. If he even had her anymore.

Meanwhile, the search for the Farzadovs went on, without success. The agency and its European cousins were working on the assumption that the Farzadovs would eventually have to surface to sell the HEU. But so far the Farzadovs had stayed out of sight. And the Kremlin was still refusing to disclose exactly what it knew about the theft.

So on his ninth night back, Wells found himself alone in a booth at the Denny's on 66. Wondering when Exley would see him again and what they'd say to each other. Wondering what he would have to give up in himself to get her back, whether he wanted to change and if he was even capable.

After an hour of drinking coffee, Wells had no answers, but at least he could feel his hands again. The teenagers had gone, leaving just him and Diane. Wells reached for his wallet, figuring he'd leave a couple of twenties under his cup and disappear, head back home. To the safe house. Then his cell phone buzzed. A restricted number. Maybe Exley was calling, reaching out. Maybe she missed him as much as he missed her. He answered—

'Hello? Have I reached John Wells?' Not Exley. A man. Some kind of European accent. Wells had heard the voice before but he couldn't place it. And then he could. The bedroom in the Hamptons,

256

a man warning him, '*You'll pay for this, what you've done tonight. Even if you think you're safe.*'

'Yes.'

'This is Pierre Kowalski.'

Wells closed his eyes and stroked a hand across his forehead and waited.

'I have something to discuss with you. Can you come to Zurich?'

PART III

CHAPTER 15

ADDISON, NEW YORK

The Repard family had owned the house for more than a century. Then, on a rainy March morning, just outside Elmira on Route 17, Jesse Repard took a turn too fast and flipped his Ford Explorer into a ravine. He was thrown through the driver's-side window and died instantly. His wife, Agnes, fractured her spine at the C-2 vertebra and was paralyzed from the neck down. In the back, their two-year-old son, Damon, was untouched, not even a cut.

The Repard house was impossible to navigate in a wheelchair and too expensive for Agnes to maintain. She had no choice but to sell it and the thirty-seven acres of land around it, quick. But upstate New York's economy was worse than lousy, and the property was too small to be farmed efficiently but too big for most families. For three months, the place sat on the market without attracting even a low-ball bid. Agnes's agent told her she needed to chop her asking price fifteen percent, maybe more.

Then a young couple came to see the property. He was in charge, Agnes saw that right off. He was a surgeon from Mercy Hospital, down the road in Corning. She walked a step behind him and didn't say much. But immediately they seemed to take to the place. They liked its thick stone walls, the heavy stand of oak trees that screened the front of the property. They especially liked the big stable behind the house.

The Repards hadn't owned horses in decades, and the stable had been crumbling when Agnes and Jesse married. A year before the accident, Jesse had started to restore it. He'd torn out the stalls and reshingled the roof, turning the stable into a giant shed, fifty feet long by eighty feet wide with dirt floors and wooden walls. Agnes had handled the exterior, painting the walls fire-engine red.

'Chose the colors myself,' Agnes told the surgeon from Corning. 'I figured we'd have lots of kids and one day we'd have horses for them. They'd grow up here and one of them would take over the house from us, keep it in the family.' She knew she shouldn't talk so much but she couldn't help herself, as if by telling him her plans she'd bring them back to life.

'Interesting,' he said.

But he didn't seem interested, much less interested than he'd been when he pulled a tape measure from his pocket and wrote the stable's dimensions on a memo pad. Or later, when he stood on the porch of the house and scanned the grass and the trees and the hills with binoculars.

'You can see,' Agnes said. 'I mean you can't see anything, you can see that. It's nice and quiet. Private.' She was nervous now. She needed a good price for the place, enough money for Damon to have a decent childhood. Damn you, Jesse, for your speeding and not wearing your seat belt. For leaving me, and for leaving me like this. She hoped she wouldn't start crying, the more so since she couldn't even wipe away the tears herself.

'Yes,' he said. 'I like privacy. Americans have a saying, the home is the castle, and I agree with that.'

He was a handsome man, tall and slightly heavy, with a soft lilting accent. He was from the Middle East, she wasn't sure where and she didn't want to ask, didn't want to take the chance of offending him. His name was Bashir, she thought he'd said. His wife wore the headscarf the Muslims liked and a brown dress that covered her from neck to toes. It was a hot June day, but the woman didn't seem to mind. Agnes supposed she was used to the heat.

Bashir visited again the next day, without his agent or his wife, but with his tape measure. He must have liked the measurements because two days after that her agent called back and said Bashir had offered to buy the place. At the asking price, and for cash.

'Said they're looking to have kids and they thought it would be perfect,' the agent said. 'They even want the furniture, the rugs, all of it. They want to move right in, and they'll pay another forty thousand for all your stuff. It's like hitting the lottery, this kind of offer. It never happens like this.'

Agnes agreed that the deal seemed too good to be true, especially since the furniture in the house was a little bit raggedy and not worth anything like $40,000. She kept waiting for the catch. But there wasn't one. The papers were signed in under a month. Her first bit of luck since that day on the road. She moved into a first-floor apartment in Ithaca with Damon and tried to forget the house and everything else that had been her life before the accident. She never went back to the place. She did see it again, though, on television. And when the reporters started calling, one after the next, to ask about it, she couldn't say she was surprised.

Not when she thought of Bashir on her porch, scanning the hills with binoculars.

The stable behind the Repard house still had the cheery red paint job. Inside, however, the place looked more like a high-end machine shop.

The strangest-looking piece of equipment sat in the very center of the stable, a black block four feet high, three feet wide, and three feet long. Handles and valves jutted from its sides, and a burnished door of inch-thick steel capped it. It looked like a washing machine built by the devil. It was a vacuum furnace, a masterpiece of engineering, able to heat metal ingots to 2,700 degrees Fahrenheit in an oxygen-free vacuum.

Beside the furnace was a metal lathe. Beside that, an open gas-fired furnace, where Bashir heated and shaped the molds that would be used to cast the uranium at the heart of the bomb. Against the back wall, a liquid nitrogen plant, essentially a powerful refrigerator that produced five liters per hour of super-cold liquid. Next to the nitrogen plant, arranged on hooks and metal shelves, Bashir's work clothes and other personal equipment: a fire-resistant coat, long rubber boots and gloves, a plastic face shield and goggles. A respirator mask. Heavy steel tongs and clamps for picking up buckets of molten metal. Three fire extinguishers. A horror movie's worth of saws: a table saw, a chain saw, a diamond-studded rotating saw capable of cutting steel or uranium. Outside and behind, a Caterpillar generator, so that Bashir wouldn't have to draw electricity from the power grid to run the equipment.

Bashir had bought most of the stuff on eBay and from machinery supply companies across the Northeast. He'd taken care never to approach the same dealer twice. No special licenses or permits were required for any of the tools, but Bashir didn't want anyone to ask why he was putting together a factory in his backyard.

Buying the vacuum furnace was more complicated. It was more than $50,000, and mainly used in steel mills and high-end university labs. After talking with Sayyid Nasiji, Bashir decided that the best way to get the furnace without attracting attention was to import it from China. American laws strictly regulated the *export* of equipment with possible military applications. That policy had been useful decades before, when the United States, Germany, and Japan had been the only countries that could produce high-end machines like vacuum furnaces.

But the laws said nothing about the import of advanced equipment. No one had considered the possibility that terrorists working on American soil might look outside the United States for the equipment they needed. After a few hours of Internet research and four phone calls to China, Bashir ordered the vacuum furnace online. It arrived two months later at a warehouse in Elmira, no questions asked.

By day, Bashir was a general surgeon in Corning, a town of eleven thousand in upstate New York, 250 miles northwest of New York City. He was Egyptian, the only son of an upper-middle-class family in Cairo. He'd gotten stellar grades at Cairo University, graduated in three years at twenty-one, and come to the United States for medical school and residency, both at Ohio State. At twenty-eight, his residency complete, he returned to Egypt to find a bride. He stayed just a few months in Cairo before coming back to Corning – and buying the Repard house.

That bare-bones résumé, though accurate, left out some facts that surely would have interested the CIA. When Bashir was eleven, his father died. With money tight, his mother sent him to live with her half sister Noor. Noor's husband, Ayman Is'mail, owned a trucking company – and secretly was a devout member of the Muslim Brotherhood, a group that favored turning Egypt into a strict Islamic state. Ayman and Noor, who had no children, raised Bashir as their own, inculcating him with the Muslim Brotherhood's beliefs.

Ayman especially hated Hosni Mubarak, the Egyptian president. 'A pharaoh,' he told Bashir. 'With his imperial court and his crumbling empire. Look at how he treats his people. How he locks up anyone who opposes him. And do you know who's behind it all?'

'No, uncle.'

'You do. You've heard me give this speech a hundred times. Tell me.'

'The Americans.'

Ayman nodded. 'The Americans. They say they want democracy for everyone. But if we Egyptians demand leaders who will stand up to them, they put us down. Who do you think pays for the prisons and the Mukhabarat?'

'The Americans?'

'Just so.'

Ayman was careful to avoid associating with the Brotherhood in public. But when Bashir was eighteen and just about to enter Cairo University, the Mukhabarat arrested Ayman in a raid on a Brotherhood meeting in Cairo. For two weeks,

Bashir and Noor did not know what had happened to him. Finally they learned that the police had sent him to the notorious Tora prison complex, fifteen miles south of Cairo. Even after they found out, another week passed before the lawyer they'd hired convinced the Mukhabarat to let Bashir visit the prison.

The concrete-walled meeting room at Tora where Bashir waited for Ayman was windowless and stifling, more than a hundred degrees. The stench of sewage soaked the air, so heavy that after a few minutes Bashir found himself pinching his nose and breathing through his mouth. Outside the room, men shouted at one another endlessly, a cacophony of voices that rose and fell as erratically as wind whistling across the Sahara. About an hour into his wait, Bashir heard, or thought he heard, a high eerie voice screaming like a teakettle's whistle. But after a few seconds, the scream stopped. It never did return, and eventually Bashir wondered if he'd imagined it.

Bashir waited two hours for the guards to bring Ayman in. When they finally did, Bashir almost wished he'd had to wait longer. The three weeks Ayman spent in jail had not been kind to him. He limped into the concrete-walled meeting room, hands cuffed behind his back, stomach poking sadly out of a cheap white T-shirt a size too small. Ayman, who had taken such care of his appearance. His skin had the grayish pallor of a plate of hummus that had sat too long in the sun. Pushed along by a guard, he shuffled to the narrow wooden bench where Bashir sat and straddled it uncomfortably.

'Won't you uncuff him? Please?' Bashir said to the guard. In response, the man pointed to a hand-lettered Arabic sign taped awkwardly to the wall: *Prisoners are restrained at all times in the meeting area.*

'Look at him. He's no threat.'

'Even so, removing the handcuffs is complicated.' Complicated. A code word for a bribe.

'A hundred pounds,' Ayman said under his breath.

Bashir had known he would need to pay bribes to get into Tora, even with the official approval from Mukhabarat headquarters. He'd come prepared with 400 Egyptian pounds, about $75. But he had foolishly spent the last of his money for the chance to bring a bottle of Ayman's blood pressure medicine into the waiting room. He had nothing left for this guard. He shook his head. The guard walked out, slamming the door behind him.

'Are you all right, uncle?'

'I miss my cigarettes. And my pills.'

'No cigarettes, but the pills I have. What happened to your leg?'

Ayman laughed. 'I banged it on a door. So they tell me.'

'They're hurting you.' Rough treatment was common at Tora, but Bashir was surprised that the guards would hurt his uncle. Though he wasn't well-connected politically, Ayman had plenty of money. And he wasn't a terrorist. He believed the government should be replaced, but peacefully, through elections.

'They're afraid, these guards,' Ayman said. 'Afraid of their masters, afraid they'll wind up in here with us if they treat us like humans and not animals.' He checked over his shoulder to be sure the guard wasn't lurking outside the door, then leaned forward, toward Bashir. 'I want you to promise me something.'

'Of course.'

'If I don't get out of here, you won't forget what I've told you. About Mubarak and especially the Americans. The Americans are behind it all.'

'What do you mean, if you don't get out?' Bashir hoped his voice didn't betray his panic. He called Ayman his uncle, but in truth the man was more like a father to him.

'I'll be fine. But I want you to promise, just in case.'

'All right. I promise.'

'Good. Now tell me about your auntie.'

'She misses you terribly.' Bashir began to fill him in about Noor, but after a few minutes the guard reappeared.

'Time's up.'

Bashir couldn't help himself. 'Time's up! We're supposed to have an hour. It's hardly been five minutes.'

'Time's up.'

'You can't – I won't—'

'Don't argue,' Ayman said under his breath. 'You'll just make it worse.'

The guard pulled Ayman up as Bashir fumbled in his pocket for the bottle of pills he'd brought. 'Uncle, here,' he said. He reached out to tuck the bottle into Ayman's T-shirt pocket, but the guard – Bashir never did find out his name – grabbed the bottle.

'What's this?'

'It's only medicine,' Ayman said. 'For my heart.'

'It's contraband,' the guard said. 'Illegal.'

Bashir couldn't believe the man was serious. Did he really think these pills were contraband? The guard shook the bottle sideways, rattling the pills inside, squinting at the words on the label. He can't read, Bashir realized. He can't read and he won't admit it.

'Please,' Ayman said. 'I swear to Allah—'

'Illegal,' the guard said again. He twisted the cap open and spilled the pills down and ground them into the concrete with his cheap black shoes. 'You're lucky I don't arrest you,' he said to Bashir. He reached behind Ayman's back and dragged him toward the door.

'I'll get you your medicine,' Bashir shouted to his uncle. 'Tomorrow.'

But Bashir couldn't keep his promise. Every day for a week, he fought through Cairo's traffic jams to return to the prison. But the guards wouldn't let him meet Ayman no matter how much money he offered. On the eighth morning, as he was finishing his breakfast and preparing to leave, the phone rang. Noor picked it up and listened. Without saying a word, she dropped the phone and fell to her knees and began to scream and beat her head against the yellow linoleum floor of the kitchen. Bashir knew immediately. On the day that his father died, his mother had screamed the same way.

The Mukhabarat officers said Ayman had been found dead in his cell. A heart attack. Nothing anyone could have done. He was unwell, as anyone could see. They offered honest and heartfelt sorrows, a thousand condolences, an endless epic in true Egyptian style, and every word emptier than the next. They'd murdered him. Whether they'd actually beaten him to death or killed him by withholding his medicine was irrelevant. They'd murdered him.

On the day of Ayman's funeral, Bashir promised he would avenge his uncle. And, intuitively, he understood the path to take. He'd been planning to study law at university, following in his father's footsteps. Now he reconsidered. Why become a lawyer in a country that had no law? The Mukhabarat had never connected him to the Brotherhood. He had no police record. His name was clean. And so he transferred to the medicine program at Cairo. Every country in the world trusted doctors, no matter their nationality or religion. If he could earn an American medical degree, even the United States would be glad to have him. He studied madly at Cairo for three years, biology and chemistry and physics, earning the best grades of anyone in his class, paving his way to Ohio State.

All along he quietly kept in touch with his uncle's friends in the Brotherhood, making sure they knew that he was still with them. Like him, they understood his potential value, and the need for patience. After finishing his residency, Bashir joined a program that offered foreign medical graduates American citizenship if they would practice in underserved areas for five years. Even the Americans needed doctors, just as he'd figured.

In the months before he started his new job, he came back to Cairo, looking for a wife. Noor, his aunt, introduced him to the daughter of her second cousin, Thalia, only nineteen, a twittering sweet girl with almond eyes and thick black hair and breasts that jutted from her robes despite her best efforts to keep them hidden. Bashir wanted her immediately. Even better, he knew she had been raised to be a good Muslim wife. America, Egypt, Pakistan; their future would be whatever he said. They were married six weeks after their first meeting.

The call Bashir had awaited for so long came just a few weeks after he and Thalia moved back to the United States. A nameless Arab, Iraqi by the sound of his voice, said they had mutual friends and asked if they could meet in Montreal.

Wandering through the big botanical garden just

east of Montreal's downtown on a fine April day, the Iraqi – Sayyid Nasiji was his name – explained what he needed. A big space where they wouldn't be disturbed, a lathe, a vacuum furnace, a PC with some basic engineering software, and a dozen other tools.

'How much will it all cost?'

'Money won't be a problem,' Nasiji said.

'And what's the point of all this equipment?' Bashir said.

'I think you can guess.'

'A bomb.'

'A big bomb.'

'The biggest?'

Nasiji stopped, put a hand on Bashir's shoulder, an oddly intimate gesture. 'Are you ready for that, Doctor? They told me about you and your uncle and I thought you would be. But you spend your days stitching these Americans together, saving the sick ones. So if this is too much—'

Bashir thought back to the casual cruelty of the guard at Tora, and about all he'd learned about the United States in his years living there. His uncle had been right. The Americans were behind it all, behind the corruption in Egypt and all over the Arab world, behind the war in Iraq, the stifling poverty in Pakistan. 'Yes,' he said. 'I'm ready.'

Learning to use the vacuum furnace, the lathe, and the rest of the equipment wasn't easy, especially since Bashir kept up his work at the hospital.

Fortunately, he'd always been good with tools, and his training as a surgeon had refined his hand-eye coordination. After ordering some basic metallurgy textbooks and videos, he got to work practicing, first with aluminum, which melted at relatively low temperatures, and then with iron and steel. He found the equipment was surprisingly finicky, especially the vacuum furnace. Too much heat, applied too fast, and the molds melted down instead of casting the material inside them.

But over a year's worth of late nights, Bashir grew comfortable with the equipment. The simplicity of the shapes he was trying to create helped him. After successfully casting several steel molds, he began training on depleted uranium. Depleted uranium was the opposite of enriched uranium, the metal left over from the enrichment process, and actually contained less of the radio-active U-235 isotope than natural uranium ore. It was useless for nuclear weapons, and so it was legal to purchase and to own without a license. But its melting point and density were practically identical to that of the uranium used in bombs, so it was ideal for practice casting.

In the years since their first meeting, Bashir had met Nasiji several more times in Montreal. But Bashir was under no illusions about who was in charge of the operation. Its ultimate success or failure would fall on Nasiji. It was Nasiji who had decided to bring the bombs in through Canada, where Bashir and his wife would pick them up, ferry them to Nova Scotia, and truck them over the United States border. In a big SUV filled with ski equipment and suitcases, the bombs wouldn't stand out. Bashir had wondered about the scheme, which seemed to him too complicated by half, but Nasiji was the boss.

Now they'd suffered disaster, no way around it. Nasiji had always told Bashir they'd have two bombs to work with. Two into one, he called the plan. And though Bashir wasn't a nuclear physicist, he understood that being short of material made their task immensely more complicated.

Well, at least they'd gotten the one bomb across the border. After the pickup, Bashir and Thalia had driven across Newfoundland through the night and caught a ferry to Sydney, Nova Scotia, a roiling two-hundred-mile trip. From Sydney they drove to Montreal. They told the border guards on the New York State Thruway that the skiing on Mont Tremblant had been great but promised that next time they'd try Lake Placid. Then they were through.

Meanwhile, Nasiji and Yusuf had taken the easy way in. After resting for a night in St John's, the capital of Newfoundland, they'd hopped a Continental flight that conveniently enough went nonstop to Newark. From there they would rent a car and drive to the farm. And the real work of making the bomb would begin.

CHAPTER 16

ZURICH

Zurich was calm and rich and Wells disliked it immediately, for no good reason. Maybe because Kowalski lived here. Maybe that was enough. Wells hadn't taken any great precautions for this trip. He'd even checked into the hotel under his own name. He had his Glock and the agency knew he was here, all the protection he needed. He couldn't imagine Kowalski had invited him just to take another shot at him.

Wells was staying at the Baur au Lac, a five-star hotel downtown. The place stank of endless wealth, fortunes that would last until the sun exploded and its flames swallowed the world. Perversely, Wells had taken a suite, handing over his agency credit card, imagining an auditor at Langley choking on his coffee as he saw the $3,000-a-night room.

As soon as the bellhop left him in the room, he reached for the phone. Kowalski answered on the first ring. 'Hallo?'

'I'm at the Baur au Lac.' Come and get me, Wells thought.

'Mr Wells. Shall we meet in the bar in the lobby, tonight at six?'

'I'll be there.' Wells hung up.

The bar was really a sitting room, a fifty-foot square with dark wood walls and a faded gold carpet. Men in dark suits and white shirts sat at tables sipping beers, reading *Die Zeit* or the *Financial Times*. In one corner a fifty-something blonde in an electric-blue blouse, diamonds glittering on her wrist and neck and ears, sat on a couch between two younger men, talking equally to them both. They leaned forward as if they'd never heard anything so interesting. Her investment advisers, perhaps. Or nephews hoping for a loan.

Kowalski sat in the opposite corner, slumped on a sofa behind a low coffee table. He was wearing a rumpled blue suit, cream shirt, no tie. He seemed smaller than when Wells had seen him last, though hardly svelte. Two men flanked him, one about Wells's size, the other tall and thin and ugly. They stood as Wells walked near, and Wells recognized the big one, Anatoly Tarasov, Kowalski's head of security. He was shorter than Wells but thicker in the shoulders. He had the cauliflower ears and flattened nose of a boxer. Wells figured he could go twelve rounds with Tarasov, but he wasn't sure he'd get the decision. The other man stood to the side and didn't bother with eye contact, focusing instead on Wells's hands. His own hands were slipped under his jacket. He was the dangerous one. He was the shooter.

As Wells reached the table, Kowalski grunted and stood and extended a hand. Wells let it dangle in the air until Kowalski pulled it back and lowered himself down to the couch.

'Mr Wells. I hope you don't mind my bringing friends. This is Anatoly, and the gentleman in the corner is called the Dragon.' Kowalski raised his glass. 'Would you like a drink? I'm having Riesling, very dry. Very nice.'

Wells saw no reason to speak.

'You know where the word *hotel* comes from?' Kowalski said. 'Six, seven hundred years ago, the Middle Ages, trade picked up and merchants began to travel, selling goods. They needed places to stay. Before that travelers had slept in monasteries or castles, but these merchants didn't know the local priests or barons. They were stuck. So in the bigger towns, the leading bars added hostels – places anyone could stay, with his safety guaranteed.'

'And hostels became hotels.'

'Exactly. Consider this such a place. Don't be afraid to have a drink. Take my glass if you like.'

'You think I'm afraid?' Wells said. 'I didn't come here for your hospitality. Or history lessons.'

'Besides, your bosses know you're here, and if I touch you all the bodyguards in the world can't protect me,' Kowalski said. 'A Black Hawk full of

Deltas will come to my house and grab me and toss me into the Zürichsee from a thousand meters up.'

'You have a vivid imagination.'

'Maybe a drink later, then. When we know each other better.' Kowalski sipped his wine. 'You like Zurich, Mr Wells? Each year we win the award for the best quality of life. Though for a man of action such as yourself, it must be boring.'

Wells wouldn't have guessed he could feel anything other than hate for Kowalski. But he did, a profound irritation that sat atop his disgust like barbed wire on an electrified fence. Kowalski reminded Wells of George Tyson, the agency's head of counterintelligence, another fat man who could never get to the point and who took more than he gave when he finally did.

'And our women are beautiful, of course,' Kowalski said. 'The Swiss misses.'

Wells thought of Exley, crying silent tears as she levered herself down the hospital hallway. Kowalski, no one else, was to blame for those tears. And now he was joking about the women of Zurich? Wells's throat tightened. Instantly, the room was twenty degrees cooler and the conversations around them no longer existed. The universe had shrunk to this corner.

Wells looked at the Dragon, the shooter, and then at Tarasov, calculating geometries. Could he get to his Glock and get two shots off, take out the Dragon first and then Tarasov? Doubtful. He'd need two guns, a cross-draw, Jesse James style. Those only worked in the movies.

The other men seemed to sense that Kowalski had pushed Wells too far. The Dragon reached under his jacket for his own weapon, a little snubnose that he held now beneath his waist, under his clasped hands. Kowalski didn't move, but his eyes opened slightly.

'I'm sorry, Mr Wells. I was impolite. But let's not disturb the peace of our neighbors.'

Wells leaned back, rested his hands in his lap. Kowalski nodded at the Dragon and the snubnose disappeared.

'Do you have something to tell me? Because now's the time.' Wells pushed back his chair. 'Now or not at all.'

'First, sincerely, I'm sorry about last month. I made a terrible mistake. What you did to me in the Hamptons, it unsettled my equilibrium. I overreacted.'

Wells stood. Kowalski raised a big hand to hold him off.

'I want peace between us. I have something for you.'

For the first time since he'd seen Kowalski, Wells smiled. 'This isn't a bribe, right? Even you aren't that stupid.'

'A bribe, yes. But not money. Information.'
Wells sat.

★   ★   ★

For the next few minutes, Kowalski filled Wells in on the call he'd gotten from Andrei Pavlov, the deputy director of Rosatom, and about his suspicion that a nuclear weapon had gone missing. Wells didn't tell Kowalski about the report that Duto had passed to him, but the details seemed to line up.

'So the Russians are missing material,' Wells said when Kowalski was done. 'Tell me something I don't know.'

'All right. Let me start at the beginning. Two years ago, a man comes to me, a Turk who lives in Germany, he wants three thousand AKs, a million rounds.'

'What's his name?'

'Let's call him the Turk.'

'Clever,' Wells said. 'So you did the deal. You weren't worried the German police were setting you up? Or someone else?'

'If the German police try to sting me, I know it before the men who are running the operation. Anyway, this wasn't illegal, what he wanted.'

'Isn't it unusual for someone to come to you like this, out of the blue?'

'Not so much. People know who I am, they know what I do, if they call me I answer. Or one of my men does.'

'But he comes to you, wants to spend a few hundred thousand on rifles, you don't ask where they're going.'

'Of course I do. He told me Nigeria, he knew

a general there, they'd done business before, used jeeps. This time, the man wanted AKs for a brigade of police, paramilitaries.'

'And this guy, the Turk, he wasn't lying about the buyer?'

'On a first-time sale like this, I don't do the deal until I'm sure. So I checked. The story was what the Turk said, Nigeria. It isn't complicated. You understand how it works?'

Wells shook his head.

'The Turk comes to me with these papers called end-user certificates, a promise by the Nigerian government that the weapons won't be resold. I check, make sure everything's in order, I set up the deal. AKs are easy to find, they make them all over the world, China, Russia, Bulgaria, wherever. I buy the AKs for $150, sell them for $220 each, including the transport. Three thousand guns, $70, a nice little profit, $210,000, plus the ammunition. A small deal, but for a few hours work, a few phone calls, not bad.'

'And the Nigerian government can't do this on its own?'

'Of course it can.' Kowalski's heavy eyes were half-closed now, as if having to explain all this bored him. 'And $220 is a very fair price for a new rifle. But you must understand, the license, the EUC, end-user certificate, it says four thousand AKs, not three thousand.'

'So?'

'So the Turk, or the general, somewhere up the

283

line they're adding a thousand AKs of their own, old bad guns, maybe cost twenty dollars each, and pocketing the difference. The general finds the Turk, the Turk finds me, everybody makes money. They don't ask me for a kick-back, even, they just want me to forget the extra thousand rifles. And I'm very good about things like that.'

'No doubt,' Wells said.

'Then, last year, the Turk, he calls me again, another order. Bigger. This time six thousand AKs, a few machine guns, plus a few SPG-nines. Just four.'

'The Spear?' Wells had seen them in Afghanistan. The Spear was a 73-millimeter recoilless rifle, Russian-designed. Basically an oversized bazooka. It was advertised as an antitank gun, but that was an exaggeration. The Spear could take out pickup trucks and medium-armored Humvees, but it wasn't much use against anything heavier.

'Yes.'

'Did he say why he wanted those?'

'No. Same deal as before. This time the license says eight thousand rifles. Okay. And the Spears, it's a little strange, they're under a separate license, but so what, who cares? It's not like he's buying a tank.'

'So you sold him the guns.'

'I am an arms dealer, Mr Wells. I do arms deals. But then, a few months ago—'

'When?'

'Six. Six months. The Turk called me again.

This time he wanted beryllium. He was coy about it, very cagey, but he wasn't joking.'

'Beryllium?'

'A metal. It's for bombs. Nuclear.'

'Can you use it for anything else?'

'Not so much. Do you understand the physics?' Kowalski explained the rudiments of bomb design, scribbling on a pad he'd brought. After a few minutes, Wells understood, or thought he did.

'So the beryllium reflects the neutrons back at the bomb?'

'Exactly. It goes around the core of the nuclear material and speeds up the chain reaction. But you can't make a bomb with it. It's useless without the plutonium or the uranium. And the Turk didn't seem to have that. His question was more in the nature of a hypothetical. If he needed beryllium, could I get it? I told him probably not, but for the right price, I would look.'

'Were you surprised he came to you? You could have gone right to the Swiss police. Or even the Germans.'

'We did two deals already, they went well, so no. Anyway, everyone knows I don't go to the authorities. If I can't make a deal, I don't make it. But that's my business, no one else's. And there's no law against asking about beryllium.'

What a fine human being you are, Wells didn't say. 'All right. He came to you. Suppose the Turk and his friends could get enough HEU or plutonium for a bomb. Would it be hard to make?'

'I'm not an expert, but I don't think so.'

'How many men?'

'Fewer than five. Remember, this is very old technology.'

Wells thought of the new Russian estimate of missing material. 'If they had the uranium, how long would it take?'

'I don't know. It depends if they know what they're doing, how much they have. Two weeks at least, three months at most.'

'*If* they have enough. Whoever they are. It's all theoretical. All smoke.'

'All smoke,' Kowalski agreed. 'But what if it's not?'

Wells looked around. This bar was the wrong place for the discussion they were having, and not because it was insecure, though it was. The room around them just didn't match the subject at hand. But then what room would? An underground bunker at Strategic Air Command headquarters, maybe. World maps glowing on wall-sized monitors. Stern-faced men with stars on their shoulder-boards watching the beast slouch closer. Not here, not with a fifty-something bottle blonde three couches away.

'You know what,' Wells said to Kowalski. 'I will have a drink.'

The Baur au Lac didn't have Bud, so Wells ordered a Heineken. The waiter's nose twitched at the order, nonetheless he returned in a few seconds with the bottle and delivered a perfect pour into a long tall glass.

'So what's his name?' Wells said.

'And what do you give me in return?'

'A truce. Your life.'

'Maybe it's your life. Maybe my men will get you this time. I don't have to do this.'

'Then why bother?' Wells said. 'This bomb, even if it's real, it won't go off in Zurich. So why do you care? Worried that it'll be bad for business?'

'A nuclear explosion? Bad for business?' Kowalski smirked. 'In New York, let's say. The United States will go mad. You'll threaten every country between Morocco and Bangladesh and actually attack half of them. New bombers, new aircraft carriers, new tanks, laser guns. Satellites that fire missiles. A trillion dollars a year in spending. More. You don't believe me? Look at what's happened since September 11. That was nothing compared to this.'

'Even if you're right, we won't be buying those weapons from you.'

'If the United States goes mad, the rest of the world has to respond. The Russians add a thousand tanks, and so the Chinese build up five divisions of their own. Then the Indians, and the Pakistanis, and the Bangladeshis, and – I believe your President Reagan called it the trickle-down effect.'

Kowalski was right, Wells realized. After the initial shock, and the promises to disarm and rid the world of nuclear weapons, after the empty words had faded, the world would get ready for

World War III. The tank factories in Russia and the missile plants in China would run overtime until America finally felt safe again. Which meant they would never stop. And here in Zurich, Pierre Kowalski would connect buyers and sellers and take his cut along the way.

Kowalski was right. But still he hadn't answered Wells's question.

'Then why tell me this? Why cost yourself money? How many men have died from the weapons you've sold? In Sudan, everywhere else? Fifty thousand? A hundred thousand? You're a little atomic bomb yourself.'

Kowalski didn't blink. 'In Rwanda, 1994, the genocide. The Hutu killed the Tutsi for a month. No one knows how many died. Let's say a million. A nice round number. They didn't use my weapons, Mr Wells. They used clubs. Clubs and machetes.'

'So what are you saying? With your guns they could have killed the million in a week, saved some time.'

'Don't pretend you don't understand. These Africans and Arabs and all the rest. They come to me for tools, tools they can't make on their own, but they kill each other or not all the same.'

'You're just following orders. Like the Nazi guards.'

'I provide a service. I leave the trigger-pulling, the order-following, to men like you.'

And then Wells found he had nothing to say.

'You presume to lecture me on morality. But I'll answer you anyway. This bomb, this isn't Africans hacking each other up for sport, as they always have, always will. This gives a few angry men the power to change the world. A great city gone. For what? Fables in a book? No. I don't want that.'

The casual racism was astonishing, but Wells found he didn't know how to argue. He hated these quick-tongued men who sliced up truth and mixed it with lies and fed it back to him. 'Why come to me with this?' he said finally. 'You must have contacts at NATO and the Pentagon. And I know you have friends at the Kremlin. Why not go there?'

'I don't need a truce with them,' Kowalski said. 'This deal, it's between us personally. If you say we're even, we're even. What you do with the information after that, it's up to you. Give it to NATO if you like, or your bosses. Though I know you prefer to work alone.'

I prefer to work with Exley, Wells didn't say. But thanks to you, I can't. 'Tell me something,' he said. 'This man, the Turk, he contacted you months ago, you said.'

'Right. Six months.'

'So why do you think he'll want to hear from you now? Don't you think he'll be suspicious if you come to him out of the blue?'

'I'm sure he'll be happy to hear from me. Because he called again two days ago, asked me if there was any chance I might have found a way to get him the stuff.'

'Another hypothetical.'

'I don't think so. Either they have enough for a bomb and they want to make it bigger, or they're a bit short and want to be sure.'

'Or you're making all this up.'

Kowalski shook his head.

'So what's the Turk's name?'

'Do we have a deal?'

Wells stood up from the table. 'I'll think it over.'

'Think fast. You know better than I do, these men won't wait.'

'Last question,' Wells said. 'So you give me the name, whatever else you have. How do you know I won't kill you anyway?'

'You're an honorable man, Mr Wells.'

'There was a time I thought so too.'

CHAPTER 17

For five weeks, the Iskander warhead had been in motion, across five thousand miles, seven countries, three continents, an ocean. Even without detonating, it had left plenty of damage. *Harmless as a Gypsy curse,* Major Yuri Akilev had said to Grigory Farzadov on the night Grigory stole the bomb. Now Grigory was dead. His cousin Tajid, too. And for his inadvertent role in the theft, Yuri was facing a court-martial sure to put him in a Siberian prison camp for the rest of his life.

Now the Gypsy curse had reached its final stop, the stable behind the Repard farmhouse. It sat on the floor beside the vacuum furnace as Yusuf and Bashir and Nasiji stood around it like thirsty college kids waiting to tap a keg. Nasiji tapped the steel cylinder, fiddled with the eight-digit locks on the panel on its side, tried to flick the arming switches up and down and found they wouldn't move.

'Wish we had the other,' he said.

'So what now,' Yusuf said. 'We open her up?'

'She?'

291

'Of course she,' Yusuf said. 'This thing's just like a woman. The sooner we get inside, the better.'

'No cutting today,' Nasiji said. 'Today we talk about how these *gadgets* work.'

The basement of the farmhouse had been refinished in the 1970s but not updated since. It was one big room with particleboard walls, a broken Ping-Pong table on one end and a pool table missing half its felt on the other, relics of happier days. In the middle, in front of an ugly synthetic couch, were three big whiteboards that Nasiji had asked Bashir to get. And in this unlikely setting, Nasiji gave them a primer on nuclear weapons design.

'The first thing to understand is that the bomb is actually two bombs.' He sketched a cylinder on the whiteboard in thick black marker, put a big *W* at its top. 'This is the warhead. In fact, to be technical, the warhead includes an outer casing. What we have is usually called the *physics package—*' Nasiji was showing off now, unable to help himself, reminding Bashir of his more irritating medical school professors. 'But I'm going to call it the warhead for the sake of simplicity. Now, inside the warhead, as I said, two bombs. Both nuclear.' Nasiji drew a couple of thick black circles inside the cylinder, one above the other.

At this Yusuf perked up. 'Two nuclear bombs? So there are two explosions?'

'There are, but they happen more or less at exactly the same time. Anyone watching would see one blast. Now the first bomb to explode' – Nasiji tapped the bottom circle – 'is called the primary. It's a very old design. Basically a fancy version of the bomb that the Americans dropped on Nagasaki. It's plutonium, and all around it is high explosive. The high explosive blows up and pushes together the plutonium and that explodes.'

Nasiji sketched the implosion mechanism on one of the white-boards, concentric circles to represent the different layers of the bomb. 'I'm leaving out a lot of detail, of course. I'll tell you more later, but the truth is we're going to try not to touch the primary at all. We don't need it. We're aiming for the other bomb, the secondary. Want to guess why it's called that, Yusuf?'

'Because it blows up second.'

'Very good. So the physics behind the second bomb are more complicated, but the bomb itself is a simple design. It's built in layers, uranium at the very center, then lithium around that, then more uranium.'

'I don't understand,' Yusuf said. 'Just uranium and lithium? Where's the trigger?'

'The first bomb is the trigger. When it detonates, it creates a wave of energy that pushes together the material in the second bomb.'

Bashir thought he understood. 'So the first bomb sets off the second bomb, just the way the explosives around the first bomb set that one off?'

'Exactly,' Nasiji said. 'And because the secondary is coming together under such force, it blows up with incredible power. So this is what's called a two-stage bomb. Or a thermonuclear, because it's all the heat from the first bomb that sets off the second bomb. You know those films of the bombs they set off over the Pacific, the Russians and the Americans, those giant mushroom clouds.'

'Of course,' Yusuf said.

'Well, those were thermonuclear bombs, just like this one. A lot bigger, but the same design.'

'So we're going to make one of them, too, once we're done taking this one apart?'

'I wish,' Nasiji said. 'No, what we're going to do is take the uranium, the U-235, from the second bomb. The secondary. And then we're going to make a bomb of our own, a simple one, a one-stager. Assuming we have enough material, that the storm and that fool captain didn't ruin it for us.' Nasiji sighed. 'But I can't think about that now. Let's talk about what we're going to see in this gadget of ours once we get it open.'

'But—'

'I know what you're going to ask, Yusuf. If these designs are national secrets, how do I know? Yes?'

Yusuf nodded.

'That first bomb was a long time ago. Over the years, the facts have come out. Mainly about the American designs. But remember, these bombs, American or Russian, they're all roughly the same, because the physics are the same everywhere. Everyone has the same design problems, and there are only so many solutions. The basics haven't changed since the 1950s.'

So for the next several hours, Nasiji sketched out, in detail, what they would see once they broke through the outer casing of the war-head. The initiator, which released neutrons into the center of the primary bomb just as the explosion began, speeding up the chain reaction. The plates of plastic explosive around the primary. The hard plastic foam that was turned into plasma by the first explosion and channeled the energy that set off the second bomb. The explanation was complex and Bashir was glad when Thalia knocked on the door and announced that lunch was ready.

They trooped upstairs for dates and couscous with raisins and carrots and fresh orange juice that Thalia had squeezed herself. She stood in the kitchen and shyly watched them eat, coming in only to clear dishes and refill glasses. 'You like it?' she said when they were done and Yusuf and Nasiji had disappeared downstairs.

'Very much.' He patted her arm tentatively, and under her headscarf she smiled.

'Good,' she said. 'I don't want you to be hungry.'

'Not much chance of that.' He ran a hand over his belly. He'd once been thin, but too many years of fourteen-hour days in surgery had filled him out.

'No, don't hide him. I like him.' She put a finger to Bashir's stomach and smiled. His pulse quickened at her unexpected touch. She'd been inexperienced when they married, a real virgin who'd never even kissed a man. Now she was becoming increasingly comfortable with him in their bedroom, but she was still shy outside it.

'We'll keep him then,' he said. She giggled. Sometimes he forgot she was just twenty-two. He was embarrassed now. 'So, back to work.'

For the rest of the afternoon, Nasiji took them through the physics behind the bomb. Bashir sensed Nasiji was talking for himself as much as for them, reminding himself of the concepts that would help him design their own bomb. The faint winter light outside the basement windows disappeared and still Nasiji talked, even after Bashir began to doze and Yusuf laid his head on the table.

'Enough,' Yusuf said, as Nasiji began to diagram the decay of a U-235 atom. 'This might as well be Hebrew for all the sense I can make of it.'

'But if something happens to me, you need to know—'

'If something happens to you, we'll shoot one piece of uranium at the other and hope for the best. That's what all this comes down to, right?' Yusuf waved a hand at the three whiteboards, filled edge to edge with equations and diagrams in smudged black ink. 'Before lunch was fine, but now we're wasting time. Let's cut the thing open and see what we find.'

Slowly, Nasiji nodded. 'It's a whole desert of sand I've given you, isn't it? And you're right. What matters is what's inside that warhead. Tomorrow we find out.'

CHAPTER 18

Wells sat in his suite at the Baur au Lac, pretending to watch television, flicking between CNN and BBC and Sky, pretending he hadn't already made up his mind, pretending he hadn't already wasted most of a day chewing over a decision that was no decision at all.

He couldn't say no to Kowalski. He needed the name. Though part of him wondered whether he and Duto and Shafer weren't overreacting. Probably this would turn out to be nothing, another in the long string of false alarms since 9/11.

But he couldn't take that chance.

Wells wished he could be certain why Kowalski had come to him, wondered if there was some double- or triple-cross he wasn't seeing. Most likely not. The simplest explanation was usually the best, and the simplest explanation here was that Kowalski feared he'd be sent straight to hell if a bomb went off and the United States found out that he had information that could have stopped it. So he'd decided to give Wells the name, get Wells off his back, two birds, one stone.

Wells had been ready, more than ready, to make Kowalski pay for Exley and all those nameless Africans who had died from the bullets that Kowalski sold. Even at the price of losing Exley. And maybe one day Exley would have forgiven him, understood that he'd needed to kill Kowalski to make sense of all the rest of the killing he'd done. Or maybe not. But though Wells always would have hated himself for driving her away, he never would have been sorry for killing Kowalski.

Or maybe . . . he would have found a way to change his mind. Maybe he would have realized that vengeance wasn't his to take. And then he could have told Exley: *I'm not going after him. Maybe it's too late, but I want you to know. I'm sorry.*

Instead Wells would lose both ways. Snake eyes. Kowalski would live. And yet Wells wouldn't be able to tell Exley that he'd found peace in his heart and walked away from the fight. Kowalski was simply buying his way out, plea-bargaining for his own survival.

As Wells had known all day. Now he was wasting time, and Kowalski was right. These terrorists, whoever they were, they wouldn't wait once the bomb was done. Wells flicked off the television and picked up the phone.

A half-hour later, the hotel's Bentley brought him through snowcovered streets to the gates of Kowalski's mansion. Wells stepped out and watched as the big black sedan, a brick on wheels, silently rolled away. Then he pushed the bell and the wrought-iron gates swung open and he walked up the gravel driveway toward the house, three stories high and wide and made of solid red brick. It looked like it belonged in Boston and not Zurich.

The front door was opened by a uniformed housekeeper. She curtseyed and stepped aside, revealing the most beautiful woman Wells had ever seen, tall and slim and high-breasted and wearing a black crepe dress that seemed molded to her body.

'Nadia,' she said, extending a hand.

'John.' Wells stood in the door, trying to brush off his long blue overcoat, feeling clumsy as a sixth-grader on his first date. He'd expected to be met by Tarasov, or the shooter whom Kowalski called the Dragon. Not this creature, whose eyes were as blue as Exley's.

'Please, come in. Let Fredrika take it.'

The housekeeper helped him out of the coat and gloves and disappeared. Nadia cocked her head and looked at Wells, a butterfly smile flitting over her face, as if he'd whispered a joke that she hadn't quite heard. 'Are you cold? Would you like a drink?'

Wells shook his head.

'Follow me, please.'

The mansion was even more opulent than Wells had expected, its walls lined with Impressionist art. Wells caught a glimpse of what looked like a

Renoir as they passed the dining room, and a Degas pastel in a dim alcove.

In front of him, Nadia's hips swung sideways and her red heels clacked on the oak floors beneath them. Her dress whispered as she walked. It was modest, knee-length, but Wells imagined Nadia's thighs underneath, could almost see them. He hadn't felt so attracted to a woman other than Exley in years, but this woman exuded sex as naturally as a lake spouted fog at dawn. He forced himself to look away. He was being cruel to Exley, and stupid besides. He was here for a deal, not to steal Kowalski's concubine.

Nadia knocked on a closed wooden door.

'Come,' Kowalski said softly.

A flare of anger burned away Wells's lust. Now that he was on the verge of making peace, he hated Kowalski more than ever. He had planned to come to this meeting unarmed, but just as he walked out of his hotel room he'd grabbed his Glock and tucked it in a shoulder holster. He was glad to have it. Though he knew he ought not to be. He was here for a name, nothing more.

Unlike the rest of the mansion, the drawing room was sleek and modern. In its center was the most striking sculpture that Wells had ever seen. If sculpture was the right word for it. It was a transparent plastic box, five feet high, eight feet long, four feet wide, with weapons inside – an RPG and an AK-47, encircled by a ring of grenades – held fast in a clear plastic goo, perfectly preserved, every detail visible. Wells rapped his fist on the plastic box. The launcher and the rifle didn't move.

'You've heard of Damien Hirst?' Kowalski said. He sat on a black couch whose sleekness seemed inappropriate for his big body. The tall shooter whom Kowalski had called the Dragon sat beside him. They made a ridiculous pair, Abbott and Costello.

Wells hadn't heard of Damien Hirst. He kept his eyes on the weapons, sealed for eternity inside the box. He feared that if he looked at Kowalski, he would lose control. In the holster below his left armpit the Glock itched, begging to be drawn.

'He's British. An artist. In 1991, he put the carcass of a tiger shark in a box like this,' Kowalski said. 'A whole shark! It made him famous. It was called *The Physical Impossibility of Death in the Mind of Someone Living*. A good title, don't you think? Since then, it's been cows and sheep and lots of other dead animals in boxes. Now he's very rich.'

Wells said nothing, and after a few seconds, Kowalski continued. 'A few years ago, I was in London at an opening of his and asked him if he might do something for me. He came up with this. A play on the original. A bit derivative, but I like it. Reminds me where my money comes from. I imagine you don't think much of it. A waste of a good AK, you probably think.'

'Why not just put a dead African in?' Wells said. 'Eliminate the middleman.'

Kowalski laughed, a short barking chuckle. 'So you do have a sense of humor. I wasn't sure. All those men you've bumped into over the years, you think they saw a tiger shark when you turned out the lights on them? *The Physical Impossibility of Death in the Mind of Someone Living.*'

Nadia was still by the door. 'Get out of here,' Wells said to her. She smiled at him, a smile that despite everything sent a surge of desire through Wells, and backed out and closed the door. When Wells glanced back at the couch, the Dragon had drawn his pistol.

'Very chivalrous,' Kowalski said. 'You must like her. Something else we have in common.'

'The name,' Wells said.

'The name for a truce.'

'The name and an introduction.'

Kowalski raised his hands. 'I'm to vouch for you? No. No, no, no. I give you the name, you do what you like with it. Have your friends from Langley trap him. Or the Germans. Cameras in the walls. Satelliters. All your toys. You think you're going to infiltrate, fool this man? I heard from Ivan Markov about your introductions.'

'Name's no good without it,' Wells said, with a patience he didn't feel. He left the sculpture behind and walked to the window. The snow was still coming down. The glass offered him a reflection of Kowalski and the Dragon on the couch.

The Dragon was tracking him with the snubnose, his body twisted sideways so he would have a clear shot if Wells spun. But if Wells kept moving along the window, the Dragon's firing angle would be partially blocked by Kowalski's bulk.

'Tell him you don't want to be involved, but you know somebody who can get the stuff,' Wells said.

'And who will you be this time? You speak Polish? Russian?'

Wells watched the window.

'You think your Arabic's going to come in handy for this?' There was a sneer in Kowalski's voice, the same sneer Wells had heard a few months before in a mansion in the Hamptons, before Wells had shut him up with a stun gun to the throat and started the mad cycle that had landed him in this room. 'You think he believes an Arab can help him? If an Arab could get this stuff, he wouldn't be coming to me.'

'You're awful brave with that bodyguard next to you,' Wells said. 'Those boys in Moscow were brave, too.' He turned to face Kowalski and the Dragon, keeping his hands loose by his sides. A shoulder holster wasn't an easy draw and the Dragon was surely quick, but Wells would take his chances. 'Tell him whatever you like. I'm a friend you know from way back when. Doesn't matter. If he needs the stuff as much as you say, he'll bite.'

Kowalski sighed, and Wells saw that for all his talk he didn't want to push their battle any further. 'And then we're even?'

Wells nodded.

'In that case. His name's Bernard Kygeli.' Kowalski plucked a cell phone from his pocket. For the next ten minutes, Wells watched in silence as he spoke rapid-fire German, Wells catching a word here and there, mostly place names – *Hamburg, Zimbabwe.* 'Gut,' Kowalski finally said. '*Gut. Bitte.*' He hung up, slid his phone shut.

'Went *goot?*' Wells said.

'Your name is Roland. You're an old friend of mine, a Rhodesian I've known a long time. I came to you because you have friends in Warsaw and the Poles have a big beryllium plant. You're not sure, but you think maybe you can get the stuff for him. At a big price. He said not to worry, money wouldn't be a problem.'

'Any hint of how close they are?'

'No. And I didn't ask.'

'The meeting,' Wells said.

'He said no, but I told him you required it. This isn't guns or grenades and you need to see him face to face. Finally, he said okay. Tomorrow in Hamburg at six p.m. The plaza outside the Rathaus, the old city hall.'

'Anything else I need to know?'

'I don't think so.'

'Then we're done.'

'You're not staying for dinner? Nadia will be disappointed.' Kowalski pushed himself off the couch and pursed his lips into a rictus grin and extended a meaty hand toward him. Before Wells could stop himself, he'd extended his own hand and they shook. Kowalski's palm was cool and dry and they stood together for a long moment, gripping and grinning for invisible, or maybe real, cameras. Finally, Wells pulled his arm away.

'Save the world, won't you, Mr Wells?' Kowalski grinned at him. 'And don't forget to save me, too.'

We're not the same, Wells wanted to say. Not even close. You can tell me we are, tell me this is all a big cosmic joke, but you're wrong. But he was through arguing. He'd gotten the name. He reached for his phone to have the hotel send the Bentley for him, then changed his mind. He would walk along the lake instead, let the snow cover him, cool him off. In this house, his emotions ran too hot.

At the door, Nadia was waiting with his coat. She slipped it over his shoulders and rested an easy hand on his back and Wells felt a shock of desire rope down his spine into his groin.

'Good luck,' she said out of the side of her mouth.

'Whatever he's paying you, I hope it's worth it. Hope you're socking every franc under the mattress.' Wells knew he ought to keep his mouth shut – she must make a gibbering idiot of every man who walked into this house – but he couldn't stop himself.

She put her hand to his face and tilted his head

and kissed his cheek. 'Good luck,' she repeated. 'Perhaps we'll meet again.'

Wells walked out.

Back in his suite, Wells found his Kyocera satellite phone, a big black handset with a finger-sized antenna poking from the top, and punched in an eighteen-digit number and listened to silence for thirty seconds. In the 1990s, Motorola had spent billions of dollars to build a satellite network called Iridium, able to carry calls from any point in the world, including both poles.

But Iridium had been a bust. The calls cost several dollars a minute, and standard cell networks worked well enough for most business travelers. In 1999, Iridium had gone into bankruptcy. But the satellites had never been shut off. Though the network was still theoretically open to anyone, it was mainly used now by the Pentagon and CIA. The number that Wells had called was known as a sniffer. Software on the other end of the line looked for abnormalities in the connection that might indicate the phone or the connection had been tampered with. Bottom line, a silent line meant a clean phone. Or so the engineers at Langley had told Wells, and he wasn't going to contradict them.

Of course, a clean phone was useless if the room was bugged, so Wells wandered back downstairs and into the silent streets of Zurich. It was not even ten p.m., but the city was as quiet as a castle with the moat up, the burghers and bankers home counting the day's profits. Wells walked down the Bahnhofstrasse along the locked stores and called Shafer, filled him in.

Five minutes later: 'Okay, spell the name for me.'

'B-A-S-S-I-M. K-Y-G-E-L-I. But goes by Bernard. Runs an ex-im business in Hamburg called Tukham.'

'Turkham? Like Turkey–Hamburg?'

'No, T-U-K-H-A-M. No R.'

'Any idea why?'

'Maybe he's not a good speller, Ellis. Focus here.'

'And wants beryllium.'

'So he says. I'm meeting him tomorrow. Six p.m.'

'John.' Shafer was silent, four thousand miles away, and Wells felt him trying to figure out what to say next. Finally he sighed, as if he knew that trying to dissuade Wells from this meeting would be pointless. 'All right. What's your cover?'

Wells explained. 'Can you get me papers?'

'To Germany in twenty hours? Sure. Piece of cake. Pick a last name.'

'Albert.'

'Albert? Okay. Roland Albert. Rhodesian mercenary. Better get you a British passport. We'll hook you up with a courier in Hamburg. Can you do a Rhodesian accent?'

'Shrimp on the barbie, mate?'

'Not Australian, John. Rhodesian.' Shafer started to laugh and stopped. 'This isn't a joke. Not with five kilos of HEU missing. You know I have to tell Duto. He'll tell the BND, get things started.'

'Give me the first meeting, at least.'

'And your fat friend? Any business left with him?'

'Deal's a deal,' Wells said. 'How's Jenny?'

'Better every day,' Shafer said. 'Sends her love.'

Wells hung up. He was directly across from the central Zurich train station now – the Hauptbahnhof, which, logically enough, marked the northern end of the Bahnhofstrasse – and he turned right and began to walk beside the narrow Limmat River, which flowed gently out of the Zürichsee. He called Exley's cell phone, a useless exercise. She wasn't answering him.

But tonight she did.

'Hello?' That voice. Smoky and sweet and husky and knowing. On nights when he couldn't sleep, she whispered to him until she herself fell asleep and even then he would hear her voice comforting him. He was ashamed of every halfpenny of lust he'd had for Nadia.

'It's me.'

'Where are you?'

'Zurich.'

'Zurich,' she said. He waited for her to ask him why, but she didn't. 'Is it safe?' she said finally. An old joke of theirs, from the scene in *Marathon Man*.

'Is it safe?' Wells laughed. 'It couldn't be safer if it tried.'

She was silent for a few seconds. Normally Wells didn't mind these pauses, but tonight he wanted her to talk, tell him she was past the worst of it, they were past the worst of it.

'How are you, Jenny? How's your back?'

'Not skiing yet, but give me time.'

'Good. That's good.'

Another pause.

'So . . . I wanted to tell you. The thing I came here for, I worked it out.'

'I don't want to talk about that, John.'

'It's not what you think.'

'*I don't want to talk about it.*' The smoke and the sweetness were gone.

'I'm sorry.'

'No,' she said. 'I'm tired, is all. Lots of rehab today. I wish you were here.'

'I can come back.' Wells tried to keep his voice steady.

'Not till you know what you want.'

'All right,' he said. 'I love you, Jenny.'

'I love you, too.' And then she was gone.

CHAPTER 19

In addition to its side control panel, the warhead had a hinged steel plate on top to allow technicians to access its guts. A tough-looking lock, a steel box the size of a deck of cards, covered half the plate, preventing it from being raised. Nasiji poked at the box with a screwdriver. 'We could try to force it,' he said. 'But I don't like the look of it. Let's cut around it, peel off the casing.'

'Ironic, isn't it?' Bashir said. 'The biggest danger we face is from the plastic and these traps, not the bomb.'

Nasiji nodded to the wall of gear in the back of the stable. 'Ready?'

'Let's pray,' Yusuf said.

So Bashir grabbed three prayer rugs from the house, and for fifteen minutes the three men prostrated themselves and asked Allah for his support, finishing with Surah 2:201. '*Oh Lord! Give us good in this world and good in the hereafter, and defend us from the torment of the Fire.*' When they were done, they rolled up the rugs and set them aside and pulled on long rubber boots and gloves and face shields and goggles and heatresistant coats.

'Before we start,' Bashir said. 'I thought, perhaps, we should film all this. One day the world will want to know how we did what we did.'

'We talked about this,' Nasiji said. For the first time, his voice betrayed impatience. 'No cameras. No more speeches, no more prayers, no more visits to the bathroom. The nitrogen now. It's time.'

So Bashir and Yusuf picked up an insulated container of liquid nitrogen, called a dewar, and carried it to a thick-sided plastic tub that sat next to the warhead. They tipped the dewar over the tub, pouring until the liquid came nearly to the brim. The nitrogen, cooled to seventy-seven degrees above absolute zero, bubbled madly as it evaporated.

'Into the bucket.'

Bashir and Nasiji picked up the warhead and lowered it into the bucket. There was no guarantee, but cooling the cylinder might make an accidental explosion less likely. Bashir felt as though he were in the operating room in Corning, about to make the day's first cut, the patient prepped and unconscious on the operating table beneath him. *It's really happening*, Bashir thought. He wanted to mark the moment, but the set of Nasiji's jaw discouraged idle chatter.

As the cylinder cooled, the only sound in the stable was the nitrogen's bubbling. Then Bashir breathed deep and picked up a circular saw, its blades diamond-tipped to cut through concrete. He flicked it on, feeling it vibrate in his gloved hands. As gently as he could, Bashir touched the saw to the top of the cylinder, avoiding the locked panel. The saw screeched and jumped back as it touched the steel. Bashir pushed down harder, hard enough that the blades bit into the steel and began to grind through it. Bashir held the saw in place for a few seconds, then pulled it up as Nasiji stepped forward with a fire extinguisher and sprayed the top of the warhead.

Bashir turned off the saw, put it down, and ran a finger over the hole he poked into the steel. It was barely a quarter-inch deep and two inches long and revealed nothing at all.

'Again,' Nasiji said.

Bashir flicked on the saw and felt it come to life. He lined it up with the groove he'd just cut. He sliced in slowly, controlling the saw through the steel, until it broke through and slipped forward—

Then, without warning, compressed air began to whoosh out of the cylinder, filling Bashir's nostrils with a strong sour smell—

Bashir pulled back the saw as Nasiji stepped forward and sprayed the casing with a fire extinguisher—

Bashir coughed wildly and twisted sideways, nearly cutting Nasiji in half. Nasiji jumped back as Yusuf reached to unplug the saw—

And then it was over. The compressed air stopped coming. Bashir counted one, two, three, four, five, waiting for the explosion. But nothing happened and Bashir put down the saw and shined a flashlight into the hole and touched the groove with his gloved fingers.

'What was that?' Yusuf said.

Bashir shook his head. He was still coughing, but the gas, whatever it was, didn't seem to be toxic. He leaned against the workbench and tried not to laugh as his fear faded. 'I don't know. Some kind of gas to keep the parts from corroding. It was under pressure inside and once we broke through the sidewall, it burst.'

'Most likely argon or neon, a noble gas, to keep the electronics inside the weapon stable,' Nasiji said. 'It's probably not dangerous, but give it a minute to air. You almost took my head off with that saw, you know.'

'I wasn't expecting it,' Bashir said sheepishly.

'It's a lesson for all of us,' Nasiji said. 'Take it a centimeter at a time. We really don't know what's inside.'

'The look on your face,' Yusuf said to Bashir. He opened his mouth, an exaggerated gasp of fear.

'Easy to be bold from across the room,' Bashir said.

Inch by inch, they opened the warhead. They weren't trying to preserve the components as a functioning weapon, so they didn't have to make perfect cuts. Even so, the work was slow and nerve-racking. As they widened the hole and exposed the inside of the shell, they poured liquid nitrogen inside, trying to freeze the bomb's circuitry.

By late in the day, they'd cut away the arming panel and exposed two flat green boards loaded with primitive electronic circuitry, capacitators and black transistors as big as quarters. They looked like they belonged in an old radio, not a nuclear warhead.

'Not like what they show in the movies,' Bashir said.

'Remember, they probably designed this in the mid-1980s, and they were far behind the United States in computers even then. And besides, for something like this, cutting-edge technology doesn't matter. Only reliability.'

'It's all going to get vaporized anyway,' Yusuf said.

'Yes,' Nasiji said. 'See, they have duplicates of everything. Two circuit boards, two altimeters, four batteries – and probably just one needed to set off the primary.'

The batteries were the size of cigarette packs, sealed in plastic and attached to the inside of the steel casing. They fed two pairs of red and black wires that snaked through a steel shield into the heart of the cylinder, the bottom half where the primary was placed. 'They want to be sure it will work even if part of the arming mechanism fails. Probably they expect ninety-eight or ninety-nine percent reliability.'

'Not one hundred?'

'Remember, they have thousands of these warheads. They can still blow up the world if a few don't work.'

'Yes, well. I'll bet they wish they had this one back.'

Nasiji yawned. 'Let's get a good night's sleep and start fresh in the morning.'

That night Bashir dreamed of sawing through the metal inch by inch. When he woke up, his fingers were inside his wife. Even before he was fully conscious, he'd slipped up her nightgown and spread her legs apart and pushed himself inside her. She was asleep when he started, but she woke up fast. The thought of the bomb drove him and he didn't last long, but he didn't mind and neither did she. She covered her mouth with her palm so Nasiji and Yusuf wouldn't hear her moans. When he was done, he fell back to sleep and didn't wake until Nasiji knocked on the bedroom door at nine a.m.

A half-hour later, he and Nasiji and Yusuf were in the stable, examining the naked guts of the warhead, trying to decide their next step. Nasiji favored cutting the battery wires before they sawed any further into the guts of the bomb. Bashir thought they might be better off leaving the wires alone.

'Didn't you say we didn't have to touch the primary at all?' he asked Nasiji.

'That was before we had a look. Now I see that the secondary won't come out easily and I'd rather be sure the detonators are asleep.'

'If there's any kind of trap, it's going to blow when we take out the batteries.'

Nasiji shook his head, and Bashir saw that he wasn't going to win this argument. 'It must have a positive action,' Nasiji said.

'How do you mean?'

'I mean, it's possible to design the plastic so that it will go off unless there's a constant flow of power from the batteries. In other words, if the power is cut, the plastic explodes. A negative action. But then what if the batteries go dead? Much too dangerous. So it must have a positive action. Goes off only if the batteries fire. And that means the safest course is to cut the power—'

Nasiji was the engineer, and Nasiji had stolen the bombs. This decision was his. So Bashir reached into the toolbox at his feet and handed Nasiji a pair of wire cutters. Then he picked up a second pair, feeling their smooth plastic handles in his hand.

'Both pairs of wires, the same time.'

'On three.' They stood next to each other and slipped the cutters' blades around the wires. 'One. Two. Three.'

The wire was brittle after being dosed with liquid nitrogen the night before. Bashir squeezed the handles together, feeling the tension – and then the plastic outer casing of the wires shattered into a hundred tiny pieces, and he tore smoothly through the copper underneath. Beside him Nasiji cut through his own wire. They waited for the bomb to sputter. Or for an explosion they would never see. But the seconds ticked by, and then a minute and then another, and the bomb sat inert.

'It's done,' Nasiji said, not triumphantly, just a statement of fact, an acknowledgment that they'd passed another way station on a very long race.

They put aside the clippers and Bashir picked up the saw and they got back to work sawing around the cylinder, trying to remove the entire top half and expose the shell of U-235 that formed the rim of the secondary. Hard work, and slow, but steady and, with the batteries removed, safe enough. Bashir was already calculating how many days they would need before they could remove the secondary and get at the U-235. One? Two? Three at most. Then they'd have the raw material to start building their own bomb.

CHAPTER 20

G ive me the bad news,' Duto said as soon as Shafer walked into his office.

'How do you know it's bad? Maybe it's good.' Shafer wandered to Duto's bookcase, plucked out *An Army at Dawn*, the Rick Atkinson book about the North African campaign in World War II, flipped through it aimlessly.

'It's never good, these chats of ours,' Duto said. 'And *you* called *me*, so it's worse than usual. Stop wasting time.'

'You may be right.' For the next five minutes, Shafer told Duto where Wells was and what had happened with Kowalski. Duto didn't say a word, the only sign of his anger a faint flush in his cheeks. Years before, when Duto had run the Directorate of Operations, now the National Clandestine Service, he'd been a screamer and sometimes even a thrower. Pens, briefing books, on one infamous occasion a laptop loaded with encrypted files. The techs had needed two weeks to recover everything. But since his promotion to director, Duto kept his anger bottled up. Shafer figured some management consultant had told him that controlled rage was more effective than fist-pounding. It was true, too.

'All right, again, from the top,' Duto said, when Shafer was done.

'Why?'

'I need to hear this twice.'

Shafer did. By the time he was done, Duto's face had turned a ripe pink, the color of a medium-rare steak. 'You're telling me that Wells already screwed us with the Russians. And then he gets a call from Pierre Kowalski and he dances over to Zurich to see him?'

'I believe he flew. Swiss Air.'

'And you signed off on this?'

'It's John, okay. You see me telling him what to do?'

'And you didn't tell me?'

'I'm telling you now.'

'And further that the real reason all this happened with Kowalski, the reason Wells and Exley got hit last month, wasn't because we screwed up Kowalski's play in Afghanistan last year. It goes back to Wells taping his head in the Hamptons?'

'Duct-taping, yes.'

'Which you and John and Jennifer, the three of you, didn't see fit to mention until now. And now Kowalski, to get Wells off his back, gave up a name. A Turkish refugee in Germany—'

'Not a refugee, a legal immigrant, a business owner—'

'Don't give a damn if he's the president of the

319

Elks Club, Ellis.' Duto picking up momentum now. 'He's trying to build a *nuke*—'

'We don't know that yet.'

'We know he wants beryllium. Desperate for it. And instead of coming straight to me on this, you tell Wells to meet the guy, Bernard, Bassim, whatever he's called, on his own?'

'Again, Wells told me.'

'And Wells is pretending to be a mercenary? From *Rhodesia*?'

'Correct.'

Duto clenched and unclenched his fists three times, like a basketball coach signaling a play in from the sidelines. 'You're two little kids, kindergarteners painting the walls with crayons. You can't help yourselves. You just push me until I have no choice.' Shafer wondered whether he was going to see an old-time explosion. But Duto breathed deep, ran a hand over his face, controlled himself. 'What do we know about the Turkish guy? Bernard?'

'He's not in the Black Book' – the CIA's database of 4,500 known or suspected terrorists – 'nor the Gray Book' – a broader list, 37,000 names in all, friends, relatives, and associates of the people in the Black Book. 'He's not in the TSC database' – yet another list, this one managed by the FBI Terrorist Screening Center, mainly for the use of local law enforcement agencies.

'Any criminal record at all?'

'Can't be sure because we don't have fingerprints,

but his name isn't in the NCIC database' – a list of fifty million names, almost everyone who had ever been arrested, convicted, jailed, or paroled in the United States. 'Interpol doesn't have anything either.'

'The NSA?'

'Still checking.'

'Germans have any files on him? BND, local police?'

'I haven't asked. Wanted to come to you first.'

'Nice of you. How about his business?'

'I've only started to look in public records, but it seems legit. He shows up in the Dun and Bradstreet corporate records for Germany, he's listed in the Hamburg phone book, he's in the Hamburg port database. Even got a Web site. Brings in rugs and machinery from Turkey, exports used cars and clothes to Africa.'

'Does he send anything to the United States?'

'Doesn't look that way, but I'm checking.'

'You're going to have a lot of other people helping you check, Ellis.'

'So be it,' Shafer said. 'Long as they don't get in my way.'

At that, Duto's fists opened and closed, three times, another play called in. 'Back to Wells. He's meeting this guy when?'

'A couple hours from now. Six p.m. in Hamburg, noon here.'

'With no backup.'

'None whatsoever.'

'And no way of knowing that Kowalski didn't triple him up, give his real name to this guy? No way of knowing that besides losing a nuke, we might wind up with a videotape of John Wells, our precious national hero, getting his head chopped off while bin Laden watches?'

'You sure you wouldn't mind? You gave us that pretty speech about how we're all on the same team, but your passion seems to have cooled.'

'Maybe I wouldn't, but the White House would.'

'Kowalski's on very thin ice and it's not in his interest to play that kind of game.'

Duto drummed his fingers against his big oak desk, horses on the backstretch, coming around the far turn, lots of race left. Shafer wasn't good at keeping his mouth shut, hated these silences, but this time he resolved to outlast Duto.

'You know the stakes here,' Duto said finally. 'Why don't you act like it?'

Because I trust Wells a lot more than I trust you, Shafer didn't say. He'd already pissed Duto off plenty. 'Worst case, he doesn't get anything, we go in, pick up this guy Bernard, we're right back where we started.'

'Worst case, Wells spooks him, sends him flying, and we miss our chance at his friends. Whoever they are. Wherever they are.'

'Vinny, he's been in tight before and it's always worked out. The BND's more likely to spook this guy than Wells is. I say we give Wells a couple days before we tell the Germans.'

'Are you kidding me?' Duto said. He smiled, a big fake grin. 'You are. You're kidding me. Ellis Shafer, you joker you. I know you and John and Jenny, you have this us-against-the-world thing going, the three musketeers, all of it—'

'But—'

'No. You listen now. Last month, one muskeeter almost got killed and now the other one's trigger-happy like a twelve-year-old playing Grand Theft Auto—'

'Grand Theft Auto?' Shafer smiled, trying to lighten the mood.

'My nephews, they're teenagers, what can I say?' Duto smiled, too, but the break in the storm didn't last. 'And you come in here with your smirk and tell me there's a guy in Hamburg wants beryllium. Then with a straight face you tell me to keep the BND in the dark, let the great John Wells do his thing. Little Boy Two blows up in Potsdamer Platz, vaporizes that fancy new Reichstag of theirs, what do you think the Germans are going to say to that?'

'The bomb's not in Germany—'

'You don't know that, Ellis. You don't know shit. And this is too important for guessing.'

'Here's what I know,' Shafer said. 'These guys don't care about Berlin. New York, D.C., maybe London, maybe Moscow – that's it for them. Max damage, max symbolism.'

'Maybe. Even so, this is on German soil and we're telling the BND.'

'You think they'll help us on this?' The CIA didn't have a great reputation in Germany these days, not after the fiascos over renditions and the Iraq war.

'They got the same report on the missing uranium as everybody else. They'll help.'

'Fine,' Shafer mumbled. He'd lost this fight. Duto had made up his mind. And part of him was relieved. Much as he disliked Duto, this mission was too important to be outside the chain of command. 'Vinny, there's something I'm not seeing here. Why won't the Russians be straight with us on this?'

'I asked Joe' – Joe Morgau, the head of the agency's Russia desk – 'the same thing. He says four possibilities. In order of likelihood. One, it's reflex. They lie to us so much they don't know how to tell the truth anymore. Two, they're embarrassed, so they're burying the truth, hoping it doesn't come back on them.'

'Sounds like something we would do.'

'Three, they don't know exactly what's missing and they don't want to scare us. Four, there's some bigger power struggle happening in the Kremlin and this is part of it in some way we can't see.'

'What do you think?'

'I think it doesn't matter. We've got to find the stuff, whatever it is, and we've got to assume the Russians aren't going to help.' Duto paused. 'Here's what I'll do for you, Ellis. It's' – Duto looked at his watch – 'ten a.m. now. Four p.m. in

Germany. I'll give Wells this one meeting tonight. I'll call Mieke' – Josef Mieke, the director of the BND – 'around six p.m. our time, midnight over there. He won't get the message until the morning. Then he'll want to talk to me, make sure it's real, that we're not exaggerating. That'll give you a few hours to get hold of Wells, tell him what's coming, so he doesn't do anything dumb and spook the Germans. But this is it. The last time.'

'You're a prick . . . but I love you anyway.' Shafer stood, aiming to get to the door before Duto could change his mind. Wells would have one night with Bernard before the Germans showed up.

'Don't make me regret this.'

'I suspect you regret it already.' Shafer grabbed the Atkinson book and left.

CHAPTER 21

The Hauptbahnhof in Hamburg was an architectural marvel, two dozen train platforms under an arched steel roof that stretched four hundred feet, the space open, no supporting columns cutting it up. The trains never stopped coming, stubby commuter S-Bahns and sleek long-distance expresses painted with the red-and-white DB logo, bound for Berlin, Munich, Paris. On the platforms, men and women lined up, quick-checked their tickets to be sure they had the right cabins, grabbed their briefcases and suitcases, and stepped up into cars, only to be replaced a few minutes later by new passengers waiting for new trains. Everyone was properly bundled against the cold, long wool coats and scarves and leather gloves, and no one pushed and no one ran. They were German, after all.

Wells watched the endless flow from a self-serve snack shop on a balcony overlooking the platforms; 4:04 turned 4:05 on the big digital clock above him. His contact was five minutes late, maybe the only person in all of Hamburg who was not on schedule. At six p.m., Wells was supposed to meet with Bernard Kygeli, and if he didn't have the right papers he might as well not show up.

Then he saw the man Shafer had told him to expect: late twenties, shoulder-length dark hair, orange Patagonia jacket. The guy sidled up to Wells's table and dropped a hotel keycard beside his coffee cup. 'Park Hyatt 402,' he murmured to the air. 'Four-oh-two,' Wells said quietly, confirming, as the courier turned and left. Wells liked the way the guy had handled the drop, how he hadn't wasted time being subtle, no need since nobody was watching. Wells pocketed the key and sipped his coffee until the clock hit 4:10, plenty of time for his contact to disappear, then pulled himself up and left the station behind.

A winter wind was flying in off the North Sea and down the Elbe, sending a shiver through the sunless city. But the stores on Möncke-bergstrasse were bustling, lit up with white lights and thick with shoppers taking advantage of the sales.

The Hyatt was only a couple of blocks from the station, and again Wells appreciated the courier's efficiency. Room 402 was a suite at the end of a short corridor, empty, a black leather briefcase on the king-sized bed. Wells turned the locks to 2004 – the year his Red Sox had won the World Series after eighty-six years of baseball misery – and flipped it open.

Inside, two manila envelopes. The first held his new papers: an Irish passport, a British driver's license, and credit cards. All in the name of Roland Albert. 'Roland Albert,' Wells said to the empty room. 'Roland Albert. Albert Roland? Roland Albert?' He wished he'd picked a better name. The license and passport had his real date of birth to make it easier to remember, a nice touch. Wells made sure he had the London address memorized, then swapped the fakes for his real credit cards and passport.

The second envelope held a two-page dossier from Shafer on the target. Wells scanned it twice, found little of interest besides the guy's real name – Bassim. He tossed both envelopes back into the briefcase, locked it, left it on the bed for his nameless courier, then walked to the Kempinski Hotel, behind the train station, to check in under Roland Albert's name, be sure his identity was live.

The Rathaus filled the south end of a plaza just off the Binnenalster, the little lake in the center of downtown Hamburg. Like the train station, the city hall was a reminder of Hamburg's prosperity, a broad building with a clock tower at its center. Wells stood beside the wooden front door, wearing a cap with the logo of the Bayern Munich soccer team, as Bernard had asked him to do.

Six o'clock came and went, and 6:15. Wells tucked his hands under his arms against the cold and watched the shoppers and commuters go by. The setup for this meeting stank of amateur hour. Wells already knew Bernard's name, after all. Why not just meet at his warehouse? But if Bernard wanted these pointless precautions, Wells wouldn't argue.

A woman with dyed blond hair turned the corner of the Rathaus, a pixie in faded blue jeans, taking short, quick tottering steps. The walk was so much like Exley's that for a second Wells thought the woman was Exley, that Exley had somehow found him here. He felt a flutter in his chest.

But of course Exley was rehabbing in Washington and didn't know where he was. And as the pixie stepped closer, Wells saw she was younger than Exley and had the wrong color eyes, brown instead of blue. She caught him looking and smiled, tentatively, almost flirting. He watched her until she disappeared, thinking of the lyrics of an old Gin Blossoms song. *You can't call it cheatin', 'cause she reminds me of you . . .*

A man walked across the plaza toward Wells. He was Turkish, but young, early twenties. Skinny under his winter clothes and pale for a Turk, faded. Three steps from Wells he stopped, cocked his head. He wore black glasses with deliberately thick frames. He looked like a programmer or a Web designer. Wells couldn't see this little guy doing business with Nigerian generals and building a nuke. And Bernard was much older, according to Shafer's dossier.

'You are Roland,' he said in English, with a heavy German accent.

'You Bernard?'

'My name is Helmut.' Said with an affected dignity.

'Helmut who?'

'No questions. Come. Please.' The kid's German manners taking over, undercutting his effort at toughness. Wells followed him along the Alsterfleet, a narrow canal that connected the Binnenalster with the Elbe. They stopped by a high-sided cargo van, a white Sprinter. The kid raised the back latch and stepped into the empty cargo compartment.

'Get in.'

Suddenly, Wells was sick of this game, sick of cutouts and fake passports, bodyguards and hard stares, pistols drawn and holstered. Helmut, Bernard, whoever you are, you're not going to win, he almost said. We'll find you, kill you hot or cold, blow up your houses, or send you to Gitmo for a trial that ends with you strapped to a gurney and a needle in your arm. Doesn't matter. You'll die either way. *You can't win.* September 11 was a fluke, you surprised us. It'll never happen again. And even if you do pull this off, somehow, even if somehow you manage to blow up Manhattan or London, what then? You think killing a million people is going to help the cause? You think you're going to roll back a thousand years of progress? What, exactly, are you trying to do? You think this is *Islam*? Wells had converted to Islam during his years in Afghanistan and Pakistan, and though he didn't pray much now, no one would ever convince him that these jihadi nihilists spoke for the religion, no matter how many surahs they quoted, how many pilgrimages they took.

'Get in?' Wells said. 'Or what?'

'Get in,' the kid repeated. But he couldn't keep his voice from breaking. And out of pity as much as anything else, pity and the knowledge that he could snap the kid in half, Wells stepped into the cargo compartment.

A few seconds later a gloved hand pulled down the back gate and locked him and the kid in darkness. Wells ought to have been worried but he wasn't. The van rolled off and he wondered whether he was overconfident, setting himself up for a fall. Locked in a truck, no backup, no tracking device. Not exactly textbook tradecraft. But if he couldn't take li'l Helmut, he deserved what he got.

The overhead light came on, a weak bulb. Helmut stood across the compartment, ten feet away, holding a pistol, a .45 ACP. Wells couldn't be a hundred percent sure in the dim light, but the pistol looked fake.

'Take off your clothes.'

Wells shook his head. He ought to feel some fear, a twinge at least, but he could only muster annoyance.

'We must be sure you're not wearing, you know, a microphone. A bug.'

'A bug. If you say so.' Wells had left his pistol in the hotel. He stripped, pulling off his jacket, sweater, T-shirt. He noticed again that he hadn't managed to lose all of the weight he'd put on for his trip to Moscow. Irritating. He stacked everything in a neat pile in a corner. The compartment was cold, air rushing in from a couple of holes punched in the floor, but Wells didn't mind.

He carefully unlaced his boots, slipped them off, his socks, his jeans, slowly, one leg at a time, Wells seeing now something he hadn't expected, Helmut's eyes shiny under the glasses.

'Take a good look.' Wells turning his flat Montana drawl into the clipped syllables of an African mercenary. He put his thumbs into the elastic band of his boxers and spun, a slow twist. As he did, Helmut took an involuntary step forward, his mouth half open.

Wells finished his turn and stepped forward and the kid stepped back as if Wells had threatened him, Wells understanding now. 'Underwear, too?' Wells said. 'Want the whole thing?'

'It's okay.' The kid tilted his head away, then back, trying to look and not to look.

'Better check, can't be sure, right? They have these little mikes, they tape them down there—' Wells slipped his fingers into the front of his shorts.

'Enough! Get dressed. Please.'

'Your call.' Wells had pushed this too far already. This guy was gay, and Wells would bet anything in the world that whoever was driving the truck didn't know it. He dressed quickly. 'How much longer?'

With Wells fully clothed, Helmut could meet his eyes again. 'I don't know exactly. Fifteen minutes. The city, there's traffic.'

'Who's driving?'

'Bernard.'

'Who's Bernard?' Wells knew he could ask the kid anything now and get an answer.

'My father.'

Wells shook his head, this job getting weirder and weirder. The guy looking to his son for help. Amateur hour. Or maybe just extreme compartmentalization, no one else Bernard could trust. 'You don't know what this is about, do you?'

Helmut shook his head. 'He asked me to bring you to the van, see if you had a wire.'

'And if I did?'

'I was supposed to knock on the front compartment.'

'Then?'

'I don't know. He said it would be an adventure, I could use it in one of my movies.'

'You make movies.'

'I'm trying. But, you know, it's very hard in Germany, all the real talent is in the United States, and the money, too, or even Berlin, I'd be better off there, but my father—'

Wells cut him off, not interested in this not-so-hard-luck story. 'The gun's fake, yeh?'

'Yes, from a film I made, a short, it won an award at the Hamburg festival, it's small, but it's something—'

And Helmut rattled on, to cover his embarrassment or his arousal or because like every other Hollywood wannabe in the world, he couldn't shut his mouth when he had an audience. Fortunately, the ride lasted only another fifteen minutes.

When the back gate rolled up again, they were inside a warehouse, mostly empty, big wooden crates scattered around the concrete floor. A middle-aged German man stood looking up at them. He wore leather gloves and held a pistol, a Glock, and this gun was real.

Helmut's eyes widened when he saw the pistol. He asked something, but the man waved the question away and barked at them in rapid-fire German.

'*Nein,*' Helmut said when Bernard was done. He stepped forward and Wells thought for a moment of keeping him in the van, using him as a shield, but then decided to let him go. Wells still wasn't sure how to play this, whether to let Bernard take the lead or not.

Helmut jumped out the back of the truck and disappeared from Wells's sight.

'Roland Albert,' Bernard said.

'Yes.'

'I'm Bernard,' he said in English. 'May I see your wallet?' These Germans, always so polite. Wells fished it out of his jeans, tossed it down. 'Your passport?' Wells sent that down, too. Bernard flipped through them. Apparently satisfied, he waved Wells down and tucked the pistol into his pants. A few seconds later, the van coughed to life and rolled away, leaving just Wells and Bernard and a Mercedes sedan that had been hidden behind the van.

Wells suddenly knew what to do. As the truck rumbled out of sight, he stepped forward and without a word jammed his heavy right fist into Bernard's gut, Bernard grunting softly, 'Ooh,' his mouth half-open, reaching for his Glock but not finding it. It was in Wells's left hand. Wells hit Bernard again, doubled him over this time; Bernard, almost sixty, was not a fighter.

'What was that, man? That bloody nonsense.' Wells didn't curse much, but Roland Albert did. 'You're lucky I don't kill you both, you and that poof son of yours. If we didn't have a friend in common, I would.'

Bernard tried to respond but could only manage a wheezy asthmatic cough.

'Amateur hour. This is amateur hour here. Bloody Helmut. Helmut and his fake poof gun.' Wells laughed, a choked half-snort, then cut himself off. He didn't want to overdo the bad-guy act. 'Your friends better be smarter than you. Let's get to it, mate? You want this stuff? You sure?'

Bernard stumbled to the Mercedes, short painful steps, and propped himself against its trunk. 'Yes.'

'How much?'

'Two hundred kilos.'

'How soon?'

'One week.'

'Christ almighty. Two hundred kilos of beryllium in a week. Why not ask for a couple MIGs, something easy?'

'I can pay.'

'Yeh. How much?'

'Three million euros.' About five million dollars. The guy had money from somewhere, another question Wells and the agency would have to answer.

'Ten.'

'Four.' Bernard coughed lightly. 'All I have.'

'Four may not get you two hundred, then, eh. We'll see. Now. I don't want to know nothing more about this. Not what you're doing with it. Not where or why. Nothing about your friends.'

'I don't know where it's going anyway.'

The flat denial stopped Wells. 'No?'

'We're not so stupid as you think.'

'Good then,' Wells said. 'Glad to hear it. Give me your mobile number.'

Bernard did.

'I'll call you in two days, three maybe, if it's possible.'

'You are not certain? Then you should know there are others looking, too.'

'Serious? Got the old Easter egg hunt going, do you?'

Bernard nodded.

'That doesn't make me happy. Best be careful. Too many on the trail, even the BND may sniff it out. Now. Two more items of business. Next time we meet in your office, yeh? And I need the saloon.'

'The saloon?'

Wells tapped the trunk of the Mercedes. 'For my troubles, chum. Whether or not I get your stuff, I keep the car.'

'*Nein.*'

'*Nein?* Try again.'

Bernard reached into his jacket, handed over the keys. Wells threw Bernard's Glock across the warehouse and clicked open the doors to the car, slipped in. 'Nice. Heated seats?'

'Of course.'

'Of course.' Wells slid the key into the ignition and rolled off, watching Bernard's face disappear in his rearview mirror. He could no longer discount the reality of the threat he and the agency faced, but he felt an unexpected elation. For the first time in months, he'd pulled off a mission exactly as planned. Bernard wouldn't question his bona fides again. And now Wells ought to be able to stall him for at least three days, probably more.

Meanwhile, though he preferred motorcycles, he had to admit the Mercedes was a great ride. He flicked on the wipers, flicked on the sedan's xenon headlights, and left Bernard and the warehouse behind.

But his mood faded by the time he found his way back to down-town Hamburg. Did Bernard really not know where his friends were building the bomb? Did he have another source of beryllium, or was he lying to bluff Wells into moving quickly?

Too many unknowns, only one certainty. Some-where, maybe just a few miles from here, maybe over the border in France or Poland, maybe on a different continent, a handful of determined men were trying to build a nuke. And though they might be wrong, they believed they were close.

CHAPTER 22

MOSCOW

The barricades at the Kutafya Tower rose and the long black Cadillac wheeled slowly up the ramp to the Kremlin, passing a handful of tourists braving the cold. Behind bullet-proof glass, Walt Purdy, the American ambassador, watched as the high brick walls loomed closer until they were all he could see. Whenever Purdy came up this ramp, he felt like Luke Skywalker approaching the Death Star and finding that he'd left his light saber back with Yoda.

For the whole of his twenty-five years at the State Department, Purdy had wanted to be ambassador to Russia. He'd found the country fascinating ever since he'd happened onto a Russian literature class his sophomore year at the University of Virginia. The assignments he'd taken in Belarus and Kazakhstan, the meetings where he'd swallowed his tongue and watched his bosses take credit for memos he'd written, the hours he'd spent perfecting his Russian, the fights he'd had with his wife when he insisted she learn the

339

language, too, they'd all been in the service of getting this job.

And he'd gotten it. The big donors had wanted cushier posts, in London and Paris and Tokyo and Buenos Aires. So the secretary of state had been able to go inside the foreign service and make the pick that the department's career officers wanted. Walter Mark Purdy. He'd been so thrilled when the call came that he hadn't slept for two days. Finally, he'd gotten his doctor to prescribe him some Ambien.

Be careful what you wish for. These days Purdy was sorry he'd ever gotten the job. He was a dog who'd been chasing a car for twenty-five years, and finally caught it, only to find . . . that he was a dog with his jaws clamped around a car's back bumper.

The Russians had never been easy. Now they were impossible. They were still seething about the nineties, when planeloads of well-meaning Ivy League political scientists and World Bank economists had come to Moscow to tell them how stupid and poor they were, how they needed to listen to their betters in Washington and London. In public, they were surly. In private, they were worse, deliberately nasty to anyone less senior than the secretary of state.

And Purdy knew now that he was the wrong man for the job. Dealing with the Russians successfully meant screaming back, making sure they knew they didn't have carte blanche. Walking out of meetings if necessary. But by nature and training, Purdy was a diplomat, not a screamer. He knew the burden that history had put on Russia, how for centuries the tsars and nobles had grown fat while the peasants starved. How in 1919 the people had destroyed their masters, only to see them replaced with a new set.

Purdy wanted to give the hard men across the table the benefit of the doubt. He wanted them to know that he'd visited all of Tolstoy's museums and read every word the man had ever written. Pushkin and Chekhov, too. He wanted them to see that he loved Russia, that he, and by extension the country he represented, were ready for a relation-ship based on mutual respect.

They couldn't have cared less.

He tried to change his tactics, toughen up, yell when they yelled. But his heart wasn't in it. He wasn't afraid of them, not exactly. He just hated these manufactured confrontations. But he knew each time he let them bully him in private, he was reinforcing their worst tendencies, goading them to believe that the United States could be bullied, too.

Purdy had always been level-headed, easygoing, reasonably happy, but after two years as ambassador he was more and more depressed. A political appointee, some billionaire Silicon Valley mogul with an ego to match his bankroll, would have made a better representative for the United States than he did. Even if the mogul didn't speak a word of Russian. Impossible but true. A political appointee would never have let himself get steamrolled. He would have screamed back. Then the Russians would have pulled out a bottle or ten of vodka and both sides would have drunk themselves silly and hugged each other good night.

He'd worked for this job his whole life, he'd gotten it, and now he'd found out he was wrong for it. It was a cosmic joke. The kind of irony that Tolstoy would have appreciated. Chekhov, anyway. Tolstoy wasn't much of an ironist.

And this assignment today. Another disaster waiting to happen. The Russians did *not* like to be questioned about the security of their nuclear arsenal. Not at all. The problems at Russian nuclear weapons depots were one of the issues that the geniuses of the 1990s had harped on the most. Even back then the generals in charge of Russia's strategic weapons had not enjoyed being told how to do their jobs. They were affronted by the American attitude that Russia was just another third-world country that couldn't be trusted with nukes. After all, Russia had successfully maintained its nuclear stockpile for more than fifty years, nearly as long as the United States.

The Kremlin grew even more suspicious when the American experts pressed for access to the weapons. The generals at the Ministry of Defense and Rosatom asked openly whether the United States wanted to leave Russia defenseless by disabling all Russia's nukes and missiles. Between 1998 and 2003, the United States had spent hundreds of millions of dollars to build a secure depot at the Mayak plant to store plutonium from disassembled nuclear weapons. The depot had concrete walls ten feet thick and could hold twenty-five tons of plutonium. By any measure, it was the most secure warehouse for nuclear materials in all of Russia. It was almost empty. The Russian government had no plans to entrust its nuclear weapons to a building that American engineers had designed. Purdy couldn't blame the Kremlin for being suspicious. If circumstances were reversed, the United States would hardly put all its nukes in a warehouse that Russia had designed. *Just trust us, boys. We're all on the same side. Really.*

Now Purdy was about to stir up this messy nest of national pride and national security again. And for what purpose? When the instructions to set up the meeting had come two days before, he'd told the secretary of state he'd be wasting his breath.

But he'd been overruled. Langley had come up with something that had made the White House sit up and take notice, and so Purdy got to put his dick on the block for the Russians to chop off. No. This time he was going to be tough. Really. He sighed and shuffled through the thin folder of papers he'd brought as the Cadillac rolled through the Trinity Gate Tower at the top of the ramp and entered the Kremlin proper.

Whatever his problems with the job, Purdy always loved this view. Unlike the White House, the Kremlin wasn't a single building. It was a complex of more than a dozen massive structures inside a

343

fort in the center of Moscow, on a hill that over-looked the Moscow River. To the south of the Trinity Gate were museums and churches open to tourists. North of the gate, toward Red Square, were government offices, closed to the public. No signs marked the two sides, but tourists who wandered toward the northern buildings were quickly warned back to the public areas.

On both sides the buildings were oversized and sturdy, covered with the snow that blanketed Moscow five months a year. This complex had survived invasions by Hitler and Napoleon, misrule by the tsars and Stalin. Some of the buildings inside were five hundred years old, mute testimony to the Russian capacity to endure. To endure foreign attackers, gulags and show trials, and endless mornings like this one, overcast and bitter, with a light snow falling from the gray sky. Somewhere behind the clouds the sun still shined, or so Purdy wanted to believe.

The Cadillac rolled on, alongside the massive Arsenal, which housed the elite soldiers who guarded the Kremlin, toward the yellow walls of the Senate, the gigantic triangular building where the president of Russia had his offices. Purdy gathered up his papers, wondering half-seriously if he should make a quick detour, pray at the Assumption Cathedral for a couple of minutes, light a candle to Saint George.

His dream job. *Hah.*

★   ★   ★

The Russians had promised Purdy a meeting with Anatoly Zubrov, the senior military adviser to President Medvedev. But it was General Sasha Davydenko, Zubrov's deputy, who awaited Purdy in a windowless conference room on the Senate's third floor. Davydenko was tall and trim and wore a flawless green uniform with enough combat decorations to stop a bullet in the unlikely event he was ever near one again.

'General Davydenko,' Purdy said. 'Will Anatoly be joining us?'

'He's been called into an urgent meeting. I assure you anything you tell me will reach him.'

Urgent meeting, right. He was probably on the beach in Brazil, and Davydenko hadn't even bothered to make an excuse for his absence. 'I was told he'd be here. This is unacceptable.'

Davydenko gave the tiniest of shrugs. 'Mr Ambassador. It's winter in Moscow. What do you expect?' Walk out, Purdy thought. Just go. But he'd come to relay a message, and the message had to be delivered.

'Unacceptable,' Purdy said again.

'Can my men get you anything? Perhaps a glass of tea? Green tea?' Davydenko raised his eyebrows, making the suggestion seem ridiculously effete. Purdy had asked for green tea once before in these offices. An instant mistake. He might as well have requested a bottle of baby formula.

'Thank you, but no. I'm sure you're busy—' Purdy gritted his teeth. Now he was apologizing for taking the time of a guy he hadn't even come to see? Davydenko nodded slightly, as though both men knew the enormity of the favor he was doing for Purdy by agreeing to this meeting.

'My government has an urgent request.'

'Yes.'

'We'd like an accounting, a full accounting, of the material that's gone missing. The nuclear material.'

'Yes?'

'The MoD originally said that five hundred grams of HEU had disappeared. Then, approximately three weeks ago, that estimate was increased to five kilograms. Where it remains. For now.'

'Yes.' Davydenko tilted his head away from Purdy, examined the ceiling, as if Purdy were barely worth listening to, a junior army officer rather than an emissary of the most powerful nation on earth. Purdy reminded himself of his vow in the Cadillac.

'General—' he snapped. 'Do I have your attention?'

Davydenko pursed his lips. He seemed faintly surprised that the mouse had roared, Purdy thought. Finally, he nodded. 'Of course, Mr Ambassador. You have all the attention you require. Go on.'

'As I said. Your country has not provided the United States or the international community with an accounting of the missing material. You haven't specified its enrichment. Nor have you given us any intelligence on the thieves. Do you believe

346

they're *mafiya*? Terrorists? Do they have the ability to use the material? Are they still within your borders, or have they escaped? Do you even have any answers to those questions?'

Purdy paused, hoping that Davydenko would speak. But the general had gone back to his earlier pose, looking at the ceiling.

'General,' Purdy said. 'I'm sure I don't need to tell you the urgency of ensuring that we never have a nuclear event on Russian or American soil. All we're asking is a candid assessment of the threat. You owe us that much.'

'The Russian government is fully able to handle this investigation, Mr Ambassador. If and when we need assistance, from the United States or NATO or anyone else, we will not hesitate to ask for it. I assure you.'

'Because we have learned that a person who may be affiliated with a terrorist group is urgently seeking a component crucial to building a nuclear weapon—'

'Excuse me?' Now Davydenko did look surprised. 'You have learned *what*?'

'Someone—'

'Who?'

'I can't say. But this person has offered several million dollars for a component of a nuclear weapon.'

'What component?'

'Again, I'm afraid I can't tell you.' Purdy allowed himself to smile. For the first time in a year, he had something on these guys. 'Ironic, isn't it, that your government has been so uncooperative and yet you demand whatever scraps of information we have.'

'What is ironic, Mr Ambassador, is that you presume to come into the Kremlin and tell us how to run our own investigation. And that you have information you refuse to share. This is not the way friends treat each other.'

'Are we friends?'

'This is not the way great nations build trust.' Davydenko banged his fist on the table and the empty glass in front of Purdy jumped. 'I ask again, do you have something to tell me?'

'I will tell you that the person who is attempting to buy this component is not here in Russia.'

'Do you have any reason to connect this person, assuming he exists at all, with our missing material?'

Purdy hesitated. 'Not at the moment.'

'*Not at the moment.*' Davydenko spoke with the sarcastic tone that senior Russian officials seemed able to deploy at any time. 'Perhaps the next moment, then? The one after that? Maybe tomorrow? Next week? Mr Ambassador, did you decide on this fool errand yourself? Did you miss seeing me so much? You come in here, you waste my time with this nonsense, no proof—'

'I speak for my government. And we want official assurance that you have full control of your arsenal.'

'Then it's your government that's wasting my

time.' Davydenko stood. 'We answer to our own president. Not to yours. Do we come to the White House demanding that you confirm that your nuclear weapons are safe in their silos? Do we? Do you play these games with the Chinese or the French or the British?'

'No.' Purdy knew he shouldn't answer, but he couldn't help himself.

'Correct. Only us. Always you treat us like children. We would never behave with such insolence. Yet you, you come in here and – Let me give you a piece of advice, Mr Ambassador. Drink your green tea and let us handle our investigation. As for this mythical person seeking this mythical component, if and when you decide to behave ethically and tell us what you know, I will be willing to listen.'

'Is that your official response, then?' Purdy wished he could come up with something snappier, but at least he was holding his ground.

'My official response is that I have business to attend to. My captain will show you out.'

When Purdy was gone, Davydenko walked down the hall to Zubrov's office, just outside the presidential suite, and relayed the conversation. Not that he needed to. The conference room was miked. Zubrov had been listening all along.

'Goddamn bombs,' Zubrov said. 'All these years we had all these missiles pointed at each other and nothing happened. We spent the fifties blowing up the Pacific, ten megatons at a time. Nothing. Now two assholes steal two two-hundred-kilo warheads and everything turns upside down. What do you think, General? This component, is it real?'

'That little man is too weak to lie. And they wouldn't have sent him unless they were worried.'

'Then why won't they tell us about this component?'

'I think what he said is true,' Davydenko said. 'They're angry that we haven't talked to them.'

'If they only knew how little we've found.'

'Is there anything new on that front?'

'I wish.' The Russian investigation had stalled completely. No one in Chelyabinsk had any idea what had happened to the Farzadov cousins. Not even Tajid's wife. The FSB had taken her into custody and spread the word to Muslim leaders in southern Russia that she wouldn't be released until Tajid turned himself in. But Tajid was still missing. Either he'd left Russia behind or he was dead. Meanwhile, the other men in the Mayak plant had been questioned, and questioned some more, by the best interrogators the FSB had. At this point, the FSB was satisfied that no one knew anything. And as for the men who must have helped the cousins outside the plant, no one knew anything about them either. No names, no descriptions, no fingerprints, no photographs. They were smoke.

'What about this component?' Zubrov said. 'What

could he be talking about? Some kind of detonator? A missile?'

'A detonator wouldn't be so expensive and I don't know why he'd call a missile a component.' Davydenko shook his head. 'Doesn't make sense. They don't need any additional components to use these bombs. Just the codes. And they don't have those. I'm not even sure this is related to the theft.'

'Call Pavlov' – the Rosatom deputy director – 'see if he has any ideas.'

'Yes, sir.'

'Thank you, General. Let me know.' Zubrov dismissed Davydenko with a salute. When the general had closed the door, Zubrov ran a hand over his thick jowls. He couldn't remember the last time he'd had a drink before noon, but today he wanted one. He wondered if he ought to tell President Medvedev that they should come clean with the United States, acknowledge the theft. But Medvedev would never agree. He wouldn't accept losing face that way. Not unless he was sure that he had no other choice. And he did have a choice. Rosatom and the generals insisted that the weapons couldn't be used without the codes. They'd said a dozen times: no codes, no bombs.

But what if all these fancy green uniforms were wrong? After all, these thieves had gotten into a depot that was supposed to be unbreakable. What if they had some way of cracking the codes?

Or getting around them? Then what? Suppose they blew up half of Manhattan, killed a million Americans? And what if the United States linked the weapons to the Russian arsenal? Would the White House demand that Moscow be destroyed in turn?

The engineers had better be right about their damn bombs, Zubrov thought. They better not have missed anything. Or else the United States and Russia might be headed for a war that would make all the others that had ever happened look like soccer friendlies. Damn the bombs. Damn the engineers, the physicists, and mutually assured destruction. 'Damn it all,' Zubrov said to the empty room.

Zubrov opened the bottom drawer of his big wooden desk, where he kept a bottle of Stoli vodka, a ceremonial gift from the president on his first day as military adviser. He reached down for it, pulled out the bottle and a dusty glass, cleaned the glass with his shirtsleeve and unscrewed the bottle for the first time. Vodka kept forever, another of its many good qualities. He poured himself a healthy shot, though not too healthy. He would have to call Medvedev after this drink. He raised his glass to the empty room, but he couldn't think of a toast. He drank it down in silence.

CHAPTER 23

The uranium-235 that Nasiji and Bashir and Yusuf had extracted from the warhead didn't look like much. A hollow sphere of gray-black metal, cut into jagged slices like an orange rind, the pieces in a plastic box on a workbench. Jumbled among them was a second sphere, solid, not much larger than an oversized grape – the 'spark plug' of U-235 that had formed the center of the secondary.

Nasiji weighed the pieces on a digital scale beside the box, first one by one, then all together. Thirty-two kilos – seventy pounds – in all. Nasiji stared at the scale, a muscle twitching in his jaw, a vein pulsing madly in his forehead.

'We'll work it out,' Bashir said. 'We're close.'

But Nasiji didn't respond. Until, finally, he put the pieces back into the box and ran his hands through his hair and smiled. His change of mood was as disconcerting as his fury had been. *Were you pretending to be crazy then*, Bashir wanted to ask, *or are you pretending to be sane now?* But he supposed he knew the answer. None of them were sane. How could they be? They were building a nuclear bomb. In a stable.

Is this right? For the first time since he'd gotten involved in this scheme, that simple question came to Bashir. Was it his place to kill hundreds of thousands of Americans, the same Americans he tried to save on the operating table?

Then he thought of his uncle, in that awful prison at Tora. Egyptians had killed him, but the United States was responsible. The Americans were the puppetmasters all over the Muslim world. Saddam Hussein had been one of their puppets, too. As long as he did what they wanted, fought wars against the Iranians, they didn't care what he did to his people. But when he stood up to them, they came after him. This place, the United States, had killed millions of Muslims. A bomb like this was the only way to stop them, to even the score. It wouldn't be pretty, but no war ever was. So Bashir forced the question out of his mind.

He hoped it wouldn't come back.

The image played over and over in Nasiji's mind, a video he couldn't turn off: the crate falling out of the lifeboat and sinking into the Atlantic. If only they'd held on to the second bomb. Instead . . . when he looked at the numbers on the scale, he couldn't help but feel as though the devil was working to thwart him.

Again he gathered up the pieces and scattered them on the scale and looked at the black numbers staring at him: 32.002 kilograms. The Russians had been precise, he'd give them that.

'Thirty-two kilos,' Yusuf said. 'What does that mean?'

'It's not enough, that's what it means.'

'Please, Sayyid,' Yusuf said. 'I know you explained before, but if it works for the Russian bomb, why do we need more?'

'Yusuf—'

'I'm just trying to understand.'

'The secondary, the bomb we took apart, the pieces fit together into a globe, right? And when the first bomb, the primary, goes off, the secondary gets smashed together, becomes *supercritical*' – that word in English.

'Super-critic-al?' Yusuf sounded like he was auditioning, badly, for a part in *Mary Poppins*.

'I told you before. Supercritical means the explosion is speeding up, more and more energy is being released. The Russians, the Americans, they've figured out how to smash the material very fast, and that means they need less material to cause an explosion. Ever since the 1940s, we've known this is how it works.'

'But we can't smash it together as fast as they can.'

'That's right. The gun that we're using, it will shoot the uranium piece at four hundred meters a second' – a quarter-mile a second, nine hundred miles an hour.

'Isn't that fast?'

'Compared to how quickly the fission reaction happens, it's slow. So we need more uranium, a bigger sphere, to make sure the bomb will go off.'

'But if it's so complicated, why don't we use the Russian bomb?'

'I should just go back to Iraq, leave this to you.'

'Sayyid—'

'I tell you again. The secondary won't go off without the primary. And the primary, I promise you, it's been engineered so it won't go off unless it's been properly armed. With those famous codes. And we can't use our own explosive to set it off either. You can't just paste dynamite around those bombs and push a big handle. The explosive has to be placed and detonated just so, or the bomb won't go off. We don't have the equipment. Synchronous detonators and high-grade explosive and a lathe that can cut to the tolerances we need. And even if we could buy them, I don't know if we have the skill to use them. It would take us six months practicing and testing to be sure. You want to live here for six months, hope no one notices?'

Nasiji pointed at the recoilless rifles stacked against the wall. 'The kind of bomb I want to make, it's so much easier. Mold the pieces into the right shapes, two masses, both just subcritical, fire one at the other. As long as you have enough material and you fire it fast enough, it's certain to work. With sixty kilos, it would have been a joke. We could have done it in a week. Now . . .'

'But isn't there a half way?' Yusuf said. 'We have half as much material as we wanted. Can't we make a bomb half as big?'

'That's not how the physics work,' Nasiji said. 'Trust me.' Why hadn't he found a way to detonate the bomb they'd stolen, instead of leaving himself in this mess? Why hadn't he listened to Bernard and Bashir and sent the bombs to New York on a container ship, instead of being tricky and sending them through Newfoundland? Why hadn't he made sure that both crates were properly locked down in the life-boat? He was so stupid. He had failed his father, failed his family, failed his people. His father . . .

He felt his anger build again and walked out of the stable and into the cold night air. He leaned against an oak tree and craned back his head and looked through the naked branches at the stars, the ultimate nuclear-power plants.

Away from the scale's figures and Yusuf's questions, his stomach began to unclench. He was being too hard on himself. Thirty-two kilograms was a massive amount of enriched uranium, more than anyone outside a weapons laboratory had ever seen. Little Boy had been sixty-four kilos, but Little Boy had been made from 80 percent enriched uranium – not nearly as pure as the material they had. He hadn't tested these pieces yet, but they were surely 93.5 percent enriched, standard weapons-grade.

At that level of purity, even a simple sphere of

uranium, with no reflector, no compression, would go critical and produce a nuclear explosion at a size of about fifty kilograms. They were short, but they were in the ballpark.

Nasiji wondered if Bernard could somehow deliver the beryllium without getting busted. Doubtful. But even without beryllium, they could try a steel reflector. Steel wouldn't be as effective as beryllium, but it would help. Maybe a double-gun assembly, to achieve maximum acceleration, if Yusuf and Bashir could somehow handle the welding.

With thirty-two kilograms, putting this bomb together wouldn't be easy. But it might not be impossible, and he knew the tricks. Slowly, over sixty-five years, first the physics and then the engineering details of building these bombs had leaked out.

Yusuf emerged from the stable, walked up to him tentatively.

'Sayyid, I must say this. I'm sorry for my stupid questions. It's confusing, that's all.'

'It's I who should apologize,' Nasiji said. 'My temper—'

'And I wanted to say, if it's really impossible with this much, we'll get more. We'll leave this here, go back to Russia, find another martyr.'

Nasiji smiled at the stars. He couldn't help but admire Yusuf's attitude, though they couldn't get within a hundred kilometers of a stockpile now.

'No need, Yusuf. We'll make do. I have some ideas.'

'Is it possible?'

'God willing. We've come too far to quit.'

The next morning, Nasiji took his physics and engineering textbooks and a sketchpad and Bashir's laptop and shut himself up in the farmhouse basement beside the Ping-Pong table. Bashir tried to follow, but Nasiji shooed him away.

'Tell Thalia to leave my lunch at the top of the stairs. Dinner too, most likely.'

'You don't want help?'

'Not for this.'

'All right, Sayyid. But you're going to see us anyway.'

'Why's that?'

'There's no toilet in the basement. Unless you plan to bring down a bucket.'

At first, Nasiji spent hours sketching out possible ways to set off the plutonium primary inside the Iskander. After all, as Yusuf had pointed out, they already had a bomb. Why not use it? But finally he gave up. He couldn't figure out a foolproof way to trigger the explosives attached to the bomb, and creating a new trigger, though theoretically possible, would take too long.

That night he went back to his original plan, the gun-type uranium bomb, the Little Boy design. One piece of enriched uranium was molded into a piece that looked like a length of pipe. A second, smaller piece was shaped into a solid cylinder that fit snugly within the larger piece. Both pieces were subcritical, meaning they were each too small to detonate on their own.

The solid cylinder was placed at the end of the gun barrel. Then the pipe-shaped piece was shot at it, creating a single piece that contained a super-critical mass of uranium, big enough to set off a nuclear explosion. The Americans had placed a neutron initiator, a few grams of beryllium and polonium, at the center of the bomb to make sure the detonation happened on schedule. But the initiator wasn't strictly necessary. The uranium would detonate on its own even without it. As Nasiji had told Yusuf, the great virtue of the design was its simplicity. If the bomb came together quickly enough and had enough uranium, it couldn't help but go off.

What Nasiji hadn't explained to Yusuf was that placing metal around the uranium core would make the explosion happen more efficiently, thus allowing the use of less uranium. The metal was called a reflector, because it bounced the neutrons, causing the chain reaction back at the exploding core. Beryllium was the ideal material for the reflector. A sphere of uranium surrounded by beryllium could produce a nuclear explosion with as little as sixteen kilograms of uranium – a crit-ical mass less than one-third that of an unreflected sphere.

So, as an insurance policy, Nasiji had asked Bernard six months ago to try to get a cache of beryllium. But Bernard had reported back that the stuff couldn't be had, not without taking a huge risk, possibly alerting the German authorities. Nasiji had told him to back off, not push too hard. With two warheads, Nasiji figured he would have enough material to make a bomb of his own.

Now, though, they were short of uranium. Beryllium was the shortest route to making a full-sized bomb. Nasiji had asked Bernard to try again. And only yesterday, in a coded e-mail message, Bernard reported he'd made contact with a man who might be able to provide the stuff. But Nasiji wasn't at all sure Bernard would come through. In the meantime, they'd have to plan on using a simpler material, something they could pick up in Rochester or Buffalo without attracting too much attention. Tungsten carbide would probably be too much for Bashir to forge. In the end, steel would probably have to do. With that thought, Nasiji spent several hours calculating the optimal thickness of a steel reflector.

The calculation was complex, but the necessary variables were available: the neutron multiplication number for steel, the average number of collisions before capture, the likelihood of a neutron emerging from a collision. He found in the end that the tamper ought to be about twenty centimeters thick – about what he would have guessed before he'd done any of the math.

Finally, he designed the uranium core and the steel tamper around it. Basically, the bomb would look like a cannonball with a hole on the top. They would weld the artillery barrel into the hole and then fire the uranium plug down the barrel into the hole. The plug would slide over the uranium core in the middle of the barrel, and – *Boom*.

At 3 a.m. that night, Nasiji was done. He had a basic design, not fancy, but a start. Bashir and Yusuf could get to work forging the molds for the reflector and the core.

When Nasiji emerged from the stairs, blinking in the light of the kitchen, he expected to be alone. But they'd waited up for him. Tried to, anyway. Bashir dozed on a rickety wooden chair, a half-eaten plate of hummus and baked chicken on the table before him. Yusuf curled up on the rug under the kitchen table.

They jerked up as he walked in.

'It's done,' Nasiji said.

'What's done?' Bashir said, running a hand across his mouth to wipe away the sleep.

'I've finished the design.'

'But . . . you said last night it wasn't possible.' This from Yusuf.

'I can't guarantee it will work. We'll see.' Over and over, Nasiji had run the numbers, tried to calculate whether the thirty-two kilos they had would be enough for a chain reaction inside a steel reflector. But the equations required a level of detail about the subatomic properties of iron and uranium that he didn't have, and the math got messy. Forty kilos would be enough, he was sure. Twenty wouldn't. Thirty-two? They wouldn't know until they pulled the trigger.

CHAPTER 24

A solid bronze knocker shaped like a lion sat in the center of the front door of Bernard Kygeli's house. Wells swung the knocker against the heavy black wood, picked it up and clanged it again.

'Hullo! Anyone home!' he shouted. 'It's Roland.'

'*Ja?*' a woman's voice said. Then a few questions in German. A woman's face, framed by a headscarf, peeked out at Wells. He was dressed for the occasion, holding a briefcase and wearing black gloves and a new gray suit he'd bought at the fancy department store downtown.

'I don't speak German. *Sprechen Deutsch nicht!* And I'm freezing my stones off out here.' Wells was hardly exaggerating. For days, the weather in Hamburg and Warsaw had been miserable, a hard wind driving sheets of rain and sleet horizontally through the streets. Wells knocked again, hard. 'Stupid woman. Is Helmut home?'

'Helmut?' The door opened a notch, revealing a middle-aged woman who wore a long-sleeved jacket that was tailored, black with gold filigree, modest but stylish. Wells put his shoulder to the door and popped it open. Its edge caught the woman and she stumbled back and dropped to a knee. Wells stepped inside and shoved the door shut. The woman yelled at him in German, less frightened than angry. He pulled her up, a hand under her elbow, and put a finger to his lips.

'Shh! I'm not here to hurt you.' Wells wasn't sure what he would do if the woman didn't quiet down. But she did. Her stare was angry but not quite furious, as if she thought he might have the right to enter the house.

'Where's Helmut? Upstairs?' Wells pointed at the stairs.

'Helmut—' she pointed at the door.

'What about Bernard?'

'Bernard—' again at the door.

'Good, then,' Wells said. 'Now be a decent girl and get me a Hefeweizen.' He pantomimed raising a bottle to his lips. Once again, Wells found the character of Roland Albert, beryllium-dealing Rhodesian mercenary, only too easy to take on. A shrink, or Exley, would no doubt have a field day watching him put his conscience aside for an hour and order this woman around. Bad guys had all the fun.

'*Hefeweizen? Bier? Nein.*'

'Right. You people don't drink. Fine. I'll make myself at home then.' Wells reached into his suit pocket, found the handcuffs he'd tucked inside it, then reconsidered. 'Whyn't you show me around? Otherwise I'll have to hook you to a doorknob or some such nonsense.' Wells pantomimed that he wanted to look around the house.

She seemed to understand and walked beside him as he wandered through the first floor. She was far more relaxed than most American or European women would be under similar circumstances. Wells had seen this passivity before in women in Afghanistan. As far as he could tell, the attitude came both from fatalism and a deep-in-the-bones understanding that whatever Wells wanted with her husband was men's business and didn't include her. The average self-respecting Western woman would have a very hard time reaching the same conclusion.

The house was expensively furnished, Persian rugs, wood-paneled walls, leather couches and bookcases loaded with texts in German and Turkish. But there were no photographs or art of any kind, aside from a few framed Quranic verses and a single photo of the Kaaba, the black stone at the center of Mecca. The lack of artwork was a sign of Bernard's piety. Observant Muslims believed that the Quran forbade the display of images, which competed unnecessarily with Allah's majesty. That prohibition didn't apply to televisions. A massive Sony flat-panel was tacked to the living room wall.

Bernard's wife – Wells still didn't know her name – acted up only once, when Wells started to open a door at the back of the living room. '*Nein*,' she said. She wagged a finger at him. '*Verboten*.'

'*Verboten?* You funning me?' Wells pressed on the

door's handle. Locked, with a simple push-button mechanism. He slipped a credit card from his wallet and popped it.

Inside, a small office, neatly organized, two file cabinets and a fine brown desk, a map of the world with shipping routes outlined from Hamburg to Istanbul and Lagos and Accra and Cape Town and Dubai, though none to the United States. Two thick leather-bound volumes with ships etched into their covers, one called *Seerecht*, the other *Gesetz von der See*. Wells figured they had something to do with maritime law. A coffee cup with the logo of the Penn State University soccer team, the Nittany Lions. Wells picked it up, looked at it curiously, set it down. A fancy pen-and-pencil set. The base for an IBM ThinkPad, though the laptop itself was nowhere in sight. A handful of papers stacked in a tray. Wells leafed through them, finding nothing of interest except a bill from a New York law firm, Snyder, Gonzalez, and Lein – $32,000 for 'insurance recovery.' Bernard's wife watched him crossly from the doorway. Evidently she'd been warned never to enter the office.

Wells tugged on the filing cabinets and was slightly surprised when they opened. Inside, neat rows of hanging folders, stacked by year. One cabinet appeared to have nothing but German tax records, the other invoices for shipments and customs forms. No nuclear weapons blueprints, though the tax forms were plenty frightening. Wells lifted the cabinets, wiggled them forward an inch and peeked behind them, ran his hand under the desk, then ducked his head under it to examine its bottom for hidden compartments. He pulled the map off the wall, checked for a safe. Nothing anywhere. The floor and walls seemed solid, though he'd need much more time to be sure and he didn't want to press his luck. The real prize was the computer and Bernard was keeping that close. 'Let's go,' he said. He left the door to the office open, but Bernard's wife closed it.

In the living room, Wells sat on the couch, stretched his feet on the glass coffee table. From his new briefcase, he extracted two bricksized blocks of light gray metal carefully wrapped in plastic. Five kilograms – about eleven pounds – of beryllium each. Wells laid the bricks on the coffee table. The metal came straight from a Department of Energy stockpile in Oak Ridge, Tennessee, though it of course bore no markings. Wells had told Shafer that he needed to get Bernard enough beryllium to buy some time, convince the guy he was serious. Shafer had gotten Duto to sign off after the weapons designers at Los Alamos agreed that ten kilograms of beryllium wouldn't be enough to make a meaningful difference to the bombmakers even if Bernard somehow got it to them.

Wells tapped the bricks. 'Don't touch,' he said to Bernard's wife. '*Verboten*. I'm serious. Got it?' Beryllium flaked into small particles, and though the metal was safe to touch, it was toxic if it was inhaled. Even small amounts of it caused a nasty inflammatory reaction in the lungs.

She nodded. 'Good,' he said. 'Tell Bernard I'll call him tonight.' Wells pantomimed putting a phone to his ear.

Wells stepped into the Mercedes he was now thinking of as his own – or at least Roland Albert's – and cruised past a Deutsche Telekom service van parked about fifty yards from the house.

Twenty minutes later, he left the Mercedes with the valet at the Kempinski, pulled out his satellite phone. Shafer picked up on the second ring.

'Ellis. I thought you said no static posts.' Wells had insisted that he work entirely apart from the BND agents monitoring Bernard's movements. But Shafer had assured him that the Germans would be cautious. Rather than watching the house from fixed positions, they would rely on drive-bys with a dozen anonymous cars, each passing the house every fifteen minutes or so.

'I did.'

'Then why is a telco van sitting down the block from Bernard Kygeli's house? Subtle.'

'Maybe somebody wants DSL.'

'Ellis—'

'I'll look into it.'

'Anything else I should know?' The BND had tapped Bernard's phones – home, cell, work – and thrown a replicator on his fiber-optic connection that allowed them to see the Web traffic that came into and out of his house and office. His trash was being searched and his tax records for the last decade examined.

'He may be an amateur, but he's cautious,' Shafer said. 'Two days ago, he bought a prepaid cell, made a couple of calls, tossed it in the river. Yesterday he went into an Internet café off the Reeperbahn for three minutes, but he was gone before we knew what terminal he was at. And that traffic isn't stored anyway. I don't think he's in charge. He's just checking in with whoever has the stuff, letting them know he's working on getting the beryllium.'

'How about the money?'

'The business looks legit. And there's been no transfers from Dubai or Saudi or anyplace. But we don't see anything like four million euros loose. In fact, it looks like he's been slipping a little bit the last year or two. We don't know why. But his bank balances have been trending down. Anyway, he's got a million-five stashed away in the accounts we can see, plus the house is worth another million. If he's got it, it's in a Swiss account or a safe box somewhere. Or maybe he's not planning to pay you at all.'

Was Bernard crazy enough to plan on killing Roland Albert after he got the beryllium? 'I can't see it,' Wells said. 'He's not a fighter.'

'Pride goeth, John. You leave him the package?'

'Yes. Took a look around his house, too. See if you can find any connection to a law firm in

New York. Snyder, Gonzalez, and Lein, it's called. They did some work for him last year. Something to do with insurance.'

'New York? Weird. All right, spell it for me.'

Wells did.

'I'll check it out,' Shafer said. 'Be safe.'

'Aren't I always?' Wells hung up.

He went back to the Kempinski, worked out for almost two hours, weights plus eight miles on the treadmill. He showered, dressed, reached for his phone to call Bernard, then changed his mind and decided to let the man stew for a few hours more. He lay on the bed and napped—

And woke to a heavy knock on his door.

'Yeh?' Even muzzy-headed with sleep, Wells remembered that in this room he was Roland Albert.

'*Polizei!*'

'What do you want?'

Rap! Rap! 'Open the door, Mr Albert!' This in English.

The voice sounded like Bernard's. Wells wished he could look through the peephole, but doing that was an easy way to get a bullet in the eye. Whoever the guy was, Wells wanted him out of the corridor before he attracted other guests' attention. Wells moved silently to the door, grabbed his Glock, unlocked the door, and in one smooth motion pulled it open with his right hand while holding the pistol across his body with his left.

Bernard stood in the corridor, pistol at his side. He tried to raise it, but Wells lunged through the doorway, knocked his arm up and back, and pinned him against the opposite wall of the corridor as quietly as he could.

Wells jerked Bernard's arm down so the pistol pointed at the carpeted floor of the corridor. 'Drop it,' Wells said.

Bernard hesitated. 'Before I break your arm, you bloody idiot.' The pistol landed with a soft plop on the carpet. Wells kicked it away. 'Now get inside.'

Bernard sat on Wells's bed, his shoulders hunched, arms folded, face an angry red. Wells had given him back his pistol after tossing the clip. The gun, the same Glock Bernard had carried in the warehouse, sat uselessly beside him.

'What do you think you're doing? Eh?'

'You come to my house—'

'Look at me, Bernard.'

Bernard turned his head toward Wells, slowly, as if the motion itself were painful.

'That's twice you've pointed that gun at me. You idiot. *Twice*. And twice I've let you live. I promise if you do it a third time, I won't be so polite. I swear on Allah, Muhammad, all the sheikhs in Saudi Arabia.'

'You insult my wife.'

'I didn't touch your wife.'

'You involved her in this. *Kaffir*,' Bernard

muttered under his breath, the Arab word for infidel.

'*Kaffir*? You think I don't know what that means? I've been in this game a long time. Watch your mouth.'

'Why did you come to my house?'

'I wanted to see who I was dealing with. You understand? Wanted to make sure you didn't have a medal from the BND on your office wall. And you weren't home, so I took a look-see. I didn't hurt your wife, did I? Instead of coming over here, trying to threaten me, you ought to thank me. You saw the present I left you? Ten kilos, 99.7 percent pure. Assay it if you don't believe me. I'll get you the rest in a week, maybe less.'

'Yes?'

'But first tell me how you figured out I was staying here.'

Bernard smiled. 'You're under your own name. This was the eighth hotel I called. When I got here, I told the concierge I was an old friend, wanted to surprise you. I gave him a hundred euros.'

'Not bad. For an amateur. Where's my money?'

'Your money?'

'I've shown you I can come through. It's your turn now. I want two million euros. Three million more on delivery.'

'I only have four. I told you.'

'Five or no go. Your boys can't get you more?' Wells hoped Bernard might give him a hint where the money was coming from. But Bernard only nodded.

'Five, then.'

'See. Easy enough. Five million euros, twenty-five thousand a kilo. And I absolutely need two now.'

'One.'

'Two or—' Wells pointed to the door.

Bernard looked at the pistol beside him. But 'When?' was all he said.

'By tomorrow night. Wire transfer. I'll get you the account number.'

'And the metal—'

'Within the week. But don't come looking for me again, Bernard. I won't be in this hotel, and I won't be under my name. And if I see you again when I don't expect you' – Wells tapped his pistol – 'I'm going to assume the worst.'

'I understand.' Bernard picked up his unloaded pistol and walked out.

'It's been a pleasure doing business with you,' Wells said after the door closed and Bernard's footsteps disappeared down the carpeted hall. 'Yes, indeed.'

CHAPTER 25

As a rule, offices at Langley were neat. Stacks of paper were security hazards, not to mention evidence of an untidy mind that might reach a conclusion at odds with what the rest of the agency wanted to hear.

Shafer's office was an exception, of course. Paper covered his desk, and files were piled on the coffee table and around the couch: estimates of China's military capability, primers on nuclear weapons design, a classified analysis of recent Russian attempts to penetrate the CIA. As Exley poked her head in, she was happy to see that most of the piles looked just as they had six weeks earlier, the last time she'd been in here. She limped in, one careful step at a time, and pushed aside a file marked 'Top Secret/SCI' to sit on the couch. She held up the file.

'Ellis. Shouldn't this be locked up?'

'Please. It's a report on this antimissile system the Jews are putting together.' Shafer, Jewish himself, insisted on referring to Israel as 'the Jews.'

'So?'

'So it was in the *Times* three weeks ago. And on

Debka' – a Web site that focused on the Israeli and Arab militaries – 'two weeks before that. You know what I think. We'd be better off if we stopped stamping 'Top Secret' on every page of dreck we write. By the way, you look great, Jennifer.

'I mean, honestly, you look like crap, like you're in agony when you twist that leg wrong, but it's good to see you. Really good.'

'You always know just how to make a girl smile, Ellis.'

'Sorry.' Shafer gave her the abashed smile of a five-year-old caught with a handful of Oreos, a face she'd seen him make before, more than once.

'Did you ask me to come in just to make me feel good about myself?'

'I need your brain.'

Exley had a glimmer of how Wells must feel. *I try to get out, but they keep pulling me back in.* Even before the shooting, she'd been trying to escape this madness-making job, seeing if she might convince Wells to escape with her. Maybe not all the way out. Maybe they could move to the Farm for a couple of years, train the bright young things who would be the next generation to keep the world safe for democracy and capitalism. Though not necessarily in that order.

Then Kowalski had reached out and touched them and Wells had proven what she'd always known, that he couldn't be housebroken no matter how hard she tried. She'd begged him to wait, and even so he'd bared his fangs and counterattacked as instinctively as a pit bull tossed into a ring. Maybe Wells was so confident in his own ability to get through the worst situations that he didn't see the danger he faced. Or maybe he simply didn't care whether he lived or died.

But she did. If not for herself, then for her kids. When she saw them at GW Hospital the day after the shooting, she couldn't stop crying. Twice in two years, they'd stood beside her hospital bed and held her hand and told her they loved her and everything would be all right. As if they were responsible for her and not the other way around. Whether God or fate or sheer luck had kept her alive, she didn't know. But she couldn't take more chances. She couldn't imagine not seeing her kids again. That day, she'd promised herself she would quit.

But quitting meant giving up Wells forever, and she couldn't imagine that either. To take her mind off the impossible choice, she'd pressed her rehab as hard as she could. If her nurses asked her to walk, she went until her legs and her spine burned and she had to lie down to recover. If they asked for fifty leg lifts, she gave them a hundred. They'd told her more than once that she wasn't helping herself by pushing so hard. But the pain distracted her from thinking about Wells.

This morning, Shafer had called and asked her to come in. He'd made the request as casually as if he were asking her if she wanted an extra ticket to a Nationals game. Even so she'd hesitated.

But then her curiosity took over; she wondered how being back would feel. As she and her bodyguards rolled by the truck-bomb barriers that guarded the main entrance to Langley, she was overcome with a strange nostalgia, as though she were visiting her old college campus for the first time a year after graduating. She loved this place and understood these people and wanted to be one of them and yet she didn't feel connected to them.

Now, in Shafer's office, Exley felt different, more engaged. Shafer was her rock at the agency. He'd hardly changed in all the years she'd known him. He was rumpled, energetic, a bad dresser and messy eater, but most of all brilliant, sometimes too brilliant. For years, she'd wondered if Shafer deliberately played up his eccentricities to add to his mystique as an absentminded genius. Today, for example, a big coffee stain covered his right shirt cuff. Could he really have done that accidentally?

Shafer had never fit in with the agency's buttoned-up bureaucracy. He'd been on the verge of being marginalized before Exley and Wells saved New York. Now he and Duto had reached an accommodation. Duto let him and Wells and Exley run their own shop. In return, Shafer did his best to control Wells. So far, the deal had worked for both sides, though Exley didn't believe it would last. Shafer didn't trust Duto, and the feeling was mutual.

'You need my brain,' Exley said now. 'Don't you know I'm done?'

'Just desk work. I'll bet after six weeks at home, you're ready for some excitement. Take your mind off things. So—' and before she could object, Ellis filled her in on the missing uranium, and then on the way that Kowalski had connected Wells with Bernard Kygeli.

'John and Kowalski are buddies now?' Exley said when Shafer finished.

'Strange world,' Shafer said. 'But Bernard's a dead end. The BND, the Hamburg police, nobody has anything on him. He pays his taxes, keeps his Mercedes polished. He probably buys Girl Scout cookies, if they have Girl Scouts in Germany—'

'I get it,' Exley said. 'Did they talk to the harbormaster?'

'The port authorities don't know much about him. He's been there a long time but he's small-time and it's a giant port and he's never been in trouble, so . . .'

'What about customs records?'

'Nothing unusual. Cabinets and rugs from Turkey. Also he sent some silverware two months ago from Poland to South Africa. The Poles checked and the factory confirms the sale.'

'He ship to the United States?'

'Not so far as we can tell.'

Exley could hardly believe how easily she was slipping back into this routine. But a few minutes of thinking out loud didn't obligate her to come back forever. Anyway, Shafer was right. No one had ever gotten shot at a desk at Langley. 'What about the general?' she said. 'This Nigerian that Bernard bought the AKs for? Any chance he's in on it?'

'Doubt it. Those look like real deals. Then when Bernard was looking for beryllium, he went to Kowalski since he had the connection already.'

'And we can't figure out where he's getting his money?'

'He makes a decent living legitimately through the business. We could go in, turn his house upside down—'

'But then he'll know we're looking and—'

'He'll tip the guys who are making the bomb. Exactly. We can't take a chance on spooking him. Same reason we haven't talked to any of his workers or gone at that law firm in New York yet. We could try to talk to them quietly, pull the national security card, but if they call him we're in trouble.'

'What law firm in New York?'

'I didn't mention this?' Shafer explained how Wells had gone to Bernard's house and found the bill from Snyder, Gonzalez, and Lein.

'Have we checked his ships?'

'He doesn't own ships. At least they're not in his corporate record or registered in Germany or anywhere else we can find. We looked. And the harbormaster didn't mention them.'

'Come on, Ellis. He has a decent-sized ex-im business, he makes regular runs, he must own a boat or two. They're not in his name, that's all. Some shell company in the Caymans or Gibraltar is holding them, with a lawyer as the corporate nominee.'

'And you think that law firm in New York is the connection?'

'I don't know,' Exley said. 'But we ought to pull the suits they've filed, see what turns up.'

'I missed you,' Shafer said.

Besides New York, Snyder, Gonzalez, and Lein had offices in Baltimore and Miami. The firm specialized in representing ship and aircraft owners against insurance companies and boatyards. Most of the suits were straightforward, and Exley didn't see any connections to Hamburg. Certainly none to Bassim Kygeli. By the end of the afternoon, her back was aching so badly that she'd been reduced to lying on Shafer's floor. 'All right, Ellis,' she said. 'I'm not sure I can stand, but it's time for me to go.'

'Give it a few more minutes. Don't you like reading about all these rich guys whining because they ordered a helicopter pad for their yacht and got an extra Jacuzzi or vice versa?'

Another half-hour crawled by. And then Shafer stood and clapped his hands. 'Check this out. Two years ago, our friends at Dewey, Cheatem, and Howe filed suit against AIG. On behalf of a company called YRL Ltd.'

'AIG, the world's biggest insurance company?'

'The one and only,' Shafer said. 'YRL looks to be a shell. Based in the Caymans. But the suit was filed in New York because that's where AIG is headquartered. YRL wants AIG to pay a four-million-dollar insurance claim for a freighter called the *Greton*, registered out of Liberia. About two years ago, the *Greton* burned up off the Nigerian coast.'

'Anybody die?'

'Doesn't look that way. Anyway, AIG won't pay. It says the *Greton* didn't have a decent fire-suppression system or an adequately trained crew. Basically that it was an accident waiting to happen.'

'So who won?'

'The lawyers. Two years gone, a dozen claims and counterclaims already and they've barely started discovery. By the time they're done, they're going to spend more on the suit than the boat was ever worth. But—' Shafer stepped out from behind his desk and stood beside Exley and jabbed at the filing he was reading. 'Lookee here.'

'Lookee here?'

Shafer tossed the filing to Exley. 'Page eight.'

On page eight, a description of the *Greton*: 'used primarily to bring cargo from Turkey to ports in Western Africa. Frequently chartered by Tukham, Ltd., an import-export company based in Hamburg.' Tukham, Ltd. was Bernard Kygeli's company.

'You are one smart girl,' Shafer said. 'And I say that in the most sexist way possible.'

'Guess we should find out who owns YRL.'

'And what other boats YRL owns.'

382

Exley checked her watch: 6:30. 'The corporate registry in the Caymans is closed for the night. We'll have to wait until tomorrow morning.'

'We? That mean you're coming in tomorrow?'

Exley didn't bother to answer.

The incorporation papers that YRL Ltd. had filed with the Cayman Secretary of State's Office were only two pages long. But they told Exley and Shafer everything. YRL's president was one Bassim Kygeli, of Hamburg, Germany.

Within the hour, they'd checked ship registries worldwide for boats registered to YRL. They found one more: the *Juno*, also registered in Liberia. YRL had bought it two years before, presumably as a replacement for the ill-fated *Greton*. It had been built in Korea in 1987 and displaced 22,000 tons, a pipsqueak compared to the newest and largest container ships. But more than big enough to carry a few kilograms of highly enriched uranium. Exley couldn't find pictures of the *Juno* online, but AIG would have some and a quick call from Langley would shake them loose.

'If the *Greton* is out of commission, that's got to be the one,' Shafer said.

'Assuming that Bernard shipped the stuff on his own boat.'

'What's the point of owning a boat if you can't use it for something like this?' Shafer said. 'Anyway, it's the first place to look.'

Exley checked the Hamburg port records. 'Shows up only twice in Hamburg in the last two years. Once last summer. And on December 31. Happy New Year. It left Hamburg with a load of used car parts. No mention of Tukham or Kygeli. It's supposedly being managed by a company called Socine Expo.' Exley looked up Socine on the D&B corporate database. 'Socine's offices are at the same building as Tukham, 29 Josefstrasse.'

'Wouldn't you know,' Shafer said. 'No wonder the German port records don't connect Bernard and the *Juno*. Where's it headed? I'll bet New York.'

'Close,' Exley said. 'Dock records say Lagos, Nigeria.'

'Then it should have gotten there already.'

'Think the Nigerians have their port records online?' With a few keystrokes, Exley sniffed out the records. 'Amazing but true. They do. Arrivals and departures in Lagos. In English. I'm not surprised about the Germans, but the Nigerians?'

'Nothing about the Internet surprises me anymore.'

'Well, this won't surprise you either,' Exley said. 'There's no record of the *Juno*.'

'Which means it's either in port here or somewhere in the Atlantic. We'd best tell Duto, get the navy looking for it. How hard can it be to find a two-hundred-foot-long boat? The Atlantic's only a couple of million square miles.'

'You going to tell John about this?'

'Not yet. At this point, the less he knows, the

better off he is. He seems to be handling Bernard decently so far.'

'How is he, Ellis?'

'Oh, no. I'm not playing matchmaker. You want to know, you ask him yourself.'

CHAPTER 26

Even waiting for the *Juno* in Newfoundland, Bashir had never been this cold. A front had blown in from Canada and encased the entire Northeast in frigid polar air. He and Nasiji and Yusuf needed heavy gloves and thick jackets for the half-minute walk between the Repard house and the stable.

But inside, the stable was as hot as Iraq in July. The gas-fired furnace at its center roared as Bashir melted steel in a thick-walled tungsten carbide pot. The steel glowed as red as the devil's own soup. Bashir stood four feet from the furnace, but even so the flames scorched his hands.

'Are we close?' Nasiji said.

'A few minutes. No wonder hell is supposed to be hot. Imagine spending eternity in those flames.'

'We won't be the ones in them.'

Bashir wished he could be so sure. As they moved close to finishing the bomb, his doubts were growing. Two nights before, with Thalia asleep, he'd crept to his laptop and read about nuclear explosions, looked at photographs of the survivors of Hiroshima and Nagasaki. The violence these bombs unleashed was unimaginable, though it didn't have to be imagined. It had already happened.

Most civilians assumed that the lethality of a nuclear bomb resulted from the radiation it produced, the gamma rays and neutrons that caused leukemia and other cancers. But radiation, though terrifying, was not the deadliest part of the blast. Even a small bomb – like the ones dropped on Japan, like the one they were making – created a fireball hundreds of feet around, with a temperature of seven thousand degrees Celsius, hotter than the surface of the sun. The fireball could burn the skin of people standing two miles away. The most horrifying pictures from Hiroshima came from the triage tents where the burn victims had gathered to die, their skin torn off, their clothes melted to their bodies.

At the same time, the explosion produced a massive shock wave that traveled at almost a thousand miles an hour, faster than the speed of sound. In other words, the blast hit before its victims could hear it coming. The wave was far stronger than the biggest tornado or hurricane, leveling buildings and tearing people to shreds. For the first halfmile from the epicenter of the blast, no human being or animal, no matter how well protected, could survive.

Along with the shock wave and the fireball came a blast of radiation. The splitting of the uranium atoms released gamma rays, high-energy particles that ricocheted through the body like tiny bullets, killing cells and damaging DNA. The rays attacked the entire body, but they were especially damaging to soft tissue and marrow. The most heavily dosed victims suffered acute radiation sickness and bled out, hemorrhaging through their skin. Other victims seemed fine for the first few weeks after the explosion. Then their hair fell out, their skin sloughed off as if they were rattlesnakes molting, their stomachs turned into bloody sinkholes. Unable to eat or drink, they starved to death. And even at relatively low doses, the radiation could kill years later by causing leukemia and lymphoma.

Bashir wasn't afraid of bloody viscera or broken bones, of puncture wounds or charred flesh. He'd been a surgeon for seven years, long enough to see all manner of horrors. An old man whose glasses had melted to his face because he'd tried to save a few dollars fixing his hot water heater himself, instead of hiring a mechanic. A motorcyclist who'd had both legs and his pelvis crushed by an SUV. Worst of all, an eleven-year-old boy who'd fallen off the roof of his house during a Fourth of July barbecue and had the terrible luck to puncture his stomach and chest on a wrought-iron fence. The firefighters and EMTs worried that the kid would bleed out if they pulled him off the spikes, so they cut the fence and brought him to the hospital with the iron still in him. He was wearing a Transformers T-shirt, Bashir remembered, and with the spikes sticking out, the shirt looked like a novelty gift gone wrong. The medics hadn't wanted to give the boy painkillers for fear of putting him into shock. When he arrived in the operating room, he was too frightened or in too much pain or both to talk. He just nodded when Bashir told him they were going to fix him, but they'd have to hold him down to get him free of the spikes. They'd put a mouth-guard in to protect his teeth and his tongue and started to pull. But the iron in his abdomen was in deeper than they'd imagined, into the muscle behind the stomach, and the kid screamed until his eyes rolled up and he fell unconscious, foam flecked at the corner of his mouth. The boy had lived, but Bashir would never forget the way he screamed. Or that when they finally wormed out the spike, bits of partially digested corn kernels were stuck to its prongs.

In his years as a surgeon, he'd saved a few lives. But this bomb would undo the good he'd done a thousand times over. The deaths would come by the hundreds of thousands, a poet's nightmare vision of the apocalypse. Only this inferno existed outside the pages of the Quran or the Bible. This jerry-rigged monster they were building from a few pieces of uranium and steel, *it was real*. No matter that they were in a hundred-year-old stable instead of a laboratory surrounded by guards and barbed wire. The physics of a nuclear explosion were the same here as in Los Alamos. They didn't need security guards, or thousands of engineers and scientists, or a billion-dollar budget. If they had enough uranium, and they pushed it together into a critical mass quickly enough, they would get a nuclear explosion. Full stop.

Hiroshima and Nagasaki had shocked the world so much that for two generations nations had come together to prevent another nuclear blast. They'd built tens of thousands of bombs. But they'd never again used one, not against civilians, not even on enemy armies. Not the Americans, not the Russians, not the Indians or the Pakistanis. Not even the Jews. They'd all kept the genie inside the bottle.

Now Bashir and Nasiji and Yusuf, and a few other men whose names he didn't even know, were going to break the taboo. Who were they to cast the world's wisdom aside? They weren't presidents or kings or prime ministers. They weren't imams whose names were known by pious Muslims around the world. They weren't even famous generals. They were a few men who'd gotten their hands on a few precious kilograms of highly enriched uranium. Now they were going to use it. They weren't going to declare war, or warn anyone what was coming. And though they had only one bomb, Nasiji was hoping to use it to start a much bigger conflict, Bashir knew.

Yet . . . why should they hold themselves to a higher standard than the United States, which hadn't warned civilians out of Hiroshima or

Nagasaki before it vaporized those cities? And why shouldn't America pay for its crimes? *They're at war with us. They kill us in ones and twos and sometimes by the hundreds. Shouldn't we be at war with them?* And the struggle long predated the invasion of Iraq. Since the first Crusade, Christians had tried to destroy Islam.

Bashir knew he was running in circles now. He'd been arguing with himself for three days, the same words and phrases chasing each other through his head. *Hiroshima. Abu Ghraib. Radiation poisoning. Crusaders. Leukemia. Hiroshima* – again, but this time as an argument for giving the Americans a taste of their own medicine.

More than anything, Bashir wished he could talk to his uncle Ayman's friends in the Muslim Brotherhood. They were wise men, honest and pious, not prone to excess, and deeply knowledgeable about the Quran and the sayings of the Prophet. If even one of them approved this mission Bashir wouldn't have worried. But he couldn't ask them what they thought. And he couldn't raise any of his doubts with Nasiji or Yusuf. Whatever had happened to Nasiji's family in Iraq, and Bashir knew only the outlines of the story, it had erased any reservations Nasiji might once have had. As for Yusuf . . . Yusuf was a perfect jihadi. He would kill until he was killed and expect heaven as his reward.

No, talking about this with Nasiji and Yusuf wouldn't be wise. That left him with Thalia, but

Thalia was a child. He would have to figure this out for himself. In the meantime, he saw no alternative but to keep working on the bomb.

'Bashir!' Nasiji said sharply. 'It was ready five minutes ago. How much longer are you planning to stir it?'

Bashir pulled himself from Hiroshima and focused on the forge. Distracted by his thoughts, he'd been stirring the steel with a tungsten carbide pole to improve its consistency. Now it was ready to be poured.

'Of course, Sayyid.'

Bashir set aside the pole and grabbed a set of tungsten tongs. He reached down into the furnace and squeezed the tongs tightly around the pot. Waves of heat blasted under his face shield and gloves.

Nasiji wrapped a second set of tongs around the pot. 'Careful, Doctor. No spills. One hundred kilos' – 220 pounds – 'of this stuff might itch a bit.'

'Yes,' Bashir said, thinking of the charred skin he'd seen on the Hiroshima burn victims. 'On three. One. Two. Three.'

They lifted the pot and took three steps to a spherical mold eighteen inches in diameter, made of high-purity ceramic. A second, smaller mold fit inside the first, to create the space for the artillery tube and the uranium plug. Bashir had sintered the molds – fused them from a powder of ceramic particles – in the vacuum furnace the day before.

'We pour on three. One. Two. Three.'

Slowly they poured the steel into the mold, their fourth pour so far. When they were done the mold was about half full. The tamper would be finished by late that afternoon. Once it had cooled, Bashir would cast the two pieces of the explosive pit – the narrow cylinder that fit inside the tamper and the larger piece, shaped like a pipe, that they fired at the cylinder and slid over it. The two shapes were relatively simple, but making sure they fit together smoothly was crucial. Before he cast the pit out of uranium, he planned to take a practice run using a steel ingot. Once he'd finished the pieces of the dummy steel pit, they would weld the steel cylinder into the tamper, then weld the muzzle of the recoilless rifle into the hole at the top of the sphere.

Once the muzzle had been attached, probably no later than tomorrow afternoon, they would fire a water glass at the plug, a test to make sure the two pieces fit together properly and that the barrel of the rifle wouldn't explode from the stress. Nasiji had insisted on the practice test. They could make another tamper easily, he said. And Bashir hadn't objected. Anything to give him more time.

That night Nasiji and Yusuf left to check their e-mail accounts, something they'd done every couple of days since they arrived, never going to the same Internet café, or even the same town, twice. When they came home, Nasiji was smiling.

'I need you to put together a second mold, Bashir,' he said. 'One that has space for a beryllium reflector. It's easy: it fits between the uranium pit and the tamper. I'll show you the design.'

'We're getting the beryllium, then?'

'No guarantees. But it's promising. Our contact says he's received ten kilos of it and thinks the rest will come soon.'

'When will we know?'

'You'll know when I tell you.'

Two days later, while Bashir tinkered with the design of the molds, Nasiji and Yusuf drove to Rochester and came back with a Sony digital video camera, a tripod, and even a spotlight. Then they disappeared into the basement. Bashir asked them what they were doing, but Nasiji was oddly coy. 'My second career,' he said. 'With Yusuf as the producer.'

The next morning, Nasiji called Bashir downstairs. The camera and spotlight were set in front of an Iraqi flag.

'I didn't want to tell you beforehand,' he said. 'I wanted you to see it with fresh eyes.' With a theatrical flourish, he flipped open the laptop and started the media player.

The video opened with Nasiji, sitting cross-legged in front of an Iraqi flag, red and white and green. He was dressed in Western clothes – jeans and a blue button-down shirt. He sat on the floor, a dagger sheathed on his hip, a beatific smile on his face, looking like a yoga instructor from hell.

'My name is Sayyid Nasiji. I was born in Baghdad, Iraq. With my own eyes, I have seen the destruction the Americans have brought to Iraq. With my own eyes, I have seen the bodies of my father and mother and sister and brothers. I represent the Army of the Believers,' he said in Arabic. 'For many years we have waited for this day. We and all true Muslims. Now we have brought the wrath of Allah on the *kaffirs*. The shortest path to freedom is the path that sheds blood far and wide. And we are not afraid of blood.'

Nasiji drew the dagger that was on his hip and scraped the blade across a cutting stone. *Scrape. Scrape.* Tiny sparks flew off the edge of the knife.

'America thought we could only use knives and guns. America thought we could not make the special weapon, that we hadn't the technology. And I cannot lie. Anyone who tries to build such a weapon faces great difficulties. So you may ask, where did this bomb come from?'

A new image filled the screen: Grigory, sitting on a couch, a black sheet as background. The video that Yusuf had filmed in Russia, two nights before he killed Grigory and Tajid.

'My name is Grigory Farzadov,' he said in Russian. 'I am an engineer at the Mayak nuclear weapons plant in Ozersk, Russia.' Grigory held up his plant security identification and his Russian passport. As he spoke, the camera's focus tightened on his identification. 'Several months ago I was approached by a group of men who told me that they wanted to steal a nuclear bomb and asked for my help. Naturally, I reported this action to my supervisor, Garry Pliakov. He is deputy manager of operations at Mayak. A week later, Garry told me that he wanted me to help the smugglers steal the bomb. He told me I was to provide the smugglers the codes to activate the weapon. I asked him why we should take this action. He told me that President Medvedev himself had made the decision and I was not to question it. He told me that if I did not do as I was told, I would be tried for treason. Naturally, I did not argue. I still do not understand why, but we have given the men the bomb.'

'Do you think Grigory is lying?' Nasiji said.

Then an image of the warhead, lying on its side on the dirt floor of the stable. The camera focused on the Cyrillic lettering atop the warhead.

'There is your answer,' Nasiji said. 'This bomb comes from Russia. The Russian government gave it to us. Could we have broken into the Mayak plant ourselves? Could we have discovered the codes ourselves? Of course not. We were given this bomb. And the Russians, they knew where we planned to use it. Remember this, America, when you are deciding what to do next. Now, I do not know why the Russians gave us this weapon. Probably they intend to attack you for themselves and are using us as a mask. Probably they didn't expect that we would expose them this way.

'But we want you to understand what's happened, America. We want you to know that it isn't just Muslims who are finished with you. It's Russians, Chinese, everyone. Everyone sees how you rule the world. Everyone wants you to pull back your armies and let us live in peace. This explosion is divine retribution for all the evil that you have committed. Do not forget your sins, America. Remember that we Muslims want to live in peace with you. We have blown up this bomb because you've given us no choice. You must decide what action to take next. But do not retaliate. Understand this lesson and make peace with the world.'

Nasiji stood and raised the dagger, holding the tip to his neck.

'You can never stop us, America. For a thousand years, we have died for Islam. If we must, we will die for a thousand more. Nothing frightens us. Now, please, take this moment to change your path.'

He pressed the knife into his neck, drew a single drop of blood. He pointed the blade directly at the camera.

'*Allahu Akbar.*'

Nasiji stopped the playback. 'That's it. I'm planning to put your names in, too. Let the world see who we are. And if you want to make your own statements, we might consider that. Though I think it works better this way. One voice, yes?'

'Genius,' Yusuf said.

'Bashir,' Nasiji said, a kid fishing for compliments. 'What do you think? Maybe I ought to use a plain black background instead of the Iraci flag. I don't want them to think Iraq is their only sin.'

Bashir couldn't take his eyes off the screen, the final image, Nasiji leaning forward, staring into the camera, the dagger held high in his hand. A madman. Or worse. Nasiji's black eyes seemed to glow red as coals. An illusion of the camera, the spotlight on his face. Had to be.

'Will it work?' Bashir said.

'Probably they won't believe it,' Nasiji said. 'They'll say I'm lying, trying to get them to attack Russia. But it's worth trying. I'm hoping we'll be done in time to set this gadget of ours off at the big speech, the State of the Union—'

'But that's hardly a week away—' *A week?* This was all going to happen within a week?

'I know. I don't think we can get the beryllium by then, and if we don't have it we'll wait. The beryllium's the only way we can be sure we'll get a full detonation. But if we can, imagine it. The whole American government is there. President, vice president, the Congress, the Supreme Court, all of them. All gone.'

'But the security must be enormous.'

'Yes, but they can't close down all of Washington. And their security, it's designed against a truck bomb. Not one of these. If we succeed, the generals will be the only ones left. And they'll want to strike back. Quickly. And if they think we're telling the truth, they'll have no choice. They'll fire all their missiles at Russia. The Russians will fire all their missiles back. The end of the United States of America. Russia, too. Every city will be gone. The two countries that hate Muslims the most, wiped away. The Crusaders, beaten forever.'

And a hundred million people will die, Bashir didn't say. More. Two hundred million. Three hundred million. More. A number so large it couldn't be counted, couldn't even be imagined.

'Sayyid,' he said. 'I want the Americans to suffer. But this . . . will Allah smile on this?'

'Losing your nerve?'

'Not at all. But isn't there anyone we can talk with, ask for guidance?'

'All these years, they've given us war. All these years, Muslims have been dying. We must destroy them, Bashir. Nothing less.'

'God willing,' Yusuf said.

'You're right,' Bashir said. He wished he could be as sure as he sounded, as sure as Nasiji and Yusuf. 'Anyway, I think you ought to have a black flag. Yusuf and I aren't Iraqi, and Iraq isn't their only sin. As you say.'

'I'll redo it.'

'Then what?'

'When we're ready, just before we go, we'll send copies to CNN and Al Jazeera and a few other places. We'll upload it to our own Web sites, too, in case they won't run it. But we'll have to time it right, so it isn't posted until afterward.'

'And if we can't get the beryllium in time?'

'We'll wait. No State of the Union. But we'll still destroy the White House, kill the president, blow up the middle of Washington. And when they see the video, they'll know who to blame. I'm only sorry we won't be around to see it.'

That night, Bashir lay beside Thalia, unable to sleep. When he closed his eyes, he saw Hiroshima and Nagasaki, the charred wooden houses and corpses in the streets, terrified even in death by what they'd seen. He wished he'd never looked.

'What's wrong, Doctor?' Thalia said quietly to him in Arabic. *Doctor.* He loved to hear her call him that. But tonight the word cut him. Doctors were meant to save lives.

'Nothing, my wife. Now sleep.'

'Bashir, tell me. And then we'll both sleep.'

Bashir wondered if he could tell her. But why not? She was his wife, after all. 'Yusuf and Sayyid, you know, this thing we're making in the stable, it's a bomb. A special bomb. Did you know that?'

'Yes.'

'You did?'

'Yes, my husband. I know I'm not very smart, but the things you and Sayyid were saying, I figured it out.'

'A big bomb. It will kill a lot of people.'

Thalia squeezed his hand. 'How many?'

'I don't know. But many.'

'Here? In America?'

'Yes.'

'So it would be *kaffirs*.' Her voice had a girlish excitement that surprised him.

'Muslims, too. It won't discriminate. And Nasiji has a plan. He's hoping to start a big war between the United States and Russia. If it works, there could be hundreds more bombs like this. Even thousands, maybe. Does that bother you?'

'*No.*' And Bashir's surprise became astonishment as his wife slid her hand down his stomach and reached for him, something she'd never done unbidden before. Bashir couldn't think of anything to say, and so he lay silent as she stroked him hard and then straddled his legs and guided him into her, all the while whispering, '*No no no.*'

PART IV

CHAPTER 27

The mission could be explained in three words. Accomplishing it required a lot more effort.

Find a ship.

A ship that had departed Hamburg on New Year's Eve, supposedly bound for West Africa, but had never arrived. A ship that was somewhere in the North Atlantic, unless it was in the Caribbean, or the Pacific, or docked, or even scuttled. A ship that was thoroughly anonymous, not a supertanker or a yacht but a midsize freighter like tens of thousands of others around the world. A ship that was called the *Juno*, unless its name had been changed. A ship that carried no visible weapons but still needed to be approached cautiously. Most of all, a ship that had to be found quickly, so its hold could be searched with Geiger counters, its crew questioned, and its captain put in a rubber room and subjected to every interrogation technique that the dark wizards of the CIA had ever invented.

The task was formidable, even with the National Security Agency and the navy making it their highest priority. Nonetheless, this was the kind of problem the United States knew how to solve, a technical puzzle that could be cracked with pure effort and brainpower. For once, no need to win hearts and minds in Baghdad or Kabul. *Just find that damn freighter.* Around NSA headquarters at Fort Meade, through the Atlantic Fleet command in Norfolk, the order went out. *By yesterday, if possible.*

Photographs of the *Juno*, along with its engineering specifications – height, length, displacement, and the shape of its superstructure – were sent to every American and British naval vessel in the Atlantic. Within twelve hours, the Atlantic Fleet had posted frigates outside the major East Coast harbors, from Miami to Portland, Maine. Meanwhile, Coast Guard cutters visited every ship that had docked in the last two weeks and that matched, or almost matched, the *Juno*'s specs.

At the same time, the Atlantic Fleet command ordered destroyers and cruisers to run alongside the main sea lanes that crossed the North Atlantic, in case the *Juno* was still somewhere en route or sailing back to Europe. The Royal Navy sent its own flotilla west. In three days, the vessels identified every ship that fit the *Juno*'s profile. Impressive work, especially considering the winter weather and the fact that the sun shone for barely eight hours a day on the main route between London and New York.

Impressive, but fruitless. The navy's efforts came up empty. The *Juno* wasn't on the sea lanes between Europe and the United States. And it wasn't docked in any port anywhere in the United States, Canada, Britain, or Western Europe.

Meanwhile, the NSA's Advanced Keyhole satellites were searching the rest of the Atlantic. The satellites could capture ships in great detail, down to their names and the foot-square patches of rust on their hulls. They could also take photographs that covered several square miles and captured dozens of boats at once.

But they had a problem. They couldn't do *both*, not at the same time. The camera capable of both super-wide and super-fine resolution hadn't been invented yet. And from Greenland to South America, the Atlantic covered more than forty million square miles. Even if the satellites photographed it in one-square-mile chunks, they would need forty million images to cover it.

To work around the problem, two dozen software engineers spent a long night at Fort Meade writing code. By morning, they'd created an application that turned the agency's face-recognition software into a crude boat-recognition program. The software couldn't find the *Juno*. But it could rule out in real time ninety-five percent of the boats spotted by the satellites as too big, too small, or the wrong shape.

The other five percent were classified as possibles and photographed again at one-meter resolution. Those images were then reviewed by the NSA's analysts, who eliminated any ship that appeared significantly different from the original photographs of the *Juno*, on the theory that the *Juno* could not have had time to undergo major structural work since leaving Hamburg.

The analysts were able to rule out another ninety percent of the boats that had gotten through the first pass. Even so, not every satellite shot was definitive. Many of the ships had gray hulls and decks that didn't stand out against the dark water of the Atlantic. They could only be ruled in or out after being seen and photographed at sea level, by helicopters, drones, or naval aircraft. Their names and locations were passed to the navy for a final inspection.

At Langley, Exley and Shafer tracked the search in the annex of the operations center in the basement of New Headquarters Building. The annex and the entire center were classified as Blue Zones, restricted to employees with Top Secret/SCI/NO FORN clearances. Originally, contractors had been excluded, too, but after the operations center went dark twice in six months, the agency gave in and hired a team from Lockheed to fix the electronics that supported it.

The annex was a high-ceilinged room, about thirty feet square, with concrete floors and a distractingly loud ventilation system. On two walls, oversized monitors projected digital maps of the Atlantic, cut up into 400,000 patches of ten square miles each. The maps divided the ocean into three colors. Green represented areas that had been searched and cleared. Red stood for areas where suspect ships had been found and needed to be checked. And yellow symbolized areas that hadn't yet been searched. An unfortunate choice. When the hunt for the *Juno* started, the Atlantic appeared to be filled with urine.

As hours and then days passed, patches of green appeared on the maps, spreading out from the East Coast along the major shipping routes like a shipborne virus. Tiny blips of red appeared, then vanished. A third monitor contained the names and photographs of suspect ships. As suspect boats were cleared, they disappeared from the screen, replaced with new targets.

On the second morning, the satellites picked up a boat off the coast of Nicaragua that looked to be almost a perfect match. But when a helicopter buzzed it, it turned out to be a freighter that had been built by the same Korean shipyard as the *Juno*.

By then, Exley was thoroughly sick of staring at the monitors.

'Ellis. We're useless here. Let's find something else to do.'

'Last week you were ready to quit,' Shafer said. 'Now you're looking for work.'

'This is it. One last job and then I'm done.'

'If you say so.'

'I told my kids and I'm keeping my word. I'm

serious.' But was she? If an interrogator had shot her full of sodium thiopental at that moment, she didn't know what she would have said.

'Uh-huh,' Shafer said. 'Meanwhile, let's go figure out where Bernard Kygeli gets his money. If anything happens here, they can call us.'

No one had officially told Henry Williams that his career was over. But he knew, as surely as if the secretary of the navy had sent him a card congratulating him for thirty years of able service and welcoming him to retirement. He imagined the card would have a golfer on the cover and say something like 'You've Knocked the Ball out of the Park – Now It's Time to Hit That Hole in One' in big block letters that his middle-aged eyes would have no problem reading. Like he was a lawyer who'd spent his career behind a desk instead of a man who'd given up his marriage and everything else on land for a life at sea. Instead of a destroyer captain, for Pete's sake.

But the navy didn't tolerate failure. And Williams had failed the summer before. Just outside Shanghai, his ship, the USS Decatur, had rammed a fishing trawler filled with Chinese college students. The ramming had killed twenty-two Chinese and pushed the United States and China to the brink of war. In retaliation, a Chinese submarine had torpedoed the Decatur, killing seventeen of Williams's sailors.

An internal inquiry by the navy found that

Williams had committed no wrongdoing in either incident. But Williams knew he would never escape the stigma of what had happened. During the months the *Decatur* was in dry dock, Williams had been persona non grata at the meetings in Honolulu and Annapolis, where senior officers discussed the future of the service. After the *Decatur* was recommissioned, it had lost its place in the *Ronald Reagan* carrier battle group and been shipped back to the East Coast to do laps in the Atlantic. And his superior officers no longer asked him what vessel he hoped to command next. No, his hopes to move further up the ranks, to earn an admiral's gold braids, had ended in the East China Sea. In two months, when the *Decatur* was done with this tour, he'd retire. Honorably, with a full pension.

He had no idea what he'd do next. The *Decatur*'s namesake, Stephen Decatur, had gone out with his spurs on, dying in a duel in 1820 – a story Williams loved telling. But duels were no longer politically correct. Williams supposed he'd wind up going home to Dallas, burning his afternoons playing golf. Or maybe he'd start consulting with some defense contractor. Either way he'd secretly be hoping for a quick heart attack.

Was Williams bitter about what had happened? His commanding officers had put him in a damn-near-impossible position, then punished him for failing to find a way out of it. In return for a career of loyal service, he'd been ditched like a rusted-out propeller. Though he could see the other side, too. The navy had plenty of commanders with spotless records. It didn't have to take a chance by promoting one with a blemish as big as his. And pissing off the Chinese wasn't in anyone's interest. Especially since America and China were both pretending that the festivities the previous summer had never happened.

In the meantime, Williams still ran the *Decatur*, and he wasn't coasting into retirement. He'd always run a clean ship. Now he was pushing his officers and crew harder than ever. He knew his sailors weren't happy, but he didn't care. He wasn't asking for anything beyond the navy's own regulations. He simply wanted them followed, to the letter. And if regulations said that officers weren't to eat until the captain arrived at meals, or that sailors were forbidden to keep pornography even in their own personal footlockers, well, rules were rules. *What are they gonna do, fire me?*

So, yeah, he was bitter. He didn't think anyone could blame him.

The orders came near midnight local time, as they were about to cross the equator on a hot dry night in the central Atlantic, slightly closer to West Africa than Brazil. The *Decatur* was to move east and north, off the coast of Sierra Leone and Liberia, just outside the sea lanes that ran between Europe and West Africa.

There, Williams and his crew would watch for

a freighter that had gone missing on a run from Hamburg to Lagos. Somebody thought this ship, the *Juno*, was carrying more than a couple tablespoons of capital-S, capital-N, capital-M Special Nuclear Material. The whole Atlantic Fleet was looking for it, as well as every satellite the NSA had.

As soon as the orders arrived, Williams lightened up some, took his foot off the crew's collective neck. Didn't take a head-shrinker to figure out why. For the first time since Shanghai, the *Decatur* had a mission. The navy still trusted him a little. And so Williams ordered the *Decatur*'s four massive gas turbines to full throttle and turned his ship east at twenty-five knots. By noon the next day, they reached their new position, the sun fierce overhead, the sea quiet, not even the hint of a breeze. Except during hurricane season, weather hardly existed in this part of the Atlantic. Fall and winter and spring were the same, an eternity of hot dry days.

Further orders weren't long in coming. Twice in two days, Williams was ordered to check on ships that the NSA's satellites deemed worthy of a closer look. Each time he'd put up the SH-60B Seahawk helicopter the *Decatur* carried, though each time he'd been sure they were wrong. In one case, the target looked too wide to him to be the *Juno*, and in the other too tall.

When the helo came back empty-handed the second time, Williams decided that he wasn't going to wait to be told what to do next. The NSA might have the satellites, but it didn't know squat about ships. He was going with his gut now, and his gut told him that the *Juno* was nowhere near West Africa. Why would it be? If it had followed the route on its original manifest, it would have reached Lagos weeks before. On the other hand, if it had made a drop off the American coast, it probably would have turned away, sailed south-east at full speed to get into the open Atlantic as quickly as possible. In that case, it would be west of him, and possibly south as well, depending on its speed. Williams decided to head southwest, back where he'd been when his orders arrived. He knew the risk he was taking, ignoring a direct order from the Atlantic Fleet command, and he didn't care.

'You sure you want to do this,' the *Decatur*'s executive officer said.

'Until they take my ship from me, I'm running it as I see fit.'

Overnight they ran southwest at twenty-five knots into the open ocean. By morning, Norfolk was asking where they were. 'Better fishing in deep waters,' Williams messaged back. Let them chew on that for a while.

He put the Seahawk in the air and ordered it to push south to the limits of its fuel tanks and to notify him of any ship that remotely resembled the *Juno*. Three hours later, it came back, dry and empty. He ordered it refueled and sent out again, this time to the southwest. The mission was a waste of fuel, a 10,000-to-1 shot. The helicopter faced the same problem as the satellites. It had to fly close to the waves so it could see the details of the boats below, but staying low limited its field of vision.

But somehow Williams wasn't surprised when the call came in an hour later. Eighty nautical miles to the southwest of the *Decatur*, the SH-60's pilot had spotted a freighter that matched the *Juno*'s basic design. 'Wants to know if they should take a look,' Stan Umsle, the *Decatur*'s tactical information officer, said.

'Go for it,' Williams said.

Two minutes later, the radio buzzed again. Umsle listened. 'You're not going to believe this, sir. The boat, it's headed southeast, 165 degrees, fourteen knots. And they're certain it's the *Juno*.'

'How do they know?'

'They say it's got *Juno* painted on the side in big white letters.'

'Good enough for me.' Somehow Williams kept his tone steady, though he wanted to howl in joy. Finding this boat might not save his career, but at least he could retire now with his head up, as something more than the captain who'd nearly started a war between America and China. 'Take us to thirty knots, heading two hundred,' he said to Umsle. 'Now.'

Then he called Rear Admiral Josh Rogers, who

was overseeing the western half of the search from Norfolk, with the good news. Rogers listened in silence, then said, 'I don't suppose I should ask why you were three hundred nautical miles from where you were told to be.'

'No, sir,' Williams said. 'You shouldn't.'

Williams half-expected Rogers to tell him to wait so the navy could bring in the SEALs. Instead, Rogers ordered him to make the interdiction as soon as possible. 'Ask nicely first. But if they don't stop, you are authorized to disable their engines.'

'I don't mean to be a stickler, but under what authority, sir? This is open ocean and they've got as much right to be on it as we do. They're not even headed for an American port.'

'If that ship is carrying nuclear material, it's violating who knows how many United States laws and UN resolutions. Tell them whatever you want, but stop them. If they're clean, we'll offer a thousand apologies for wasting their precious time.'

'Yes, sir, Admiral. We'll get it done.'

'Roger that.' Rogers hung up.

Williams looked at Umsle. 'Lieutenant, get a tac team ready to board the *Juno*. I'm not sure what law or UN resolution or intergalactic ordinance we're going to use as an excuse, but we're going in.'

'Intergalactic ordinance, sir?'

'Just get a team together. Make sure they know what they're looking for.' Williams went up to the *Decatur*'s bridge and sent his executive officer

416

down to manage the combat information center. He wanted to see this ship for himself.

Intercepting the *Juno*, which was traveling in a straight line at a piddling eleven knots, was almost embarrassingly easy for the *Decatur*. Within two hours, the freighter was visible from the destroyer's bridge, a speck on the ocean to the southwest. A half-hour after that, the two ships were less than five nautical miles apart, and the *Juno* was clearly outlined against the sea.

In another fifteen minutes, the *Decatur* and the freighter were sailing parallel. The destroyer towered over the *Juno*, twice as long and almost three times as high. Even if the freighter had been larger, the missile launchers and guns that sprouted from the deck of the *Decatur* left no doubt which vessel was in charge.

'We have radio contact?' Williams asked the bridge communications officer.

'Yes, sir.'

Williams grabbed his headset. 'This is Captain Henry Williams of the United States Navy. To whom am I speaking?'

'Captain Alvar Haxhi.' Haxhi had a heavy Eastern European accept. No surprise. Lots of ship captains were from Romania, Bulgaria, and Albania.

'You are the commander of the *Juno*, registered in Monrovia, Liberia?'

'That is correct.'

'Captain Haxhi, by order of the United States

Navy, you are commanded to stop so my men can board and search your vessel.'

'Under what law of the sea do you make this demand?' The captain sounded surprisingly unworried given the circumstances.

'We have reason to believe your vessel is carrying sensitive material that belongs to the United States government. If you don't allow us to board, I've been authorized to use deadly force.'

A pause. 'Then I suppose I have no choice.'

The boarding went smoothly enough. Over the radio, Williams asked Haxhi to come to the *Decatur* so he could be interviewed about the *Juno*'s movements.

'I will not leave my ship,' Haxhi said.

'Under any circumstances?'

'You and I both know this boarding is very much illegal, Captain. I allow it because I must. But I will not leave my men.'

Williams had to respect that attitude. 'Then I'll come to you.'

A half-hour later, Williams was sitting with Haxhi in the captain's cabin on the *Juno*, an unadorned white-painted room ten feet square. The cabin stank of Eastern European cigarettes and was furnished with a metal desk, a full-sized wooden bed, and a dresser, all bolted to the floor. Two photographs of a pretty young woman were taped over his desk, Haxhi's wife or girlfriend or maybe even his daughter, and a couple of Albanian novels lay on his bed. Otherwise, the cabin was devoid of any signs of personality, except for the putting green nailed to the floor.

'You like to golf?' Williams said.

'Of course, Captain. Do you?'

'I think it's a big waste of time. Tell me where you've been.'

'The stupidest of trips,' Haxhi said. 'We were on way to Nigeria. When we reached a hundred kilometers from Lagos, my manager called, said, Head west to Caracas.'

The story was implausible to the point of being insulting. 'When was this?' Williams said evenly.

'Ten, eleven days. I can check.'

'Has that ever happened before?'

'One time.'

'And who is your manager?'

'Name is Serge.'

'Serge what?'

'I just call him Serge. But, sure, we have his name on the manifest.'

'What's the company?'

'Called Socine Expo.'

'You have a phone number, address, e-mail?'

Haxhi gave him all three.

'How'd you end up here?'

'I told you, after Lagos, they tell us Venezuela. We go there, all the way across the Atlantic, and then when we're two hundred kilometers from Caracas, they tell us, back. To Jo'burg this time. So we turn around again.'

'Not a very well-run company. You wasted a lot of diesel.'

'Bosses change their minds. Why they're bosses.'

'And when we found you?'

'As I said, on way back from Caracas.'

'You short on food or fuel?'

'Have plenty of both.'

'Your crew must be sick of this.'

'My crew, they do what I tell them.'

That much Williams believed. 'You have logs to support this story of yours?'

Haxhi nodded at his desk. 'Of course. Maybe you tell me what you looking for? Maybe I can help.'

'You get to wait here until we're done looking around. It may be a while. I'm going to put a sentry outside the door, so don't be stupid.'

'Mr American Captain. You must be kidding. Look at my ship and look at yours. Maybe I am stupid but crazy I am not.'

For the next six hours, the *Decatur*'s crew combed the *Juno* with radiation detectors, looking for any hints that uranium or plutonium had been carried on the ship. But they found only the car parts that were listed on the manifest, a hull of crates packed with gear shafts, tires, brake drums, and shocks. The destroyer's medic examined the sailors on the *Juno* for radiation sickness but found nothing unusual. Williams tried to talk to the sailors but got nowhere. To a man, they claimed they couldn't speak English. He went back to Haxhi's cabin, now clouded with smoke.

'Captain, may I get you anything?'

'My ship. Get it back to me.' Haxhi offered Williams the pack. 'Cigarette?'

Williams shook his head.

'Have you found it yet, what you're looking for?'

'No, and we're not going anywhere until we do. And neither are you.'

'What about my delivery?' Haxhi asked the question with a straight face.

'Those poor South Africans, waiting for your precious car parts?' Williams almost laughed. 'They'll have to hang on a few more days. Let me tell you something, Captain. Pretty soon half the U.S. Navy's going to be here. If we have to put this rustbucket in dry dock and cut holes in it from stem to stern, we will.'

'Whatever you like to do, you will do. But I am sure, this thing you're looking for, you will not find it.' Haxhi exhaled a cloud of smoke in Williams's direction, though not exactly at him. He was too confident, Williams thought. Whatever contraband the *Juno* had been carrying, loose uranium, a bomb, whatever, it was long gone.

Then Williams knew what he needed to do. He should have thought of it before, but better late than never.

'Sit tight, Captain,' Williams said. 'I'll be back.'

He ordered the *Juno*'s crew assembled on the front of the freighter's deck, in two lines. To starboard the sun was setting, turning the sky a brilliant crimson. 'Red sky at night, a sailor's delight,' Williams said to the crew, pointing at the sun. 'Red sky at morn, sailor be warned. I know some of you know what I'm saying. I know some of you speak English. And if you don't, there are men on my crew who speak French, German, Spanish. They're going to translate.'

One by one, the *Decatur*'s bilingual sailors repeated Williams's message to the men. They stood still, their mouths shut, hardly moving even to breathe.

'I know you all are pretending you don't understand. I see you standing there like a bunch of damn deaf-mutes who've been commanded to sail the oceans until the Second Coming. And I know it's a bunch of bull. Let me explain this to you. We didn't want to board your vessel, but we must find the contraband you were carrying. We don't blame any of you. We understand that you probably didn't know what you had. But *we must find it.*'

A pause for translation.

'Now, we could separate you, interrogate you one by one, pick a few of you to put in our brig. But we're low on time. So I'm going to extend a one-time offer. On my authority as a captain in the United States Navy, and on my honor as commander of the USS *Decatur.*'

Translation. The sailors in the *Juno* looked curiously at one another as they heard Williams's words.

'I promise that any man who gives us the truth about your route, helps us find the cargo you were carrying, will receive American citizenship. Your immediate family as well. Wife, children, parents, all to the United States. Right now. No red tape. You have my word, and the word of my crew.' Was he allowed to make this deal? Surely not. No more than the *Decatur* was allowed to leave its position off the African coast. But if he could get the information his admirals needed, no one would care. And if they did . . . *what are you going to do, fire me?* 'I'll take two men. The first two to come forward, no more, so decide quickly.'

Williams signaled for his translators.

But even before they could speak, two men stepped out of line.

CHAPTER 28

Wells banged the brass lion knocker against Bernard Kygeli's front door.

'Hullo? Hey?'

'*Ja?*' Bernard's wife.

'It's Roland.'

'*Nein.*'

'Open up, you handkerchief-wearing twit. I need Bernard.' Wells hadn't seen Bernard in almost a week, since the meeting in the hotel. Two days before, Wells had called Bernard and briefly updated him on the progress he was supposedly making in getting the beryllium and promised to deliver the rest within seventy-two hours. Bernard had seemed satisfied. Wells figured he'd try to string Bernard along for a few more days, give the agency as much time as possible to find out where the bombmakers were hiding.

But this morning, Shafer had called Wells, told him he needed to get hold of Bernard. Immediately. Bernard wasn't answering his phone. So Wells had come to the house.

'*Nein.* Not here.'

'Where is he then?'

424

But the house stayed silent. Wells waited a minute more, then dropped to a crouch and scuttled along the front porch. He vaulted over the rail of the porch and ran into the backyard, which was hidden from the neighbors by a high white wall. Most of the yard was taken up by a little garden, the plants wrapped in blue plastic to protect them from the winter. Three recycling bins stood tidily beside the back door of the house, which opened into the kitchen. The savory smell of Turkish coffee wafted into the yard through a half-open kitchen window.

For this visit, Wells had brought his Glock. He unzipped his jacket and started to pull the pistol from his shoulder holster. Then he changed his mind. He left the gun in the holster and stepped to the door and peeked inside. The kitchen was empty. Wells tested the door. Locked. He pushed on the window but couldn't raise it.

Wells was wearing a black wool knit cap low on his head. He pulled off the cap and wrapped his gloved hand in it and punched through the window beside the door. The glass cracked with the sweet tinkle of a distant ice-cream truck. Wells reached in and opened the door and stepped inside. 'Bernard,' he yelled. 'It's Roland.' Heavy steps thumped through the house toward the kitchen. Wells pulled his pistol. Helmut, Bernard's son, skidded into the kitchen on black dress socks. He held a poker in both hands. He stepped toward Wells but stopped when he saw the Glock.

'Put it down,' Wells said.

'We're calling the police.'

'No you're not. Put it down, boy.'

Helmut laid the poker on the kitchen table.

'Good.' Wells tucked away his gun and stepped toward Helmut.

'Where's your father?'

'At the warehouse.'

Wells lunged and grabbed the poker as Helmut shrank back against the refrigerator.

'I was just there. Where is he?'

'I don't know. I swear.'

'Bloody hell. Do you have any idea what he's gotten us into?'

Wells pressed Helmut against the refrigerator and put his gloved left hand around Helmut's neck and lifted and squeezed—

To his right, Wells sensed as much as saw a shape coming at him through the doorway—

Still holding Helmut, he swung the poker diagonally downward, a quick blind slash that ended when the iron rod thumped solidly into bone—

A woman screamed and a knife clattered to the floor and Helmut swung his skinny arms wildly at Wells like a puppet trying to slip its strings—

But Wells kept his grip until Helmut's shoulders drooped and he gave up—

Wells loosened up on Helmut and kicked the knife to the far end of the kitchen. Meanwhile, Bernard's wife, his would-be attacker, held her damaged hand to her chest and groaned. Wells wasn't sure if he'd broken any bones, but she'd be black-and-blue for sure. He jabbed at her with the poker to keep her at bay.

'Tell your mother to step back,' Wells said. 'Before I start shooting.'

Helmut fired German at his mother. Wells was surprised that they didn't speak Arabic or Turkish with each other, but maybe Helmut had never learned it. Finally, the woman retreated. Wells stepped back to the far end of the kitchen and dropped the poker and drew his Glock.

'Crazy family,' he said. 'Helmut the screenwriter, his killer mom, his disappearing dad. What's her name, anyway?'

'Ayelet.'

'Tell Omelet I need her husband.'

'Ayelet.'

'I don't give a rat's ass. You two talkee-fastee and find me Bernard or we're all in trouble.'

But after talking to his mother, Helmut shook his head. 'She doesn't know. And I don't either.'

'Lying.'

'No. He left yesterday morning and he hasn't been home since.'

Did the BND know where Bernard was? Wells wondered. They had to. Then why hadn't they told Shafer? Or had the Germans somehow lost him? 'Let's go,' Wells said. 'I want a look around.'

'I don't understand,' Helmut said. 'Are you *Polizei*?'

'Do I look like the constabulary? Your father owes me three million euros. I want my money and I don't want to wind up in some Kraut jail.' Wells walked through the living room to Bernard's office. The door was locked, but Wells put his shoulder to it and popped it.

Inside, the file cabinets were empty and the papers on Bernard's desk were gone. So was his laptop dock. Only the maps and the volumes of maritime law remained.

'Bloody hell,' Wells said, not acting anymore. *The BND* better know where he is. 'Did you know about this?'

'No.'

Ayelet murmured something to Helmut. 'She says he burned his papers.' Wells walked back into the living room. Heaps of charred ash filled the fireplace. Wells kicked through them but found nothing of value. Then, deeper in the fireplace, a lump of melted plastic. Bernard's laptop, permanently rebooted. Bernard had taken advantage of the cold weather to get rid of his records without attracting the BND's attention.

'When did he do this?'

'Last night.'

Wells backhanded Helmut across the face, hard enough that the kid nearly banged his head on the marble fireplace mantel. 'You told me he left yesterday morning.'

'He came back last night to burn the stuff. Just for an hour.'

Wells pulled Helmut close, got a faceful of the kid's cologne. 'Who else was in on this?'

'I don't even know what you're doing here. You think my father talks to me?' Helmut's voice was a piteous but truthful whine.

'You don't know what we're doing? I'll tell you, then. Your dear old da' asked me to find him some beryllium. Know what that's for, Helmut? Atomic bombs. Try that in one of your movies. Your dad wants an A-bomb.'

'That's—' But Helmut had nothing else to say.

'You ever seen anyone from the BND with your dad?' Wells said. 'Think hard.'

Helmut shook his head.

'Then who's it for, Helmut?'

Helmut hesitated. His eyes flicked at his mother, at the floor, and then finally back at Wells. 'I don't know.' He knew something, maybe not a name, but something. Even so, Wells decided to hold off on pushing the question. Finding Bernard was the key. Wells grabbed Helmut and pulled him close and stuck the Glock under his chin. Helmut's cologne could no longer hide the reek of his sweat. Wells didn't like scaring civilians this way, but he didn't see any choice.

'Your dad and me, we had a deal. And I intend to get paid. And if he goes down, he had best keep his mouth shut and never mention me to anyone. Otherwise I will kill you and your ugly twit of a mother and your sisters. So find Bernard and tell him I want to see him in person. Do you understand?'

'You have a foul mouth,' Helmut said through clenched teeth.

'And an even fouler mind at that. But I keep my promises. Tell him.'

And with his message delivered, Wells flung Helmut aside and stalked out.

An hour later, from his hotel room, Wells called Shafer. 'Bernard is AWOL.' Wells told Shafer about the empty office and his run-in with Helmut.

'That's a problem,' Shafer said.

'Why did he run?'

Shafer told Wells about the *Decatur* and the *Juno*.

'And you didn't tell me about this?'

'I wanted you outside the loop so you wouldn't blow your cover. Anyway, we didn't find the *Juno* until yesterday, so there was nothing to tell.'

'And it wasn't carrying anything.'

'Clean. But the crew members say it sailed from Hamburg to somewhere off eastern Canada and that there it dropped two guys off. Both Arab. They hardly talked to the crew during the trip, mostly stayed in their cabin, and the captain gave strict orders that they weren't to be disturbed. Like ghosts, one of the crew said.'

'Names or faces?'

'We've shown the crew a couple hundred possibles. No matches yet. Anyway, these guys were carrying four wooden crates. Two as big as steamer trunks. Much more than you'd need to carry a few kilos of HEU. Which means the Russians are lying. I'm sure you're shocked.'

'If they have that much material, why do they need the beryllium?'

'We asked the boys at Los Alamos the same question. Their best guess was that maybe these guys have a few hundred kilos of material, but not military-grade. The way the physics work, if it's sixty or seventy percent enriched, you need much more uranium than if it's 93.5. Or it could be components for a bomb, or some kind of shielding. Outside chance they have a finished bomb, but we think that's unlikely. It would have gone off already.'

'And this was when?'

'January 10 or 11. More than two weeks ago.'

'So where exactly did the drop happen?'

'No one on the crew can tell us.'

'How is that possible?'

'The navy says these freighters, they're not democracies. Officers' orders aren't questioned. Ever. And this time, only the captain and the first mate knew exactly where they were. And the first mate went overboard when they were bringing the crates in. Maybe intentional, maybe an accident. That leaves the captain. Haxhi is his name. Albanian. And he's not talking, not yet. But we're guessing it must have been Nova Scotia. Highways from there lead straight to the U.S. border. The Canadians are checking their naval records for suspicious contacts. But they haven't found anything, and considering this was a couple weeks ago, they probably won't.'

'They still have to get it over the border.'

'Unless they have a hard-on for Montreal, yeah. We're figuring they drove. Why go to so much trouble, sailing these crates across the Atlantic, and then try to airmail them from Canada? Plus the crates, whatever's in them, FedEx or DHL would notice. So they drove. Probable entry points are Maine and New York. We've checked the border records, looking for pairs of Arab guys. We even checked immigration records for Arab men who flew in from Canada on passports from Middle Eastern countries or Europe. And we've found a couple of hundred since January 1. We're trying to track them down. But there's nobody who pops out. Nobody who crosses with the Gray Book or the Black Book. No surprise. They would have been flagged and arrested at the border. So whoever these guys are, they probably have American or Canadian passports.'

'We checking those?'

'Close to fifty thousand people fly between the United States and Canada every day. A four-day window, that's two hundred thousand people. Even if we just go for the obvious Arab names, cut out everyone else, we're stuck with maybe five thousand to check. And we're three weeks late, which means bad forwarding addresses, or no addresses at all, for ninety percent of them. It's impossible.'

Wells digested this bad news in silence. Four crates. Carrying uranium, bombs, who knew what? Now, most likely, on American soil.

'Still there, John? It gets worse. The crew of the *Juno* says that Haxhi, the captain, after the *Decatur* showed up, but before it boarded the *Juno*, he made a call on his sat phone. Then he tossed the phone. Probably he and Bernard were running a traffic light, an indirect. A preset alarm.'

'I get it, Ellis.' The goal was to eliminate direct links between the *Juno* and Bernard but still have a way to let Bernard know if the *Juno* ran into trouble. The solution was a cut-out voice mail, one that Haxhi would call only if he believed he was in serious trouble. Bernard would check the voice mail every day. As long as it was empty, he'd know that Haxhi was safe. The light was green. But if Haxhi thought the *Juno* was going to be boarded, he'd leave a message, a yellow signal. If he didn't call back with an all-clear within twenty-four to forty-eight hours, the signal went red. Bernard would assume that Haxhi had been taken down – and that he was next on the list.

'When did the *Decatur* find the *Juno*?'

'Yesterday afternoon.'

'Makes sense,' Wells said. 'Bernard checks the voice mail, gets the message, burns his stuff, takes off. I'm useless here now, Ellis. Bernard probably thinks I'm with the BND. Even if he doesn't, he's not going to look to me for help. The Germans should move in, take him down. Assuming they know where he is. I'll catch the next flight to Washington.'

'You going commercial or you want an Air Force ride?'

'Whatever's quicker. Probably commercial.'

'Sure you wouldn't rather stay in Hamburg? It's outside the blast radius.' *Click.*

Wells checked the flights. Continental had an evening nonstop from Hamburg to Newark, getting in around 10 p.m. Eastern. From there he could grab the last connection of the night to Reagan. He still had a couple of hours, plenty of time to make the flight. He made the reservation and began to pack. But just as he finished and zipped up, his second phone, Roland Albert's phone, rang.

Roland's phone? Only Bernard had that number. The caller identification showed a local Hamburg exchange. 'Roland here.'

'I need to see you.' The voice was Bernard's. '*Now.*'

CHAPTER 29

The bomb was ungainly-looking, a sphere of steel with the long barrel of the Spear recoilless rifle sticking from its side. More than ungainly. Ugly. It looked like an oversized, broken barbell, like a bowling ball attached to a stovepipe. It looked like an Introduction to Sculpture 101 project produced by a particularly dismal student. It looked like anything but what it was, Bashir thought.

Bashir had the stable to himself this morning, after two long days of working beside Nasiji and Yusuf, forging the steel tamper and welding the barrel of the Spear to the hole that tunneled into its heart.

'You don't know the trouble you're about to cause,' Bashir said to the bomb. Even now, he couldn't believe that this jerry-rigged heap of metal could have anything like the destructive power that Nasiji expected. Bashir stared at the bomb. 'Don't you have any manners, Mr Gadget? You must know ignoring me isn't polite. Especially since I'm the one who made you. And it was tiring work.'

Indeed, Bashir had hardly slept the last few days. He hadn't been so exhausted since his first year as a surgical resident, when he'd caught himself more than once in the middle of rounds leaning against a wall and trying to sleep standing up. Bashir took another look at his handiwork, trying to decide if he was proud or ashamed. The steel ball was solid and strong, its seams invisible.

Bashir and Nasiji and Yusuf had tested the design three days before, using steel in place of the uranium that would be at the center of the live bomb. For the test, they loaded the outer half of the dummy steel pit and the 73-millimeter explosive round into the breech of the barrel. Then they covered the Spear and the tamper with heavy wool blankets to dull the noise from the blast. To be safe, they'd already moved all their equipment – and, of course, the partially disassembled Iskander warhead – out of the stable.

The Spear was fired by a trigger inside a pistol grip attached to its barrel. They would blow the real bomb simply by pulling the trigger. No point in trying to set it off from a distance. When it went, so would they. But for this practice firing Bashir soldered the tip of a flexible spool of thin steel wire to the trigger. Then Yusuf cut a hole in the wall of the stable and ran the spool through it.

Outside, Bashir walked through the woods, unspooling the wire until the slack was gone. He stood behind a tree, shivering, pulling lightly on the wire. The steel felt almost alive under his gloved fingertips, tensing and loosening as if a fish were hooked on the end of the line. Dusk had fallen and night was coming quickly, the weak winter sun disappearing into the hills behind them.

'Ready?' Bashir said.

Nasiji reached for the wire. Bashir wanted to pull the trigger himself. He was the one who'd forged the tamper, after all. But without a word he handed it over. Nasiji held the wire, closed his eyes – he might have been praying – gave the wire a sturdy tug—

And *boom*!

The explosion echoed through the woods, sending squirrels chittering angrily from the trees around them. A bird, big and black and fast, some kind of crow, took off from a stand of pines and flew straight at Bashir before turning up into the night. The stable shook, and though it held, a piece of the wall disappeared, sending shingles in their direction.

'Bang-bang,' Yusuf said. He grinned and squeezed Nasiji's shoulder like a proud father.

They walked together back into the stable and looked at their handiwork. The steel tamper had held, but the force of the explosion had bowed it slightly. It was no longer a perfect sphere. The back-blast had split the Spear from the tamper and smashed it into the side of the stable, leaving a jagged hole in the wall. The steel barrel had crumpled in half. It wouldn't be of any use to them except as scrap, but they had a second tube in reserve.

Nasiji shined a penlight into the hole in the tamper.

'Not bad,' he said.

Bashir peered inside. The high-explosive round and the pieces of the pit had fused into a single mass, still warm to the touch, in the center of the tamper.

'Looks like a scrambled egg,' Yusuf said.

'Not perfect, though,' Nasiji said to Bashir. Nasiji reached in with pliers, tugged the crumpled, charred mass of steel out of the hole. 'You can still see the outlines of the two pieces.'

'So?'

'So the live pit needs to come together more closely, within a millimeter. The tighter the fit, the less the chance of predetonation.'

'A *fizzle*,' Yusuf said in English. Bashir had learned that Yusuf used the word *fizzle* at every opportunity. He seemed to find it hilarious.

'You can do a better job, yes, Bashir?'

'Of course.' Bashir didn't like Nasiji talking to him as though he were a child, but what could he say? Nasiji had controlled this project long before Bashir had ever been involved. *No excuses*, Bashir told himself. The truth . . . the truth was that until the last few days, he hadn't minded letting Nasiji run this operation. That way he hadn't had to think over what they were doing.

★   ★   ★

438

Yet even after the practice firing, even as they forged the replacement tamper, Bashir kept working, not a word about his doubts to Nasiji. For the next two days, standing over the forge, washed by its infernal heat, he tried to sort out the reasons for his silence: a runny mix of fear, confusion, esprit de corps, and anger. Fear of what they would do if he tried to stop them. More important, fear of what they would do to his wife. He had signed up for this project with eyes open, and he would accept the consequences if he tried to back out. But he wouldn't allow Thalia to suffer.

At the same time, Bashir wasn't sure if he had the right to undo Nasiji and Yusuf's work. The time for doubt had come and gone. How could he substitute his judgment for theirs? They were a team. If the Americans found them together, they would certainly die as a team.

Bashir couldn't forget his uncle either. The old man in the visitors' room in Tora, heavy and gentle and about to be destroyed. Bashir no longer thought that all Americans were evil – he'd seen too much compassion, too many tears in his emergency room – but they were certainly heedless. Nasiji wasn't wrong to hate them. They'd caused great misery all over the world, especially for Muslims. Maybe this bomb was the answer.

Or maybe he wouldn't have to take any action. Maybe the bomb would fail on its own. Maybe they'd be caught before they were done. And so Bashir procrastinated, putting off any decision, forgetting that procrastination was a choice in and of itself.

While Bashir worked with Yusuf to reforge the tamper, Nasiji had his own project. He was installing emergency flashers in the grille and rear of the used black Chevy Suburban that Bashir had bought a few months before, a private sale. Bashir had paid cash and never reregistered the Suburban, so it couldn't be connected to him. Nasiji also picked up a couple of scrap Washington plates. Nothing intimidated other drivers, or even cops, more than a black Suburban with D.C. plates and hidden flashers, the combination preferred by the FBI. The lights wouldn't get them onto the White House grounds, but they might get them close enough to make a difference.

Bashir also spent a day forging a second tamper, this one with a hole at its center big enough to accommodate a beryllium reflector as well as the pit. Nasiji insisted they make both, though he no longer seemed certain they would get the beryllium. His contact in Germany still hadn't gotten the second shipment of the metal. And even if it arrived now, sending it to the United States before the State of the Union would be impossible.

'At least this way we'll have time to make sure the design is perfect,' Bashir said. He was secretly glad for the holdup. Without the State of the Union as a deadline, they might not blow the bomb for months.

'Whatever happens with the beryllium, I want us to be ready,' Nasiji said. 'If we wait too long, we'll wake up with the FBI breaking down our doors.'

So they came to the stable before sunrise and worked until close to midnight. They returned to the house only to eat. The kitchen smelled of chicken and lemon and chickpeas, Thalia's contribution to the cause. She'd asked Bashir twice if she could see the bomb. Both times he'd refused. Now, at meals, she was strangely focused on Nasiji. She even made sure his plate was full before turning to her husband. Bashir reminded himself that she was young and impressionable and probably in love with the idea of having this secret.

After forty-eight hours of nearly nonstop work, they finished the tampers. Nasiji and Yusuf drove to Binghamton to find an Internet café and check on the beryllium. Bashir turned his attention to sintering the mold for the uranium pit. As Nasiji had demanded, he was trying to shrink the gap between the pieces of the pit – the cylinder that fit in the center of the tamper and the pipe-shaped piece that they would fire at it – to less than one millimeter.

Bashir finished the first piece around lunchtime, melting the precious pieces of uranium, then pouring the molten metal – a thick gray-black soup – into the ceramic mold he'd created and transferring the mold to the vacuum forge. Through the inch-thick window of the forge, he could see that the uranium was setting perfectly. He turned down the gas until the metal solidified. Then he removed the mold from the forge and laid it on a steel plate to cool. He was just beginning to work on the second piece when Nasiji and Yusuf ran into the stable.

'Sayyid,' Bashir said. 'Take a look—'

'How long before you're done?' Nasiji's eyes were narrow, half-shut, his jaw thrust forward.

'I've just finished the first part.' Bashir pointed to the piece cooling on the tungsten plate, a dark gray cylinder of uranium, just six inches long, less than three inches in diameter. Nearly pure U-235, it weighed nineteen kilograms.

'That's it?' Nasiji reached for it.

'Don't touch. It's still cooling.'

'How long for the rest, the cylinder?'

'It's more complicated. It will take another day or so, at least.'

'No. You finish it tonight.'

'What's wrong, Sayyid?'

'The Americans, they found the ship that brought Yusuf and me over.'

'How do you know?'

'I know. It was far from here, but somehow they discovered it. We have to assume that Bernard has been arrested or will be soon. The message came yesterday. Very bad luck we didn't see it until now. Bernard should have called me directly, but he must have been afraid to take the chance.'

'But he doesn't know where we are. They don't know me or you. They can't track us here. We have plenty of time.' Bashir hoped his voice didn't sound as desperate as he felt. In his head he heard a clock ticking, so loudly that for a moment he wondered if it was real. The moment of decision was here, far sooner than he'd expected. He wasn't sure whom he feared more, the Americans or the men beside him.

'If they've found him, they're only one step from us. We have to get the gadget done as quickly as possible, get it out of here.'

'Can you reach him? Find out whether he's been taken?'

Nasiji laid a hand on Bashir's bicep and squeezed, his fingers digging in as though he wanted to snap Bashir's arm in half. 'Stick to your forge, Doctor. Let me worry about this.'

'Yes, Sayyid. But what about the beryllium? I thought you said—'

'If we don't move now, we're going to lose everything. Anyway, we'll try for the State of the Union.'

'Tomorrow?'

'Yes, tomorrow.' Nasiji leaned back, opened his eyes, looked Bashir up and down. 'Is something wrong, Bashir? Losing your nerve?'

'You asked me that before, and the answer's the same: no. Now, take your hand off my arm so I can get back to work.'

'Good,' Nasiji said. 'I'm glad there's some fight in you yet. God willing, we'll finish this pit tonight, get the pieces together, be ready to travel in the morning.'

'God willing.' *And then what?*

CHAPTER 30

'I need to see you.' The voice was Bernard's. 'Now.'

'Where are you?' Wells said.

'I have your money. The final three million. It's yours. I don't want you to hurt my family.'

'Wire transfer it like the two.'

'It's cash. I must hand it over face-to-face.'

'BND watching you? You setting me up?'

'I don't think so, no.'

'Let's meet somewhere nice and public.'

'That wouldn't be safe for either of us. You want your money, come to the Stern Hotel. Room 317.'

'Three-one-seven?'

'On the Reeperbahn.' Bernard hung up.

This meeting would end badly, Wells knew. He'd done too good a job scaring Bernard. Now Bernard thought he had only one way to be sure that Wells wouldn't come after his family.

Wells stripped to his gray T-shirt and pulled on the bulletproof vest he carried and put a heavy wool sweater on over it. The vest offered limited protection, but it was better than nothing. He strapped his shoulder holster around his sweater and tucked in his Glock and hid the holster with a loose-fitting leather jacket. Cold weather made carrying pistols easy. He headed for the door, reconsidered, grabbed his phone, called Shafer.

'At the *Flughafen* already?' Shafer said.

'The Germans know where Bernard is?'

'Not at the moment.' Disgust dripped across the Atlantic. 'So the associate director of the BND just informed me. *Not at the moment.*'

'I do.' Wells explained the call he'd just received.

'Good. The BND can bring him in.'

'I'll get him.'

'Thought you were done freelancing. Let the Germans handle him.'

'He's expecting me. He sees anybody else coming, he'll jump out the window. I show, it'll slow him down. He's still not sure what side I'm on.'

'The best way to do this is with a tac team and some flash-bangs.'

'That worked great in Munich.'

'Nineteen seventy-two was a long time ago. The Germans have learned a few things. You're not the only one who can do this, John. You keep making the same mistake. Definition of insanity and all that.'

'Save me the fortune-cookie wisdom. I'll bring him in, get back to Langley before tomorrow morning.'

'You planning to fly commercial or just flap your cape and go?'

'Funny, Ellis.'

'I have to call the BND. But I'll give you an hour. Plenty of time to get there.'

'Two hours.'

'Two hours.'

The late-afternoon Hamburg traffic was heavy, and Wells wished he had left the Mercedes at the hotel and taken the U-Bahn. Forty minutes passed before he reached the Reeperbahn, quiet and gray in the twilight. The long cold winter nights were enough to keep even the most debased whore-mongers at home. On the south side of the avenue, he saw the Stern—

Surrounded by German police cars and dozens of officers in riot gear. Wells looked twice, hoping that the cops were there coincidentally to bust an unlicensed brothel or a heroin-dealing kebob shop. But as he watched, three men in helmets and face shields ran into the hotel. Shafer hadn't given him two hours. Shafer hadn't given him five minutes.

Wells parked the Mercedes in an alley off the Reeperbahn and grabbed his sat phone.

'Tell me I'm not seeing this.'

'I had to, John. Their country, their op.'

'*Their op?* Who found him? Who's been playing him?'

'What are you gonna do with him? You can't arrest him. And they say no renditions.' A delivery truck turned into the alley behind the Mercedes and honked, a quick double-tap, *move along*. 'He's a German national, he stays on German soil. I promised them.'

'You promised *me*, Ellis. Two hours.' Wells hung up. He would deal with Shafer later. Betrayal and betrayal and betrayal. He jumped out of the Mercedes, ignoring the shouts of the delivery driver, and dodged traffic as he ran across the Reeperbahn, heading for the armored police van parked outside the hotel's entrance.

'Halt! Halt!' A big man in a black flak jacket, *Polizei* emblazoned across the chest in white, trotted at Wells, right hand hovering over the pistol on his hip. Wells slowed.

'I need to talk to the agent in charge, whoever's running the show—'

'You are American?' the officer said. 'This is a police action. Very serious. You must leave.'

'I know the guy in there,' Wells said desperately. 'I gave him to you.'

The officer put a heavy hand on Wells's shoulder and steered him away from the hotel.

'Listen, my name's John Wells—'

From above, the *thump* of a flash-bang grenade, and then another. Wells and the officer swung around, watching as a window blew at the west end of the hotel, three stories up, glass pouring like confetti toward the pavement, a pair of hookers screaming and shielding their mascaraed eyes—

Then a single gunshot.

The officer pushed Wells to the street, landed on top of him, 250 pounds of German cop protecting him. Wells barely restrained himself

448

from rolling the guy over and punching him in the face. 'Let me up.'

'When it is safe.'

'It's safe now,' Wells said, staring down at the Reeperbahn pavement, cigarette butts and crumpled beer cans. 'Unless that guy up there can shoot when he's dead.'

The officer rolled over and Wells stood. A team of medics ran into the hotel, carrying a stretcher and a defibrillator. Too late, Wells was sure. They'd gone in hard and slow and given Bernard plenty of time to take the coward's way out. Or the hero's. Depending on who was telling the story. Either way Bernard wouldn't be much help.

Three minutes of explanations later, Wells found himself outside the hotel's front door, pleading with the BND agent in charge to let him inside.

'You want to see the room? But the man inside is dead. He killed himself, yes?'

'No doubt. Maybe he left me something.'

'We will find it.'

'I'd like to look for myself.' You guys blew this top to bottom, so please don't make me beg, Wells didn't say.

But the agent seemed to understand. 'As you wish. Jergen will accompany you.'

The *stern* catered to British chavs who piled into cheap charter flights for weekend vacations in Hamburg: all the pilsner they could swallow and a stop at the brothels on Herbertstrasse. Good times.

449

The thirdfloor carpet had once been blue. Now it was closer to black and covered with cigarette burns. The plaster in the hallway was laced with fist-sized holes where guests had traded punches with each other and maybe a few unlucky hookers. A dozen BND agents stood outside the room, murmuring to one another, knocking around what had happened, what had gone wrong, the stories they would tell their bosses and the internal investigators who would second-guess every decision they had and hadn't made. They fell silent as Wells passed.

And in Room 317, Bernard Kygeli, the top of his head split like an overcooked egg. He lay on his back on the queen-sized bed, his blood soaking through the cheap wool blanket. The medics weren't even pretending to work on him. Bernard hadn't taken any chances when the BND came through the door. He'd put his pistol in his mouth and swallowed eternity. His brains were splattered on the grimy yellow wall behind the bed.

Wells knew he ought to feel a touch of pity for Bernard, or at least disgust at the ugly way he'd died. But he could muster only annoyance, the annoyance of a district manager whose top salesman had just quit. Bernard should have stuck around a little bit longer, instead of bailing this way, leaving him shorthanded with the end of the quarter coming up. Not a team player.

From the neck down, Bernard was undamaged, oddly dapper in a blue suit with a pale pink shirt and dark red tie, his black leather dress shoes hanging limply off the bed. A bitter wind blew in through the shattered window, carrying in the rising blare of European sirens – Ooh-*Ooh*! Ooh-*Ooh*! – from the flotilla of police vehicles below. Wells peeked out the window. A television truck had already appeared at the end of the block, just beyond the east edge of the hotel.

'Anyone search him yet?'

Jergen consulted with the other cops. 'No.'

Wells grabbed latex gloves from one of the medics, strapped them on, sifted through Bernard's pockets, hoping for a cell phone, a flash drive, an engraved pen, a business card, a hotel receipt, any clue at all. In Bernard's inside suit pocket, he found six keys – house, office, and warehouse, most likely. In the right front pants pocket, a wallet, smooth black leather. Wells flipped through it. A gold Amex card, seven 50-euro notes, a creased headshot of two young women, pretty, both wearing headscarves. His daughters, presumably.

And in the left pocket, a thickly folded piece of lined notebook paper. Wells unfolded it and found a scrawl in Arabic, shakily written in thin blue pen—

Why, when it is said to you, Go and fight in God's way, do you dig your heels in the earth? Do you prefer this world to the life to come? How small the enjoyment of this world is, compared with the life to come! If you do not go out and fight, God will punish you severely and put others in your place, but you cannot harm Him in any way. God has power over all things.

'What is it?' Jergen said.

'A suicide note. From the Quran.' The ninth Surah, if Wells remembered right. He tucked the paper and Bernard's wallet and the keys where he'd found them. He pulled open the squeaking closet doors, looked inside the particleboard dresser, stuck his head in the bathroom, ducked his head under the bed. He found nothing but two roaches in the tub and a couple of dusty condom wrappers, surely predating Bernard's arrival.

'He say anything when you came in?' Wells said to the agent in charge. '*Allahu Akbar*? Anything at all?'

The cop shook his head. 'Just the pistol in his mouth, and—'

'Yeah.'

When Wells and Jergen returned to the front entrance, they found a tall man in a gray suit. He extended a hand to Wells.

'Mr Wells,' he said. 'I'm Gerhard Tobertal. Assistant director of the BND for Hamburg—'

'Yeah, you're the one who lost him.' Wells leaned forward, put his face close to Tobertal's, staring into the German's blue eyes. 'Get your men out of here. All of them.'

'Excuse me?'

'Don't you see anything?' Wells knew that his rage was counter-productive, but he couldn't help

452

himself. First Shafer and now this. 'You blew the surveillance and the takedown, too, and now you want CNN here, talking about how a terrorist killed himself on the Reeperbahn? So all Bernard's friends know he's dead.'

'Mr Wells—'

'Make it go away. Pull your guys and make it a no-name junkie overdose. And when you hit his house, do it fast and quiet in the middle of the night. If you know how. Maybe we're lucky and the compartmentalization saves us, and his buddies don't find out for a few extra hours.'

'I don't appreciate being talked to this way—'

'Then do your job.' Wells turned away. If he hurried, he could still make his flight.

CHAPTER 31

This time Wells had no problem at immigration. The opposite, in fact. A Homeland Security officer waited for him when the flight arrived at Newark. 'Mr Wells,' she said as he walked out of the companionway, the first passenger off. 'This way.'

She led him along the glassed-in second floor that overlooked the C Concourse, a long walkway, no exits, that connected international arrivals with the Newark customs hall. She was young and strong and Wells had to jog to keep up. He felt heavy and slow. He'd lost a night's sleep – it was nearly 10 p.m. in Newark, 4 a.m. in Germany – and even the frigid jetway air hadn't shocked him awake. Maybe he was getting old.

When Wells had come home after his decade in Afghanistan and Pakistan, the wealth of the United States had overwhelmed him. Not just the size of the stores, aisle upon aisle of products for every conceivable desire, but the buildings themselves, high-ceilinged and fitted tightly together. Even the lights, banks of bright fluorescents where Afghans would make do with a single sixty-watt bulb. Americans might complain about the price of electricity but they sure weren't afraid to use it. For his first few months back, Wells found himself wondering whether he had landed in a fifty-state Potemkin village, if the malls and office parks and highways he saw were nothing more than stage sets. So much abundance couldn't be real.

Fortunately or not, the feeling faded. Now, after two years of motorcycles and perfect teeth and flat-screen televisions and grocery stores filled with fresh fruit, Wells was again used to, if not exactly comfortable with, his country's riches.

Tonight, though, he felt a different dislocation, a kind of real-time nostalgia for the people on the concourse below him. The family clumped together slurping sodas outside the Subway, two tiny kids dressed identically in puffy red jackets and jeans and white sneakers, not a fashion statement, just a sale at Wal-Mart. The sales rep in a demure gray suit-and-skirt set, leaning against a wall, checking her Black-Berry, then pumping her fist in quiet triumph, deal closed and bonus won. The middle-aged man with the darkest skin Wells had ever seen, stepping up to gate C-89 to hug an equally dark woman wearing a bright orange and green dress under her winter coat.

No matter where it blew, the bomb would destroy this place. The buildings would be rebuilt. Maybe, eventually, the economy would recover. But the *idea* of the United States as the world's lighthouse, the land given peace and justice and prosperity so that it could export those gifts everywhere else, would never return. And maybe America had never lived up to that promise. Maybe it had never become the shining city that the plastic patriots claimed. But dreams had power even if they didn't come true. The world would be a poorer place if the American dream died.

When they reached customs, Wells didn't even have to hand over his passport. The agent simply guided him through to the booths, and then he was back officially on American soil. Five minutes later, he was at C-101, catching the last flight of the night to D.C.

At National, another surprise, Shafer waited. He extended his hand, a wrinkly paw sticking from his too-short shirt cuffs. Wells let it dangle until Shafer pulled it back.

'All right,' Shafer said. 'I earned that. You want to talk about it? Hug it out?'

Wells ignored him and headed for the exit. Shafer trotted behind him, yapping at his heels. 'I wanted you to see that you can't fly solo all the time. An object lesson. Unfortunately, it didn't work out how I expected—'

'Enough,' Wells said. When this ended, if it ever ended, they'd have a chance to discuss what Shafer had done. Or, more likely, to bury it along with all the other miscommunications and fibs and flat-out lies that Wells and the agency had traded over the years.

At the front of the terminal, a Crown Vic and two SUVs waited, black Suburbans with armored windows and antennas jutting from their roofs. Two agents in suits stood outside the lead truck. As Wells and Shafer approached, the back doors to the front Suburban popped open. Wells and Shafer slipped inside and the Suburbans took off, their red-and-blues flashing, roaring up the George Washington Parkway at eighty miles an hour.

'Subtle, Ellis.'

'Duto's orders.'

'So tell me where we stand.'

'Maybe two hours ago, we got good news. They broke Haxhi. The captain. Don't ask me how.'

Wells didn't need to ask. He knew. A few months before, in China, he'd been on the receiving end of a torture session that had left his ribs broken and his shoulder loose in its socket. Even now his ribs ached at the thought. Round and round it goes, he didn't say. Where it stops nobody knows.

'He gave us the names of the smugglers?'

'Not that. Says he doesn't know and maybe it's true. But he did give up the drop point. It's not Nova Scotia. Southeastern Newfoundland. Near St John's. That's the capital.'

'Newfoundland?' Wells tried to picture eastern Canada. 'That's an island, right?'

'Correct. Best guess, they went in that way

because they thought there wouldn't be a big Canadian navy presence. Which there isn't. So they land those crates, ferry them to Nova Scotia, drive them in.'

'But somebody's got to meet them.'

'Looks like it.'

'Anything else? The magicians' – the NSA – 'have any luck?'

Shafer shook his head. 'There was one sat phone left on the boat. Not activated. The cell number you have for Bernard didn't go anywhere. Neither did his e-mail addresses. The Germans hit his house and office and warehouse while you were in the air, but so far they haven't gotten anything useful.'

'The laptop?'

'Tough to recover anything from a melted hard drive. Though they're trying.'

'The son, Helmut, he knew something,' Wells said. 'I'm sure of it. Maybe a name.'

'They'll push him. Anything else, John? It's the fourth quarter now, late.'

'Yeah, and they got the ball.'

Wells closed his eyes, tried to think. But sleep was on him like a glove and all he could remember was the airport, the family on Concourse C—

'You're assuming the crates came in by land, but maybe the courier handled the crossing and the bad guys flew in. Anybody check flights from St John's?'

'I don't know if it's happened yet, but it's on

the top sheet. If there's a direct flight between the United States and Newfoundland, so they didn't get lost in a transfer in Toronto or somewhere, maybe we'll catch a break.'

Five minutes later, they reached Langley. And then the biggest surprise yet. Exley, on Shafer's couch, leaning forward, staring intently at a wall map of the North Atlantic and North America that was posted to a corkboard in the middle of the office. She'd cut her hair. Wells had never seen it so short, cropped on the sides and almost spiky on top. She looked like a punk singer. Wells didn't know what the haircut meant. Otherwise, she was as beautiful as ever. The short hair accentuated her blue eyes and she'd lost a few pounds, not many, but she hadn't been very big to start with and now her cheeks had a sorrowful sharpness to them. She stood when she saw him and he crossed to her and picked her up and hugged her like he was trying to meld their bodies together. She put her arms around him, but when he tried to kiss her she ducked her head. He set her down and she put a hand on his arm.
'You stayed,' Shafer said.
'Couldn't miss this,' she said. A smile flitted across her lips, narrow, quiet, almost maternal. 'The prodigal son returns.'
'You look great,' Wells said. He ran a hand over her hair.
'Last time it was this short, I was in college,' Exley said.

459

'But I thought—' Wells broke off, not wanting to say the wrong thing, or anything at all, just to look at her.

'Old habits,' she said. 'I swore I'd just come in to see Ellis, and then I swore I'd only work for a day or two, and then I swore I wouldn't be here when you got back, and look at me. Nothing changes but the hair and the hole in my liver. But now I swear when this one's done, so am I.'

'Yeah?'

'Yeah.' She smiled and Wells felt his heart take two beats at once. Maybe they would find a way to be together after this, maybe they wouldn't, but he was sure she would always love him.

'Reunion's over, kids,' Shafer said. 'Work to do. Anything new?'

'We gave the RCMP what we know' – the Royal Canadian Mounted Police – 'and they're hitting the ferry offices now. They'll get records of trucks that sailed from Newfoundland to Nova Scotia since January 1. We can check those against our border crossing records. But they're telling us not to expect much. Passenger vehicles don't register and there aren't any cameras on the boats or the docks.'

'What about the flights?'

'Better news there. One nonstop a day out of St John's to Newark.'

'That's the only nonstop to the United States?'

'The one and only. The FBI is getting a warrant for the manifests. And we're sorting the immigration records at Newark. If they came in on that flight, we ought to have their names and faces and passports within a couple of hours.'

'Then we can start checking car rentals, airlines, credit cards, cell phones,' Shafer said.

'No problems with a warrant?' Wells said.

'We'll get a finding from the president. I think even the ACLU won't mind.'

'Any decision on releasing the names of the bombmakers publicly, if we get them?'

'Duto and the rest of the big-boy club' – official title, the Homeland Security Emergency Interagency Executive Committee – 'are heading to the White House to talk about that now. You know the problem.'

The problem, as always, was that publicizing the manhunt might push the terrorists to immediately detonate whatever they had. But putting out their names was also the quickest and most efficient way to find them. The problem was made even more complicated by the fact that the State of the Union was scheduled for the next night. Allowing it to proceed with a nuclear bomb potentially loose would be insane. But canceling it would be as good as telling the terrorists to blow the bomb immediately.

'So what can I do?' Wells said.

'You? Let the machine crank for a couple hours, get some sleep,' Shafer said to Wells. 'There's nothing for you to do now and tomorrow's going to be a long day. Dream about Bernard if you can. These guys have been careful the whole way and

461

I don't think we're going to find them right away even with their names. Bernard's the closest we've come so far and you're the closest we came to him.'

'I'll do my best,' Wells said. He lay down on the couch and tried to rest his head on Exley's lap, but she pushed him off.

'Not now.'

So he shuffled down the hall to his office and lay on the floor and closed his eyes and dreamed of Bernard. Bernard, lying on his deathbed in the Hotel Stern, trying through his cracked skull to tell him the secrets of the bombmakers. Where they were. What their crates held. But then a German agent wearing a bear suit suddenly parachuted into his office and Bernard disappeared. Then Wells was in Bernard's office again, tapping on the melted keys of Bernard's laptop, looking at the burned-out screen. He reached down for a sip of coffee—

And suddenly woke.

In Shafer's office, Exley and Shafer were hunched over his screen.

'Ellis. Jenny. Can you think of any reason why Bernard Kygeli would have a coffee cup from Penn State?'

'Penn State as in Pennsylvania State University in Happy Valley, Pennsylvania? Not a good one.'

'He did. In his office.'

'Kids go there?' This from Exley.

'Don't think so. They live in Hamburg.'

'Cousins, nephews?' Shafer thinking out loud now. 'The BND can give us the names of any relatives he has in Germany. And I guess we get the FBI to look for students with Arab names. Though I'm not sure we'll be able to bring anybody in without some kind of connection. You're sure it was Penn State.'

'I'm sure.'

'Forty thousand students just in undergrad. Too bad it wasn't Swarthmore.'

'There was something else . . .' Wells shook his head. The memory, whatever it was, lurked just outside his consciousness.

'Go back to dreamland, John, see what else you get.'

CHAPTER 32

Bashir lay awake, his fingers interlaced behind his head, his wife snoring gently beside him. His last night as a husband. His last night as a surgeon. His last night.

He saw now that he had agreed to help build this gadget without believing they would succeed. Like every Egyptian child, he'd dreamed of scoring the winning goal in the World Cup finals, bringing the trophy home to Cairo. Through grade school, he worked on his kicks, his footwork, even his headers. But on the day he turned nine, playing with his friends and cousins in a dusty park around the corner from his apartment, he'd realized he wouldn't have the chance. He wasn't the slowest player on the field, but he was far from the fastest. And though his footwork was solid, his friends – two of them, anyway – controlled the ball so easily that they seemed to have it leashed to a string.

And this was just one little field. All over the neighborhood, all over Cairo, millions of kids were playing soccer. He wasn't even the best here. How would he ever be the best in Egypt? The realization didn't spoil Bashir's love for soccer. He still

464

played, and he still dreamed of playing beneath the lights in Paris or London or Barcelona. But for the rest of his childhood, he knew his vision was nothing more than a pleasant fantasy.

Somehow he'd deluded himself into thinking this project was equally impossible. Even as the stable turned into a machine shop, even after he learned how to forge steel, even after Nasiji and Yusuf arrived in Newfoundland, even after they disassembled the warhead and built the molds and crafted the dummy bomb, even this week as he'd molded the pits, he'd somehow failed to accept the reality of the project. He didn't know whether his imagination had been too strong or too weak.

Now the bomb was done. He and Yusuf had finished the second piece of the uranium pit three hours before. Bashir had surprised himself with his speed, but then Nasiji's scowl and Yusuf's dead eyes were powerful motivators. Nasiji had briefly slid the two pieces of the pit over each other – a step that was safe as long as the pit was in the open air and not surrounded by the reflective steel tamper. The pieces fit together as lock and key. Then they had fused the bottom piece to the hole in the tamper, using a steel cap to be sure that it was exactly centered. The penultimate step, welding the recoilless rifle with the tamper, took only a few minutes. Finally, they'd used high-strength epoxy to glue the waterglass-shaped cap of uranium to the Spear's high-explosive 73-millimeter round.

465

And then they were done. The bomb could be fired as quickly as Nasiji or Bashir or Yusuf could load the round into the barrel of the Spear and pull the trigger. After they were finished, Yusuf and Nasiji silently examined their handiwork, backyard barbecuers contemplating a perfectly cooked steak. Bashir puttered around the stable, putting tools in place, wiping down the welding torch.

Finally, Nasiji whistled sharply at Bashir.

'Quit that,' Nasiji said. 'There's no point. We won't be making another one.'

'Yes,' Bashir said. 'I suppose my surgical training, I always neaten up after the operation—' he was stammering now.

'It's late,' Nasiji said. 'Let's have supper and then to bed.'

Over dinner, Nasiji outlined their final steps. In the morning they'd load the bomb and the remains of the Iskander into the Suburban, drive to the final safe house – a place Bashir hadn't even known about before tonight, a temporary spot where they could stay for a few hours but no longer – and hole up for their final run to Washington. The State of the Union started around 9 p.m. and Nasiji didn't want them on the D.C. streets for very long beforehand. If the State of the Union was canceled or postponed, they'd assume that their plot had been discovered and that they were being hunted. In that case, they'd head for New York City and try to hit midtown Manhattan. Philadelphia, the city closest to their safe house, was the third option. Before they left, they would upload the video they'd made to several jihadi Web sites, and FedEx copies of the DVD to CNN, *The New York Times*, and other Western media outlets. Without the beryllium, the detonation probably would be too small to be confused with a real Russian weapon, but the video could add to the Americans' confusion and increase the pressure for a retaliatory strike.

'Before you sleep, make your absolutions,' Nasiji said, as Thalia cleaned the table. 'Tomorrow we won't have much time. Make your peace with Allah tonight. Think of the reasons you've chosen this path. Think of what the Sheikh' – bin Laden – 'said before the Crusaders came to Iraq.'

Nasiji pushed back his chair. 'Come with me,' he said. He walked outside.

In the dark, under the clean pale starlight, the three men stood shivering. A thick crust of snow covered the trees and the earth, white and silent, reminding Bashir how far he was from home.

'*I shall lead my steed and hurl us both at the target,*' Nasiji said. '*Oh Lord, if my end is nigh, may my tomb not be draped in green mantles. No, let it be the belly of an eagle, perched on high with his kin. So let me be a martyr, dwelling in a high mountain pass among a band of knights.*'

Nasiji reached out his hands for Yusuf and Bashir.

'Tomorrow we descend from the pass.'

★　　★　　★

A fine, knightly moment. Then Bashir had come to his bed and his wife had clutched at him with the same ardor she'd displayed all week, grinding her hips against his and making the fluttering noises that he'd thought until now existed only on the banned pornographic channels that half of Egypt watched on satellite television. He wondered if she was making love to him, Nasiji, the bomb, or all three at once.

When they were done, she wrapped her arms around him and whispered, 'Tomorrow.'

She was nervous, Bashir thought. Understandable. 'My love,' he said. 'I wish this weren't all happening so fast. If we had time, I would have sent you home. But it'll be safer for you to stay here. You'll just have to tell the Americans when they come that you didn't know what we were doing, that we kept it secret from you—'

'My Bashir. My husband. I'm coming with you.'

Bashir was silent. He couldn't have heard her right. 'No,' he said finally. 'I won't allow it. You don't understand what these bombs do—'

'I do.'

He rolled atop her, pushing her down. 'You don't. And as your husband, I order you—'

'I'm coming. Bashir, if they find me here, do you think they'll believe I had no idea? Why shouldn't I come? Why shouldn't I be part of this?'

'All right,' Bashir said. Nasiji wouldn't possibly allow her along, but for tonight Bashir decided to let her think she'd be included. Otherwise she would never sleep.

'Are you scared, my husband?'

'Why would you think that?'

'There's no reason to be. This, what you've built, it's Allah's will.'

'Yes? Did you speak to him?' Bashir tried to smile in the dark, to make his words a joke, but he couldn't.

'I'm not a *prophet*, Bashir.' Not a hint of laughter in her answer. 'But this I know.' She kissed him again. A few minutes later, her breath eased and he knew she was asleep beside him, one hand wrapped around his arm, her nostrils fluttering, her full lips opened slightly. The sleep of a child. His wife, blessed with a certainty he couldn't imagine.

CHAPTER 33

The Black Hawks from Langley and the Pentagon arrived on the back lawn of the White House just as the armored limousines from the FBI and Foggy Bottom rolled through the E Street gates. One by one, a string of grim-faced men made their way into the west wing of the White House. Midnight had already passed, but each visitor had independently chosen to wear a freshly pressed suit and a smoothly knotted tie. The gravity of this meeting demanded formality.

Inside the White House, they were directed not to the Situation Room, as they'd expected, but to the Oval Office. No one questioned the choice. Like the suits and ties, the Oval Office seemed appropriate. Anyway, the Situation Room was cramped and low-ceilinged and not particularly comfortable compared to the double O.

The meeting had been scheduled for 12:15 a.m. and the president didn't like latecomers. Duto, the last to arrive, slipped in at 12:13 and took his seat beside the secretary of defense. Everyone else in the room was equally senior: the director of national intelligence, the director of the FBI, the secretaries of state and homeland security, and the national security adviser. Principals only. The director of Los Alamos and the general in charge of Strategic Air Command were waiting by their phones in case the president had questions, but they weren't part of the meeting.

Duto had been in this office hundreds of times before, but he couldn't remember a situation as serious as this one. The confrontation with China had been tricky, but they hadn't realized how tricky until after it ended. At the time, no one had really thought they were facing a nuclear threat. This time they knew better. And until they could narrow down where the bad guys were hiding, they had only two options: tell everyone in the country and create a national panic, or hold the information close while they searched in secret.

Duto didn't mind letting someone else make the decision. The way he saw it, his job was to lay out the options, maybe pushing one a bit more than another, but never explicitly expressing his opinion unless asked. After the president decided what to do, the agency would carry out his orders as best it could. In truth, though, the CIA's powers were more limited than either its critics or its supporters believed. Want to invade a country? Call in the army. Hoping for a prediction of what Afghanistan will be like twenty years from now? Get a crystal ball. The agency was neither all-powerful nor all-knowing. It gave its best guesses, did the nasty work that no one else would, and tried not to embarrass the United States along the way.

It was a big, heavy bureaucracy, and Duto spent much of his time just trying to keep it going, and much of the rest keeping it afloat in the even bigger bureaucracy that was the American intelligence community. He didn't set policy, and he didn't try to embarrass the president. And so he survived. He'd survived two administrations, a mole, Guantánamo, and that near-miss in New York. He'd survived long enough to defend the CIA's turf, his turf, from the FBI and the Defense Department, which had tried to muscle in on the covert operations that by right and custom belonged only to Langley. And yet some of his own agents, the very men and women whose turf he was protecting, had the gall to call him a lapdog.

Like John Wells. Duto knew exactly how Wells saw him. And Wells had proven useful the last couple of years, no doubt about it. But he didn't like Wells and he never would. The guy grated on him. Wells was like Kobe Bryant, Duto thought. Big skills and an even bigger ego. Guys like that always imagined they were indispensable. And they were, for a while. But no one was indispensable. These guys, they lost a step and the game moved past them. The teams were eternal, but the players came and went. One day, Wells would lose a step, too. And when that moment came, Duto would gladly show him the door.

★　　★　　★

But first they had to get through this night, and the next day.

In the Oval Office, Duto and the other six men waited in silence. No one wanted to be caught bantering about the weather or the Super Bowl when the president arrived. He showed at 12:17, wearing khakis and a blue shirt, thumbs looped into his belt, as if he were about to host a late-night card game instead of discussing the most dangerous nuclear threat the United States had faced since the Cuban Missile Crisis. His chief of staff, a tall man with pasty skin trailed a step behind. The chief of staff's name was Bob Hatch. Inevitably, and accurately, he was known in the top ranks of the government as Hatchet.

The president nodded at each of the men in the room and sat down behind his massive desk. Tucked under his arm, Hatchet held the briefing book that the CIA and FBI had prepared two hours before. At a nod from the president, Hatchet dropped – not placed, dropped – the book on the desk. It thumped against the wood, the sound of failure. The president put a finger on top of the book.

'Here's my executive summary. We don't know where these men are. Nor their names. Nor who's paying them. Nor if they have a working bomb. Nor their targets. As for the Russians, they're lying to us, but we don't know why.' The president's eyes had locked on Duto. 'Director, would you say I've accurately summarized the report?'

'Mr President, I can't disagree with what you say. However, we have made great progress in the last six hours. We believe that in the next few hours, certainly by sunrise, we will have the names and passports under which they entered the United States. We're pursuing every possible avenue to get answers to your questions. As to whether they may attempt to use the bombs for ransom, we judge that possibility unlikely, sir.'

The president took his eyes off Duto and glanced around the room. 'I hoped this report would help me decide whether I should postpone the State of the Union. Or evacuate New York and Washington, God forbid.' He tapped the book impatiently. 'Instead I get this. I can't order any evacuations, not off this. I'm not going to terrify the country until I'm certain what we face. I'm not going to cancel the State of the Union either, though I am going to order the Vice to stay home. Just in case. Until we get more information, I don't think we should make anything public at all. We're going to treat this as a law enforcement matter. BOLOs, right? That's what they're called?' He was looking at the head of the FBI now.

'Yes, sir. Means be on the lookout for. We send them to the agencies, counterterrorism units at the big police forces—'

'I know what it means and what you do. So we'll start with that. And if you can nail these guys down to the point where going public would actually make sense, I'll reconsider.' Again he looked around the room. 'I'm not going to do anything as juvenile as threatening to fire any of you. We're way past that. I am simply going to tell you something you already know. We need to find these men before they blow this bomb. Or it's *over*. Understand?'

Silent nods.

'Now, let's turn to another equally pleasant topic. If we don't find it. And it takes out midtown Manhattan. Or the Loop. Or this very office. *What then*? If it turns out that this weapon has come from the Russian arsenal, what then? Do we hit back? With what? We're going to talk this out for fifteen minutes. Then you're going to go back to your offices and make sure it never happens. But first. This is a yes-or-no question. We'll discuss it after. How many of you think nuclear retaliation is justified in the case of a nuclear attack on American soil?'

Duto had thought he'd understood the danger they faced. But he realized, as the president asked his question, that he hadn't. Not really. The late-night helicopter ride to the White House, this meeting, they'd all seemed almost unreal. No, they hadn't found the bombmakers yet. But they would, and then the world would go back to normal, and this night would seem almost a dream. Or, more accurately, the crowning moment of his career, the moment that would put his memoirs on the best-seller list.

But now the president was asking about nuclear

retaliation. The president believed this bomb might go off. And if he believed it, Duto had to believe it, too. A nuclear bomb on American soil.

'I want a show of hands,' the president said. 'If you believe nuclear retaliation is justified, raise your hand.'

There were seven of them in the room, not counting the president and his chief of staff. Seven hands rose. 'Now, what if it's a Russian nuke but we can't be sure the Russians were involved? What then?'

Christ, Duto thought. *Can I? Can we?* But he kept his hand up. There could be no excuses. No honest mistakes. Someone would have to pay. And as he looked around the room, he saw he was in the majority. Only the secretary of state and the director of the FBI had lowered their hands. Five-to-two in favor of retaliation.

'Doomsday it is,' the president said. He didn't smile.

CHAPTER 34

*N*o. Bashir heard a voice, not inside his head but a real voice, a man speaking. Had he fallen asleep? The clock said 1:58, so he must have. But he hadn't. He was sure. He sat up and looked around, but the room was empty. It had spoken with such power. Allah? Muhammad? Whoever had spoken, he needed to obey.

No. He couldn't allow it. He would go to the stable and take the the uranium and disappear. Maybe he would go directly to the police. Or he would simply vanish. In a day or two, he'd call Thalia and tell her to go back to Egypt, call Nasiji and Yusuf and tell them to leave, that the police would be raiding the house and the stable.

Either way, Washington would still be standing tomorrow. Yes. He breathed slowly, inhaling and exhaling five times, a step he sometimes took before entering the operating room. He waited for doubts but felt none. He was making the right decision. He touched his wife's forehead and she stirred in her sleep. And then he rolled out of bed and noiselessly padded to the rocking chair – a relic of the house's previous owners – where he'd stacked his jeans and sneakers and sweater.

He padded down the second-floor hallway, sneakers cradled in his hands, trying not to set off the creaky wooden planks. He edged past the bedroom where the Repard kids had once lived and where Nasiji and Yusuf now slept in twin beds decorated with Star Wars blankets.

A plank groaned lightly and Bashir pulled his weight off it and leaned against the wall waiting for Nasiji or Yusuf to rouse. But the rhythm of their breathing didn't change. So Bashir slipped down the stairs and pulled on his shoes and walked out the kitchen door and—

Creak!—

How had he forgotten the soft plank on the porch? He waited for the house lights to come on, for Nasiji and Yusuf to emerge. *I heard something outside. I wanted to check.*

The house stayed silent. After a minute, Bashir headed down the path connecting the house and the stable, a river of brown brick between the snow-covered ground on either side. Yusuf cleared the path every day. He seemed to enjoy shoveling. Bashir wondered what Yusuf thought of the bomb. He'd never said. He reminded Bashir of a tiger at the zoo in Cairo, a big lazy beast. Once the tiger had strolled to the front of his cage and pushed himself up on his hind paws and leaned against the bars. He towered over Bashir, three meters from his paws to the black tip of his nose. He yawned and turned his head and looked Bashir up and down, slowly, almost gently. *Meat*, his eyes said. *And I'm hungry.*

Yusuf had eyes like that. Bashir would be happy never to see them again.

In the stable, Bashir flicked on a penlight, followed its narrow beam to the Spear round with the uranium cap attached. It sat on a steel workbench beside the bomb, just where he'd left it. He would need less than a minute to grab it, get to the Suburban, be gone. He fingered his car keys, safe in his pocket. Good.

Was he sure? He was. He walked across the stable, picked up the cap.

He was halfway back to the door when the lights clicked on—

And Yusuf walked in, pistol in hand.

Bashir froze. 'Yusuf,' he said. 'I was worried. So stupid of us to leave it out—'

'Hush.'

'You must have the wrong idea.'

'Thalia said this might happen. She told Sayyid.'

Bashir found himself shaking his head. 'Thalia . . .' *My Thalia? My wife?*

His wife had betrayed him? Impossible. But apparently not, because here came Yusuf, stalking toward him, blocking the door—

And Bashir ran.

Not for the door. Running for the door meant

running toward Yusuf. He ran for the blue tarp they had put over the hole in the stable wall, the hole blown open when they tested the dummy bomb. The hole was narrow and splintery and Bashir wasn't sure he would fit but it was his only chance. If Nasiji had wanted to talk things over, he would have come, too. Instead he'd sent Yusuf, gun in hand, with one order and one order only.

Yusuf didn't shoot when Bashir started to run. Bashir guessed he was afraid of hitting the bomb. Bashir dropped the uranium plug and tore at the tarp, tugging it from the nails that held it to the walls. He squirmed through, the splinters from the wall cutting at his hands—

And heard Yusuf's pistol bark and felt the burn in his right shoulder at the same time. The impact of the shot shoved him through the hole and into the snow behind the stable. He landed hard, and when he tried to catch himself with his right hand, a blast of pain shot up his arm and through his shoulder and stole his breath. He couldn't even scream.

Then he heard the second shot. It missed, scattering the snow in front of him, giving him the strength to pull himself up and run for the woods. A few hundred meters to the south, on the back side of this hill, a narrow creek marked the boundary between the Repard property and the state park behind it. Eventually the creek reached the state road that connected Addison and Corning. If he could just get to the road . . .

He blundered through the woods, cracking branches and scattering snow with every step. He knew he was leaving a trail, but he couldn't help himself. His shoulder still hurt, but instead of an electric charge, now he felt a solid lump of heat and pain, as though a charcoal briquette had been sewn into his back.

Behind him, and not far, he heard Yusuf, blundering through branches. His one hope: Yusuf wasn't used to this terrain either. Every thirty seconds or so, Yusuf's flashlight caught Bashir, but each time Bashir ducked and turned sideways to escape. He forced himself not to look back. Whether Yusuf was ten meters away or a hundred didn't matter. The creek. And then the road.

Even so, Bashir felt himself fading as he topped the hill and made his way down to the creek. The snow was thicker here, and Bashir's jeans and sneakers were soaked and his feet had turned to blocks of wood. Though he wanted to run, he had to step carefully. He couldn't risk a fall. Yusuf would surely be on him. His shoulder was still leaking blood, a warm trail down his chest and right arm.

'Stop,' Yusuf yelled behind him. 'Stop running. Let's talk about this.'

'The tiger speaks,' Bashir yelled back, but his breath was faint and he wished he'd said nothing.

'What?'

Bashir saved his breath and ran, step-step-step,

through the woods, lifting his legs as high as he could, thinking of the soccer drills that he'd done as a kid, bouncing the ball off his knees. A thin cloud cover had blown in but the stars still threw off enough light to reveal the contours of the rolling earth under the snow.

Step-step-step . . .

'Stop!' Yusuf yelled again, his voice stronger, angrier. 'You can't escape. Be a man.'

The truth. No false promises of safety. The glare of Yusuf's flash-light caught Bashir again, more powerfully now, and Bashir knew he must be only a few steps ahead. A surge of adrenaline and fear powered through him and his steps came more quickly, and though his shoulder and arm and chest were slick with blood, somehow he drew away. Behind him, he heard Yusuf stumble and curse, and for the first time since the stable lights had snapped on he thought he might live. He reached the bottom of the hill and the creek and turned and—

His *right* leg slipped through the thin creek ice and onto the slick stones underneath. He lost his balance and fell and landed square on his shoulder and the charcoal in his back burned hotter than ever. He screamed, a vicious sound that seemed to come from somewhere outside him, and he knew he needed to try to stand, but the pain was overwhelming . . .

The flashlight caught him and he heard Yusuf coming down the hill. He made one more try, grabbing the trunk of a birch beside the creek with his good left hand and pulling himself up. He reached his feet and stumbled forward in the thin snow alongside the creek . . .

But the light got stronger and stronger and he knew the tiger had him now . . .

Then his feet were kicked out and he crashed down and knew he wouldn't be getting up again. His burial ground would be a bed of pine needles in a country that wasn't his.

'Turn around,' Yusuf said above him, and Bashir didn't argue. The time for argument was through. He pushed himself against a log and rolled over and stared into the blinding glare of Yusuf's flashlight. Behind the light, Yusuf's breaths came fast, and despite his terror Bashir congratulated himself for making Yusuf run.

Yusuf reached down for him and Bashir promised himself that whatever happened he wouldn't beg and then—

Yusuf reached under his good left arm and pulled him up and frogmarched him back to the stable, retracing his steps. Bashir could hardly see the path and twice needed to lean against a tree to rest. He supposed he was going into shock from the blood he'd lost.

The third time he tried to rest, Yusuf reached over and squeezed his bad shoulder and the pain brought him back to reality for a few seconds. 'Coward,' Yusuf said. 'We're almost there.'

★   ★   ★

In the stable, Nasiji waited for them.

'Sit down, Bashir,' he said, and Bashir stumbled gratefully down.

'Stable floor,' he said. 'No better or worse than pine needles.'

'Shut up and look at me,' Nasiji said. Bashir raised his head. 'Are you a spy, Bashir?'

'No. Are you, Sayyid?'

'Then why?'

'It's too much,' Bashir said. 'Much too much.'

'So you tried to destroy all we've done? All of us, you included? Yusuf always said you were weak.'

Bashir's head drooped. But he did mean to ask something. What? Then he remembered. 'Did Thalia—'

'Tell us? Of course she did.'

Bashir closed his eyes. 'Do what you want with him, Yusuf,' Nasiji said, and Bashir heard him walk away. And then Yusuf's steady breathing was the only sound in the stable.

'You shouldn't have run,' Yusuf said. 'I would have made this easier. Traitor.'

Bashir opened his eyes to see Yusuf whetting a blade.

'Don't worry, Yusuf,' he said. 'It'll be easy enough.'

And when Yusuf kneeled astride him and dug the knife into his gut and tore open skin and sinew and arteries—

And then repositioned himself and raised and

lowered the blade into Bashir as rhythmically, mechanically as a jackhammer cutting concrete.

Bashir didn't argue, didn't even scream. He just closed his eyes and saw the tiger in the Cairo zoo. And, sure enough, the pain rose like the whine of a teakettle and then disappeared.

Then only a man and a corpse were left in the stable, twined as lovers, and Yusuf's breath came fast and hot as he worked the knife into Bashir's throat and face. Yusuf chopped until the body underneath him no longer had a nose or ears or eyes or a mouth. Even then Yusuf wasn't satisfied, even then he wanted to do more, but he couldn't think of anything else. So he dug the blade into Bashir's chest and left it there and stood and walked out of the stable and into the clean white snow.

CHAPTER 35

Wells opened his eyes and woke, as sharply as a bat snapped in half over an angry batter's knee, to find Exley standing over him. He didn't know how long he'd slept but he felt strong and ready, his reflexes fueled by the sure knowledge of combat to come.

'Time is it?'

'Eight.' Six hours. He'd been out longer than he thought.

'Did you sleep, Jennifer? You shouldn't push like this.' She looked slack, exhausted, her face shiny with sweat. Even as he stood up, she sagged against his desk.

'We tracked them into the country,' she said. 'They flew from St John's to Newark. January 13. Canadian passports.'

'We're sure.'

'Checked their pictures with the crew on the *Juno*. It's them. They came in under the names Jad Ghani and Kamel al-Bachary. From Montreal. The Canadians have addresses and are waiting for our go to kick down doors up there. That's the good news. Bad news is there's nothing on this end.

The airlines and rental agencies don't have anything in their databases. They used other names for the rentals, or didn't fly or rent a car. Or didn't use a national agency.'

'These guys.'

Exley closed her eyes. 'FBI has every agent between Boston and Washington hitting rental companies, see if anybody recognizes their pictures. They're trying to get them done by noon, then on to hotels and motels. Meanwhile we got a warrant for the credit card companies. But those databases are so big it'll take some time to check their names.'

'Anything else?'

'All the toll takers at the bridges and tunnels into New York and up and down Ninety-five have their pictures. Though if they have an E-Z Pass, it won't make a difference. We put some radiation sniffers on the Beltway and the tunnels, too, but if the bomb's properly shielded, they won't do much. Specially if it's HEU and not plutonium.'

'So basically if we can't find them before they leave whatever safe house they're at . . .'

Now Exley looked at Wells. 'The odds are bad, yes. Not impossible, but bad.'

'The Germans get anything yet?'

'The kid, Bernard's son, Helmut, he's talking, confirms he saw one of them. The guy who came in under the Jad passport. Says the guy spoke German and that Bernard always called him Sayyid. But nothing more, no phone numbers or e-mails or anything.'

'How about Penn State? Anything there?'

'Nothing yet.'

'So when do we go public?'

'Hasn't been decided.'

'What about the Russians?'

'We gave them the names and pictures and they said they'll get back to us. Last I heard, they still haven't told us what's really in the crates or even confirmed these guys are connected to the missing material. The president's going to talk to Medvedev directly as soon as possible, but who knows what that'll do. And the White House is trying to figure out whether they should cancel the State of the Union tonight. So there's your update.'

Wells laid the back of his hand on Exley's forehead to test her temperature and found her running a fever. 'You ought to lie down, Jenny.'

'I'll sleep in the infirmary for a couple of hours.'

'Why don't you go home?'

'Why don't you come with me?'

He was silent. Her eyes went wet and then her cheeks and eyes hardened, her face becoming a mask, the emotion disappearing inch by inch. *Say yes*, he told himself. *You don't have to do this*. But he did.

'You know,' she said. 'I'll go home, wait for you. You don't even have to come. If you can promise me one thing. Promise me when we find these guys, you won't go after them. You'll sit tight here with Ellis.'

'It's my op.'

'They'll put half the army in the air. They don't need you. You're in the way. And it goes off, what then? You going to outrun the fireball?'

'I can't ask someone else to take a risk I won't take myself.'

She put her arm around his neck. A peace offering. 'You've taken enough risks. Some might say you've gotten greedy. Let someone else have this one. Come home.'

He didn't know how to convince her. Probably because she was right. After a minute of silence, she ran her hand down his arm, took his hand.

'This thing you have in you, this thing that won't let you stop, I have it, too,' she said. 'I came back here. I swore I wouldn't, but I did. The difference between you and me is that I have some other things, too. My kids. I thought I had you. You, you just have this.'

'I have a son. I have you.'

'You haven't seen Evan in how long? And you don't have me, John. You don't.' She stood and kissed him on the lips, a wet openmouthed kiss that brought him back to their very first kiss, barely two years before, on a day when she'd saved his life and nearly died in the process.

The kiss went on and he closed his eyes and pulled her to him. But she put a hand on his face and pushed him away. And without another word, she walked out.

★　　★　　★

489

The call came three hours later. An FBI team had found the Avis office in Morristown, New Jersey, where 'Jad' and 'Kamel' rented their car. The agent who'd been working on January 13 wasn't at the office when they arrived. But when they tracked him to his apartment, he immediately recognized the photographs. Jad had rented a Pontiac G6, dark blue, 11,347 miles, for a month. He'd used an international driver's license and a Turkish passport and a MasterCard, all in the name of Dawood Askari. How exactly he'd gotten those useful items was a question they'd answer later.

For now they had the name he was using in the United States. And something even more precious. Avis equipped its vehicles with LoJack, the antitheft system, which could be activated remotely to broadcast a stolen car's location. According to the system, the G6 was parked on a farm outside the town of Addison, New York – three hundred miles from Washington, and slightly closer to Manhattan. The farm belonged to a surgeon named Bashir Is'mail, who worked at a hospital in Corning.

Now two companies of Rangers had been scrambled from Fort Drum, a big army base about 150 miles north of Addison. FBI agents were en route from Buffalo and Albany. The New York State Police had been given the plate number and description of the G6 and asked to set up observation posts – not roadblocks – on the highways and state roads around Corning. And a half-dozen

F-16 fighter-bombers were being put in the air from Andrews Air Force Base.

Meanwhile, the job of taking the house had been given to a Delta unit that was officially called the 9th Special Operations Group/Emergency Response and unofficially known as Red Team. Red Team had two squads, one based at Andrews and the other at West Point. It worked alongside the Nuclear Emergency Search Team, a group of scientists responsible for finding and defusing nuclear and dirty bombs. The Red Team soldiers carried gamma and alpha ray detectors and radiological protective gear and were authorized to shoot on sight anyone they reasonably suspected of carrying a nuclear weapon. Each Red Team squad had twelve soldiers and two Black Hawks dedicated to its transport and was ready to scramble within thirty minutes, twenty-four hours a day.

'When are they taking off?' Wells said. He'd been sitting in Shafer's office as Shafer flicked between calls and e-mail and IM to track the plan. But Shafer was focused on his screen and paid no attention to the question. 'Ellis.'

'Company C is shipping out in fifteen from Andrews,' Shafer said. 'They're gonna set down in Corning, switch over to SUVs that the state police will have waiting, go in on the ground instead of helicopter so whoever's at the farm won't hear them coming. I don't want to tell you this, but they've got a spot for you. They've got eleven guys and you'll make twelve. You want to ride with them?'

491

'What do you think?'

'What I think and what I wish are two different things.'

'Aren't they always?'

Twenty minutes later, Wells stood on a helipad at Langley, shielding his eyes from the winter sun as the Black Hawk swept in. He wore a helmet and his lightweight bulletproof vest and carried an M-4, an automatic rifle with a grenade launcher attached below the barrel.

The helicopter touched down and Wells ran through the frigid windstorm whipped up by its blades and jumped into the cabin. He strapped himself in and the crew chief hopped out to check on him and then they took off. He didn't expect to know any of the men, but as he looked around he recognized one, Brett Gaffan, a sergeant he'd met a few months before in Afghanistan. Gaffan and he had spent a long night together, pinned on open ground under fire from Taliban guerrillas.

After the mission, they'd traded e-mail addresses and vowed to stay in touch, but they hadn't. Wells guessed that his reputation intimidated Gaffan, who wouldn't want Wells to think he was sucking up, keeping in contact in case Wells could do him a favor. But Wells had no such excuse. He'd simply forgotten. He remembered the men he killed but forgot the ones he saved or fought beside. *You just have this*, Exley had said. He didn't want to believe her, but she was right.

The Black Hawk's cabin was frigid as they flew over the hills of western Maryland and then into Pennsylvania, roughly tracking U.S. 15. They passed a stretch of open fields, two low ridges facing each other, the landscape as familiar to Wells as a dream, and as the helicopter swept by he realized he was seeing Gettysburg. But even before he could imagine Grant and Lee and the armies in blue and gray, the fields were gone. They were running at 170 knots, roughly 200 miles an hour, the effective maximum cruising speed for these modified Hawks.

They rolled north along ground that was heavily wooded and hilly, blurred towns disappearing as fast as they came, heating oil tankers and tractor-trailers chugging on the roads beneath them. At Harrisburg, the State Capitol flashed before them and then was gone. For a while they flew along the Susquehanna, the river flowing wide and sluggish, chunks of ice floating in its dark brown water. In front of them, the hills grew until they were the Appalachians and the patches of snow on the ground thickened until they weren't patches anymore.

No one in the cabin spoke and no one smiled. Wells understood. The quickest reflexes and all the Kevlar in the world wouldn't matter if this bomb blew. So Wells closed his eyes and listened to the music in his head, Springsteen asking, *Is a dream a lie if it don't come true? / Or is it something worse? . . .*

Would he ever see Exley again? Whether or not he survived?

The helicopter slowed and Wells opened his eyes. They came down in an empty parking lot outside an abandoned factory, its bricks cracking and its smokestacks stained. The other three Black Hawks were already down, and eighteen soldiers stood beside them, checking their gear, along with about fifteen state troopers. Four Suburbans, two marked and two unmarked, and two unmarked Crown Vics waited for them, lights on and engines running.

As the fourth Black Hawk landed, the Deltas began to huddle around a tall man who, unusually for a Special Operations officer, wore a standard camouflage uniform, a lieutenant colonel's oak leaves on his shoulderboards, and *Giese* on his name tag. As Wells joined the huddle, Giese looked at him and nodded. Wells nodded back, all the introduction he needed, and all he would get. Giese spread a four-foot-square satellite photo of the Repard farm on the hood of one of the Suburbans. The property had two buildings, the main house and a stable behind it. The G6 was clearly visible, parked in front of the main house, along with a second vehicle, a Ford Expedition.

'We're guessing that whatever they have is in the back building. But it could be in the basement of the main house or even hidden somewhere else on the property,' Giese said. 'We put up a sniffer'

– a plane with equipment that could detect radioactive particles – 'but it didn't find anything. So we really don't know.

'C Company's going in first. We'll leave the Black Hawks here, drive to the perimeter of the property and move along the driveway on foot. The state police have blocked the road that leads to the farm where it runs across Route 417. The police are giving us a ride, but they're not going in. Meanwhile, B Company will ride in and land between the house and the stable. But only after C has hit the buildings. I don't want these guys to know we're coming.'

Giese handed out wallet-sized copies of the Newark immigration photographs. 'Our primary targets. Our ROE' – rules of engagement – 'say you can shoot on sight, no warning. We don't know what they have, whether it's a bomb or just material. But I want you to assume the worst. Assume they have a megaton bomb and they can trigger it remotely. And act accordingly. Any questions?'

'Whose property is it, sir?'

'According to the records, it belongs to a surgeon from Egypt. He bought it a couple of years ago and we can assume he's part of whatever they're doing. We're still getting a photograph of him, but it doesn't matter what he looks like. Once we cross that perimeter, everyone you see is subject to the ROE. Women and children included.'

'Children, sir?'

'If a child has the detonator, then he's more dangerous than any adult. Other questions?'

Silence.

'All right. I'm going to ride lead. We don't have time for any fancy speeches, and I don't have to tell you what this means. So I won't. But I would like to offer a quick prayer. If you want to join, huddle up and bow your heads and close your eyes.'

Every man did. Including Wells.

'Dear God, please help us overcome the enemy we face and keep our country safe from this most dangerous weapon. And please return us this night to our families and homes. Amen.'

'Amen,' twenty-three voices said in return.

'Saddle up.'

The troopers drove fast, lights flashing but no sirens. Wells and Gaffan sat in the rear Crown Vic.

'Sergeant.'

'Mr Wells.'

'What did I tell you about calling me mister? Or sir? I wish I'd known you were in D.C. We could have had a beer.'

'I just got moved a couple months ago, sir. I mean John.'

'Who'd you piss off to wind up on this detail?'

Gaffan laughed. 'I requested it. My wife was joking about divorcing me if she didn't start seeing me more, and after a while it didn't sound like she was joking. Anyway, I was tired of Afghanistan.

Chasing those Talibs around the caves. It never ends, does it?'

'It does for some. When we get through this, we're going out for a drink. And this time, I want you to hold me to it.'

'I'll do that. Think they have a bomb?'

Wells shook his head. No point in guessing.

The convoy turned off 86 and onto 15. Then onto 417, and five minutes after that through a roadblock and left onto a nameless narrow road into the woods. A minute later, they pulled up outside the driveway, a rutted asphalt track that disappeared through thick woods over a low rise. A gray wooden mailbox beside the road announced 'Repard' in faint black letters.

The Suburbans and Crown Vics pulled over and the soldiers threw open the doors and stepped onto the road. When all twelve men were out, the vehicles rolled away. The only sound was the trickle of snow-melt dripping off branches. Without a word, the Deltas dropped the safeties on their M-16s and M-4s, checked the slides on their pistols, adjusted their Kevlar and bulletproof vests. They nodded to each other and lined up in pairs by the side of the driveway. Then Giese threw two fingers forward, and they began to run.

At the top of the rise, they threw themselves down. The house was two hundred yards down the driveway, the Pontiac and Ford parked in front. The lights were out and Wells saw no signs of motion inside. Now they had to choose.

They could run up the driveway, moving quickly but visible to anyone inside the house. Or they could spread into the woods, a slower and noisier but better hidden route. After a few seconds, Giese pointed his fingertips down the path. Two by two, the commandos ran toward the house. The first six men ran around it and toward the stable in back. The next four set up on the porch with a battering ram, preparing to break open the front door. Wells and Gaffan ran to the back of the house.

The back door was unlocked. Wells slung it open and followed Gaffan into the kitchen. Three plates sat on the table, along with a dish of cucumber slices, a carton of orange juice, and a basket of pitas. Wells pulled open a cheap wooden door that looked like it led to the basement. Bingo. Gaffan took the stairs two at a time and Wells followed.

In the basement, three clean whiteboards, a broken Ping-Pong table, three cans of Coke. No bomb, no terrorists hiding in corners. They ran back up the stairs and into the kitchen, where the other two teams waited. The other soldiers shook their heads. The house was clear. The stable, too, apparently. They hadn't heard any shots or explosions or calls for help. These men, whoever they were, had eluded them again.

Then Gaffan's radio buzzed. 'The stable,' he said.

★　　★　　★

Giese poked with his foot at the brutalized corpse on the floor of the stable. 'Seems they had a falling-out,' he said.

'We know which one this is?' Wells said.

Giese shook his head. 'You find anything?'

'The house is empty but there's food in the kitchen,' Wells said. 'Looks like they ate breakfast and left. It's' – Wells looked at his watch – 'one-thirty now. Say they left between seven and ten.'

'In six hours, they could get three hundred, four hundred miles,' Giese said. 'They could be in New York already, or Washington. Halfway to Chicago.'

'Unless we shut down the whole eastern half of the country, we can't freeze them. And if we do, they'll know where they stand and they'll blow this thing wherever they are.'

'That's a White House decision,' Giese said. 'But in a couple hours, they're going to have to cancel the State of the Union and then the game's going to be up anyway. And for all we know, word's leaking already. Too many people have bits of it.' He sighed and reached for his phone. 'I have to call in. They'll probably bring us back to Andrews, let the Rangers and the state cops take over here. You going to ride with us?'

Wells shook his head. He wanted to look around the house and the stable, see if he could connect anything he saw with Bernard Kygeli. There was something he wasn't remembering. Maybe the house would spark it.

'Mind leaving me Gaffan?' he said. 'I know him from Afghanistan.'

Giese tilted his head. 'Guess we'll make do with ten. Here's my cell.' He passed on the number. 'You think of anything, let me know. Time's short.'

'Indeed.'

CHAPTER 36

'What are we looking for?' Gaffan said.

'We'll know when we see it. Wear gloves and leave everything how you found it.'

They went back into the house, looked into the closets, under the beds, inside the heavy wooden furniture. With its rocking chairs and patchwork quilts, the house looked more like a bed-and-breakfast than a terrorist camp. The closet in the master bedroom was filled with skirts, long and modest, and long-sleeve blouses. Four people had been here – the two terrorists, Bashir, and a woman. Three were gone, one dead. Wells didn't understand. Had they fought over the woman? Had one lost his nerve? And why had they left? Had Bernard gotten an alarm to them? If this house had the answers, Wells couldn't find them.

Sirens began to scream up the driveway. In minutes, cops and FBI agents would be overrunning the place. Maybe he should have gone back to Andrews after all.

Wells's phone buzzed. Shafer. 'They're not here,' he said.

'I heard. You decided to stay, enjoy the scenery?'

'Give me some good news.'

'There isn't any. If we haven't found them by five, the president will announce that the State of the Union has been canceled and release their names and photographs publicly. It's going to leak by then anyway. Already there's stuff on the Internet, rumors. Nobody's put it together yet, but they will.'

Wells looked at his watch: 2:15.

'We know what they're driving?'

'The only car registered to Bashir is that Ford. If I had to guess, I'd say they bought something else and didn't retag it. It's got to be something big, though. A van or SUV.'

'There's only about fifty million of those.'

'I told you no good news. What, they didn't leave a map with a big X marking safe house?'

'You think they have another safe house?'

'Maybe not a true safe house, but these guys are too smart just to be driving around, especially if the car's not registered. They've got someplace to crash.'

Wells thought of the coffee mug in Bernard Kygeli's office. 'How about Penn State? From there, it's interstate to New York and D.C.'

'We're looking, but we can't find anybody connected to Kygeli.'

'All right. If anything happens, call me.'

'If anything happens, you may hear it all the way up there.' *Click*.

'Who was that?' Gaffan said.

'My boss.'

'What now?'

The keys to Bashir's Expedition were in a candy dish on the kitchen table. Wells picked them up. 'We're going to Happy Valley.'

Gaffan shook his head. 'I don't get it.'

'Happy Valley, Pennsylvania. Penn State.'

A New York State trooper escorted them in a Suburban, calling ahead so that the Pennsylvania troopers knew they were coming. They rolled down 15, and at the state border were handed off to a Pennsylvania trooper in an unmarked Mustang. The highway was narrow and the Expedition was wide, but somehow Gaffan kept the speedometer pinned at 105 most of the way down. They'd get to Penn State by four, give or take, Wells thought. Then what? He had no idea.

The place was sparsely furnished and small, two rooms and a galley kitchen. Cheap, simple college housing. Nasiji let them in with the key that Bernard had given him. They parked the Suburban in the parking lot directly outside, no need to be fancy. They'd taken out the two back rows of seats. The gadget was in the back, facing backward, the tamper close to the back gate. On the way down, Yusuf had driven, with Thalia next to him. Nasiji lay in the back, next to the Spear, hidden by the tinted windows, the uranium round between his legs.

No one could track them here, and all they needed to do was wait. The woman who lived here had no idea what they were planning, of course. Nasiji hoped she wouldn't show up until they arrived. She would only complicate things.

In the apartment, Nasiji watched CNN with the sound off, waiting for the screen crawl that might tell him that they'd been found, that the State of the Union had been canceled or a farm in upstate New York had been raided. But the afternoon rolled by quietly and he began to think that they'd gotten away. They would leave just before sunset and head southeast to Harrisburg. There they would decide whether to turn south toward Washington – if the State of the Union was still happening – or east toward Philadelphia and New York. Once they were on the road, they ought to be unstoppable. He couldn't imagine how anyone could connect them with the Suburban, and the police lights would help.

The mission hadn't gone according to plan, he had to admit. They'd lost the second bomb. The Americans had found the *Juno*. And then, last night, Bashir's unforgivable treachery.

Even so, they were close. By the end of this night, the American government might no longer exist. *If.* If they could get into Washington, get close to the Capitol. If the bomb didn't fizzle. If Allah smiled on them. Nasiji lowered himself to the floor and began to pray.

★ ★ ★

Ten miles outside state college, a billboard for Penn State football towered over Route 220. *Go Nittany Lions.* And then Wells remembered. The coffee mug in Bernard's office hadn't been for Penn State. It had been for Penn State *soccer.*

He called Shafer.

'Ellis. Have the FBI call Penn State, get the soccer team roster. That's the connection.'

'You sure?'

'Do you have a better idea?'

'I'll Google it . . . Penn State athletics . . . It's all football . . . Soccer . . . No Arab or Turkish-sounding names, nobody from Turkey or Germany or anywhere in the Middle East.'

'Try the J.V.'

A few seconds later, Shafer came back. 'No, John. You still want me to call the FBI? They've got a few other things to do.'

'What about women?' Gaffan said.

Wells clapped a hand to his forehead. 'Of course.'

'Of course what?' Shafer said.

'Check the women's roster.'

Shafer clicked away. 'Wouldn't you know? Aymet Helsi. From Blankenese, Germany. Says here she's a goalie. You want to bet your buddy Bernard knows her family? Maybe he's helping with her tuition?'

'You have an address?'

'As soon as I hang up, I'll get the FBI to get a warrant, get her address from the registrar. Meantime let's see if she's got a, yes, she's listed. The last twenty-year-old with a landline.'

'Address.'

'Ten Vairo Boulevard, unit 239–04 . . . Looks like it's part of a big apartment complex called Vairo Village. You want me to stay on the line, give you directions?'

'We've got a GPS.'

'I'll call the army. But you're going to get there first, no matter what. I don't suppose I can convince you to wait.'

Wells was silent.

'John, do me a favor and don't get killed. She'll never forgive you. Or me.' *Click.*

Following the GPS's chirped orders, Gaffan turned right onto the Mount Nittany Expressway, Route 322, the east-west highway that ran along the northern edge of town. At Waddle Road, less than a mile from the apartment, Gaffan pulled off. Wells tapped his shoulder. 'Pull over.' Wells hopped out, told the trooper what had happened.

'I gotta call the State College cops,' the trooper said.

'Sit tight for five minutes. We'll go in first, no sirens.'

'But what about evacuating—'

'There's no evacuating from this,' Wells said. 'Let us go in first.'

At 4:25, the news crawl on CNN began to promise a major announcement from the White House at 5 p.m. Then the crawl reported that the FBI would

506

hold a briefing following the White House announcement. Nasiji didn't need to see more.

'We're going,' he said to Yusuf and Thalia. 'Now.'

Wells and Gaffan rolled down Oakwood Avenue. The GPS informed them that Vairo Boulevard was ahead on their right. They reached a stop sign, turned right onto Vairo. The apartment complex was across the road, dozens of brown-and-white buildings around a long cul-de-sac.

Gaffan started to swing in. 'No,' Wells said. 'Next one.'

He pointed to the sign in front: 'Phase 1 – Units 1–100.' Wells lowered the window of the Expedition and cradled his M-4. His mouth was dry, his fingers gnarled. If his hunch was wrong, he might be about to shoot an innocent college student. And if it was right . . .

They reached the next block: 'Phase 2 – Units 201–300.' Gaffan swung in. They rolled slowly down the street, which was really just a big parking lot for the complex. The buildings were identical, each two stories, white and brown, laid out roughly in a rectangle that extended several hundred feet around the parking lot. They were moving up the longer side of the rectangle, north from Vairo Boulevard, as the parking lot divided into four rows.

'We know what kind of car we're looking for?'

'Something big,' Wells said.

And Wells saw it. A black Suburban at the far

end of the complex, moving south away from them, toward the exit. He touched Gaffan's shoulder.

'Let's see what building they came out of.'

They swung right, down the northern edge of the complex, the top of the rectangle, as the Suburban rolled away. Number 239 lay at the northeastern flank of the complex, where Wells had first seen the Suburban. Gaffan slowed down. 'We going in?'

'No.'

Nasiji lay on the floor of the Suburban, the uranium pit tucked between his legs. On the ride down from Addison, the position had left him vaguely carsick, but it allowed him to load and fire the Spear in seconds. *Inshallah*. How silly to worry about a bit of stomach pain when he was about to give his body to a nuclear fireball. He wasn't afraid . . . Or perhaps he was. Anyone would be. But he had chosen this course, and unlike that coward Bashir, he would see it through. His father, his mother, they hadn't asked to die either. He and Yusuf and even Thalia would join Mohammed Atta and the other martyrs who had given themselves to liberate Islam.

Nasiji clutched the pit tight and closed his eyes. They stopped, waiting for traffic to clear so they could join the traffic on Vairo Boulevard. Soon they would be on the highway, just another anonymous black SUV traveling through the

Pennsylvania night, burning the gasoline that the Americans had invaded Iraq to steal. In half an hour, he would hear what the president had to say and then he would decide where to take their precious cargo.

The suburban stopped at the intersection of the parking lot and Vairo Boulevard, stuck behind a car that was waiting to make a left turn.

'Ram them,' Wells said. 'Hard.'

'Yeah?'

'Yeah.'

Gaffan stamped the gas pedal and the Expedition surged, its big engine roaring—

Crash. The Expedition's massive grille buckled the rear of the Suburban, shattering the back windows. The collision threw Wells forward but his seat belt caught and airbags popped from all over, front and side. He didn't even drop his M-4. He juddered back into his seat and even before the steam started to rise from the Expedition's crumpled radiator, he'd unbuckled his seat belt. For a moment, he couldn't open his door, but he put his shoulder to it and popped it out. Through the Suburban's broken windows, Wells saw a man in the back of the truck, crawling toward what looked like a big rocket-propelled grenade tube, a Spear, maybe. A strange ball was attached to the muzzle of the Spear.

'Stop!' Wells yelled in Arabic. He stepped out of

the Ford and dropped the safety on the M-4, wondering if he really was about to start shooting, without warning, at three people in an SUV he'd never seen before. The man in the Suburban didn't look back. He inched forward and stretched out his right arm for the barrel of the Spear.

The collision tossed Nasiji backward, throwing him into the Suburban's rear doors. Shards of glass covered him and he dropped the pit. No. Somehow, he couldn't imagine how, but they'd been tracked. Only one choice left. This stupid place wasn't Washington or New York, but it would have to do. He reached around and found the pit and inched forward. Outside the car, a man yelled '*Stop*' in Arabic, and Nasiji remembered the American soldiers in Iraq, always giving orders. He pushed himself forward. If he could just load the pit.

The suburban lurched forward, metal tearing metal, pulling apart the grille of the Expedition. In a moment, it would be free. Wells stepped forward and propelled himself onto the hood of the Expedition and began to shoot, first at the man in the back, tearing him open, three in the chest and then two in the head to be sure, and switched to full auto and tore up the driver and passenger seats until blood and brains splattered the front windshield and the Suburban was still.

★　　★　　★

And then Wells leaned back against the hood of the Ford and looked at what he'd done. A hand squeezed his shoulder and a voice, Gaffan's, said his name. But Wells only shook his head and sat in the cold, shivering, as the police arrived in ones and twos and then by the dozens, and Vairo Village turned into a mad clanking, flashing carnival, with him the main attraction, its mute and beating heart.

EPILOGUE

The bomb would have worked.

So the engineers at Los Alamos calculated after oh-so-carefully taking it apart and simulating its explosion on their supercomputers. They calculated an 87 percent chance of a Hiroshima-sized 10- to 15-kiloton explosion, a 4 percent chance of a 2- to 10-kiloton explosion, and a 9 percent chance of a fizzle.

To avoid panicking the public, the results of the simulation were never released. The White House and FBI publicly said only that the weapon found in the back of the Suburban was an 'improvised radio-logical device,' never calling it a nuclear weapon. Wells's role in finding the bomb was also kept secret. Reporters were told only that he and Gaffan were 'U.S. government employees,' a statement that was true enough as far as it went.

Meanwhile, the video that Nasiji had made caused a stir across the Internet when it was aired on Islamic Web sites. The United States and Russia quickly issued a joint statement calling the video 'a total fabrication intended to stir hatred between us.' A few conspiracy theorists insisted that the

512

bombs and Grigory's identification both looked real, but they were ignored.

Privately, of course, the White House blamed the Kremlin for the near catastrophe, and for once the Russians didn't try to defend themselves. The director of Rosatom was quietly relieved of his duties and given a new job overseeing nuclear waste cleanup in Siberia.

Finding the source of the financing for the plot proved more complicated. After several false starts, analysts at the CIA and Treasury linked a bank account that Nasiji had used to a twenty-thousand-barrel oil shipment from the Yanbu terminal in Saudi Arabia. But despite extraordinary pressure from the White House, the Saudi government insisted that it could not determine who had authorized the shipment. A few weeks later, Ahmed Faisal, a minor Saudi prince, burned to death when his Land Rover exploded in a fiery crash on the desert road connecting Riyadh and Jedda. The accident surprised Faisal's friends, who'd always known him to be a careful driver.

None of this mattered to Wells, though he did vaguely wonder what would happen to Bernard Kygeli's family. For three days, he stayed at Langley, where he was interviewed by the investigators who were working to pull the weeds of the rest of Nasiji's network. There was no word from Exley, and all along he had only one question: *Where is she?* Finally, Wells lost patience and told them that they'd gotten all he knew and that if they had specific questions they knew where to find him. He showered and shaved and drove off campus in a standard-issue agency Pontiac G6. He insisted on no protection, no chase cars or spotters, and they seemed to agree; as far as he could tell he was alone.

When he got to their house, the usual tinted-glass Suburban was parked in front. But the windows were dark and her minivan was gone. Wells let himself in, knowing before he did that the house would be empty.

'Jenny?' he said. 'You there?'

Upstairs the bed was neatly made, an envelope tucked under his pillow. In her neat script, nine words:

'I love you. I miss you already. Be safe.'

Wells sat on the bed and turned the note over and over in his fingers as if hoping to make the words disappear, vanish like a shaken Etch A Sketch drawing. But they didn't, and after a while he tucked the note in his pocket and looked in her closet. Her suitcases were gone and so were most of her clothes. He couldn't stay in this room anymore. He walked downstairs and turned toward the kitchen, then to the front door, wanting to be out of the house.

He knocked on the SUV's windows.

'Where is she?'

The guard shook his head apologetically.

Wells leaned into the truck. 'I need to talk to her.'

'She requested that we not tell you, sir.' The guard looked embarrassed, Wells thought, embarrassed to be seeing the famous John Wells this way, like a lovesick high school senior dumped the night before the prom.

'Is she with her kids?'

'I'm sorry, sir.'

Wells turned away before he could humiliate himself further. He slipped into the Pontiac and screamed off with no good idea where he was headed. A half-hour later he found himself at Dulles looking at a departure board full of choices, none he wanted to take. Should he go to Zurich, see Kowalski? And then what? Thank the man for saving the world? Shoot him and break the last promise he'd made? Try to forget Exley in Nadia's cool blue eyes?

Or Missoula to see Heather and Evan, his ex-wife and son? This time insist on meeting his boy, whatever Heather said?

Or somewhere else?

No. Montana or Switzerland it was. Neither made sense. But all he really wanted was a place to go, a place that wasn't here. He pulled a quarter from his pocket, picked heads and tails. Heads, Zurich. Tails, Missoula.

All around him the hall bustled, arrivals and departures, purposeful motion. Wells flicked the quarter high into the air and watched it spin, watched it catch the lights overhead as it rose and rose and finally topped out and fell. He should have reached out to catch it but instead watched it land at his feet and spin neatly around until it plopped over. Heads? Tails? He leaned down and looked at the quarter as if it could give him an answer that mattered.

ACKNOWLEDGMENTS

At the end of *The Ghost War*, I encouraged readers to e-mail me at alexberenson@gmail.com with comments, suggestions, and complaints. I had no idea I would get so many responses. More than five hundred of you wrote, and I learned some things that I should have known already – I can promise I will never again use the phrase 'knots per hour' – as well as some things that I don't think anyone who wasn't a C-130 pilot could have known.

Best of all were the notes from soldiers, both active-duty and veteran, some of whom said they identified very much with Wells, for better and worse. Wells isn't real, and yet his emotions are: his sense of duty, his loneliness, his anger at injustice in all its forms, his strength, his patience, his ability to keep his emotions under wraps for as long as necessary. He is a soldier as much as a spy, and I hope I have rendered him honorably.

I tried to reply to every e-mail, and I'm sorry if I missed anyone. Please keep the notes coming, and I will try to continue to respond individually to each one, though if the volume of e-mail continues to grow exponentially I may not be able to keep up. Let me know also if you'd like to see improvements to my Web site – I'm considering a forum for people to discuss the books and other spy novels, but if it won't be used I won't bother. (Few sights are sadder than a message board with three entries.)

Now, on to the actual acknowledgments (which haven't changed much since *The Ghost War*, a sign of either stability or ossification).

Ellen and Harvey, my parents and closest readers.

David, my brother and best bud.

Neil Nyren, whose suggestions are always on point – and the rest of the folks at Putnam and Berkley, who somehow made *The Faithful Spy* a number-one bestseller in paperback.

Heather Schroder, who makes the deals that keep John Wells alive, and Matthew Snyder, who is still working to get Wells his close-up.

Tim Race, Larry Ingrassia, and the rest of the fine folks at *The New York Times*, who are far more patient than I have any right to expect.

And: Jonathan Karp, Douglas Ollivant, Deirdre Silver, Andrew Ross Sorkin, and Mark Tavani, all of whom have helped nurture John Wells along the way. Thanks to all of you.